Hope For TOMORROW

Joi Copeland

Comfort PUBLISHING

Hope For Tomorrow

First printing

Book cover design
by Colin Kernes

ISBN: 978-1-936695-07-2
Published by Comfort Publishing, LLC
www.comfortpublishing.com

Printed in the United States of America

Dedication

I dedicate this book to my husband, Chris, and my boys, Garrison, Gage, and Gavin. I also dedicate this book to the Ferris Family, Russell, Steffanne, Josiah, and Dylan.

Acknowledgements

Without the love and support of people, there was no way I could have written and finished this book.

Chris, my wonderful husband and best friend, without you, this would not have happened. You have been my encouragement throughout this entire process! Thank you for supporting me, loving me, and being my sounding board! Thank you for helping me accomplish my dream! You are amazing!

Garrison, Gage, and Gavin, you boys gave me the gift of time. Thank you for letting "Mommy be" for a few hours a day so I could write! You are a blessing!

Steffanne and Russell, you two and Chris told me I needed to write. You read the book and gave me feedback. You caused me to search deeper and write from my heart. You challenged me, encouraged me, and pushed me to do the "unthinkable." Thank you!

Josiah and Dylan, you were there, listening to the chapters and reading them. You frequently asked me how the book was coming, and I thank you for taking an interest in my dream! Because of your questions, I was able to come up with new ideas! Thank you!

Kristy Huddle, and the team at Comfort Publishing, I thank you! God gave me the desire to write, you gave me the opportunity! Thank you for being patient as I went through this process!

And last, but certainly not the least, thanks be to Jesus who put the desire in my heart for writing years ago. His love and grace has filled my heart to overflowing! Without Him, none of this would have been possible!

Hope For Tomorrow

Sue sat on her couch, tears streaming down her face. Her whole world was being   torn apart, and she had no way of knowing how to stop it. The blue scrapbook was open. She didn't know why she was torturing herself this way, looking at a book with precious memories she had painstakingly put together. In one single moment, everything had changed. Sobbing quietly, she flipped another page, one that took her breath away. The page showed her family, all together, happy and joyful.

Will we ever be that way again? Her family was about to be destroyed, never to be the same again, all because of one choice.

Why, Lord? Why is this happening? No answer came. Sue was devastated. Her heart felt as if it were being smashed into tiny pieces. How could things have turned out this way? How could one person change the course of their lives without even realizing the consequences of their actions? Sue sighed and closing her eyes, she leaned heavily against the couch.

Her mind drifted back to how it all began.

Chapter 1

*J*osephine Johnson stumbled through the front door and caught a glimpse of herself in the mirror. Her short, bleach blonde hair looked frizzy today, probably due to the moisture in the air, but the blue jacket made her deep blue eyes stand out against her rosy cheeks.

She took off her jacket and then went into the kitchen to make some hot chocolate. This December was colder than usual. Lakewood, Colorado had received more snow this winter than any other she could remember. Now, she really loved Colorado and every season in this glorious state, but winter was a favorite and usually kept her filled with delight.

Today, however, she struggled with an emptiness she felt building up inside of her. She brought her hot chocolate and plopped down on the couch, exhausted from a long day at work. She had been working extra hours all week, trying to save more money for Christmas gifts for her family but actually, just trying to stay busy, trying to keep her mind off her personal situation. The longer she worked, though, the more her heart ached of loneliness.

It had only been a month since she and Jim broke up and she had moved out. Josephine could still see her sisters standing in the kitchen of this new apartment, putting the dishes away they had bought her as a house warming gift. They were laughing and talking about the things the Lord was going to do in Josephine's life. She had rededicated her life to the Lord and knew she needed to be on her own. Josephine smiled a sad smile, remembering that day. She wished her sisters were with her this very moment. Perhaps she wouldn't feel so lonely tonight. She had experienced an extremely emotional day at work.

As a hairdresser, Josephine had her normal clients, of course, and they always took really good care of her. Being a beautician, of course one relied on the tips. But it was the few walk-ins who were so difficult for her heart to bear.

A teenage couple had come in. The girl was playfully tousling the boy's shaggy brown hair, laughing and making jokes about what her grandparents would say when he came over for Christmas dinner. Another couple had come in. The gentleman, Josephine found out, was treating his wife to a day of relaxation and pampering. He had taken her to get a manicure and pedicure already. He wanted her to have extra special treatment while getting her hair done and tipped generously in advance to make sure that this happened. His wife talked the whole time about how thoughtful and caring her husband was. Next, she told Josephine, he was taking her shopping for a few Christmas outfits.

When Josephine asked why all the special treatment, the wife smiled and shrugged her shoulders.

"He said it's just because he loves me and wants to spend the day pampering me."

Josephine had just smiled and mumbled, "That's great," but deep down, she felt a pain of sadness and couldn't wait for the day to end.

As she sat sipping her hot chocolate now, she flipped through the channels on television. "It's a Wonderful Life" and "White Christmas" were both on. She quickly changed the channels. The last thing she wanted to do was watch something that would cause her more loneliness during this holiday season. She picked up her phone, wanting to call one of her sisters.

They are probably busy with other things, Lord. I don't want to be a burden. Maybe, she thought, suddenly, Jim could come over and she could share the Lord with him. Maybe, she thought, that would make me feel better. She reached for the phone and dialed his number.

"Hello?" he answered.

o o o o

Josephine sighed and rolled over. As she stretched, memories from the previous night raced through her mind. Jim had come over just a few minutes after she had called him. He had complemented her on how she looked. Josephine had invited him in, made him something warm to drink, and sat down on the couch to talk. They started watching the rest of "White Christmas," and before she knew what was happening, he was kissing her. She didn't resist.

Josephine shook her head, utter hopelessness filling her very soul this morning.

She looked over and saw a note from Jim.

"Thanks for last night. Call you later!" it read. Shame and regret flooded over her. What had she done? She lay in bed, weeping with remorse and repentance, begging the Lord's forgiveness. She glanced at the plaque her sisters had given to her after she rededicated her life to Christ.

"Create in me a clean heart and renew a right spirit within me. Cast me not away from your presence, O Lord. And do not take your spirit from me."

It was from Psalms 51:10. As she got ready for work the verse became an intense prayer.

o o o o

Weeks passed. Josephine began to feel forgiven and cleansed. Jim called a few times. She had asked his forgiveness but informed him that could never happen again. After about a week, he stopped calling altogether. She felt some relief but sadness, also, knowing she had blown her witness for Christ.

Christmas was spent with her family. Her sisters, Sue and Brittany were there, along with Sue's fiancé, Nate, Brittany's husband, Luke, and their daughter, Joslyn. She enjoyed herself immensely, spending a lot of time laughing at Nate's silly jokes. Nate was one of the funniest people she had met. He was so laid back and good-natured. Looking at her sister, she knew Nate was a good match for her. Nate was taller than Sue, but only by a few inches. His sandy blonde hair was always done perfectly, seldom a hair out of place. His blue eyes often sparkled with delight as he spent time with the family.

Her eyes traveled to Luke, normally so serious. On this festive occasion, however, he had four Christmas bows stuck to his forehead. He was an observer and processor by nature, which sometimes was mistaken for rudeness, but certainly not meant that way. He stood up to help clear the table. Josephine had never really noticed how tall he was until today. His slender frame made him look taller than usual. With his short, blonde hair and intense blue eyes, one could easily be intimated just by looking at him. She was never intimidated, though. She loved Luke, and looked up to him as the big brother she never had.

Her niece, Joslyn, was a little over a year old and as cute as a button. She had her parents' good looks: blonde hair and deep blue eyes. Josephine laughed as Joslyn decided to sing her own version of "Jingle Bells". Instead of singing "Jingle Bells" she kept singing "Jinker Bells".

It started to get late, and Josephine had to get up early. She kissed them all good-bye and headed for the car. She never told them what happened between her and Jim. She did not see the need to since it would never happen again.

New Year's Eve was busier than usual at work. People wanted to look just right for their plans that evening. By the time Josephine got done, she was totally exhausted and she went straight to bed. She woke up the next morning, tired and nauseous.

Must be something I ate, she thought. She turned on the Rose Parade and waited for her sisters to arrive. They were going to have a New Year's Day Parade breakfast and spend the day watching movies and hanging out.

Just then, the doorbell rang.

Brittany walked through the door looking stunning as usual. Even in a pair of sweats and t-shirt she looked beautiful. Her long sandy blond hair hung loosely around her shoulders. Though she had no makeup on she could have been mistaken for a model.

"Jo," Brittney said, "you ok? You don't look well."

"I think it's something I ate last night. I feel sick to my stomach." She answered placing a hand on her stomach and ushering Brittney and Sue into the living room.

Sue felt her forehead, motherly as usual. "No fever. Sit. We'll take care of you today." Sue walked into the kitchen. .

Josephine couldn't help but notice how slim Sue had become. Her vibrant red hair set off the sparkle in her soft, beautiful blue eyes.

"Must be because of the upcoming wedding," Josephine thought to herself.

Her sisters made breakfast. She ate very little. They watched the parade and reminisced about Christmas. Luke was a source of entertainment that day. The bows on his head and the funny little dance he did made Josephine laugh so hard her stomach hurt. Nate had challenged Luke to a "house building contest" with cards. Nate lost, and the sisters laughed remembering the good-natured teasing he endured the rest of the day from Luke.

"How are you feeling, Jo?" Sue sipped her diet coke.

"Exhausted. I just don't know what is wrong with me!" Josephine flopped her body onto the couch.

Brittany took a bite of chocolate cake. "You remind me of how I felt when I was first pregnant with Joslyn. Remember? I was exhausted and nauseous."

The color drained from Josephine's face. "Oh no!" She groaned softly. Her thoughts drifted to the night with Jim. "Oh no!" She covered her face with her hands and started to cry.

Her sisters looked at her with shock at the sudden outburst.

Brittany set down her cake and put her arm around Josephine. "Sweetheart, what's wrong?"

Through sobs, Josephine told her sisters what had happened the night Jim came over. By the time she was finished, tears were streaming down Brittany's cheeks, and Sue sat in stunned silence.

"Ok." Sue stood up and gathered her purse and keys. "I'll go get a pregnancy test."

"Hey Sue," Brittany smiled through her tears, "could you get two?"

Sue mustered up a smile and hugged her. "You bet." She walked out the door a second later, leaving Brittany and Josephine alone to talk.

While Sue was gone, Josephine recounted her story to Brittany about repenting and seeking God's forgiveness.

"I thought it would all be ok. I mean I thought that I was forgiven." Her lip quivered. Tears threatened to escape once again.

"It is ok and you are forgiven, but remember, being pregnant isn't a sign of not being forgiven. Being pregnant just means that your sin got found out. Remember though, that doesn't mean this baby isn't a gift. God has a plan for its life, and yours, Jo." Brittney hugged her. "I love you, little sister.".

Josephine sniffed and nodded her head. "Thank you. I love you to."

Just then Sue walked through the door. "Well, that was fun!" She rolled her eyes, setting the bag down. "I thought it might be awkward buying one pregnancy test. You should have seen the look the cashier gave me when I bought two."

Josephine chuckled softly and grabbed the test.

"Here goes." she headed for the bathroom.

When she came out, her eyes were red from crying. Suddenly, the world she knew so well was about to change. She looked at her sisters and tried to tell them the test was positive. Instead, all that came out was a cry of despair. They both ran to her side and wrapped their arms around her.

"It's going to be all right," they both kept saying.

"How?" Josephine was weak and needed to sit down. The edge in her voice caught even herself off guard. But she didn't care. Why would God allow this to happen? She thought she was forgiven! How come she didn't feel it now?

"How is it going to be all right?" The room started to spin. "I'm twenty years old! This isn't what was supposed to happen!"

Josephine sat down quickly and put her head between her legs, trying to stop herself from passing out. Her breathing was quick. Her heart was beating so rapidly, she felt as if it was going to burst from her chest.

"Jo, you need to breath." Brittany's voice was calm and collected. She sat beside Josephine and rubbed her back. "It is going to be fine. It doesn't seem that way now, but it will. You messed up, yes. However, God has a plan. You need to trust that."

Josephine's breathing began to slow down. She knew what Brittany was saying was true. Even in her sin, God had a plan. Her head knew these things, but her heart was still conflicted. Josephine chose to believe what her head was telling her. Even when things look bleak, she knew she could trust God would lead her and guide her. But still, she was scared. How could she raise a child on her own? This wasn't how she pictured her life turning out. She wasn't supposed to be pregnant, without a husband!

Josephine sat up slowly. She inhaled deeply and looked at each of her sisters. What they must think of her!

"Are you upset with me?"

Sue spoke first. "Are we upset with your decision to sleep with Jim? Yes." She paused for a brief moment. "Are we going to judge you? No. What's done is done. We love you, little sister, no matter what. We'll help you as much as we can, okay?"

Josephine nodded. Smiling a weak smile, she looked at Brittany.

"Sis, it's your turn."

"No way. I'll take it when I get home." Brittany shook her head emphatically.

"No," Josephine insisted, "I want to be one of the first people who know if you're pregnant or not. Now go, Brit." She gave her a gentle push toward the bathroom.

"You need to tell Jim, Jo." Sue's voice was gentle but firm.

"Huh?" Josephine was obviously distracted. She nodded slowly. "Oh yeah, I know. I'll call the doctor tomorrow for an appointment just to confirm and then tell him."

The bathroom door opened and both girls looked up. "Well Brit?" Sue asked as Brittany walked toward her sisters.

Her eyes glowed with excitement. "Positive!"

The three sisters squealed with delight and hugged one another. No matter what her situation, Josephine was thrilled for Brittany.

After her sisters left, Josephine felt physically and emotionally exhausted

"*Lord*," she cried as she covered her face with her hands, "*what am I going to do?*"

She waited, and when no answer came, she sighed and lay down for a restless night of sleep.

○ ○ ○ ○

As Sue drove home, her heart ached for her sister. At the same time, her heart ached for herself. She was going to be getting married in just a few short months. She was excited to be marrying Nate. He was the most incredible man she had ever met. He loved Jesus with all of his heart. He was compassionate, gentle, yet strong, and the handsomest man she had ever laid eyes on! He had a great sense of humor and kept her laughing. He reminded her so much of her father. She knew he was the man for her!

Sue sighed now as tears threatened to spill onto her cheeks. She knew they were not able to have children. That was the cause of the ache inside of her heart. Nate had survived testicular cancer as a teenager, but unfortunately, he was unable to father children. Sue knew early on in their relationship. They had often talked about adopting children from third world countries. They had considered adoption from the United States, but one of the reasons Sue wanted to adopt internationally was because she wanted to give children hope. She wanted them to have a good future, and she wanted them to feel the love of Jesus. She could do that in America,., but the survival rate of children from third world countries was very low. Sue was happy with plans for adoption but knowing both of her sisters were pregnant caused a deep pain in her heart. Seeing the excitement on Brittany's face when she told them the news was thrilling! Brittany and Luke were already great parents. They loved their daughter and would be great parents to any child. Sue so enjoyed spending time with Joslyn. She was adorable, and was going to look precious as the flower girl in her wedding.

Josephine's pregnancy was a shock, to say the least. When Josephine had decided to rededicate her life to the Lord, Sue and Brittany were ecstatic! They helped her find an apartment in a good neighborhood; they helped her move out of Jim's place and set up her new home. They even bought her some house warming gifts. Sue and Brittany prayed for Josephine everyday, desiring her to be the woman God designed her to be. Now, she was pregnant. Sue wasn't angry or even disappointed with Josephine. Everyone has struggles, and right now, Josephine's was loneliness. She was just sad that her baby sister, who was not ready to be a parent, was going to have a baby.

Lord, she cried, as she pulled into her garage, *please help me be an encouragement to Josephine and her baby. Help me not to dwell on these negative thoughts. Help me to be content with what you have given me. I am grateful I have such a great husband-to-be. May I find joy in that!* She walked into the condo, took out her cell phone, and called Nate.

"Hi Nate." Sadness hung on her every word.

"Sweetie, what's the matter?" Nate's voice was filled with concern.

"Jo just told Brittany and me that she's pregnant." Sue knew she shouldn't be talking with Nate about this. But at this moment, she had no one else to turn to.

"Whoa, wait a minute. What?" Nate sounded as shocked as she had felt.

Sue told Nate the story Josephine had told her hours earlier. Then she finished by saying, "Brittany is pregnant, too."

"Ahhh." Understanding etched through his voice.

"I'm sorry, Nate. I shouldn't be talking to you about this." Sue felt a twinge of guilt pass through her heart.

"Honey, it's all right. I understand how you feel. I go through this every time I hear someone is pregnant. What can I do for you?"

"Nothing, Nate. It is just something that I need to continue to pray about. I'm fine, hon. Really. I would rather spend the rest of my life with you than have my own children. I look forward to the day when we can become husband and wife."

Sue desperately wanted to change the subject.

"Me, too, Sue, me, too. You are the greatest thing that has happened to me, aside from Jesus, of course." Nate's tone softened. Sue loved it when he used that tone of voice with her.

"I feel that way, too. I love you, Nate Danes."

"I love you, too, Sue **Johnson**."

○ ○ ○ ○

Brittany drove home with mixed emotions. She was so happy to be having another baby! She could hardly wait to tell Luke! He had wanted another baby so Joslyn could have with a playmate, to bond , grow and connect over the years. Now, that was actually going to happen. She was going to be a mom again! She was going to have another little one to hold. Joslyn was a little over one already. Sometimes, Brittany missed the baby stage. Now she was able to go through that all over again. Joslyn is going to be a big sister! She is going to love it!

God, I pray my two children will be the best of friends!

On the other hand, her baby sister was going to have a baby. Brittany knew Josephine was nowhere near ready to have a baby. Being a single mom would be difficult. She had friends who were single parents, and they often told her how blessed she was to have someone to share the load. She wanted to talk with Josephine more about what she was going to do, how she was going to take care of the baby, what she would do about Jim. She knew it was too soon to discuss anything with Josephine. She needed to have time for the shock to wear off.

Brittany took a deep breath to try to relieve the tension that was building inside of her.

Well, Lord, she prayed, *You have a plan. I pray you will have me, Luke, Sue, Nate, and myself help out as much as possible and do what we can for Josephine. Give Josephine strength as she faces this new challenge. I pray You will be in control of all that happens. Bless that little baby that is growing inside of Josephine. Bless the little baby growing inside of me, too! I can hardly wait to tell Luke!*

She pulled the car inside of garage. Luke opened the door from the house to the garage. He met her with a smile.

"Hi, beautiful!" he said. "I missed you today!"

Brittany threw her arms around him. "I missed you, too. I have some news for you!"

"Yeah? What's that?"

"I'm pregnant!" she squealed.

"You are? Really?" Luke picked her up and swung her around. "This is great!"

They hugged and kissed and ran to tell Joslyn the good news.

Once Joslyn was all tucked into bed, Brittany snuggled next to Luke on the couch.

"Hey, since you have been home, have you seen my Coke?"

Luke looked around the living room.

"Nope! You are such a nut! Can't keep track of your sodas these days, huh?" Brittany teased.

"Apparently not! So, how did the rest of today go?" Luke found his Coke. He sat down beside Brittany and took a sip. Then he began rubbing her back.

"Mm. I don't really know. It was good and bad, I suppose." Brittany was thoughtful before continuing.

She knew she needed to tell Luke about Josephine's pregnancy. He had taken the news pretty hard when Josephine decided to move in with Jim. He had spent many hours lying awake at night, heart broken over her decision to walk completely away from the Lord. Brittany knew Luke would be sad about this news, as well. Brittany took a deep breath.

"Josephine's pregnant," she said quickly, watching her husband's reaction. "That was tough news to take."

Luke nodded slowly, rubbing his chin. "Yes, I suppose it was. I must admit, I am not surprised, though."

"What do you mean?"

"Well, the warning signs were all there. She has been incredibly lonely for some time now. Since she and Jim broke up, she has struggled with being by herself. I wondered if she would go back to Jim. I'm glad she didn't. I'm just sorry she didn't call one of us instead."

Brittany nodded her head. "Yes. I wish she had called one of us, too. But what is done is done. She has truly repented, and that's good. I wonder what she is going to do now that she is pregnant."

"Do you think she will give the baby up for adoption?" Luke sipped his coke again.

"I don't know. I wish we could raise the baby, but with this new little one on the way, that's a little too much for us to handle." Brittany really wanted to adopt the little one. She just knew that for her, two babies would not be a good thing.

"Well, we will just have to pray God shows her what to do."

"I'm surprised you are taking the news so well." Brittany raised an eyebrow.

"Well, Josephine is a big girl now. She makes her own choices. I learned shortly after she moved in with Jim that I have to place her in God's hands and leave her there. It wasn't easy, and I still struggle with it every so often."

Luke stopped talking. A comfortable silence settled between them. Finally, Luke spoke again,

"C'mon, let's go to bed." Luke helped her up off the couch. "I love you, Brittany."

"I love you, too, Luke."

Chapter 2

*T*he doctor's appointment came. Josephine sat in the waiting area, wringing her hands. She was nervous, although she already knew the results..

Why am I so scared? She knew the answer. This wasn't how it was supposed to be. She should be sitting here with her husband, holding her hand in joyful expectation, excited to receive confirmation that indeed, they were going to be parents. Instead, she was sitting by herself, alone, waiting to confirm she was indeed pregnant. All of this was happening because she made a mistake with Jim.

Oh, well. It is what it is. She thought with finality.

No sense in dwelling on the past.

But what am I going to do about the future?

Finally, she was called in and within a few short minutes, the nurse returned with official confirmation of her pregnancy results. Tears sprang to her eyes. Her due date was mid-September.

Ugh, she thought, *big and pregnant during the summer! Could this get any worse?*

In a daze, Josephine walked to her car. She climbed into the driver's seat, her stomach feeling queasy ,and not entirely due to the pregnancy. She knew what she had to do, but felt uneasy about doing it. Slowly, she picked up her cell phone and dialed. Jim answered within seconds.

"Hey Jo," he said tentatively. "I thought you said we shouldn't call each other anymore."

"I know what I said, Jim." She hesitated. "But I need to see you. Can we meet somewhere public and talk?"

"I don't know, Jo. Is that such a good idea?"

"Jim, please. It's really important," she practically begged him.

"Okay. When and where?"

She suggested meeting that night at a restaurant for dinner. She looked at her watch. Now she just needed to waste three hours before they met. She began driving. Without realizing it, she ended up in front of Brittany and Luke's house. She got out of her car and walked up the steps. When she rang the doorbell, she heard giggling and laughter coming from inside.

God, I can't give my child what Luke and Brit give theirs, she prayed. *Help me to do the right thing. Show me what the right thing is. I don't even know how Jim is going to respond to this bombshell I am about to drop in his lap!*

Brittany answered the door, out of breadth. "Sorry, Sis. I was chasing Joslyn around! What's up?"

"I'm meeting Jim tonight for dinner to tell him the news. I just needed a place to go before we met. I don't want to be alone right now."

Brittany hugged her sister. "Come on in. Let's see if you and I can catch Joslyn together!"

Josephine smiled and agreed. "Joslyn, Auntie Jo has come to get you!" she sang out.

After playing with Joslyn and talking with Brittany, Josephine began to feel much better. She hardly noticed when it was time for her to go and meet Jim.

"I'll be praying for you, Jo." Brittany hugged her sister for a long time.

"Thanks! I will need it!" Josephine was grateful for the prayers on her behalf. She had no idea what to expect, but something told her it wasn't going to be good.

She drove to the restaurant a few minutes before she and Jim were to meet. As she was escorted to her table, her mind began to take on thoughts of their own.

What if Jim decided he wanted to get back together because of the baby? What would I do? Nothing has changed. I still do not want to be together anymore. But would I, for the sake of the baby? Ugh, Lord, give me wisdom!

Her stomach was in knots as she waited for him to arrive. To keep her hands steady she held on tightly to her drink. She was nervous about his reaction. He never wanted kids while they were dating, but now? Will his opinion change now that he is going to be a father?

She looked across the restaurant and saw the booth she and Jim had sat in on their first date. Her mind drifted back to that night. She still remembered Jim's easy smile and the sparkle in his eyes when he saw her. He had complimented her on her outfit and told her she was the most beautiful girl he had seen. Jim had driven them to this restaurant, a quiet place where the two of them could get to know each other. Josephine was nervous at first. It had been a long time since she had been out on a date. She knew her parents would not approve of Jim, but she quickly pushed that thought out of her mind. They were gone, weren't they? It didn't matter what they thought anymore. She sat across from Jim and liked how easy it was to talk with him. Jim was different than any guy she had dated. They didn't have a lot in common, and she liked that. Jim liked motorcycles and had tattoos on one of his arms. He was going to school and working part time and lived on his own. Josephine liked his independence and how he didn't rely on anyone. She was definitely attracted to him from the very beginning.

Josephine shook her head and brought herself to the present. Glancing out the window she saw him pull up in his car. As he got out and sauntered through the front door she thought, *Poor guy, he doesn't have a clue what's about to hit him.*

"What's going on, Jo? Why the sudden desire to meet?" He lounged in his chair.

Not being able to hold it in for another moment more, she blurted,

"Jim, I'm pregnant!"

"What?" he stammered, as he bolted upright.

"I'm pregnant. You're going to be a father." Her voice sounded calmer than what she felt at the moment. She couldn't read Jim's reaction, but instinct told her it wasn't a good one.

"When did you find out?" He rubbed his eyes with the palm of his hands.

"A few days ago." She studied him, trying to figure out what was going on in his mind.

"Okay," relief flooded his face as he leaned back and ran his hand through his hair. "so you can still terminate it right?"

"What?" Josephine shot straight up. She almost knocked over her drink. Realizing that she was making a scene, she quickly sat down. This is not what she'd expected. When they were dating, he never talked about abortion. She always assumed he felt it was wrong, like she did.

"Look, Jo, nothing has changed. I do not want to be a father. You know that."

"Jim, I'm not having an abortion! I am not going to end this child's life!"

"Look, this isn't my fault. You called me that night, remember? You were the one who allowed this to even take place. Once we broke up, that was it for me. And all of a sudden, I get a call from you. Now you are telling me you are pregnant with a baby I don't even want? Why didn't you use protection that night?" Jim slammed his hand down on the table in frustration.

People looked at them from around the room. Josephine blushed, embarrassed.

"Jim, please," she whispered, not wanting to draw anymore attention to them, "Let's not play the blame game. The fact of the matter is this: I am pregnant with your child. The question is what are we going to do about it?"

She leaned forward, hoping they would come to an agreement.

"I'm not going to have any involvement with this kid. I don't want it." Jim's voice was hard.

"You can't mean that, Jim!" Josephine's hand flew to her mouth as tears rushed to her eyes.

"I can and I do. I told you from the beginning I never wanted kids. What made you think now would be any different?"

Her voice rose. "Because now I am actually pregnant! That's why!" Josephine answered quickly. She looked around and lowered her voice. "Jim, I didn't want this to happen, either. I'm not ready to be a mom!"

"So why not an abortion, then? Neither one of us wants this thing. Just terminate it." Jim was calmer now. He leaned back in his chair.

"I can't. This child shouldn't suffer for our mistake. I thought you knew me better than that!" Josephine wiped the tears off of her cheeks.

Jim was impatient.. "And I thought you knew me better. You can raise this baby for all I care, but I'm out. I'll contact a lawyer and send over the paperwork." Jim got up to leave.

"Jim, wait! Please! Can't we talk more about this?" She grabbed his hand, her eyes pleading for him to stay with her.

Jim yanked his hand away. "There's nothing to discuss anymore, Jo. Good luck with everything."

With that, he stormed out of the restaurant.

Josephine sat there stunned. This is not what she had anticipated at all. She slowly pulled money out of her wallet and left it on the table. In a daze she walked out, got in her car to drive home.

Oh God! She leaned against the steering wheel. *What am I going to do? I can't be a single parent! I can't do this on my own! I'm only twenty years old! I'm not ready to be a mom! This baby deservers more than what I have to offer. Help me, Jesus! Please, tell me what you want me to do!*

No response came.

With tears streaming down her face, she drove home.

A few weeks passed. True to his word, Jim sent over legal papers giving up parental rights to the baby. She felt no emotion. Josephine prayed again.

God, I don't want to be a mother. Not now. Not anytime soon. I need your guidance. Please show me what to do.

An hour later she grabbed her keys and headed out the door.

○ ○ ○ ○

Sue had the day off of work. With her upcoming wedding,

she needed to prepare some of the house for Nate's stuff. Nate didn't own a lot of things, but she wanted to make sure her home turned into their home. Now, standing with her hands on her hips in the walk-in closet of her three bedroom condominium, she wondered if she would have enough room for Nate's clothing. She cocked her head to one side.

"I think this should be plenty of room," she said aloud to herself. "At least, I hope it will be plenty of room!"

Just then, she heard a noise from downstairs.

"Knock, knock!" She heard Josephine say.

"Hey, Jo! You startled me!" Sue called from her room. "I'm upstairs. Come on up!"

I hope everything is all right, Sue thought to herself as her sister made her way up. She prayed silently for wisdom. Josephine seldom made unannounced visits. Whatever the reason for Josephine being there, Sue needed wisdom from above and prayed she would receive it quickly.

Josephine loved coming to her sister's house. She walked through the entry way toward the stairs. As she walked up, she studied the pictures on the wall, pictures of her and her sisters, of Sue and Nate, even one of their parents. Tears sprung to Josephine's eyes as her gaze settled on the picture of her mom and dad.

Not now, she thought. *I can't think about them right now.* She sighed and looked over the banister. Even cluttered with all the wedding stuff in the house, there was a sense peace.

Lord, I need your peace, too, right now! Josephine silently prayed.

"Sue, I need to talk to you. Do you have a minute?" Josephine came into her room and sat down on the edge of the bed.

"You bet! Sit down on my bed. I'll be right there," Sue called from the closet. "I was just going through my clothes trying to make room for Nate's stuff when he moves in," she laughed.

"Good luck with that!" Jo giggled. "Nate has far more clothes than you ever had!"

"No kidding," Sue smiled sitting down. "What's up, Jo? Are you feeling alright?" Concern filled her eyes.

"I am, thanks." Josephine sighed a heavy sigh. "Sue, I need to talk to you about the baby. Nothing's wrong," she quickly added. "Jim was true to his word. I got the papers today."

"Oh, Sis," Sue reached over and took her hand and gave it a gentle squeeze. "I'm sorry. I prayed he would change his mind."

"It's okay. That's not why I am here, though," Josephine continued with a wave of her hand. "I know you have a lot on your plate right now, and I hate to add more. I just don't know what else to do." She paused as her eyes swelled with tears.

Sue's eyes were compassionate. "Go on".

"I can't do this, Sue. I'm just not ready, to be a parent, I mean." She got up and paced back and forth. "I know you and Nate have talked about having a family. I know you guys can't have kids, because of Nate's cancer when he was younger, so you were going to adopt." Josephine took a deep breath before continuing,

"Would you both consider adopting this baby?" Josephine blurted.

Sue's mouth dropped open. "What?" Her eyes grew wide.

"I know Sue; it's a shock that I would ask you. You'll be a newlywed by the time this baby arrives. I am sure you hadn't planned on starting a family this early in your marriage. But I can't keep it! I want it to go to a good family." Josephine paused and waited. "Please, Sue, say something." Josephine reached for her sister's hand once more.

"I...I don't know what to say. You know we wanted to adopt internationally. We never even considered adoption in the state." Sue paused. "But Jo, are you sure you want to do this? Shouldn't you pray about it?"

"Sue, I have prayed about it. I just won't be able to give this baby all it deserves. But you could." Josephine got up again and began pacing once more. "I want to do the unselfish thing for a change. I want to put this baby's needs before my own. Yes, I know it would be hard to raise a child by myself, so partly, I am being selfish. But on the other hand, I really want what is best for this baby. Besides, you would be a great mom, and

Nate is such a great man! You both love the Lord and would cherish this child." Josephine stopped. She sat back down on the bed again. "Please, Sis, pray about it. Talk with Nate. Let me know what you decide. We'll do everything by the book, legally, I mean. Will you think about it? Please?"

Sue nodded thoughtfully. "This is a lot to take in, Jo. But yes, I will seek the Lord, talk to Nate, and let you know."

Josephine hugged Sue. "Oh, thank you, Sue! Thank You!"

"Don't thank me yet, Jo!" Sue sighed and rubbed her forehead.

Josephine left Sue's house with a feeling of peace and relief.

This is the right thing to do, she thought. *I know it is!*

○ ○ ○ ○

Adopt Josephine's baby? Lord, is this what You really want for us?

Sue picked up the phone and called Nate. He promised he would be over as soon as he got off of work. Sue watched the minutes tick away ever so slowly. Finally, after what seemed like an eternity, Nate showed up at the house.

"Hey, Sweetie." He kissed her on the cheek. "The wedding stuff looks like it's coming together!"

Sue nodded. "It is. But, Nate, I need to talk to you about something. Josephine came over a little bit ago. She, well, you better sit down for this."

As she spoke, Sue was moving things off of the couch so he could sit down.

Sue took Nate's hand as she launched into the reason Josephine had come over and her request.

Nate's eyes bulged out in shock.

"She, she wants us, you and me, to adopt this baby? Only after a few months of being married? Is she serious?"

"I know. It's a lot to ask of a person." Sue watched as Nate got up and walked to the refrigerator. He pulled out a Dr. Pepper, opened it, and took a long drink. He slowly walked into the living room.

"Sue, this is crazy! Is she serious?" he asked again. "I understand why she would want to give the baby up for adoption, but to us? Us? Why us?"

"Okay, honey. I know you are in shock. But take it easy." She patted the couch next to her. "Sit, sweetie." Sue took his hand again and waited for him to relax a little. "She wants the baby to go to a good home, one where she knows it will be loved and cherished and valued. We could do that. She doesn't want to always be wondering what happened to the baby."

"Oh, Sue, there are so many things to take into consideration!" He ran his hand through his thick hair. "How is she going to respond when the baby calls her Auntie and not Mommy? How is she going to feel when she sees the baby every birthday party, holiday, or family gathering? How is she going to feel when she will be the one going through the pregnancy and labor and then to hand the baby over to us? What if, down the road, she realizes she wants the baby back? What then?"

Question after question came out of Nate's mouth.

Sue shrugged her shoulders. "I don't have all of those answers, not yet anyway. But I do know she wants this to be done legally, so she is going to have the appropriate papers drawn up, if we decide to do this."

Sue watched her husband-to-be wrestle with the thoughts overtaking his mind. She gave him a small smile. "I can ask her those questions that you just brought up, though."

Nate took a deep, long breath, and leaned back. "We need to ask God if this is His desire for us. I know we wanted to adopt. I just didn't think it would be this soon. I also didn't think we would be adopting a baby from a family member!"

"I know. This isn't exactly the way I pictured it." Sue loved how quick Nate went to the Lord for guidance.

Nate shook his head. "Let's take the week to fast and pray and seek godly wisdom. We will see if God answers us by then. Then you can call her and give her an answer."

They got on their knees right then and there and began praying.

Two days later, Brittany and Luke sat across from Sue and Nate, astonished looks on their faces.

"Let me get this straight," Luke started, trying to put all the pieces together, "Jo wants the two of you to adopt her baby?"

"In a nutshell, yes." Sue nodded her head. She began playing with the hem of her shirt.. "What do you both think?"

Brittany and Luke looked at each other, speechless. Brittany held up her hand.

"I need a second to process."

"So do I!" Luke sighed.

They sat in silence for a few minutes, each silently praying for wisdom. Finally, Luke spoke up. "What have you two decided?"

"We haven't yet. That's just it. We fasted yesterday, and will do so again in a few days. We've been praying about it, but don't know what to do yet. We know we need to seek Godly counsel, and that is where the two of you come in." Nate leaned over and patted Luke's shoulder.

"I can't say it is a terrible idea." Sue could tell Luke was contemplating his words. "I would hate to see this baby grow up without a dad, and I would hate to have her give the baby up for adoption outside of the family."

"We actually thought about adopting the baby, but since I am already pregnant, we thought it wouldn't be a good idea." Brittany added.

Now Sue and Nate showed their shock. "Really?" Sue knew Brittany could handle twins, even though her sister didn't think so. Brittany was great with kids! She had a patience most people didn't even posses.

Brittany nodded her head. "Really. Jo had told me Jim never wanted to have kids. He said they were too much of a burden. When she told us she was going to tell him she was pregnant, I really doubted he would change his mind. So, Luke and I considered adopting the baby, but with this little Davidson coming, we thought it wouldn't be wise." She rubbed her belly, although she wasn't even showing yet.

"So, what do you think about the two of us adopting the baby, being newlyweds shortly after the baby is born?" Sue respected Brittany and Luke more than any other person. Their opinion meant the world to her.

"I think we need time to pray about it. It's a lot of work, that's for sure. And it won't give the two of you much time together. But," Luke added, rubbing his goatee, "I don't think it's a bad idea. If there is any couple who could do it, it would be the two of you. What do you think, Brit?"

"I agree with everything Luke just said. Continue to pray about it and fast. But know you will have our support no matter what you decide to do." Brittany's smile lit up her face.

"I do have one more thing to say, though," Luke said, a serious expression on his face. "Has anyone seen my Coke? I can't seem to find it!" Sue, Nate, and Brittany laughed, shaking their heads. "I'm serious! I really want my coke!" They laughed some more and got up from the couch.

Leaving their house hand in hand, Nate looked at Sue. She looked at him and blushed. "What are you staring at?"

"I just keep thinking you would be a great mom, sweetie." Nate tenderly took her in his arms and kissed her.

A gentle smiled caressed her face. "Thanks. The more I think about it, the more I want to adopt this little baby!"

"I was thinking that same thing. Let's not get ahead of ourselves, though. Lets continue to fast and pray the remainder of the week, and then we can decide, ok?"

Sue wrapped her arms around his neck and squeezed him a little tighter. "Ok!"

A week went by and Josephine still hadn't heard from Sue.

I need to be patient. She needs time to think it all through.

Just as she walked through the door to her home, her cell phone rang.

"Hey, Sue!" Josephine tried to calm her racing heart..

"Hey, Jo., Nate and I talked about it and prayed and fasted. We decided that if this is really what you want....we'll adopt the baby."

"Oh, my gosh! Thank you! Sis, you are truly the best! I will get the paperwork all drawn up and then----"

"Wait, Jo," Sue interrupted. "You need to carefully think through this, though. Nate brought up some very good points. The baby will call you "Auntie" and not "Mommy". Every birthday party and holiday, you are going to see this baby. Are you going to be able to handle that? How are you going to feel going through the pregnancy, and going through the labor only to hand the baby over to us when it is all over? And Jo, once it is done, it's done! You cannot just take the child back if you suddenly decide you want him or her."

"Sue, I've thought through all of that. First, I am not going to take the child back. Once those papers are signed, we're done. I am not ready to be a mom. I'm just now getting my life together, mentally, financially, spiritually. I could not offer this baby what the two of you could."

"Second," Josephine continued, taking a deep breath, "I will be fine seeing the baby because I know he or she went to a good home. I will still be a part of the child's life. I won't ever have to wonder if he or she had a good life, I'll know because of you. I will try hard not to get too attached to the baby during pregnancy. I know this is the right thing to do, Sue, I just know it! Thank you, Sue! Thank you!" Josephine started to cry, all the stress of the last few months finally being released.

○ ○ ○ ○

Nate and Sue went to every doctor's appointment with Josephine. They didn't want to miss a thing when it came to the baby. They heard the heartbeat for the first time and marveled at the miracle of life. Sue was so excited to be a mom! She and Nate had already started reading parenting books, as well as adoption books. One of the things the books suggested was that they get involved in an adoption support group. Sue and Nate decided after the wedding they would locate a local adoption support group and join it. They needed the support of people who had either gone through adoption or were in the process of adopting.

Sue could hardly wait for the day they could take the baby home. It was a good thing she had her wedding to distract her from counting down the days. Now that Josephine and Brittany were going to be pretty pregnant for their wedding, she had to make some adjustments for their gowns. She wanted them to be as comfortable as possible during her ceremony. She made sure they had stools set up for them in the case they got too tired to stand during the wedding.

The day for their wedding came. It was a beautiful day. Sue had always wanted an outside wedding. Sue looked out the window from the room she was getting ready in. The sun was shining, which can be a rare thing in Colorado! Normally, thunder storms were a daily thing. She smiled. Not a cloud in the sky! Sue tore her eyes away from the window and stared at herself in the full length mirror. The only thing missing, she thought holding back her tears, were her parents.

She wished her mom and dad could be there, as they had been with Brittany during her wedding, making sure everything was going according to plan. She wished her dad could be there to walk her down the aisle. Sue was thrilled that Luke had agreed to walk her down the aisle. It had taken some time to convince him to do it, but after a little while, he finally relented.

If her dad wasn't able to do it, then Luke was definitely the next best thing. But still, she missed her father. She missed the way his eyes shown when he was proud to be her dad. She missed the way his arms felt around her, calming her fears. She missed his godly wisdom and advice. Sue thought back to the day her father met Nate. Nate and Sue were just friends back then, just going to see a movie together. Her father had sensed something more was developing between them and asked Sue about it. Sue's cheeks had turned a bright shade of pink.

"I don't know, Daddy," she had answered truthfully. "Sometimes I think there is something happening between us, and then other times, I think I am just imagining things."

"Would you like there to be something?" her dad had asked, his eyes softly studying his daughter.

Sue smiled. "Honestly, yes."

Her dad hugged her. "Then he would be a fool not to be interested in you." Sue laughed. "I love you, Dad. Just do me a favor, okay?" Her father pulled away. "What's that?"

"Don't tell Nate that!"

Her dad put his hand to his heart. "What? Me? Do anything to embarrass my daughter? Never!

Sue had laughed and gently pushed her father toward the living room. Of course, her mom and dad loved Nate from the moment they met him. Sue had known they would all get along wonderfully!

Sighing, she glanced at the clock. The time came for her to meet Luke outside. As she walked up to him, he kindly whispered to her,

"You look lovely, Sue. Your dad would have been so proud!"

Tears sprung to her eyes. "Thanks, Luke. Thanks for doing this for me. I appreciate it more than you know!"

As she walked down the aisle, she only had eyes for Nate. His broad shoulders filled out his tuxedo nicely. He looked extremely handsome! She couldn't take her eyes away from him, and he couldn't tear his eyes away from her.

When their hands touched, he said to her softly, "You look absolutely gorgeous!"

Her eyes met his. "So do you!"

The pastor did a fantastic job at officiating the ceremony. He told of how they met, how they got engaged. He had them repeat their wedding vows after him, all the while Nate was crying. Sue was deeply touched at his display of emotions.

"You may kiss your bride, Nate," the pastor said.

Nate's kiss was sweet and gentle, yet filled with passion.

"Ladies and gentlemen, I introduce to you for the very first time, Mr. and Mrs. Nate Danes!"

The audience clapped and rose to their feet as Sue and Nate walked down the aisle together.

It was one of the best days of Sue's life.

○ ○ ○ ○

As Josephine watched them walk away together, she thought

her sister looked amazing in her wedding gown.

I've never seen her look more beautiful, Josephine thought, standing next to Brittany. Nate looked more handsome than ever. During the ceremony, Nate cried.

I would love to have a man that sensitive!

She watched Nate wipe his eyes. She pulled out a tissue hidden in her bouquet of flowers and dabbed at her own eyes. Josephine could tell this day was what he had always wanted and prepared.

There was a quick reception, and then the happy couple headed off to their honeymoon.

Josephine was surprised to learn they cut their honeymoon short so they could prepare the baby's room in their condo .With the baby being due in just a few months, she was touched.

Josephine felt truly blessed by Nate and Sue. They paid for all of her doctor appointments, maternity clothes and legal fees. Josephine was thrilled when all the paper work was finally signed and done. She would not allow herself to get attached to the baby. Sometimes it was difficult for her, but she knew it would be easier letting go if she did not get attached.

She spent a lot of time with Sue. Every time the baby kicked, Sue would rush over to feel it. The look of utter joy on her sister's face confirmed Josephine was doing the right thing in giving up the baby.

o o o o

Nate and Sue walked into the adoption support group, a little tentative. They had been talking about doing this for weeks, but finally made the decision to just go.

"Everyone- I want to introduce Sue and Nate Danes," the leader of the group announced.

Everyone said hello and the group began. The group became a special place for Nate and Sue to express their concerns and joys over adopting. They received encouragement and advice. They were made aware of problems that could potentially arise. Because of the support group, Sue became fast friends with Kayla and Brad Musso.

Kayla became one of Sue's best friends. After the meetings, Sue and Nate would often go out to dinner with Brad and Kayla. Brad and Kayla had wanted to adopt a child for years. They had been married for five years, and finally decided it was time. They were in the process of adopting a little girl, almost one year old. Her name was Taylor Joy. Kayla was thrilled and could hardly wait for the day that they would bring her home.

Sue and Kayla would talk of their kids being the best of friends. They would plan play dates for future events, knowing that because they would be friends for life, so would their kids. Kayla often asked if Sue wanted a boy or girl.

"Truthfully, Kay," Sue admitted once, "I pray it's a boy. That way," she continued with a sly grin, "we could arrange their marriage! Just to make sure we would always be connected!"

Kayla threw her head back and laughed. "Sounds like a plan to me!"

○ ○ ○ ○

The day came when they were to find out the sex of the baby. When they found out the baby was going to be a boy, Nate and Sue cried. Sue had always pictured herself with a boy.

On the way home from the appointment, they decided to go grab a bite to eat.

"Well, you two," Nate broke the silence, "I think it is time we decide on a boy's name, don't you?"

Josephine looked surprised. "What do you mean? Don't you think you and Sue should do that?"

"We already talked about it, Jo." Sue took a bite of her salad. "We decided no matter what the sex of the baby would be, you would help us figure out a name for him or her. So, what are your thoughts?"

Josephine's eyes were misty. "I can't believe you two! You amaze me, you know that?"

"As amazing as we are," Nate teased her, "we still need a name. Let's brainstorm, shall we?"

"What about Nathaniel?" Sue suggested.

Nate shook his head. "Nope. Too close to my name."

"Hm. What about John?"

"Too ordinary," Sue wrinkled her nose.

"What about James?" Josephine suggested, carefully.

"Oh, I like James for a middle name!" Nate nodded his agreement. "That's one of your favorite books of the Bible, right?"

Josephine nodded. "It is! It is a life changing book in the Bible. I can only pray your son will change lives, as well!"

"Me, too," Sue said softly. She wiped her mouth with her napkin, a light dawning in her eyes. "Hey, I know this is totally sentimental, but what about Daniel?"

Josephine gasped as her hand flew to her mouth. It was perfect! "Daniel James."

Nate's eyes were tender as he laid his hand on Sue's. "Perfect. I couldn't have chosen a better name myself."

All three agreed on Daniel James, DJ for short.

Daniel, Sue thought, ***Dad's name! How I wish he were here!***

○ ○ ○ ○

Sue woke with a start. Today was the day! Looking over at Nate, she saw that he was sleeping soundly.

How can he do that? She wondered.   Today the social worker was coming over to give the home inspection. They had already gone through so much. This was the final phase of the adoption.

Did we really do everything we needed to do? She quickly made a checklist in her head. They were already fingerprinted. That was the easiest and first thing they had accomplished. Along with completing their paperwork, they had to have their personal reference letters done. They had their physicals done, along with the TB test. *What else?* She tapped the tip of her nose.

What else did we need to have done? Oh yes! She suddenly remembered. They had been certified in CPR. Plus, they had to have their car checked and approved. Whew! She brushed her hand across her forehead. She knew they had done so much more than just those few things. The paperwork was huge on top of all the other things. She could hardly believe they had done everything that was asked of them including the twenty one hours of   pre- certification classes. With planning their wedding, going to doctor's appointments, and the classes, they were a busy couple! Sue was sure they would pass the house inspection. Now, if only she could go back to sleep!

"Jo!" Sue called her sister later that day.

"Yeah?" Josephine asked.

"We passed! We passed the inspection!"

Josephine laughed. "I had no doubt that you would, sis!"

○ ○ ○ ○

As the months flew by Josephine became more and more uncomfortable. She did not enjoy pregnancy and the pain it caused her body. Being on her feet because of work was killing her back and by the time she got home, her feet were always swollen. Her friends at work tried to get her to take more breaks, but she insisted on standing.

"When I sit, I feel all squished. It's not a fun feeling!" she would complain.

It was humbling, going to work day after day, knowing she had sinned terribly with Jim and had her pregnancy to show for it. She felt like she blew her witness to her friends at work, but no one judged her. She told them she was wrong in sleeping with Jim. She said she did not regret getting pregnant, though. She just regretted the decision she had made. She prayed it would not hinder them from accepting Jesus one day. Perhaps it had shown her friends that even Christians sin. One of them, Bobbi, had expressed an interest in going to church with her. Her heart swelled with gratefulness to God for an opportunity to share despite her sin.

One day after work, she came home completely wiped out. She headed straight for the recliner Brittney and Luke had bought her.

Brittany....she hadn't talked to Brittany in a few days. She eased her way onto the recliner.

"Ahhh!" Her whole body relaxed as she reached for the phone and dialed the number.

"Hello?" Luke answered.

"Hi Luke! It's Josephine. How are you?"

"Good, Prego! Except I can't seem to find my Coke! Why does this always happen to me?" He pretended to be exasperated.

"You just can't sit still, that's all! You are always walking around with a Coke in your hand, and then you put it down. Think about when the last time it was that you had it?" Josephine crossed her feet at her ankles.

"I don't even know. Hm. Anyway, enough about me. How are you feeling?" Luke's voice carried concern over the phone.

"Ugh! Don't ask. How Brit did this twice is beyond me. Is she there?"

"Yep. Hang on a sec."

A few moments later Brittany got on the phone.

"Hey, sis! It's only two o'clock. How come you are home so early? Are you feeling alright?" Josephine could tell Brittany was worried.

"I'm fine. It was just a slow day, and I didn't mind leaving work a little early. Let's not talk about me. Let's talk about you. How are you?"

"Good! I've been having contractions off and on today. I figure that sometime tomorrow, this baby will be here!" Brittney sounded excited.

"Lucky you! I am so done being pregnant!" Josephine loved talking to her sister. Brittany always had a positive outlook on life, no matter what her circumstances. After chatting for a few minutes Brittney started to have a contraction.

"I know this isn't a good time. I'll let you go. Call me if you need anything okay?" Josephine hung up the phone.

Brittany was already having contractions, and here she was, not having started.. Her heart was disappointed and frustrated. Why couldn't she have contractions now, too? It would be so neat to have the two kids have the same birthday! Not that she would be the one planning Daniel's birthday party, but she would be there celebrating him.

She suddenly felt the pang of giving up her son. She would never be able to tell him he was hers. Was she doing the right thing in giving him up? In her heart of hearts, she knew she was doing the right thing. At the same time, her heart was breaking, knowing in just a few short days, she would be sitting at home, no longer pregnant, all alone while Nate and Sue celebrated a new family member. Josephine reached for the remote control, doing anything to take her mind off of the feelings that were all jumbled inside of her.

A few hours later she received a call from Sue. Brittany was in the hospital having the baby. Off Josephine went to the hospital.

As she waddled down the corridor, she kept getting curious glances.

"I'm not here for me. My sister's in labor!" she kept explaining to the nurses.

"People are giving me the oddest looks!" Josephine was exasperated, slowly sitting down in the chair next to Sue.

"No kidding," Nate replied, dryly, looking up from his book. "It's because you look like you belong here right next to Brittany!"

She stuck her tongue out at him and made a face. "Whatever. Just because I look like I belong here doesn't mean I should yet. Although, let me tell you, I wish I were right next to Brittany!"

Nate chuckled. "Don't worry, Sis. All in due time. It'll happen when it's time!"

Sue patted her leg. "We'll be there for you when it does, Jo. In the meantime, if it doesn't happen soon, why don't we take you miniature golfing tomorrow? That could take your mind off of not going into labor and might even help walking around. "

Josephine gave Sue a grateful look. "Thanks, Sue! I would love that!"

She was only there a few hours when Luke announced they had a boy! Gideon Henry! Josephine smiled as she held her newest nephew. He looked so much like Luke! He had sweet little fingers that would clench into a fist when he cried. She gently stroked his head, praying Gideon and DJ would be the very best of friends. The feelings welling up inside her were too much for her to handle. She handed Gideon back to Brittany.

"You did great, Brittany Josephine wiped her eyes with the back of her sleeve.

Brittany looked tired, but happy.

"Thanks. You're next."

"We can only hope," Josephine commented back. It would be a bittersweet moment, after all, when her turn finally arrived.

Just then, a nurse entered the room.

"Okay, family," she said, shooing them out the door. "I need to check on the mommy and the baby."

Josephine, Nate, and Sue walked to the waiting room and sat down.

Once they were in the hallway headed back to the waiting room, Josephine needed to be by herself.

"I need a Sprite or something. Can I get either of you something?"

"No, thanks," Sue waived her hand. "We're good."

As she was just about to walk away, a weird sensation came over her. Within seconds, she knew, her water had broken.

"Uh, Jo, I think you got your wish!" Nate pointed to the floor. "About wanting to have the baby, I mean."

Suddenly contractions began to hit. Josephine doubled over in pain. "Hey, Sue? I think we may have to cancel our miniature golfing tomorrow!

"Ow!" she exclaimed, grabbing her stomach again.

Sue giggled and then turned her attention to Nate. "Nate, go get a nurse. Grab the paperwork, too!" she reminded him. "Do you have your bag in the car?"

"Yeah. I've been bringing it with me in the case I go into labor," Josephine laughed nervously.

"Good. When Nate comes back, I will have him go to the car and get it for you, ok?"

Josephine just nodded and began breathing through the pain like the Lamaze instructor told her to.

The contractions were the worst feeling she had ever had. She doubled over once more. Sue eased her into a chair. The pain was excruciating!

"Where is that nurse?" Josephine was getting impatient.

"Right here," Nate answered, coming up from behind her.

The nurse came with a wheelchair. Josephine sat down, holding onto her belly and breathing.

"Nate, please go to the car and get Jo's bag. Also, stop by Brittany's room and let her know what's going on. Tell her these cousins could be born just a few hours apart! Thanks, Hon!"

She was quickly admitted into the hospital and given her own birthing room.

Good, she thought, breathing through a contraction. *Now strangers won't have to see or hear me go through this pain!*

Sue was right beside her the entire time, encouraging her, praying for her. She was so excited, she could barely contain herself. This was it! In just a few short days, she would be taking home her son! She could hardly believe it! Knowing Josephine was going through such pain, she decided to keep her excitement to herself. She stood in amazement, watching Josephine breath through each contraction. She would watch the monitor and prepare Josephine when a contraction was about to hit. Josephine would squeeze Sue's hand so hard she thought it was going to break. She knew Josephine was in a tremendous amount of pain, and when the nurse came in asking if Josephine wanted an epidural, Sue had to turn away as she administered the needle. It wouldn't do Josephine any good if Sue was to pass out! Sue kept praying, asking God to keep her strong for Josephine. It was the least she could do, since Josephine was giving up her son to her and Nate.

In no time at all, everything would be over, and Sue would be a mom!

Finally, after what seemed like an eternity, Josephine held

DJ in her arms. She looked at his tiny fingers and smiled sadly. Through her tears she said,

"Hey little guy. I'm your Auntie Jo."

Glancing over at Sue and Nate, who both had tears in their eyes, she cleared her throat.

"You better take your son, Nate. He wants to meet his daddy."

Nate carefully took Daniel James out of Josephine's arms. "Jo, thank you very much for giving us this opportunity." He looked at her briefly before turning his eyes to his son.

Turning his back, he began whispering to DJ only words audible to the baby.

Sue gently eased her way down on Josephine's bed. "Sis, you were amazing, you know that?"

Josephine shook her head. "I couldn't have done it without you being here. Thank you," she stopped, choking back tears.

The sisters hugged each other.

One was grateful for the gift of motherhood.

The other was grateful for the gift of family.

Chapter 3

*S*ue stayed all through the day with Josephine in the hospital. When she needed to get out of bed to use the bathroom, Sue was right there, helping her up. When DJ needed to be fed, Sue would get the bottle ready and feed him. Sue had asked Josephine if she wanted to feed him first, but Josephine declined. She felt it would be better for DJ and her if neither one of them grew attached to the other. Josephine looked at Sue, sitting in the rocking chair, feeding DJ his bottle. She was humming "Jesus Loves Me" as he was gulping down the formula.

She looks like she has been doing this most of her life! God, help her in this new role as a mom!

Once DJ's diaper was changed, and he was put back into the bassinet, Josephine patted the spot next to her on the bed. "You are a natural, Sue. If I ever had doubts about this, that moment just wiped them completely away."

Sue sat next to Josephine. "Thank you. I know this is hard for you. I am so proud of you for doing what you felt God called you to do. You are amazing, you know that?"

"Thank you." Josephine's lip began to quiver. She knew she needed to change the subject or she would break down. "Have you seen Brittany?"

"Yes. Luke took her and Gideon home already. She didn't want to stay another night in the hospital, and since Gideon is her second child, the doctor on duty felt comfortable enough for her to go home. Luke said he will take you home when you get discharged, too."

Tears came to Josephine's eyes yet again. It seemed to be

the norm for her the last few days. "That was really nice of him. I should be able to drive myself, though, don't you think?"

"No way! The doctor says no driving for at least two weeks! You need to let your body heal, Jo!"

"Okay, okay!" Josephine held her hands up in resignation. Josephine slept peacefully that night. She knew she didn't need to worry about DJ because Sue was there, taking care of both of their needs.

The next day, the doctor told Josephine she was doing well enough to be released to go home. Sue called Luke, who showed up an hour later. After the paperwork was signed for Josephine and DJ to be discharged from the hospital, the nurse put Josephine and DJ in a wheelchair and took her to the entrance of the hospital. Josephine tried arguing with the nurse that Sue should carry him out, but that was against hospital policy. Sue and Nate walked behind the nurse, Luke following with Josephine's bag. At the front of the hospital, Luke ran to get the car for Josephine. Sue gently took DJ from Josephine's arms. Before she let go, she kissed his head.

"I love you, little man. Be good for your mommy and daddy," she whispered to the sleeping baby. She sucked in her breath, trying to gain control over her raging emotions.

Luke carefully helped her up and into the car. Nate put DJ in his car seat and Sue climbed in the front seat of their car. As Luke pulled away from the curb, so did Nate. Luke turned one way, Nate the other. Josephine felt a deep ache in her soul. She placed her hand on the window, silently saying her good-byes one more time to the son she would never raise.

Nate and Sue were going home to start a new family.

She was going home to an empty, lonely apartment.

○ ○ ○ ○

"We're home, little one," Nate softly sang to DJ as he carried him into the condo.

"I can hardly believe we're already parents!" Sue closed the door behind her.

"I know. It's wonderful already, isn't it?" Nate marveled. He walked up the stairs.

"Where are you going?" Sue was puzzled. She had thought they would sit downstairs and get acquainted as a family.

"I am going to show little Daniel his new room." Nate's face showed mock annoyance.

"Oh. Wait. I'm coming, too!" Sue hurried up the stairs behind them.

When they entered the room, Sue was surprised to see Nate had done more work on it. The walls were painted blue and green, which they had done together. But he added a gliding rocking chair with a foot stool in the corner of the room. On the wall closest to the window, Nate moved the changing table. On the long wall, Nate and Sue had put the crib.

"When did you get that rocking chair?" Sue slowly sat down and rocked back and forth.

"I got it yesterday when you were at the hospital with Jo. I thought it would be a nice surprise and touch to the room." Nate carefully handed her DJ.

"It is! I love it!" She rubbed the tip of her finger over DJ's sweet cheeks. "Thanks! Hey," she added carefully looking at his watch. "It's almost dinner time. Do you want me to make something or should we just go grab something to eat?"

"Let's grab something. I want to enjoy every second with DJ today." Nate took DJ back, tenderness pouring from his eyes.

Sue got up and put her hand on his shoulder. He looked up, tears in his eyes. "When we talked about adopting, I never expected to adopt at this age. It's a miracle, isn't it?" She had tears in her voice.

Nate nodded his head, unable to speak.

"I'll go get dinner. I'll be back soon, all right?"

Nate nodded again. Sue smiled. Things were going so well already! She got in the car and pulled out her cell phone.

"Kayla!" Sue exclaimed, pulling out of the garage. "It's Sue! Daniel's here! We're at home already!"

"Oh, Sue! Congratulations! I'm so happy for you!"

"How's Taylor?" Sue turned right on Wadsworth.

"Great! She is absolutely adorable! She's going to be so thrilled to have Daniel here!" Kayla told Sue about how well Taylor was adjusting to herself and Brad.

"I am so glad, Kay. I'll have you guys over in a few days to play, okay? Well," Sue laughed, "Daniel won't be able to play, but at least you guys can see him!"

"Sounds good, my friend. Try to get some sleep tonight!" Kayla advised.

Sue grinned and went through the drive through of their favorite fast food place.

When she got home, Nate was still in DJ's room, singing songs of love to their new son.

○ ○ ○ ○

The weeks that followed were difficult. Josephine had no idea how painful it would be to have a baby and recover from it.

Sue, Nate, Brittany, and Luke had paid for a caretaker to come help her while she was healing.

Caretaker, she thought. *Mom should have been here.*

Without warning, her thoughts drifted back to that horrible day. Mom and Dad were going on a trip together. Josephine had already graduated from high school, at the early age of 16, due to being home- schooled by her mom. She was already in cosmetology school, and had been for two years already. She had often wondered if her parents would be disappointed she wanted to be a hair stylist.

"Honey," her father wrapped her in his strong arms, "there are no such things as bad jobs as long as you work hard and it is pleasing to the Lord. We are proud of you. We are thankful you found a career that you love and that you would be used for God in the process!"

Not only had that brought a smile to her face, but tears to her eyes, knowing she wasn't a disappointment to her parents.

"Mom, I'll be fine," she said after a series of questions from her mother. "I am a big girl now. I am 18, not 12! Don't worry!"

"I know, Sweetie," her mom pated her on the arm. "It's just

that I do worry. I will always worry about you, no matter what. It is just something I have to continually give to the Lord."

Her mom smiled a sad smile. She looked older than Josephine had remembered. Her dark brown hair had touches of gray in the front and around her temples. Her blue eyes seemed sadder than normal.

"Are you all right, Mom?" Josephine took a step closer to her mom. "You look worn out."

"I'm fine, dear. I am just a little tired, that's all. Back to the conversation at hand, though. I want you to be extra careful this week. I know we will only be gone a few days, but I want you to be careful. Call your sisters if you need anything. I already told them to look in on you."

Josephine groaned and rolled her eyes. "Oh, Mom."

"Promise me you will call them if you need anything."

"I promise, Mom," she had answered.

"She better promise," her dad's voice came through the door way.

"Daddy!" Josephine said, startled, and laughed. "I will call them if I need anything. Don't worry!"

Her father came to her then and gave her a sideways hug. "We will pray for you while we are gone. Continue working hard in school. It will all pay off. We are so proud of you, Jo! You are loved very much, you know that?"

"I know, Dad. I love you, too!"

As her dad walked away to put the rest of the luggage in the car, she noticed how strong he looked. He had always been a symbol of strength in her eyes, demanding respect, but always available and compassionate and tender-hearted.

That's the kind of man I want to marry, Lord, she thought. She cocked her head to one side and studied her father. He had black hair, but oddly enough, he was blonde as a child.

Must be where I get my blonde hair. His eyes were a hazel color, often changing from brown to green without a moments notice. He had broad shoulders, which were perfect particularly when a few tears were shed.

As her father came back, he smiled his old, playful smile.

"What are you thinking about, Josephine? You look so serious!"

"Just thinking about how blessed I am to have you and Mom for parents. I have great sisters, too. Life is pretty good." Josephine sighed and smiled.

"Just remember that no matter what happens, God will use it for good in your life, even if things go wrong." He crossed his arms.

"I know." But deep down, what could possibly go wrong?

"We said good-bye to your sisters earlier today. We will call you when we get to the hotel. We love you, Jo!" Her mom paused and hugged her. Then she walked to the car.

"Love you, too, Mom!" Josephine waved good-bye to her parents.

"Goodbye!" Her mom waved back.

As they drove out of sight, Josephine felt a wave of sadness engulf her. She glanced up at the dark, gloomy clouds that were threatening to unleash its rain at any moment. She ran into the house as the rain started pouring down.

A few hours later, the phone rang.

"Mom! I thought you would never call! I was getting--" Josephine began, but was interrupted.

"Jo, its Brit." Brittany sobbed. "Mom and Dad were in a car accident. Honey, they didn't survive."

The room began to spin. Josephine could not get her breath, no matter how hard she tried. She crumbled to the floor, all the strength gone from her body. Tears streaming down her cheeks, she listened quietly as Brittany described the awful details of her parents' car crash. It had been raining so hard, her dad could barely see out of the window. He had a green light and began driving through the intersection. Little did he know, that due to a malfunction because of the storm, all four lights were green, as well.. The driver of the other vehicle couldn't stop without sliding and ran into the side of the car. The two cars collided, each coming from an opposite side. The blow to her mom's side of the car had killed her instantly. Her dad would have survived had the car not spun around and smacked his side of the car into a light pole. He had hit his head pretty hard on the side of the car.

By the time the ambulance arrived at the scene, her parents had gone home to be with the Lord.

"God!" she cried in desperation. "Where were you when they needed Your protection? Why didn't you stop this from happening? Why?"

It was at that moment that her faith in a "loving" God began to waiver. How could a loving God take her parents away from her? How could He leave her without their love, support, and guidance? She stopped praying and reading her bible, and she stopped going to church. Josephine felt angry and alone. It wasn't fair and it wasn't right. If God loved her and her parents, He would have had the city fix the lights when the first calls were made, making the city aware of the problem. But God didn't do anything about it. He didn't stop them from going through the intersection. Nor did he stop the other driver from slamming his car into them.

Her sisters tried telling her bad things happen. She was so angry that everything they said fell on deaf ears, and a cold heart.

With school finally out of the way, she had more time to spend at work, which she welcomed. She found it difficult going to a new apartment, with no one waiting for her like her parents used to. She was lonely, and missed her mom's smiling face when she would walk through the front door. She and her sisters decided to sell the house and divide up the proceeds from it. Josephine knew it was the right decision, but hated it all the same. The house shouldn't have been sold, but her parents shouldn't have died.

Six months after her parents' funeral, she met Jim. He had come into the shop for a hair cut. She had just worked her way up from being the receptionist to a hair stylist. Jim was a welcomed distraction. He was extremely handsome and charming. He had won her heart right away. Her sisters warned her to be careful, to wait before jumping into a relationship, but she ignored their advice. After a few months of dating, they moved in together. Her sisters tried talking her out of moving in with Jim, but she would not listen to them. They told her it wouldn't heal the pain she was feeling. She ignored their advice. She had her job and her inheritance to help pay for the bills. She thought if they moved in together, she would not be as lonely and heart broken from missing her parents. After two years of living together, though, she began to realize that Jim couldn't fill the void in her heart.

Looking back now, she could see God moving. One of her clients, Mr. Sorenson, was a born-again Christian. He would come in for a haircut every month and talk with her about her life. When she had first begun working there, he asked her about family. She told him all about her parents and sisters. When her parents' had died in the car accident, he cried with her. When she told him she was angry with God and had walked away from God, he had tears in his eyes, but loved her all the same. He had told her he prayed for her everyday. Even when he didn't need a haircut, he and his wife would stop in with an encouraging word or an invitation to spend dinner with them when she was off of work. She loved Mr. Sorenson as if he were her own grandfather. Because of the Sorensons, Josephine knew she needed to get her life right with Jesus. It was the love and the example of people outside her immediate family that caused her eyes to be opened. She went back to church, talked with a pastor about her hurt and devastation, started reading her Bible again, and started praying, too.

When she told Mr. Sorenson she rededicated her life to Jesus, he cried, and called his wife, who met them at the shop with a fresh batch of cookies. They took her out to dinner to celebrate. When he found out she was pregnant, he never condemned her. He wrapped his arms around her, cried a few tears, and told her it would all be alright. He and his wife bought DJ an outfit, even after she told them she was giving him up for adoption. Josephine thought they would tell her it was a horrible idea, but instead, they praised her for doing the unselfish thing. The Sorensons even stopped by her home when the caretaker left, just to bring her dinner and sit with her.

She sighed and shook her head. *Thank You, God, for using them to bring me back to You!*

What started out to be sad and depressing thoughts turned out to be thankful ones.

○ ○ ○ ○

Sue sat in DJ's room, feeding him his midnight feeding- or at least trying to do so.. Getting him to wake up was more work than feeding him! Thoughts flooded her head as she rocked him back and forth. Sue's mind took an unexpected turn for the worse. She sat there, holding DJ, thinking of her mom and dad. Oh, how she missed them, ,especially during this time! She wished her mom were alive, able to talk with her about what to do with a newborn. Now that she was a stay at home mom, she could use some advice! She wished her dad were alive to know that they named the baby after him. She could picture his sparkling eyes, looking tenderly at DJ. She would love to see him, holding her son, talking to him about Jesus, just they way she knew he would have done.

She wished her mom were there, also, guiding her as she charted into unknown territory with being a wife. She needed a mom right now, telling her that marriage was hard but worth the effort. Sue got up from the rocking chair, put DJ back to bed, and went to sit in the living room. She didn't want to wake Nate up. As she sat in the dark, she wept silently.

Oh, God, I miss them so much! I wish they were here! Lord, I know they are with you, but sometimes, I wish they were with me, instead!

Sue covered her face with her hands, trying to console herself enough to go back to bed. She jumped when she felt a gentle hand on her shoulder.

"Thinking about your mom and dad, huh?" Nate's soft voice startled her.

She nodded her head. "I didn't mean to. I just miss them so much, especially now!"

She sobbed some more.

Nate sat down next to her and held her in his strong arms. "I know, honey. I'm so sorry."

Sue sniffed, starting to calm down. When they had sat there for a long time, she finally spoke.

"Let's go back to bed. We need to get some sleep tonight." She smiled a half-hearted smile that didn't quite make it to her eyes.

Sue called Brittany the next day. She confided in her the thoughts that ran wild in her head during her long night.

"I understand, Sue," Brittany empathized. "I felt that way when Joslyn was born. It hurt so much; I thought my heart would literally break."

"That's how I felt last night. Brit, this is all so new to me! I am a wife and a mom now, all within a few months of each other."

"I know, Sue. I wish there was something I could say to make it all better, to ease your pain. It will take time, though. And hey, if you need anything, you just let me know. I'm here for you. And Nate's mom is there for you, too."

Sue sniffed. "Thanks, Sis. So, how are things with Gideon? Does Joslyn just love her new brother?"

"She does! She wants to hold him all of the time. She doesn't want to share him with anyone, even me and Luke! It's so funny to watch her!"

Brittany told Sue how after they brought Gideon home, Joslyn looked at him lying in his car seat, and said,

"Chase me, Brother, chase me!" When Gideon just stayed there and didn't move, Joslyn started to cry.

"Mommy! Brother won't chase me!"

Sue started laughing.

"Really? Oh my goodness, I love that little girl!"

Brittany laughed. "I had to tell her he needs to grow a little bit more before he would be able to chase her!"

Sue felt better after talking with Brittany. She hung up the phone and called Josephine to see if she wanted some company that evening.

○ ○ ○ ○

Josephine hadn't expected her first encounter with DJ to be a difficult one, but it was. Sue and Nate came by after Nate got off of work. They had called first to ask if they could bring her dinner. Of course, she agreed. The moment they walked through the front door, a longing filled her heart. She wanted to take DJ in her arms, tell him she was his mommy, and take care of him the way she would have had circumstances been different.

"I'm so sorry, Jo," Sue had apologized when she saw the pain in her sister's eyes. "I didn't even think about how hard this would be on you! We'll just go." She started to get up.

"No, Sue, don't." Josephine took her sister's hand. "It's all right. I need to get used to this. I guess I just didn't realize how hard it would be at first. Really, stay. I will be fine."

She paused a moment before continuing. "Sue, do you miss Mom?"

"I do, especially now. I was just telling Brittany that this morning." Sue's eyes grew watery.

"I have been thinking about Mom and Dad a lot lately. Do you think they would be disappointed in me?" Fear clouded Josephine's blue eyes.

"Jo." Sue sensed the hurt in her sister. "They knew people made mistakes. They made mistakes themselves! They wouldn't be disappointed in you. They loved you, always, so much. For instance, even when you were floundering a bit in high school, remember how you wanted to take classes at the high school around the corner from the house?"

Josephine nodded. "Yeah. I loved being homeschooled, but I knew I needed a bit more than what Mom could give me."

" That's right. And remember how you started taking an interest in the guy, what was his name?"

"Justin," Josephine said.

"A-huh. Justin. Mom and Dad knew he didn't love the Lord. They knew he would be bad news. Remember all the talks the three of you had? They knew if you dated him, you would make a huge mistake, but they never told you they were disappointed, did they?"

Josephine shook her head. "They trusted you to do the right thing, and you did. You may have wanted to date that guy, but you chose the best thing: to say no to your feelings, and trust God."

"Yes,, but I didn't say no to my feelings the night Jim came over. I went ahead with them."

"True, but you haven't done that since, right? And when a righteous person falls seven times, he still gets up. Remember that proverb? Jo, you need to remember how much Mom and Dad loved and cared for you. Don't let thoughts of low self-worth invade your mind."

Josephine nodded. "Sometimes, I just need to be reminded."

"I understand. Look at Nate over there," Sue whispered. "He and DJ are sleeping!"

Josephine laughed as Sue took DJ out of Nate's arms.

When DJ woke up, Josephine played with him, all the while calling herself "Auntie Jo." She talked with her sister about how the nights were going for DJ and asked if she and Nate were getting any sleep at all.

"Obviously   not," Sue pointed to Nate."He's not getting enough sleep.

It's funny," Sue continued, remembering their check up with the pediatrician. "We just had our two week check up with the doctor. Dr. Cacnio is a really great pediatrician. I told him DJ had to be awakened from sleeping in the middle of the night to eat, you know, because we are on the schedule thing. He looked at me like I was crazy! He said, "If DJ is sleeping through the night already, do not wake him up to eat! He will be just fine!" I laughed so hard when Nate and I left!"

Josephine laughed. "Well, he doesn't appear to be too thin now, does he?"

"Being in the 90th percentile of his weight? No, I don't think so!"

The sisters laughed. They talked for a few more minutes. Sue woke Nate up, who announced with defiance, "I wasn't sleeping! I was resting my eyes!"

Josephine chuckled. "Sure you were. You keep telling yourself that, pal! We know the truth!"

Nate laughed, packed up their belongings, and then the new family left.

Josephine cried when they were gone. She knew she had to get through the first time seeing DJ, not as her son, but as her nephew. She knew her feelings were natural, but deep down, she knew she had done the right thing in giving him up. She didn't just cry for DJ, but for herself. She wished she had that "someone special" to sit with and share her heart with. She wished God would provide her the man of her dreams. She felt secluded. Her sisters had the men of their dreams, and now the families of their dreams.

When will it be my turn, Lord? She thought dejectedly. *I don't want to be alone forever!*

Oh, God, she prayed earnestly, *please help me get through this! Please do not allow life always to be this hard!*

Chapter 4

*P*ost-partum recuperation took less time than Josephine had imagined. In less than two months, she was back at work.

Her first day of work was more fun than it was work! All of her regular clients had come in, including Mr. Sorenson. He bought her a journal and a Bible with her name on it. She was overcome with emotion as tears spilled down her cheeks and she hugged him. Her coworkers had decorated her work area with "Welcome Back" signs and even brought in a cake for her. She was so grateful to be working in such a caring atmosphere. Tears swelled in her eyes as she gathered her things to go home. *"God,"* she prayed, *"may I bless these people as much as they have blessed me."*

October arrived. Josephine loved the season of autumn.. She loved watching the leaves in the trees change to beautiful yellow, orange and red colors. She marveled at how creative God was in designing the seasons!

Dressed as a pirate for this occasion, as she drove to work, she was excited to see what costumes her friends at work would have.. Dressing up was always something into which everyone put a lot of energy. Last year, she dressed up as Ariel from the Little Mermaid. Two other girls dressed up as Belle from Beauty and the Beast and Snow White, as well. It was so much fun being princesses! They laughed with delight when they saw each other and sang Disney songs the rest of the day!

Josephine walked into work and gasped with surprise. Instead of the traditional Halloween decorations, the entire shop was transformed into a autumn wonderland! A scarecrow leaned against the receptionist desk. There was a giant tree taped to one of the walls with orange and red leaves draping from its branches. Cornucopias were placed on the coffee tables near the magazines. It was breathtaking!

"Great job, ladies!" She walked to the back of the store to put down her bag..

Bobbi, dressed as Princess Lei, turned around and smiled.

"Thanks! It was so much fun decorating! We decided not to do the spooky thing. Sometimes that takes all the fun out of the season! We can hardly wait for Christmas!"

Amber laughed and pointed at Josephine.

"Yep. We've already got plans coming together. You get to dress like Mrs. Claus," she added, putting on the final touches to her costume.

When Josephine looked up, she saw that this year Amber was dressed as Little Bo Peep.

"Where's your sheep?" Josephine giggled.

Amber waved her hand in front of her face like a southern belle would and replied with mock sincerity, "Why, I must have lost them!"

The three women laughed.

"Any plans for tonight, Jo?" Bobbi began sweeping the floor around her chair.

"My sisters and their families invited me to go to a Fall Festival with them at their church. Last time we had gone, everyone was dressed up, including the adults, so we thought we would all be pirates this year. Their church goes all out! They have bounce houses, cake walks, carnival games and everything. It should be a lot of fun!" " She stole a sideways glance at her friends, wondering if they were going to comment.

"Sounds fun." Bobbi cleared her throat. "How are you with all of that?"

"I have my good days and my bad. I know it was the best decision, though. But every time I see DJ, he changes a little bit more, and my heart aches. But then," she continued, joy filling her eyes, "I see Sue and Nate with him. I see their faces so full of love and appreciation. I always leave feeling this was the right decision."

Bobbi placed a comforting hand on Josephine's shoulder. "Seriously, Jo, we're proud of you. It took strength and courage to do what you did."

"Thanks, but that was God's doing, not mine. Without Him, I wouldn't have been able to put DJ's needs above my own." Josephine hugged Bobbi. "I appreciate the encouragement, though. It does get easier the more I am around him."

"Good." Bobbi squeezed her once more and turned back to her work station.

Work ended quickly. The day was so busy! People flocked to the store, wanting to dye their hair for the festivities that awaited them. Some just needed a plain haircut, but by the end of her shift, Josephine was ready to rest.. It felt good sitting and driving to Brittany's house. It allowed her body and mind time to relax before getting back on her feet again.

When she arrived at Brittany's, Luke came to the door dressed as Captain Jack Sparrow. She knew this year would be a lot of fun, being a family of pirates. Seeing Luke all dressed up just confirmed it.

"Arrggg," he growled, holding a soda in his hand.

"Arrgg, Captain Jack. Hey! You found your soda!" She gave him a hug. "Where my sister be?" she sneered back, stifling a giggle.

"Indeed I have, Matey! But I be not Captain Jack! I be his brother, Captain Bob!" Luke growled once more.

Josephine laughed and pushed her way past him.

"Hi, Jo! Pizza should be here any minute!" Brittany called from the kitchen.

"Great! Need help?" Josephine offered.

"Sure. Will you grab Gideon for me? I need to get Joslyn's hair done." Brittany walked out of the kitchen. She looked great dressed in a short skirt, fish net stockings, a white shirt that fit loosely enough for her to have a belt draped across her hips. She wore a bandana on her head and big hoop earrings dangled from her ears.

"You look awesome, Brit!" Josephine picked up Gideon.

"Thanks! So do you!" Brittany returned the compliment.

"Hi, Gideon! Don't you look adorable?"

Gideon was a little too small to dress as a pirate, but not wanting him to feel left out, Brittany dressed him in all black sweats with a sweatshirt that had skulls on it. She had a bandana on his head to keep it warm.

"Ahoy, there, me Matey!" Nate's voice boomed through the house.

Nate walked in, dressed as the traditional pirate from head to toe. A bandana was wrapped around his head, too, with a gold earring hanging from his ear. His white pirate shirt hung over his black pants that were tucked into leather pirate boots.

Josephine smiled a teasing smile. "You look like a bigger version of Gideon."

"Arrggg. As well as DJ, too!" He held up the car seat so Josephine could see DJ's outfit. It was exactly like Gideon's!

"Did Sue and Brit plan that?"

"We sure did," Sue laughed, coming in behind Nate. "You look great! How was work?"

"Good, good. Glad to be done, though." Josephine blew her bangs out of her face.

"Pizza man!" Luke called, carrying in two large boxes.

Dinner was quickly eaten. In no time at all, they were all headed to the cars for the quick trip to the church.

"Auntie Jo." Joslyn batted her big blue eyes at Josephine. "You go wif me?"

"Sure, Sweetie." Josephine buckled her into her car seat and sat down beside her.

They spent the next hour and a half, enjoying all the festivities the church had to offer! Josephine even won cupcakes during the cake walk.

Josephine carried Joslyn to the house once they arrived back at Brittany's house.

"Auntie Jo," Joslyn put her sleepy head on her shoulder, "thanks."

Josephine kissed her niece and nephews goodnight and drove home.

Climbing into bed, she thanked God for family. Lord, may we always be close! Don't allow anything to tear us apart!

○ ○ ○ ○

Josephine poured a cup of coffee and breathed in the scent of the holiday brew she had made that morning. Thanksgiving. It was a wonderful holiday. A time to stop and give thanks for the many things the good Lord had offered. That was one thing Josephine's parents had taught her.

"Be thankful for what God has given you," she could still hear her mother say.

Thanksgiving was a time to remember, with fondness, her childhood. It was a holiday full of tradition which Josephine remembered from parents. Traditions she hoped to embrace when she had a family of her own. Her mom. would have fall decorations displayed throughout the house. Orange, yellow, and brown were a dominant theme. She had a beautiful table cloth she would proudly put on the table every year, and a self made cornucopia filled with plastic fruit and vegetables, would be the final touch of the Thanksgiving decorations.

Josephine used to love waking up to the smell of pumpkin pie baking in the oven on Thanksgiving morning.Her mom woke up early Thanksgiving Day to prepare the pumpkin pie. Her dad thoroughly enjoyed cooking and preparing the turkey. Once the pies were out of the oven, the "big ole bird", as her dad called it, would go right in. Josephine recalled her dad having a bowl of shelled walnuts set on the coffee table with a nut cracker next to it for anyone to enjoy once they came through the door. She and her sisters used to have so much fun cracking open the walnut shells, and sometimes, pinching their siblings fingers. Their house was always full for Thanksgiving dinner. Her grandparents, before they passed away, would come and celebrate with them. It always struck Josephine odd that neither of her parents had any siblings. Friends who did not have loved ones to celebrate with were always welcomed at her mom and dad's house. Neighbors would stop by on their way to their own festivities just to say hello and to receive an encouraging word.

Mom was always good at encouraging others, Josephine thought sadly. *I miss her encouragement, Lord.*

During the Thanksgiving dinner, all would sit around the table, and her dad would start off by giving thanks to God for His many blessings. After the prayer, each person would tell why they were thankful. Josephine loved that tradition and was excited that Brittany had made that a part of Thanksgiving since her parents had passed away. Josephine sipped her coffee and thought of what this Thanksgiving was going to bring.

This year was going to be extra special! There were, there two new family members, DJ and Gideon. Plus, the Sorensons had accepted her invitation to spend this holiday with Josephine and her family. She felt they were a part of her family already and wanted her sisters and their families to get to know them, as well. She looked forward to this time she was able to spend with her family and friends. Mr. and Mrs. Sorenson's son lived on the east coast, and she knew they would be lonely. They told her after they volunteered at the soup kitchen, they would head right over to her place and carpool with her to Luke and Brittany"s home.. Josephine eagerly anticipated their arrival.

She set down her coffee just as the door bell rang.

"Happy Thanksgiving, Josephine!" Mrs. Sorenson gave her a tender hug.

"Happy Thanksgiving, to you, Mrs. Sorenson!" Josephine loved Mrs. Sorenson's hugs. They reminded her so much of her mom's hugs. It was hard not to get teary eyed thinking about it.

"Dear," Mrs. Sorenson stepped back and patted her hand. "We've been talking, and we think it's time to have you not address us so formerly. We're past that stage in our relationship, don't you think?" Mrs. Sorenson walked with Josephine to the car and took her arm in hers.

"That would be fine with me! But what would you like me to call you?" Josephine studied Mrs. Sorenson thoughtfully.

"We know you don't have grandparents. We were thinking of maybe having you, and even your family members if they desire, call us Grandpa Jake and Grandma Em, short for Emily, of course."

"Or you can call us just Grandma and Grandpa," Mr. Sorenson interjected, opening the door to the car for the ladies. "How does that sound?" Mrs. Sorenson buckled her seat belt and glanced back at Josephine.

"That sounds wonderful, Mrs.—oops!" Josephine's hand flew to her lips. "I mean, Grandma!"

"Good!" Mr. Sorenson interrupted. "Now, where am I driving?" Mr. Sorenson asked, pulling out of the apartment complex.

Josephine gave him directions as they made small talk. A few minutes later, they pulled up to Luke and Brittany's house and walked up to the front door.

"Hello!" Josephine called, walking in through the front door.

"Happy Thanksgiving!" Brittany called from the kitchen as she walked toward them.

"Same to you, Sis! Brittany, this is Mr. and Mrs. Sorenson." Josephine introduced, watching them shake each other's hands. "They wanted us to know we can call them Grandma and Grandpa, since we no longer have ours."

Josephine's eyes shown.

Brittany nodded, a gentle smile crossing her lips. "Nice to meet you both! Won't you come in?" Brittany waived her hand toward the living room.

"You have a lovely home, Brittany," Mrs. Sorenson complimented. "I love the way you have decorated!"

"Thank you, Grandma! Can I get either of you something to drink? "We're fine, thank you." Mr. Sorenson sat down on the couch near Gideon. "Who is this little fellow?" he asked, placing his giant finger in the baby's.

"That is our son, Gideon Henry." Pride rang in Brittany's voice.

"He is a cutie, isn't he?" Josephine bent down, playing with his foot.

"He is! May I hold him?" Mrs. Sorenson clasped her hands together in anticipation.

"Absolutely!" Brittany took him out and placing him in her arms.

"I haven't held a baby in so long," Mrs. Sorenson said wistfully. She played with his fingers and watched him make funny faces. "Remember when Steven was this small, Jake?"

He grunted. "I'm not sure Steven was ever that small!" Mr. Sorenson put his fingers on Gideon's chest and began walking them up to his nose singing,

"Wocky-pocky, wocky-pocky," and paused for dramatic effect. Once he got to his nose, he let out a loud, "Bing!" and gently tapped Gideon on the nose. Gideon was mesmerized the entire time, and when Mr. Sorenson got to "Bing!" Gideon cooed softly.

Josephine laughed. "Hey, Luke, these are the Sorensons." Luke shook hands with both of them, a grin tugging at the corners of his mouth. "Where are Nate and Sue? They aren't here yet?" Josephine looked around, noticing for the first time they were missing.

"Nope. Not yet." Luke shook his head. "Hey, has anyone seen my soda?" He surveyed the room. Luke sighed. "Anyway," he said looking around the room. "They called a few minutes ago and said they were just leaving Nate's mom's house. They should be here any minute."

"They are eating two Thanksgiving meals today?" Josephine asked, amazed. "Now that is something to be thankful for! Not many people have the chance to even eat one meal!"

Just then, Sue and Nate walked through the door.

"Whew! I am stuffed!" Nate exclaimed, patting his stomach.

"I told him not to eat that much at his mom's, but he just loves her cooking!" Sue laughed. "It smells so good, Sis! Here are my contributions to tonight's meal."

"Thanks!" Brittany took the dishes out of Sue's hands. "Come into the kitchen and we can get the table set."

Sue followed Brittany into the kitchen while Josephine made introductions again. "Nice to meet you, Nate. This must be little Daniel James." Mrs. Sorenson said as Nate sat the car seat down.

"It's nice to meet you, too. Yes, this is DJ. He has had a very exhausting day today!" Nate commented, looking at the sleeping baby.

○ ○ ○ ○

"So, why did you really want me to come in the kitchen, Brit?" Sue raised one eye-brow.

"Is it that obvious?" Brittany's smile took up her face.

"It is. What's going on?"

"I've been thinking. It's the holiday season, and we know what happened last year." She glanced over her shoulder in Josephine's direction. "I know Jo struggles with loneliness. She has struggled with that most of her teenage and adult life. I don't want her to keep falling into the same ritual year after year. I was thinking that maybe this season, we should try extra hard to keep her busy and not be alone so much. What do you think about that?"

"That's a good idea. But won't her being around us all of the time make her even lonelier? I mean, you have a husband and two kids; I have a husband and one kid. Don't you think that would put a longing even more so on her heart?" Sue didn't want to do anything to add more loneliness to her younger sister.

"It might. But if we are all together or if someone is with her a lot of the time this season, maybe it won't be so hard. I'm just thinking of ways to get her to not be alone. This time of year is very difficult. Maybe we can pull in the Sorensons, too." Brittany shrugged.

"Pull us in on what?" Mrs. Sorenson walked into the kitchen.

"Sorry. I didn't mean to eavesdrop. I was coming in to see if I could help in any way, and I overheard my name."

Brittany blushed slightly. "We, uh, were talking about Josephine being lonely during this holiday season." She didn't know the Sorensons, and didn't want them to get the wrong idea of her.

"Ah, I see." Understanding registered in Mrs. Sorenson's

eyes. "I take it you don't want to have happen what did last year?"

"No, we don't," Sue shook her head firmly. "Don't get me wrong. We love DJ, and he is a blessing beyond all measure. We know she loves the Lord, but my family struggles with reacting to how we feel at the moment." Sue lifted one shoulder. "It is a struggle we all share. We don't want to be women controlled by our emotions. And Jo, well, she is just now really starting to walk with Jesus. We want to help her as much as we can; especially since we know most of her life, she has dealt with feeling lonely."

"I understand where you ladies are coming from. And I must say, I agree. So, what's the plan?" Mrs. Sorenson sat down on a stool, leaning her head on her hand as she rested her elbow on the island in the middle of the kitchen.

"I just thought if we kept her busy during the holiday season, asking her to go shopping with us, taking her to the holiday socials we have at church or with the kiddos, something along those lines." Brittany turned around and took plates from her cupboard. "Maybe it won't be so hard on her."

"Ladies, it sounds like a plan!" Mrs. Sorenson clapped her hands together. "I think this might help her a bit."

Just then, Joslyn ran in. "Mommy! Daddy says when food time is?"

"Tell Daddy, almost time!" Brittany laughed softly.

〇 〇 〇 〇

Sue laid down in bed, snuggling next to Nate and laying her head on his chest.

"Today seemed to go well, don't you think?".

"Mm, hm," he replied sleepily.

"I really like the Sorensons." Sue rubbed Nate's arm.

"So do I. They fit in really well with the family, don't they?" Nate gave her a gentle squeeze.

"They do. I really felt a connection with Grandma. She was just so willing to jump right in and be apart of our family! She is even collaborating how to make Jo not feel so lonely during this time of year."

"That's what you ladies were talking about in the kitchen. I wondered what that was all about!" Nate chuckled, rubbing Sue's back.

"Yep. It was Brittany's idea. She is always thinking ahead like that. Brittany reminds me so much of my mom sometimes. There are times when it is difficult because she reminds me so much of her, and then there are times when I am so glad Brittany is so much like Mom because I can still feel her, you know?".

"I wish I had more time getting to know your mom. I was only around a few months before she passed away." Nate sighed, an unspoken regret she shared with him.

"I know. You remind me so much of my dad, though. He had a lot of your personality. It makes me so thankful that I have you in my life!" Sue kissed Nate's cheek.

They heard a tiny cry coming from DJ's room. "I'll go see if he is okay." Sue started to get up.

"No. I'll check on him this time." Nate climbed out of bed and walked down the hallway toward DJ's room.

Nate walked into DJ's room, and gently picked him up. "Not hungry. Perhaps you are wet?" Nate put DJ down on the changing table and took out a fresh diaper. "Little man, I am very lucky to be your dad. I love you, you know that?" he whispered.

DJ, looking up at him, made baby sounds that touched Nate's heart. Picking him up again, he sat down in the rocking chair and sang softly to him. "I love you, DJ, oh yes, I do, I love you, DJ, it's always true!"

DJ started to calm down a bit and got a sleepy look on his face. Carefully, Nate put DJ back to bed. Walking out of the room, he saw Sue standing in the hallway, watching his every move.

"You scared me!" He jumped back, startled.

"Sorry! I just really enjoy watching you bond with DJ. You are already a great dad, you know that? You are so gentle and tender with him. I just love watching you in this role!"

He took her hand and led her back to bed. Lying beside her, he said, "I just never thought it would be like this; this good, I mean. I thought we would adopt a child a little older than DJ, one with a few more issues we would need to deal with. I still want to adopt more children, and I wouldn't mind adopting older ones, either. I just never expected this, I guess."

Sue kissed Nate's cheek. "I understand what you mean."

They lay in silence. "Good night, honey."

Nate kissed Sue's forehead. "Good night, love."

○ ○ ○ ○

The next morning, Josephine's phone rang.

"Hello?" she answered, groggy.

"Jo? Sorry to wake you." Brittany's voice sounded apologetic.

"It's ok. Is everything alright?" Josephine looked at the clock. 3:00 a.m.! Something must be wrong. She sat up with a start.

"Everything's fine. Do you work today?"

"No. I have today off. Why?" Irritation rang in her voice.

"Sue and I are coming to pick you up. We are going to venture out in the "Black Friday" sales. You know. The day after Thanksgiving shopping that only crazy people like me does?"

"Are you kidding me? You called and woke me up for that?" Josephine sat up, completely annoyed.

"C'mon, Jo! It will be fun! We can go grab coffee and get in line. There are a few stores with incredible deals. Please!" Brittany begged.

"Ugh. Fine. When will you be here?" She got out of bed and turned on her light.

"We're already here! See you in 5 minutes!" Brittany sang joyfully.

Sisters can be such a bother! Josephine thought, quickly getting dressed and walking outside.

"I'm not happy about this!" Grumpiness was written all over her face. "The sun isn't even up yet! Are you two nuts?"

"This will be fun, Sis, and you know it! How often do we get to do this together, huh?" Sue turned around and looked at her.

"Let's just go get some coffee so I can wake up a bit. And it is so cold! I need to warm up!" Josephine's teeth chattered.

They drove through the drive through at the coffee shop

and each had a warm cup to hold while waiting.

"You know what I think is awesome?" Sue took a sit of her coffee. "I love that the stores let everyone in so we don't have to wait outside in the cold. That's just so cool to me!"

"I had no idea they would do that!" Josephine moved her cup around in her hands. "What are we shopping for?"

"I want to get the kids some things, and Sue wanted to get Nate and DJ some stuff. We thought we would all pitch in on some gifts for the Sorensons. You know them better than we do. What do they like?" Brittany said.

"They like lots of stuff. I know Grandma wanted some new towels for the kitchen, and Grandpa needed a new tool box, one he can carry. He was saying that he needed one to take to people's houses when he does ministry with his church. They have a program called 'No Longer Silent.' The program helps persons who are and are not members of the church who need their houses fixed up and just can't afford it. Those are the only things I can think of that they had mentioned recently. Wait until my brain wakes up. I may think of something more," Josephine added.

Brittany and Sue laughed. "Look!" Sue pointed to the employees. "They are unwrapping things! Here we go!"

The sisters were being pushed as the crowd of people headed toward the displays. They felt like a herd of cattle, but had a great time doing their shopping. Even though Josephine was wakened before the sun was up, she was glad her sisters had called her. They laughed as they saw people pushing and running through the store, just to get an item discounted. They rolled their eyes at some of the rudeness of people, but they did find what they were looking for. By the time they paid for their merchandise, the sun was up, and all three were hungry.

"Let's go get some breakfast, my treat." Josephine had her bags in her hands as they headed toward the car.

Sue smiled. "Oh, look who's not so grumpy now! Aren't you glad we got you up?"

"Yes, I am. But next year, can you tell me we are doing this before I leave Brittany's house on Thanksgiving instead of calling me at the crack of dawn?" Josephine climbed in the backseat of the car, setting her bags down beside her.

"It's a deal," Brittany giggled.

○ ○ ○ ○

December came, and along with it, a lot of snow. Sue enjoyed looking out of her living room window, seeing the gentle fall of the snow. The fire was lit in the fireplace. She had her teapot brewing water for some hot tea. A candle was burning in the dining room, letting out a sweet aroma of Christmas. She loved this time of year. It had always been her favorite. Sitting on the couch, she held her cup of tea and remembered her Mom. Mom had always loved tea. Whenever Sue had come to the house just for a visit, her mom would put the teapot on the stove and sit and talk with her daughter for hours. Sue sighed. Remembering Mom always brings a fresh pang of loneliness. How she missed her! Sue glanced over at the pack and play, watching DJ sleep.

He is such a sweet baby, Lord. My mom would have loved him!

Nate was at work, and Brittany was out with Luke's mom, doing some more Christmas shopping. Brittany loved having Luke's parents visit from California! She always looked forward to seeing them. Josephine was working, which left Sue alone with her thoughts. Her memories suddenly came to life about the day she told her mom and dad she would be moving out. Her parents never forced them out of the house, but Sue and Brittany had felt that they should get a place of their own. They wanted to move in together. It had been a dream of theirs since they were kids. Both of them had saved enough money to get an apartment. They had so much fun living together! Then Luke had proposed to Brittany. She knew she needed to save money and decided to move back home. That was fine with Sue. She had wanted to buy a condominium anyway, and when the opportunity presented itself, she jumped at the chance. She had gotten a killer deal on her condo, and with a little work, it turned out to be a great home, especially now that she and Nate were married and had a little baby. She looked over at the fireplace. Her dad had helped strip it of its white paint. Now, it looked amazing! The brick added a nice touch to the living room. Her mom and dad had spent a lot of time painting the house, putting new cabinets in the kitchen, and her dad had even paid for the new carpet as a house warming gift. Sue loved her home. She was so thankful her parents had a hand in fixing it up. It made her feel closer to them somehow, even though they were no longer with her. DJ's movement brought her back to the present. She walked over to him.

"Hi, sleepyhead!" she sang softly. "Did you have sweet dreams?" Picking him up, she cuddled with him on the couch. He made the goo and ga sounds all babies do, and then smiled a sweet smile. Sue had fun having alone time with him. When Nate was around, he would spend time with her, but rarely did he share DJ with her.

"You get him all day to yourself," he announced one night after dinner. "It's only fair you share him at night with me." She laughed. It made her heart explode with joy that he loved DJ so very much. "I'll share him with you. But he has to share you with me," she jokingly added.

"Sounds good," Nate responded, kissing her.

Holding Daniel James now, she felt like the luckiest woman in the world.

God, she prayed, *thank you for the many blessings you give to me! May I treasure them always!*

○ ○ ○ ○

Josephine answered her phone. "Hello?"

"Josephine, it's Grandma. How are you today?"

"Good Grandma! How are you?"

"Good, dear. I was wondering if you would like to go caroling with me and Grandpa tonight. We are going over to a senior citizens home this evening after dinner. Would you like to join us?"

"That sounds like fun! I haven't been caroling in a long time." Josephine smiled. Not that anyone would want to hear her sing, but she had a good time doing it anyway.

"Great! Why don't you come over for a bite to eat and then

we can head over? Grandpa is making his famous chicken and noodles!" Mrs. Sorenson offered.

"Mm. Wonderful. I will be there. What time?"

"Six o'clock. We'll see you then!"

Josephine hung up the phone. This had been the busiest Christmas season ever! Her sisters had her going with them to whatever Christmas function they were attending. The Sorensons had invited her caroling just now, but over the last week, she had been invited to spend time with them also while addressing Christmas cards, serving at the soup kitchen, and just having dinner together.

She loved being busy and did not mind at all. It helped her with the loneliness she faced. She had a feeling her sisters kept her busy because they did not want her to feel so lonely. She appreciated their thoughtfulness, and often took them up on their invitations. She was happy to keep herself occupied. Caroling sounded like so much fun, too! With only a week away until Christmas, Josephine wanted to spread a little more Christmas cheer to those who might be lonely, too. Her mom and dad had always told her serving was the best way to not feel so depressed.

She realized now how right they were.

The dinner Mr. Sorenson made was scrumptious! Josephine could hardly move after she had eaten two bowls full! Now, as she was standing with the Sorensons, singing 'Silent Night', she was so thankful to be there at that moment. The senior citizens to whom they sang were so filled with joy! They smiled their sweet, gentle smiles as they all sang. They clapped and applauded, even as she sang off key! The Sorensons had brought blankets that Mrs. Sorenson had made and passed them out as special gifts. She couldn't remember a time when she had felt so blessed to be a part of something bigger than herself. With each song they sang, her heart burst more and more at the wonder of the season. To think that Jesus came as a child, to sacrifice Himself as an adult, just to bridge the gap between God and man. Josephine's eyes had tears in them as they sang, 'What Child is This?' and 'O Holy Night' The latter was her favorite Christmas carol. And as Christmas quickly approached, Josephine thought of Mary, the mother of sweet Jesus, and the pain she felt as she had him. She remembered the time she was pregnant. Somehow, this Christmas, the miracle birth became more real to Josephine than ever before.

Experiencing pregnancy, labor, and healing allowed Josephine to understand Mary a little bit more.

○ ○ ○ ○

DJ's first Christmas, Sue thought excitedly. She knew he wouldn't understand it all yet, but she was thrilled to be spending this time with him. Nate was dressed and ready to go. They were going to Nate's mom's house first, and then over to Brittany's to exchange gifts. She was looking forward to spending time with family this year.

Lloyd opened the front door, his eyes dancing merrily.

"Nate! Sue! Merry Christmas!" He took the car seat that still held DJ from Nate's hand.

"Merry Christmas to you, Dad!" Sue smiled up at him.

Sue loved Lloyd like he was her own father. He was tall and slightly plump. His round face was offset with glasses that rested gently on his cheeks. His short brown hair was disheveled from preparing the house for company.

"Sportin' the farmer look today, huh, Dad?" Nate teased.

Lloyd grinned. "What? You don't like my overalls today?"

Nate and Sue laughed.

"Oh, Dad," Sue said, putting her arm around him, "don't listen to Nate. Not everyone can pull off the farmer look!"

Lloyd's shoulders shook from silent laughter. "Oh, now I am getting it from you, too!" He gently shoved her away. "I'm taking DJ and leaving you alone with Mom and Becca!"

Sue laughed as he carried DJ away.

Becca came in as Lloyd walked away. "I tried to get him to change his clothes! But you know how my dad can be!"

Sue enjoyed Becca. She was nine years old and already had a style all of her own. Her straight, blonde hair hung just below her chin. She had her dad's height, but looked more like Nate's mom.

Nate hugged his little sister. "Well, at least you tried! It's okay. It'll give us something to laugh about in the years to come!"

Becca smiled and walked toward the kitchen. "Mom's in here, putting olives in a bowl. I told her just to leave them in the can since we all know they will be gone as soon as she places them on the table!"

Sue walked into the kitchen to help Martha prepare the rest of the Christmas meal. She smiled to herself, grateful she had a wonderful mother-in-law. Martha had embraced Sue from the moment they met. She was kind, tenderhearted, and a godly woman. Sue knew her mom and Martha would have become fast friends. Now, working side by side with Martha, the pain of losing her mom lessened. No one could replace her mom, but she was glad Martha was there, filling a void in her life.

After lunch was eaten, everyone gathered around to open gifts. Nate's mom took it upon herself to spoil not only DJ, but Sue and Nate, as well. She had made them all 'crazy quilts', including DJ. His was extra small, but sewn with lots of love. Nate's mom loved the fact she was a grandma and took extra special pride in it. It did not matter DJ was adopted. She loved him just the same as she would a biological grandson. She never even asked from whom they adopted him. She had said it wasn't important. She just thanked the good Lord the mom had decided to give DJ a good home, one where he would be loved more than anything. Sue loved Nate's mom like she were her own mother. It was comforting to have her around when her own mom was no longer with her.

Sue sat back in the comfortable chair and sighed. She surveyed the family sitting around her. A gentle smile tugged at the corner of her lips. Lloyd was holding DJ, and instead of looking at Lloyd, DJ kept staring toward the light behind Lloyd. He had done everything he could to get DJ's attention, but nothing worked. He finally gave up and was content in just holding the baby! Sue took pride in being a part of Nate's family. She knew that she would be loved and cherished, just like her own parents had loved and cherished her.

○ ○ ○ ○

Josephine sat at Luke and Brittainy's, happy to be a part of such a great family. She enjoyed opening gifts, having a ham dinner, and celebrating Christmas with her sisters. The Sorensons had said they would come by for dessert, which they did. They opened more gifts from them and gave them theirs.

It certainly was fun to watch Joslyn with the Sorensons.

They spoiled her tremendously! They gave her more gifts that she had gotten in her entire lifetime! Brittany tried to protest, but the Sorenson's were insistent.

"Our son doesn't have kids yet. We feel we need to spoil somebody, and we just adore Joslyn. Please, Brittany," Grandma pleaded. "Don't take this away from us!"

Reluctantly, she agreed. Josephine laughed. It was such a great time being together. Luke asked Mr. Sorenson if he would read the Christmas story, just as Josephine's father had done. It was the perfect way to end the day!

Josephine went to bed later that night, not feeling alone, like last year. She was so glad God had blessed her so much with her family.

Chapter 5

Brittany knocked on Sue's door.

"Sue?" Brittany walked in, glancing around the living room.

"Come on it, Sis! I'm in the kitchen!" Sue just finished putting the final touches on the table.

Brittany carried the cake into the dining room. "Wow! The dining room looks great!" Her eyes sparkled with excitement.

"It's our boys' second birthday. I really wanted everything to be perfect! Oh!" Sue looked at the cake of their two boys, awe filling her eyes. "The cake looks absolutely wonderful! Look at our two crazy boys!"

Brittany laughed. "I know. I think it turned out pretty good, too!" She put the cake down in the center of the table. "What can I start doing?"

"I have balloons that need to get placed through-out the house. Nate picked them up from the party store earlier today." Sue went to the kitchen to get the refreshments together.

"You got it. How about the streamers? Did you get some of those, too?" Brittany grabbed the balloons and strategically put them in the living room and dining room.

"Yes I did. They are in the bag next to the balloons." Sue pointed to the bag lying on the floor. "By the way, Nate's mom invited someone to the party. Is that all right with you?"

"Who is it?" Brittany took the streamers out of the bag and began taping one side to the wall. She twisted the streamers until she got to the other side of the room and taped the end in the corner.

"His name is Mark. He's a swimming teacher. You know how

Nate's little sister was taking Competitive Swim lessons this summer?"

Sue set bowls of chips on the table near the cake.

"Uh-huh," Brittany replied, criss-crossing the streamers.

"Well, after the swim lessons, Mark would play with DJ in the water. From Martha's description of it, Mark really enjoyed hanging out with DJ. So she called and asked if she could invite him." Sue lifted one shoulder. "I didn't think you would mind."

"That's fine with me." Brittany tilted her head to one side. "Does that look good to you?"

Sue glanced around the room. "It looks great!"

"So, how did Becca like the swim lessons?"

Sue paused. "I think she was glad she did them. But I think she realized it's not her thing."

"Better to realize that now than later, I guess. Oh, Luke is going to bring the kids in an hour or so." Brittany suddenly realized Nate and DJ were missing.. "Where are Nate and DJ?"

"Nate took DJ to the park so I could get some decorating done without him under foot. He is so active now that he is two! I can hardly believe it!"

"I know. I was looking at Joslyn and Gideon the other day. Joslyn is four now. How crazy is that?" Brittany shook her head. "She is getting to be such a big girl! And now Gideon is two! The last two years have certainly gone quickly, haven't they?"

"They have. It seems just like yesterday we brought Daniel home." Sue smiled. "Sometimes I forget that Josephine was his birth mother."

"I think that, too. DJ seems to fit so well with you and Nate. Nate has such a way with DJ. I have fun watching all three of you together! You are a great family." Brittany put her arm around her sister's shoulders. "Have you thought about adopting any more?"

"Yes. We've talked about it. We have kind of started the process to adopt internationally. We know it'll take awhile, so we thought we would start now. That way, DJ can be the oldest still." Sue stopped and cocked her head to one side. "Yep. I definitely want to adopt again! But we haven't told anyone except the Sorensons."

Brittany smiled. "Oh, I totally understand that one! I won't say a word, I promise."

"Thanks. So, anymore kiddos for you and Luke?"

"No, I think we're done. We've only wanted to have two kids, anyway. So, next week or so, Luke is going to make an appointment." A sly grin played at Brittany's lips.

"Ah, yes. That appointment. It will definitely help you not get pregnant. I bet Luke is really excited about that!"

Sue nodded her head in understanding, her eyes twinkling.

"Oh, he can hardly wait!" Brittany giggled.

By the time the sisters were done talking, the house was decorated. Nate walked through the door with the DJ just as Luke came in with Joslyn and Gideon.

"Auntie Sue!" Joslyn cried, throwing her arms around Sue.

"Hi Joslyn! How are you today?" Sue squeezed her niece tightly.

"I'm good! Today is Gideon's birthday!" Joslyn told her. Her big eyes were dancing with joy at the thought of celebrating her little brother.

"I know! Are you excited to celebrate?" Sue knelt down and made eye contact with her.

"Yes! Gideon, come show Auntie Sue your new shoes!" Joslyn told him.

Gideon came over with DJ in tow. "Hi Auntie Sue! See my soos? They fast soos!"

"Wow, Gideon! That's cool!" Sue tousled his hair.

"Mommy! I wike soos!" DJ jumped up and down happily.

Sue hugged DJ. "I know, buddy. Why don't you go ask Daddy to go get your new shoes out of your room?"

"Otay!" DJ's eyes lit up as he ran away. "Daddy!" Sue heard him call.

The guests began arriving for the birthday party. The Sorensons were the first ones to arrive.

"Grandma and Grandpa! I am so glad you two were able to make it!" Sue greeted them both with a hug.

"Thank you, dear! We didn't know if we would be able to

come! Steven's plane was supposed to come in last night, but it got delayed. So, he will be flying in late tomorrow afternoon." Mrs. Sorenson handed the presents to Sue.

"How is Steven?" Brittany took their jackets and hung them up in the closet. "I feel like we already know him since you have talked about him so much!"

"He feels the same way." Mrs. Sorenson paused a moment. "But to answer your question, he's good. He's thinking about moving closer to us. He said his company is relocating to Colorado, and that he would rather be near us. He said its lonely back east, and he misses us. Such a good boy." She placed her hand over her heart. "He's only 26, and he is doing well on his own."

"26? Really? I always pictured Steven a little older than that," Sue said thoughtfully.

"We had him when we were in our thirties. We wanted to get established before we had kids. He is our only one. He's not married, yet, either, which is why I am glad I get to spoil these three precious children!" Mrs. Sorenson held out her arms as Gideon ran into them. "I love you, Gideon! Happy birthday!"

"I wuv you too, Gramma!" Gideon rubbed noses with her.

Brittany and Sue exchanged glances, tears in their eyes at the picture. Both women knew what the other was thinking. Their mom and dad were missed, but God blessed each of them with the Sorensons!

Brittany was the first one to find her voice. "Grandpa, Luke and Nate are outside, setting up the barbeque, if you want to help them. I know standing here talking with us women folk isn't always fun!"

Mr. Sorenson smiled. "I do enjoy Nate and Luke! Oh," he leaned in to whisper softly to Brittany and Sue, "does Luke know where his soda is or should I just bring him a new one?"

Brittany answered him through her laughter. "You might want to bring him a new one! If nothing else, he'll get a kick out of that!"

"Come on, Gideon!" Mr. Sorenson took his little hand in his big one. "Let's go grab Daddy a Coke!"

The three women sat down to talk a little bit more before the other guests were to arrive.

○ ○ ○ ○

I can't believe DJ and Gideon are already two! Josephine thought as she drove over to Nate and Sue's house. *Where has the time gone?*

She thought about the last two years. A gentle smile caressed her face. She recalled the family gatherings she had gone to when DJ and Gideon would be rolling over onto their bellies and then couldn't roll back over to their backs. She laughed remembering how they would crawl side by side, like they were racing each other to see who would cross the imaginary finish line. She loved taking both boys to the park and pushing them on the little kid swings. When they began walking, she was so afraid they would bump their heads as they lost their balance and would topple over. Now they were two!

Two!

Gradually, the idea of DJ ever being her son had begun to dissipate. She no longer felt a motherly connection to him but really took on the role as an aunt. She didn't know when it had happened, but over the course of time, she had truly let go of DJ and she truly saw him as Nate's and Sue's son.

It's freeing, Lord, knowing DJ really is loved. Bless Sue and Nate! Provide for them in ways that only You can!

So much has happened in the last two years! Josephine thought about how well her sisters and the Sorensons had been getting along. She was excited to see the Sorensons at every family gathering, even if it was just an impromptu dinner. The Sorensons had helped fill a void in her and her sisters' lives that their parents left behind. They were much needed in her sisters' lives! Josephine thought about how wise the Sorenson's were. She had gone to them, telling her how lonely she had been the through out the last two years. They prayed with her and told her the best way to cure loneliness was by getting involved with serving others. Josephine thought that was a great idea, and offered to serve as much as she could in her church. It did help some, but the initial loneliness never did go away. It was still there, building up inside of her. She knew if she could just meet the right guy, her desire for compatibility would be gone. She had thought by now, she would have found the right guy for her. Unfortunately, no one seemed to even notice her. It was depressing, but she tried not to dwell on those thoughts.

As she walked up to the condo, Josephine heard joyful commotion coming from the inside. The house was decorated just the way Josephine had pictured. There were balloons with the number 2 all over the house. Streamers went from one corner of the room to the other. One side of the room had a table for Gideon's gifts along with his picture. The other side of the room had a picture of DJ on a table for his gifts. After placing her gifts on the appropriate tables, Josephine entered the dining room. The table was pushed against the wall. A blue table cloth decorated the table along with a picture of Gideon with his arm around DJ, both boys smiling a cheesy smile. Josephine laughed. She saw the same picture was put on the birthday cake that was sitting in the middle of the table. People were all over the room, some holding cups of soda or water bottles in their hands, others just munching on chips and carrots. Her sisters' in-laws and friends waved hello to her as she passed them by.

"Josephine!" Nate's mom called from the other side of the room.

"Hello, Martha!" Josephine walked over to where Martha was standing. "How are you?"

"Fine, dear, just fine." Martha Kepler gave her a warm hug.

Josephine spent the next fifteen minutes talking to Martha. She was an older version of Nate, easy going and easy to talk to. Martha was in her late 40's. Her red hair matched Sue's, and more often than not, people mistook Sue for Martha's daughter, not just her daughter-in-law. Josephine recalled one of her earliest conversations with Martha. It was at the engagement party Brittany had thrown for Nate and Sue.

"I got pregnant with Nate when I was 19." Martha sighed heavily and Josephine could tell she was struggling with her emotions. "I told Nate's dad, and we decided to go to a free clinic to find out if I was really pregnant or not. The doctor came in and told us the news and asked when we would like to make the appointment. At first, we were confused. Appointment? For what?"

Martha shook her head. Her voice suddenly had an edge to it. "He proceeded to tell us for the abortion, of course. I can still see the smug expression on his face. My head was spinning." She sniffed back her tears. "And Nate's dad, Eddie, said no, absolutely not. We walked out of there and decided the best thing to do was to get married."

Josephine was touched by her story and her willingness to be so open. "So what happened with you and Eddie? You're no longer married, right?"

"No, sweetie, we aren't. Neither one of us knew Jesus at the time. We both said and did things that destroyed the other. We divorced when Nate was ten. Eddie ended up getting remarried and so did I. Eddie is happy. I am happy." Martha's eyes tenderly found her husband. "I love Lloyd. He is such an amazing man! And because of Nate's witness, Lloyd and I dedicated our lives to Christ." She smiled, dabbing her eyes with a tissue. "God uses our pain and sadness to teach us and to draw us closer to Him."

Three and a half years after that conversation, Josephine knew exactly what Martha meant.

"Hello, Mrs. Kepler." A deep voice brought Josephine back to her recent conversation with Martha.

"Mark! I am so glad you could make it!" Martha looked behind Josephine and motioned for Mark to join them. "Josephine, sweetie, this is Mark Littleton. Mark, Josephine is DJ's aunt."

Turning to Josephine, she added, "Mark was Becca's competitive swim instructor this summer. He met DJ a few times when I was babysitting him and had to take Becca to swim class."

"Nice to meet you, Mark." Josephine extended her hand.

Her heart skipped a beat when their hands shook.

"And you." Mark gave a lopsided grin.

"Every week after swim class, when I had DJ, Mark would play with DJ in the pool for a bit. He said DJ is a natural swimmer. Of course, being the proud grandma that I am," Martha placed her hand over her heart before continuing, "I couldn't agree more. I brought DJ a few more times, and then on the last day, I invited Mark to the birthday party."

Josephine had a hard time peeling her eyes away from Mark so she could pay attention to what Martha was saying. Mark was extremely handsome. His green eyes captivated Josephine. He had dark, curly hair and a smile made her knees weak! His bronze arms revealed he spent many hours in the sun.

"And how did Becca do?" Josephine put her hands in her back pockets of her jeans.

"She did great! Becca was a fast learner." Mark locked eyes with Josephine.

"Hey, Everyone! Burgers are done! Come and get 'em!" Luke waived to the back patio where he and Nate were serving up the burgers.

One by one, people filed outside and stood in line, waiting for their food. Martha glanced from Josephine to Mark. "If you two will excuse me, I have a husband to find."

Josephine nodded absently. "No problem, Martha. Tell Lloyd hi for me!"

Josephine stood next to Mark in line, wondering what to say next. She didn't have long to wait. Mark broke the silence.

"So." Mark ran his hand through his hair. "What do you do?"

"I'm a hair stylist." Josephine looked up at him and then quickly turned away, silently hoping her eyes didn't give away her attraction to him. "I work just off of Jewell and Wadsworth Streets."

"Do you enjoy your job?" Mark kept his tone light.

"I do," Josephine eyes lit up. "I really feel blessed to work there. The ladies I work with are so amazing, and I love my clients. God has truly blessed me."

"Hm. God. Are you a believer?" Mark held out his plate for the burger to be placed on. He waited for Josephine to do the same.

"I am! And you?" Josephine found an empty table and sat

down. Mark sat down across from her.

"Yes. I grew up in a Christian home and accepted the Lord at a young age."

"That's awesome!" Josephine could feel them connecting already.

They took a few bites of their food without saying anything.

Mark wiped his mouth on his napkin. "I've met a lot of people here today but I haven't met your parents yet."

Josephine averted her eyes. "They passed away a few years ago."

Mark's eyes softened. "I'm so sorry to hear that. I didn't know."

"Thanks."

"Do you mind me asking you what happened?" Mark patted Josephine's hand tenderly.

The hurt was so raw in her eyes, Josephine was sure the pain radiated from her. "They were in a car accident and died before the ambulance even arrived on the scene." She told Mark the tragic story leading up to her parents' death. From the look in his eyes, she could tell he felt her pain.

"Josephine, that's terrible. I really am sorry." They sat in silence.

Josephine didn't know how to make the conversation lighter. Just as she was about to excuse herself, she saw Gideon come running up to her.

"Auntie Jo!" Gideon had a guitar in his hands. "I sing for you, ok?"

"Sure, sweetie!" She was relieved to have a distraction. She never knew how to go from the story of her parents' tragic death to a normal conversation. Gideon was a welcomed sight.

"Jesus, wover of my soulllll.....Jesus, I will never wet you go! You taken me from miry clay, set my feet up on a ROCK!!" and he clenched his fist to signify a rock. "I wuv you, I need you, I will never wet you gooo!!"

"Wow, Gideon! That was cool! Good job, buddy!" Josephine encouraged her nephew and hugged him.

"Thanks!" and with that, he was gone.

Mark and Josephine laughed. "Kids are great." Mark chuckled.

Josephine nodded in agreement. "So, tell me about you and your family."

"Well, I grew up in a Christian home. I am 24 years old. My parents have loved the Lord most of their lives. I have one sister and one brother. Both of my siblings are married. My sister just got married in the summer and my brother has been married for two years now."

"Any nieces or nephews?" Josephine sipped her soda.

"I have one niece. My brother and his wife are thinking about having more kids in a year or so." Mark leaned back in his chair casually.

"And what do you do, aside from swimming lessons?" Josephine toyed with her napkin.

"I go to school right now. I live with my parents so my bills are minimal. I work part time at our church." Mark bit into a chip.

"Sounds like fun." Josephine needed to occupy her hands so she sipped her soda again.

"Yeah, it is. I love children. I wanted to be a pastor, but I decided to teach instead. At the church, I help the children's pastor."

The more Josephine talked with Mark, the more she took an interest in him. When there was a break in the conversation, Mr. Sorenson walked over to them.

"Hi there." He sat down beside Josephine.

"Hello, Sir," Mark replied, standing up briefly.

"Grandpa, this is Mark Littleton. Mark, this is Mr. Sorenson."

Mr. Sorenson shook Mark's hand. "Nice to meet you, Mark."

"You, too, sir." Mark sat down again.

"After the party, Jo, Grandma and I were wondering if you would like go out for a cup of coffee." Mr. Sorenson tapped his finger on Josephine's hand.

"I would love to Grandpa." Josephine squeezed his hand.

Spending time with the Sorensons had become one of her favorite past times!

Mr. Sorenson looked at Mark and back to Josephine again. "You are more than welcome to come, too, young man."

"Thank you, sir, but I have plans this evening. Maybe I could take a rain check?" Mark's eyes showed regret.

Josephine's heart sank. She was hoping he would accept the invitation so she could get to know him more.

And plans? What kind of plans? Is it with another girl? Does he have a girlfriend? I don't even know if he is single! Am I possibly interested in a man who is already taken? Oh, God, that would not be good!

Mr. Sorenson nodded and stood up. "Some other time then." Placing a hand on Josephine's shoulder, he gave her a little squeeze. "We'll leave in about an hour. Is that all right?"

"Perfect, Grandpa." She smiled up at him.

"Your grandpa seems like a nice man." Mark's eyes held hers for a moment.

"Oh, he's not my real grandpa. My real grandparents died years ago. I met Mr. Sorenson and his wife while I was working at the salon. A few years ago, they asked if my sisters and I would call them 'grandma and grandpa' since we no longer had any." Josephine's heart skipped a beat. She had to be careful or she was going to get lost in his eyes.

"I see." Mark nodded his head. "So, the only family you have are your sisters?"

Her eyes softened. "Yes. It's been that way for about four years now." She angled her head. "Do your brother and sister live around here?"

"Not to far from here. I am going to my brother's tonight to celebrate my mom's birthday. My family is big on celebrating birthdays and holidays. We go all out!" Mark sipped his bottled water.

Josephine felt her heart lighten up a bit. *Ok,* she thought, *so Mark doesn't have plans with another girl tonight. That makes me feel a little bit better!* She began to feel more hopeful.

"Are your siblings older or younger than you, or both?"

Josephine wanted to know as much as she could about Mark before she left with the Sorensons'. She had less than an hour to get as much information as possible and she intended to use every moment of it!

"My sister and I are twins. We are twenty four. I have one older brother who is twenty six.. What about you?" Mark wiped his hands on his napkin.

"I am almost twenty three and the youngest. My sister, Brittany, is 26, and my other sister, Sue, is 25."

"Wow. Your parents had your sisters pretty close, didn't they?" Mark observed.

Josephine laughed. "Sue was their little 'surprise'. That's what they liked to call her."

"Surprises aren't all bad." He flashed her a grin. Was it her imagination or was he actually flirting with her? Her heart jumped.

Sue appeared just then in the middle of the crowd. "Everyone, we are going to sing happy birthday and have the boys open their gifts now. Would you all join me in the house?"

Side by side, Mark and Josephine walked into the house. They sat together on the couch. They watched the boys open their gifts, sang happy birthday, and ate cake. They continued talking until, glancing at her watch, she noticed it was time to have coffee with the Sorensons..

"Well, Mark, it was nice talking with you. I need to find Mr. and Mrs. Sorenson." She stood up to leave.

"Wait," Mark hesitated, slightly touching her hand. "Would you mind if I called you sometime?" He suddenly appeared shy.

"I would love that." Josephine wrote down her number on a napkin that was near by and handed it to him. "I had a nice time talking with you today."

"Me, too." Mark grinned.

Josephine waved good-bye and searched for her nephews to say good-bye to them. She was intercepted by Brittany.

"So, who is this Mystery Man you have been talking to most

of the party?" Brittany raised her eyebrows.

"His name is Mark Littleton. Nate's mom introduced us. He's cute, huh?" Josephine blushed as she glanced his way.

"If you say so! Did you have a nice talk?"

"I did." Josephine sighed. "He's going to call me!"

Josephine excitedly told Brittany their conversation.

"Wow, Jo!" Brittany smiled. "He sounds like a nice guy. Just a quick word of caution... takes things slow."

"It's been two years since I have been in a relationship, Brit!" Josephine's gentle tone suddenly had an edge to it. She placed her hands on her hips. "How slow do you want me to go?"

"Sis," Brittany gently reached out and took Josephine's hand. "Please don't get defensive. I know you have been lonely lately, and the last few years have been hard."

Brittany sighed, tears coming to her eyes. "Since Mom and Dad have been gone, well, I just feel I need to watch out for you. You're my baby sister. I want only the best for you."

"I know." Josephine hung her head. "I'm sorry. I don't mean to be defensive. Someone has finally noticed me, though! I just want you to be happy for me!"

"If this is who God has for you, I will be happy for you. Just pray about it and go slow." Brittany hugged her sister. "Call me later, ok?"

"I will." Josephine smiled but it didn't quite leave her lips. "Besides, this guy could end up being a really good friend, and that's it."

A look of doubt crossed Brittany's face but she didn't say anything more.

Josephine found the Sorensons talking with Sue. "Ready when you are." She linked her arm with Mrs. Sorenson's.

"Great. Let's get going. Do you want to drive together or separate?" Mr. Sorenson turned to leave.

"We can drive separately. That way, we both can go straight home when we are done." Josephine turned to Sue. "The party was fun. I will call you later, ok?"

"You better! I saw you talking with Mark! I want details, Jo, details!" Sue slapped the back of her hand into the palm of her hand.

Josephine smiled. "All right..okay!"

As Josephine drove to the coffee shop, her thoughts ran away from her. She pictured herself and Mark, strolling hand in hand along a beautiful trail, hiking together. She pictured herself snuggling up to him while they watched a movie together. She envisioned him down on one knee, asking for her hand in marriage.

Who am I kidding? She asked herself. *Lord, I am already having us walk down the aisle! This is ridiculous! God, help me take every thought captive!*

Josephine walked into the coffee shop. "Hi, you two! Sorry I didn't get to talk with you at the party!" She apologized, sitting down.

"No problem. We saw you talking to a gentleman." Mrs. Sorenson sipped her coffee and raised her eyebrows over the top of the cup.

"I was. But let's not talk about him right now. I want to make sure I spend a lot of time in prayer about that." Josephine stopped and was thoughtful. Something was missing. And then it hit her! "I thought Steven was supposed to be coming in today?"

"His flight was delayed. He'll be coming in tomorrow afternoon. We were hoping to have a special dinner for him. I asked the girls already, and they said they wouldn't mind coming over on Monday night for dinner. Are you free to join us?" Mrs. Sorenson set her coffee on the table.

"I don't have any plans yet. I think I can make it. What time?" Josephine took out her phone and hit the calendar button.

"We'll say six o'clock. We'll eat as soon as you all arrive. Sound good, Jake?" Mrs. Sorenson looked at him.

"Mm, hm. Sounds fine with me."

They talked for a bit more, finished their coffee, and left.

Driving home, Josephine prayed about Mark. She really wanted to keep her thoughts in check.

God, I pray You will guide me and show me what You want for me.

Chapter 6

*J*ust as Josephine was leaving for work two days later, her cell phone rang.

"Hello?"

"Josephine? It's Mark, Mark Littleton."

"Oh!" Her heart beat rapidly in her chest. "Hi, Mark! How are you?"

"I'm fine. Is this a bad time?"

"No, not at all. I'm just on my way to work." Josephine fumbled with her seat belt.

"Sorry about that." Mark sounded apologetic. "Should I let you go?"

"No, no. We can talk until I get to work. What are you up to today?" She turned on the car, trying to distract herself from getting too excited.

"I have class this afternoon. That's about it. I just thought I would call to see if you were available on Friday night? I would like to take you out."

"I'm free Friday night. I work until four. What time were you thinking?" Her pulse quickened. A date! I'm going on a date!

"I can pick you up at six. Is that all right?"

"Yes, that's perfect. How should I dress?"

"Josephine, I imagine you look great no matter what you wear," Mark complimented. "But dress casually."

"Thanks." She suddenly felt herself get shy. "I look forward to seeing you."

"I look forward to seeing you, as well. Have a great day at work." His voice carried a hint of a smile.

Josephine was grinning from ear to ear when she walked

through the door to the salon.

"Well, well." Bobbi eyed Josephine curiously. "What happened to you?"

"I met a really neat guy this weekend! He just called and asked me out on a date for Friday night!" Josephine dropped her bag near her station and sighed.

"Who? What? When?" Amber turned in Josephine's direction, questions written all over her face.

Josephine giggled. "I feel like such a school girl! I am so excited!" Dreamily, she sat down in a chair.

Josephine tried to contain her excitement as she told Amber and Bobbi about Mark, how they met, and how thrilled she was he called her so soon after their first meeting.

"So," Bobbi tossed her hair over her shoulder, "what does dream boy look like?"

"Um, I think I can answer that," Amber began, whispering. "He's tall, with dark curly hair, very tan, and a great smile, right?"

"Wait a minute." Josephine sat straight up in her chair. "How did you know that, and why are you whispering?"

Amber pointed to the front door. "Because he just walked through the door!"

Josephine stood and turned around in surprise. Her face showed her delight as he walked toward her.

"Mark! What are you doing here?"

"I remembered you telling me where you worked. So, I thought I would bring you these." He handed her a bouquet of yellow and white daisies. "I just wanted to let you know how excited I am about Friday, and to encourage you to have a wonderful day today." He smiled at her.

Josephine inhaled the lovely aroma of the flowers.

"She'll have a wonderful day now," Bobbi said under her breadth. Amber giggled and turned away.

Josephine's face turned pink. "Thank you, Mark! The flowers are beautiful!" Josephine set the flowers down and guided Mark into the waiting area.

"Anyway, have a good day. I will call you this week, okay?"

Mark turned to leave.

"Mark!" Josephine stepped forward.

"Yes?"

"Wait. I'll walk you to your car." She glanced over her shoulder, giving her friends a look saying *don't even think about following us*! The girls' giggles were full of mischief.

As they walked, her arm brushed his and she got goose bumps. "That was really sweet of you, by the way."

"I just wanted your day to be special."

"It is already, believe me. I really appreciate your thoughtfulness."

They stopped by his car. "Thanks again for stopping by. I still can't believe you did this!" She shook her head, hoping her eyes didn't betray her.

"I just wanted you to know you are special, and that I would be thinking about you." He brushed her hair away from her face.

She tilted her chin down and smiled, blushing. "You are so full of compliments today!" She glanced back at the salon. "I better get back to work. I'll talk to you later."

He unlocked the door and climbed into his car. "Bye, Josephine."

She waved. "Bye, Mark!"

As she walked toward the salon, she saw Amber and Bobbi's faces pushed up against the window. She laughed and shook her head. Friday night couldn't come fast enough!

Josephine was practically walking on air when she walked up to the Sorensons house that night. She saw her sisters cars parked on the street and knew she was the last one to arrive.

She rang the doorbell and a tall man opened the door.

"Josephine?"

She was caught by surprise. "I'm sorry." She stammered when he repeated himself. "I was expecting Grandpa to open the door!" She looked into his dancing eyes.

The man laughed. "No problem. I'm Steven."

"Hi, Steven. And yes, I'm Josephine. How did you know?"

"Process of elimination, I guess. Your sisters are already

here, and I have heard so much about you and your family the last two years."

"Oh, I see. Yes, that explains it!" She laughed and followed him into the living room.

"Auntie Jo!" all three kids exclaimed, running over to her, and wrapping their little arms around her legs.

She bent down. "Hi kiddos!" Looking up at the adults, she added, "Sorry I'm a few minutes late. I got off of work later than expected."

"No problem, dear. How was work?" Mrs. Sorenson was in the kitchen but could hear the conversation.

"Good. It was a long day, but it went well." She thought about Mark coming in and bringing her flowers.

"Why don't we all go to the dining room?" Mr. Sorenson stood and led the way.

One by one, everyone entered into the dining room. Mr. Sorenson sat at the head of the table, Mrs. Sorenson beside him. Everyone took their seats. The kids had a special card table set up for them.

"Looks like we need to get a bigger dining room!" Mr. Sorenson surveyed the room, joy spilling from his eyes. "We can't all fit around our table anymore!"

Everyone laughed. Mr. Sorenson thanked God for their food. When the prayer was finished, Mrs. Sorenson got up and went into the kitchen. She came out with a can of Coke in her hands.

"Luke." She placed the Coke in front of him. "Don't forget where this is!"

Steven had a perplexed look on his face. "I don't get it."

Luke groaned and everyone laughed.

Josephine leaned over and told him Luke's problem of forgetting where his Coke was. Steven laughed. He slapped Luke on the back.

"I have a lot to learn about this family!"

Dinner was a wonderful time of getting to know Steven. His company back east had decided to relocate to Colorado. Steven wanted to be closer to his parents so he was considering coming back to Colorado.

"When would the move take place?" Nate bit into the cake Mrs. Sorenson had served for dessert.

"In less than a year. The company wants it to be quick and easy. It would make things easier on my company on my behalf because I would already have a place to stay until I got a place of my own. I wouldn't have to have the company look for an apartment or house for me, so that would benefit them, that's for sure."

"Is it a large company?" Josephine sipped her water.

"Not too big, but they are growing larger every month." Steven wiped his mouth. He turned to his mom.. "Mom, that was the best cake ever! I'm not used to having dessert right after dinner anymore! It's been a long time!" He leaned back in his chair.

The gang all laughed. Mr. Sorenson had to have dessert right after dinner. He would always say "I have a wedge shaped cavity!" Meaning that he needed to have a piece of pie. Unfortunately for him tonight, Mrs. Sorenson had baked a chocolate cake because it was Steven's favorite.

"I will settle on a piece of cake, I guess," Mr. Sorenson had playfully teased.

Everyone adjourned to the living room. They sat down and continued talking with Steven.

"I feel like I know you all already! Mom and Dad have talked about nothing else except this family! Mom has said how excited she is to have grandkids to spoil. I am very thankful for that because now maybe she will stop bugging me about settling down and having kids!" The group laughed. "Seriously, though, I am so glad you all were here to spend time with them. My work kept me busy over the last few years, including holidays." Steven sighed and looked at his parents. "My folks are pretty special, and I have missed being close by. I am happy to be moving back to Colorado!"

Mrs. Sorenson squeezed her son's hand. "We are happy, too, Steven. We will continue to pray this is what God has for you."

"Thanks, Mom!" Steven squeezed his mom's hand in return.

They talked a little while more. Then the families with children decided to leave since the kids needed to be put to bed.

"Steven, how long will you be in town?" Brittany put her coat on.

"Just until Sunday." Steven stood by the front door. "I need to get back before Monday so I can be ready for work."

"Can we all get together one more time before you go?" Sue knelt down and helped DJ put on his jacket.

"Sure! That would be wonderful," Steven turned to his parents. "Is that fine with you?"

They nodded their consent.

"Great! How about Friday night?" Brittany picked up Gideon.

"I can't Friday night. Can we make it Saturday night instead?" Josephine felt the heat rush to her cheeks when all eyes turned to her.

"What are you doing Friday night?" Nate teased. "Got a hot date?"

"Actually," Josephine blushed even more, "I do. Well, not a hot date, but a date with Mark, the guy at the boys' birthday party."

"Okay," Brittany said, trying to hide her surprise. "Will Saturday work for you, Steven? We can do it at my house this time, so your mom won't have to go through all the work."

"Saturday it is." Steven hugged each of them as they walked out the door.

Josephine quickly said her good-byes before being questioned any further on her date with Mark for Friday. She knew she would have to fill her sisters in on the details of how that came about. She knew they would tell her to be careful, to take things slowly.

I'll wait until after work on Tuesday to call them, she thought as she drove home.

○ ○ ○ ○

Steven closed the door to his parents' house and turned around.

"Well?" his mom raised her eyebrows in expectation. "What do you think of them?"

Steven sat down on the couch and smiled. "They seem pretty fun! I love the way they can all laugh together!"

"Laughter is not one of the things missing from this family, that's for sure." Mr. Sorenson sat opposite of his son. "I just wish we were able to meet their parents before they went home to be with the Lord."

Steven's eyes were compassionate as he spoke, "I can't imagine my life without the two of you."

"I know what you mean." Mrs. Sorenson sighed. "Those girls only have each other now."

"Not true, Mom," Steven disagreed gently. "They have the two of you, and although you can't take the place of their parents, you sure do come pretty close!"

Mrs. Sorenson's eyes filled with grateful tears. "You are a good son, Steven."

"Thanks, Mom. I look forward to getting to know everyone more." Steven rubbed his chin. "Nate, Sue, Josephine, Brittany, and Luke all seem very special. They seem to be the sisters and brothers I never had."

"Oh, Steven, I'm so glad. This is an amazing, god fearing family. I know we joked around tonight, so you probably didn't get to see it. But this family is very special."

"Oh, Mom, I saw it, make no mistake about that." Steven stood and stretched. "I think I'll turn in early. It's been a long day. A good day," he quickly added. "But a long one. Good night, folks."

Mrs. Sorenson watched her son walk away. He was such a good boy. She loved the way he showed his love for God in everything he did. She leaned her head back and closed her eyes. Now if only she could find him a good girl to date and marry. He needed someone in his life, someone who could love him, encourage him, and challenge him in his walk with Christ. Steven was a good looking boy. Well, she chuckled to herself, maybe not boy; man would be the right word. He was tall, with thick hair. His eyes were the color of the ocean, blue and gray mixed together.

Mrs. Sorenson couldn't figure out for the life of her why girls weren't knocking down his door. To be truthful, she had hoped perhaps Josephine would have taken an interest in him tonight. After hearing she had a date for Friday, she let that thought go as quickly as it had come. Perhaps soon God would provide the right woman for Steven.

At least, she hoped He would.

○ ○ ○ ○

Brittany's phone rang Tuesday afternoon.

"I have been waiting for your call!" Brittany chided her with mock irritation. "So, Mark asked you out, huh?"

"He stopped by the salon on Monday morning. I haven't had the chance to tell you. He remembered where I worked and brought me flowers just to tell me to have a good day! Isn't that sweet?" Josephine's excitement could be felt through the phone lines.

"Wow. That is nice of him. What are you going to do on your date?" Brittany could tell by the sound of Josephine's voice she was already falling for Mark.

"I don't know. He said dress casual. He told me I would look good in anything I wear!"

Brittany sat on the stool in her kitchen. She was glad Josephine couldn't see her. She was pretty easy to read, and right now, her eyes would have given her away. She was worried already about Josephine. Worried Josephine would jump in with two feet, and not take things slowly. Worried that Josephine was going to get her heart broken in two. She didn't know how she felt about Mark just yet; she didn't even know him. It had been a few years since anyone had taken any interest in Josephine, and Brittany's fear was Josephine will jump into a relationship a little too quickly. She was so impulsive sometimes. Brittany hoped Josephine would take things slowly, get to know him before deciding he was the one she was going to marry.

"Well, I am definitely looking forward to hearing about your date on Saturday! Will you come over to the house early and tell me all about it?" As soon as she asked the question, Brittany knew the answer.

"Brit, you know me. I don't do anything early. But how about if I tell you all about it over dinner. Anyway, I am just walking through the door to my home, and I am exhausted. I will talk with you later. Will you call Sue and tell her the news for me?" "You got it. Love you, Jo," Brittany said before hanging up. "Love you, too," Josephine answered.

○ ○ ○ ○

"Have you ever spent anytime with this Mark guy?" Brittany was quick to ask as soon as Sue answered the phone.

"Well, hello to you, too!" Brittany could tell Sue was being mildly sarcastic..

"I'm sorry. It's just that I just got off the phone with Jo. She has a date with him on Friday night. She seems pretty excited, and I was just curious what you know about him." Brittany ran her hand through her hair.

"He seems pretty normal to me," Sue's voice was nonchalant. "I just think Jo's excited about him, that's all. It has been a long time since anyone has shown any interest in her."

"Yeah, I know you're right. I just really want her to make good choices, and she hasn't had the most wisdom in the area of men."

"I know. But we need to be careful that we don't push her to make the wrong choices, just out of spite, you know? Lets pray about it and see what we should do, all right?"

"Ok." Brittany talked with Sue a bit more about Steven, and then Sue said she needed to go. DJ was just getting up from his nap and she wanted to have snuggle time with him.

When Brittany hung up the phone, she walked to her window and took a deep breath. Why did she feel so on edge when it came to Josephine dating again? She knew Josephine just wanted to find love like she and Luke had or like Sue and Nate. Brittany was just concerned. She thought back to the other relationships Josephine had been in. Not relationships, but relationship. It was just Jim. Brittany hadn't liked him from the beginning, and let Josephine know it. Jim had scoffed at anything that had to do with Jesus. He never showed any respect whatsoever when it came to prayer at family gatherings. When he did go to the family functions, he spent most of the time by himself, not trying to get to know anyone, and if anyone tried talking to him, Jim mostly answered in one word phrases. Jim definitely was not her type, and was not what Jo had needed. Is Mark anything like Jim? Would he be friendly, outgoing with the family? Would he encourage Jo in her walk with Christ? Brittany didn't know. The only thing she could do was pray for her sister to make wise decisions when it came to dating.

And pray she did!

○ ○ ○ ○

The week drug by ever so slowly. Josephine woke up Wednesday morning, anticipating her date with Mark. As she was getting ready to leave for work, she noticed she had missed a phone call. It was from Mark. She quickly checked her messages.

"Hi, Josephine! Just calling to say Hi! Call me if you have time today. If not, I will see you on Friday!"

She was about to return his call, and then she changed her mind. Instead, she called Sue.

"Sue? It's Jo. Do you have a minute?"

"Sure, Jo. Everything ok?"

"Yes, everything's fine," Josephine reassured her. "I just got a voicemail from Mark. Brittany told you about our date for Friday night, right? "Yes, Brittany filled me in."

"Well, how much do you know about him?" Josephine ran a brush through her hair.

"Mm. Not much. Only what Martha told me. I know he is 24 and going to school to become a, what was it? A teacher of some sort. How come?"

"I just don't know much about him. He seems nice and all, but I just want to make sure I am not going out with a crazy man, you know what I mean?"

"I understand," Sue empathized. "Just take things slowly.

Don't look too far ahead. Take each day as it come, and pray, pray, pray."

"Thanks, Sue. I will see you Saturday and tell you the details of the date!"

Josephine was thankful her sisters were always there, giving her wisdom and encouragement for any situation she might face. "You'd better or else!" Sue playfully threatened.

Josephine hung up the phone and called Mark. She took a deep breath. His answering machine went on.

"Mark, its Josephine. Sorry I missed your call. I was getting ready for work. I won't have much time to talk today, so I thought I would return your call now before I got too busy. I guess I will talk with you on Friday!"

When she hung up, she prayed, *Lord, please allow the next two days to fly by!*

Finally, Friday arrived, and with it, butterflies in Josephine's stomach. She hadn't been this nervous in a long time! She had forgotten what it was like to be so excited about something! She could barely concentrate on work. Amber and Bobbi often teased her about accidentally giving a woman a Mohawk by mistake or dying an older man's hair blue. She knew they were kidding, but she was on edge. What if the date didn't go well? What if he was some maniac who would take advantage of her? What if he was the one for her? What if? What if? What if? The what-ifs kept coming and wouldn't stop no matter how many times she tried praying, meditating on Bible verses, or busying herself with conversation with her clients.

Finally, when she thought she could stand it no more, two friendly faces came through the front door.

"Grandma! Grandpa!" Josephine felt relief run through her entire body. She ran over to them and threw her arms around both of them.

They laughed by her unexpected display of affection. "What's the matter, Josephine?" Mrs. Sorenson's face was masked with concern.

"I have that date tonight, and I am so nervous! I haven't felt this way in a very long time! I have so many things going through my head right now! I can't seem to settle my thoughts down!" Josephine blew her bangs out of her face in exasperation.

"Well, tell us all about it. Do you have time?" Mr. Sorenson glanced at his watch.

"I can take my break now. Would you both walk over to the restaurant with me? We can sit for a bit and talk." Josephine was so glad they had come in at that moment. She needed to talk through her emotions with someone.

"Absolutely." They walked hand in hand.

"Where's Steven today?" Josephine fell into step beside them.

"He said he wanted to go look at some apartments. He is going to live with us at first, but he wants to know how much things cost and how big places are." Mrs. Sorenson walked through the door of the restaurant.

"That's awesome!" Josephine was grateful her mind was preoccupied with Steven. "Tell him if he needs any help next time he's here, I would love to go with him."

"We will. Now, tell us what's going on?" Mrs. Sorenson sat down at their table.

After they had ordered lunch, Josephine poured out her heart to her beloved friends. They sat there, attentively listening, not interrupting her, but allowing her to share her feelings and thoughts with them. When she was done speaking, she took a deep breadth.

"I think you are just nervous, Jo." Mrs. Sorenson patted her hand. "But don't be! This Mark fellow seems like a nice man. Don't worry. Philippians 4:6-7 says for us not to be anxious for anything. Just continue to pray and give thanks to God and His peace, which surpasses all understanding, will guard your heart and mind."

Mr. Sorenson took a sip of his coffee. "And take it all slow. Spend time getting to know each other before you have convinced yourself you are going to marry this fellow. There is no hurry. There is no rush. Enjoy this time of courting."

Their food arrived, and Mr. Sorenson prayed, "God, we thank you for this food. Please take it to nourish our bodies and bless the hands that made it. We ask You, Father, to give Jo a peace of mind today. Give her your joy. We pray she is not nervous about her date. We pray she and Mark will have a good time getting to know each other. Please be with them and keep them safe tonight. May your will be done in their lives. We love you, Jesus. Amen."

She reached over and took the Sorenson's hands. "Thank you both! I love you dearly!"

After lunch, she walked back to work feeling a renewed peace of mind. She said a quick prayer, thanking God for the blessing of friendship with the Sorensons. She knew God had placed them in her life, and was grateful because of it!

Chapter 7

*J*osephine opened the door. Mark was standing there in a dark green sweater, a pair of blue jeans, and a dark leather jacket. He looked absolutely gorgeous. She caught her breath.

"Wow! You look amazing!" She blurted out and then blushed.

"I was just going to say the same thing about you. I love the way your sweater brings out the deep blue in your eyes." Mark's compliment made it all the way to Josephine's soul.

"Thank you. So, where are we going?" Josephine closed the door behind her and walked to Mark's car.

"I thought we would go to dinner first. There is this nice Italian restaurant I have wanted to try. Do you like Italian?"

"I do! It is one of my favorite foods!" Josephine thought how well the date seemed to be starting out. "What then?" She climbed into the car and buckled her seat belt.

"Well," Mark closed the door and quickly got into the driver's seat, "I thought we would go to a corn maze. Have you ever been to one?"

She smiled. "No, but it sounds like fun!"

"Before we leave, I would like to pray. Is that acceptable?"

"Of course. That would be great!" Josephine took a breath, trying to steady her nerves. Was this really happening? Was she really about to pray with an amazing man before she went on a date?

Mark reached over and took her hand. "Lord, thank you for this time I get to spend with Josephine. I pray you will bless our date and our conversation. Keep us safe tonight. May You be glorified through out this evening. We love you, Jesus. Amen."

Josephine tried really hard to concentrate on the prayer. The fact that Mark had taken her hand in his was very distracting. He occasionally rubbed his thumb on the top of her hand. The sensation of her hand in his sent excited shivers up and down her spine. Josephine opened her eyes, half expecting to see Mark gazing at her tenderly. What she saw was complete horror instead.

"Mark! What is it? Are you all right?"

"Oh my gosh! I am so sorry, Josephine!" Mark was beet red from embarrassment, She gasped and did her best to stifle a giggle. There, smack dab on her leg was a wad of snot! He frantically searched for a tissue.

"It's no problem." Josephine kept her tone light. "Really. It happens."

"Ugh! What a way for the night to start!" He wiped off her leg and turned on the engine and starting driving to the restaurant.

"Mark, lets not allow that to ruin our night. We'll have a good time tonight. I already am." She reached out and touched his hand. When she did not get a response, she drew her hand away.

If this is how this guy acts because of a little embarrassment, maybe I don't want to continue this date! She sank deeper into the seat and crossed her arms in front of her chest, looking out the window. *But*, she argued with herself, *I would be totally embarrassed if that happened to me, too. Ok. I will cut the guy some slack.*

There was an awkward silence until they got to the restaurant. As she was about to get out of the car, he gently grabbed her hand.

"I'm sorry. You're right. From this point on, I will have a good attitude. Please forgive me." He smiled at her.

Her cheeks warmed under his gaze. "Sounds good to me."

They walked together, talking about the weather and how excited they were for the snow that was soon to be coming. They gave their names to the hostess and took a seat to wait for their names to be called.

Fifteen minutes later, they were seated at their table. Water was brought to them with fresh baked bread from the bus boy. They were looking at their menus when the waiter sauntered up to their table.

"Hi folks," a voice familiar to Josephine said.

Where have I heard that voice? Josephine pondered.

"My name is--"

Oh no! Josephine couldn't believe her ears. "Jim?"

Jim looked up from his pad of paper. Mark looked over the top of his menu, and saw Josephine's face turn pale.

"Josephine? Are you all right?" Mark voice was filled with concern.

"I'm fine, Mark," she said bleakly. "Jim, what are you doing here?"

"I started working here about a year ago to make some extra money." Jim turned to Mark. "I'm-"

"Jim, yeah, I got that." A shadow fell across his finely chiseled features.

"Josephine and I used to date." Jim pointed his pen at Josephine.

Josephine cleared her throat. "Jim, this is Mark. And I think we need a few more minutes before we order."

"Sure thing." Jim winked at her and walked away.

"Mark, I am so sorry! I had no idea he worked here!" Josephine leaned across the table, desperately trying to ease the situation. "Should we just leave?"

"No. It's not your fault." Mark was clearly trying to push aside feelings of uneasiness. "I planned the date. It'll be fine. After we order, maybe you can tell me more about you and Jim."

"I don't know, Mark." A sudden warning began to make its way into her heart. "This is a little too soon to be talking about past relationships, don't you think?"

"Josephine," Mark laid his hand on hers, "I want us to be honest with each other. I already know you two went out. I don't know how long or how serious your relationship was. Should I worry that after seeing him you may want to get back together with him? Do I even think about asking you out for a second date or do I need to just walk away at this point? I just want a few details, that's all."

"A second date?" She lifted her eyebrows up hopefully.

Mark nodded. "Yes. I would like to go out with you again. Is that all right?"

Josephine nodded. "Yes. Okay. After we order, I will tell you know about me and Jim."

"Great! Now, lets order!"

Jim came back a few minutes later and took their order.

"So," Mark began, an edge to his voice. "How long did you and Jim date?"

"It's kind of a long story," Josephine said. She was a little nervous about telling him about Jim. What if he decided he didn't want a second date?

What if this is my only chance at having a relationship and I blow it by offering up too much information?

"I'm all ears." Mark rested his elbows on the table.

"Remember when I told you my parents died in a car accident a few years ago?" Mark nodded slowly, urging her on. "Well, my world crumbled after that. My faith is God was shaken to its very core. I couldn't believe God would take my parents away from me." She took a sip of water. "So, six months after their death, I met Jim. I wanted to fill the void that was left in my heart. I wasn't walking with God at the time." Josephine looked down, shame and regret filling her eyes and face.

"What happened?" Mark pried gently.

"We moved in together." She lowered her eyes, unable to look at Mark.

Just then, Jim walked up with their food.

"Sorry for the interruption." He glanced from Josephine to Mark.

"Can I get you two anything else?" He placed their food in front of them.

"No, thank you," Mark answered before Josephine could say a word.

Jim walked away. Josephine began to wonder if it was

a mistake telling Mark she lived with another man before marriage. She could tell he was struggling to get a grip on his emotions.

"Say something, Mark," she pleaded.

Mark cleared his throat. "I'm not really sure what to say. I understand the implications of you and Jim living together. In today's society, I know that is the norm. But, I think it is sad. My heart aches for you that you thought that was the way to fill a void only God Himself could fill."

"So, what does this mean?" Josephine expected Mark to say he didn't want to date someone who wasn't pure until marriage. "Does this change your mind about having another date with me?"

Mark shook his head. "No. It doesn't. I'm just glad you are walking with God now and not living in sin any longer."

"Me, too!" Josephine breathed a heavy sigh.

"All right. No more serious talk." Mark's tone of voice became lighter. "Let's have fun the rest of the evening. Agreed?"

"Agreed!" Josephine wanted nothing more than to have a great rest of the date.

○ ○ ○ ○

"Ugh! This is not my idea of fun!" Mark exclaimed forty-five minutes later. Red lights flashed in his rear view mirror. "I seriously cannot believe this!" He pulled the car over and threw his hands up in the air.

The policeman got out of his car and walked toward Mark's window. "May I see your license and registration, please?" The officer's voice was rough.

"Yes, sir. May I ask what this is all about?" Mark handed them to him.

"Son, do you realize you were going ten miles above the speed limit?" The officer looked at his license and registration.

"No, sir, I did not." Mark glanced at Josephine who shrugged her shoulders.

"What is the hurry, may I ask?" The officer handed Mark back his things.

"We were heading to the corn maze. You see," Mark took a

deep breath, "This is our first date, and so far, sir, it isn't going very well. It all started with me accidentally blowing a booger on Josephine's leg."

Josephine waved when the policeman looked in at her.

"Then, I took her to a restaurant I have wanted to try, and our waiter ends up being her ex-boyfriend! And now this!" Mark put his head in his hands in exasperation.

The officer's mouth hung open. He quickly covered his mouth with is black note book. Josephine could tell he was trying really hard to hide his laughter! He peered in at Josephine again, who nodded slowly with a half grin on her face.

"Uh, okay, look," the officer cleared his throat. "I won't give you a ticket this time. I will give you some grace here. But next time, I won't go so easy on you, no matter how hard your day was, got it?"

"Yes, sir!" Mark nodded emphatically.

Mark drove carefully the rest of the way to the corn maze. After a few moments, he turned his gaze on Josephine, his mouth drawn in a tight line.

"Why didn't you tell me there was a cop behind me?" His eyes were cold.

Josephine's defenses shot up. "I didn't know there was one behind you. I was listening to you talk. Why didn't you notice there was a cop behind you? You are the one driving," she pointed out.

Where does he get off blaming me, Lord?

Josephine shook her blonde head, her anger beginning to build. Is this really the way Mark was? She knew she didn't know him that well, but this was ridiculous. It was not her fault he spent too much time talking and not enough time paying attention to driving. Maybe she should just tell him to turn around and take her home. She had had just about all she could take of Mark Littleton!

Mark took a deep breadth and exhaled slowly.

"I'm sorry, Josephine. This night is not really going how I had planned. I just wanted it to go perfectly, you know?"

Josephine calmed down a bit. "I understand." She gave him a stale smile. "It's all right. Let's make the rest of the night a good one. I have never been to a corn maze, and I look forward to it!"

He flashed a heart melting smile. "I'm glad I get to experience this with you. I think we'll have a great time!"

They pulled up to the corn maze. People were milling around, some waiting to go inside the maze, others just coming out with smiles on their faces.

Josephine was utterly amazed. Whatever she had expected, it wasn't this! The corn stalks were as high as twelve feet. She expected the corn maze to be smaller somehow!

As they were about to enter, Mark came up with an idea.

"Hey, let's race. Let's see who can get out of the maze first. What do you think?"

"I don't know, Mark. We haven't had the best of luck this evening. Don't you think we ought to do this together? I have never been to one of these before." The last thing she wanted to do was add tension to their night.

"Oh, c'mon," he coaxed her. "It could be fun. Where is your sense of adventure? Besides, the employee said there is only one way out of the maze. Wouldn't it be fun to see who can find their way out of the maze first? Plus, we said we wanted the rest of the night to be fun, remember? What could be more fun than a little friendly competition?"

"All right." She exhaled slowly. "But know that I don't think this is a good idea."

"Duly noted." Mark put his hand on the small of her back and led the way to the booth.

He paid for them to go into the maze. Mark went left, and she stopped to look around. Right? Left? Straight? Everywhere she turned looked like a sea of yellow and gold. There were two employees high above the maze, one on a bridge and the other on a lift. They were there to help people find the exit if they got lost. What did the employee say at the front? He said no path should be taken more than twice.

No problem there, she thought. *I just started! Oh well. I can't remember what he said, but I will try to do this anyway!*

Josephine traipsed through the maze for a half an hour. She was positive she had taken the same path a few times. Everything looked the same, no matter which way she turned. Before long, she finally saw the exit sign. She expected to see Mark standing there, with a cocky smile on his face. To her surprise, he was not there. She grinned. *I beat him!* She thought happily. She sat down on a bale of hay and waited. Families walked out, laughing and talking about how much fun going through the maze was. Groups of friends exited, giggling and teasing each other about one of them misguiding them. A couple walked out, hand in hand, enjoying each other's company. Josephine watched them a little longer and saw them head straight for the funnel cake booth. Her mouth watered just at the thought of a funnel cake! Maybe she and Mark could grab one when he came out. She looked at her watch and was shocked to see thirty more minutes had gone by. Josephine started to get worried.

What if something had happened? Should I get a corn cop to go find him? As she was about to stand up and go search for the security guard, Mark came out of the maze, looking around to see if he had beat her.

"What?" His voice was filled with disbelief. "How did you get out before me? I thought you said you had never been to one of these before."

"I haven't been to one of these before. I was telling you the truth." She put her hands on her hips. "I just found my way out before you did, that's all."

"Oh great. Rub it in my face, why don't you." He glared down at her.

"Hey, I told you this wasn't a good idea." Josephine pointed her finger at him. "It was your idea to race. If I would have known you were such a sore loser, I wouldn't have agreed to this at all!" She stamped away, fuming.

Who does he think he is? I told him this wasn't a good idea, and now he is blaming me for making it out before him! Good grief! God, what have I gotten myself into?

She stood beside his car, tapping her foot impatiently. He finally reached the car and opened her door. "Thank you." She didn't bother looking at him as she got in.

He got in the car and sat silent for a moment.

"Josephine," he began, "this is not how I wanted the date to go at all."

"Oh, and I suppose I'm to blame for that, too?" Anger spilled from her words. She had to do everything she could not to let the tears spill down her cheeks.

"No. Not at all." He shook his head. "I had envisioned the date going a lot better than this. From the very beginning, it seems this date has been jinxed. I didn't mean to get so upset with you. I shouldn't have been so upset you beat me out of the maze. It's just that," he paused, his voice turning from apologetic to defeat, "with everything that has happened tonight, I think I just blew up. It isn't an excuse. I know I was wrong. I also figured I would beat you out since I have been to corn mazes before, and you hadn't. Please, please forgive me." He reached out to touch her hand.

She searched his eyes and face. She saw a remorseful heart, yet again. She squeezed his hand. "I forgive you."

"I do have one more thing I would like to do with you tonight." He looked at his watch. "I know it is getting late, but can I take you out for dessert? Maybe we can end this night on a positive note. Would that be alright with you?"

She nodded, really wanting the date to end well. "That sounds good."

They drove to a fifty's diner and walked in. They shared a sundae and talked about the night.

"Oddly enough," Mark grinned, "I had a good time tonight."

Josephine almost choked on her ice cream. "You did?"

"Uh-huh. Didn't you?"

"I guess I did. I would have liked things to go more smoothly, but it could have been worse, I suppose." Josephine smiled half-heartedly.

"I would love to go on another date, to redeem myself." Mark's eyes were hopeful.

"I think that can be arranged." Josephine set her spoon down and laughed.

As they walked to the car, Mark slipped his fingers between hers. Josephine felt her heart twitter at the touch of his hand.

He drove her home. They got out of the car and walked to her front door.

"Josephine," he whispered, brushing the hair away from her face, "I really am sorry about tonight." He ran his hand down her arm and tenderly held her hand.

"I know. Me, too." His very touch gave her goose bumps.

He kissed her hand. "Can we go out Sunday night, please? I would really like to make this up to you."

She smiled gently. "That sounds good to me."

She hugged him good night and turned to go inside. Closing the door behind her, she prayed, *Lord, that was the weirdest date I have ever been on!* She sighed. This was not exactly her idea of a romantic date, but certainly an experience. She completely understood why he was so frustrated. She could only imagine how frustrated she would have been if all those bad things happened to her. How would she have handled the snot incident and running into an ex-girlfriend of his. Add being pulled over and losing in a competition to her.

Yes, Lord, I would not have handled that well, either. I do thank You, though, that Mark wants to go out again! Perhaps we can have a better time, Lord? Please let Sunday night be a lot better than tonight! She paused, remembering the way her body felt when he touched her. *And Jesus, it felt so great to finally have someone to be with. Oh, Lord, did You see the way he touched my arm and my hair*

As Josephine crawled into her bed, a soft smile crossed her face as she drifted off to sleep.

o o o o

"Jo?" Brittany said when she had answered the phone. "Are you on your way yet?"

"I'm just leaving now. Why?" Josephine pulled her car onto the street.

"I need some French bread for dinner. Will you pick up two loaves?"

"Sure. I'll be there shortly."

She pulled into the grocery store parking lot. Walking into

the store, she glanced around. She spotted the sign for bakery and walked toward it. She searched for the French bread and started going to the check out.

"Hi Josephine!" Steven walked up to her.

"Steven! You startled me!" Josephine placed her hand over her heart and laughed.

"I'm sorry! I didn't mean to. You looked like you were deep in thought." Steven tilted his head.

"I am I guess. What are you doing here?"

"Mom and Dad are already at Luke and Brittany's. They asked if I would stop by and pick up a six pack of Coke. I guess this is a running joke with Luke?" Steven held up the soda.

"It is! That man is crazy when it comes to his Coke!" Josephine paid for the bread and waited for Steven.

"Do you want to drive over there together? You could leave your car here and I could drop you off after dinner." Josephine took her keys out of her purse and headed toward her car. She hadn't noticed how much Steven's eyes looked like the ocean on a stormy day until now. She quickly looked away.

"Sure," Steven agreed. "So, what were you thinking about when I ran into you?"

"I had a date last night that didn't go very well." Josephine smiled sadly.

"What happened?" Steven climbed into her car.

"Oh, I'll tell you all about it tonight at dinner. My sisters will want to know, too." She shook her head. "It just wasn't a great date, that's all." Josephine sighed. "So, to change the subject, how did house hunting go?"

"Not bad. I think I will take you up on your offer for help, though. I should be back next month. Can we set a day after I know more of my schedule?"

"Sure. No problem. I would be glad to help you." Josephine gave him a sideways glance, taking in his handsome features. She shook her head ever so slightly, not allowing herself to be attracted to Steven.

They pulled up to the house and walked up the steps. "We're here!" She walked into the house, carrying the bread.

"We? Who's we?" Luke called from the kitchen.

"Me and the guest of honor, silly! We ran into each other at the grocery store." Josephine put the bread in the kitchen.

Steven handed Luke the twelve pack of Coke. . "My folks asked me to pick this up on my way here." He grinned.

Luke rolled his eyes. "Oh brother! Well, it should be a lot harder to lose a twelve pack as opposed to just one can!"

Steven laughed. "True! True! Can I help with anything?"

"Nope. Just putting the final touches on dinner." Brittany poked her head out from the kitchen.

Luke and Steven sat down. "So you and Jo ran into each other, huh? Any word on how the date went?" Luke whispered as Josephine walked into the kitchen.

Steven leaned forward. "Not good, I hear. She said it didn't go very well. She wouldn't go into detail, though. Why do you ask?"

"We haven't met this guy yet. Sue met him briefly, but didn't get a chance to talk with him at the party. I guess we will find out more at dinner."

Steven nodded his head. "I guess so."

"Dinner time, folks!" Sue announced.

Everyone gathered around the table and the prayer was said.

"All right, Josephine," Sue knitted her brow together sternly, "we all want to know how the date went with Mark. Spill the beans, little sister!"

Josephine looked around the table. "You may want to get out your tissues. I have a feeling this one may bring out some tears!"

"What do you mean?" Brittany bit into her food.

"It didn't go well?" Mrs. Sorenson leaned forward in anticipation.

"To say the least!" Josephine began relating the events of the evening.

When she got to the part of the booger on her leg, everyone laughed hysterically.

"Who does that?" Astonishment was written all over Luke's face.

Josephine laughed. "Apparently, it happens all the time!"

"It's, I mean, not that bad, right?" Nate roared with laughter.

The group joined in. When the laughter subsided a bit, Josephine was able to continue on with her story of how things went. When she got to the part of Jim, Sue and Brittany gasped.

"No!" Sue covered her mouth, shock pouring from her eyes.

"Seriously?"

"Who's Jim?" Steven wondered aloud.

"Josephine's ex-boyfriend," Mr. Sorenson answered. "How did Mark handle that?"

"Not too well," Josephine admitted. "He wanted to know about my relationship with Jim. I was very worried at first, but he said that it made him sadder more than anything that Jim and I lived in sin together." She blushed, realizing Steven may not know this about her. "Sorry, Steven. I know this is a lot of information about a girl you just met."

"Don't be." Steven patted her hand. "We all have a past, right? Not one of us sitting here is perfect."

"Amen!" everyone agreed.

"So, we finally managed to get through dinner with the promise that the rest of the night we would make fun. And then," she paused for effect.

"No! What more could go wrong?" Brittany wiped her mouth with her napkin.

"Oh, believe me, it gets far better." Sarcasm filled her voice. "And then, Mark gets pulled over by a policeman!"

Luke laughed pounding his hand on the dining room table. Nate cracked up, tears rolling down his cheeks. Mrs. Sorenson's mouth hung open, and Mr. Sorenson's eyes were as big as saucers.

"Seriously?" Steven looked hard at Josephine, making sure she was being honest. "You're joking now, right?"

Josephine only shook her head. "I wish I were. The cop was nice, though. He didn't give Mark a ticket. But then, on the way to the corn maze, Mark got mad at me and tried blaming me! He told me I should have told him a cop was behind him."

The laughter quickly came to an end. Sue gave Brittany a sideways glance, making sure she was not going to say anything. Brittany put her hand to her mouth to stop herself from saying something.

"What did you say after he told you that?" Mrs. Sorenson chose her words carefully.

"I told him I wasn't the one driving, he was. I was so mad at first."

"At first?" Nate's eyebrows came together.

Josephine nodded. "He did say he was sorry, that he wanted to have fun. So, we went to the corn maze. He decided he wanted to have a race to see who would come out first." Josephine's hair flopped as she shook her head. "I didn't think it was a good idea, but agreed to do it anyway. He seemed so excited about it, and I really wanted the night to end well. I should have stuck to my guns."

"Why?" Brittany voiced what everyone else was thinking.

"Because I ended up coming out thirty minutes before he did!"

"Oh! Beaten by a girl!" Luke laughed, throwing his head back.

"How did Mark take that?" Nate covered his eyes with his hands and shook his head.

"Again, not well. He accused me of lying to him about not having been to a corn maze before." Josephine was indignant.

The room got quiet. Josephine looked around.

"To his defense, though," she added quickly, "I can see why he was so irritated. I mean, look at all the bad things that happened right from the start. I don't know how I would have handled any of those things." She tried to make light of the situation. "I may have ended the date right after dinner!"

"Maybe that would have been best," Brittany said under her breath.

"What?" Josephine looked at her.

"Nothing. So, what happened after that?" Brittany waived her hand.

"I walked to the car angry. He followed behind me after a

few moments, and once we got in the car, he apologized. He said it was a lousy date and that's why he got so frustrated. We had dessert at a fifty's diner, and then he drove me home. He said he wanted to make the terrible date up to me, so he asked if we could go out on Sunday night." Josephine finished with a smile.

"Are you?" Sue leaned forward, her arms resting on the table.

Josephine nodded. "Yep. I thought I would give him another chance since the circumstances dictated how the night would go. I felt so bad for the guy. How could I say no?"

Brittany leaned forward. "Jo, are you sure that's a good idea? I mean, even though circumstances weren't the greatest, he seemed to take his frustration out on you a lot."

"I know. But wouldn't you have done the same thing? So many bad things happened last night. I was even frustrated about how the date was turning out."

"Hm," was all Brittany would say.

"I know he probably seems like he isn't the greatest of guys." Josephine stood up to clear the dishes. "But I really think he needs another chance. Sue, how many times have you told me you snapped at Nate for something that wasn't his fault?" Josephine pointed out, walking into the kitchen.

"I think we all have those moments, Josephine." Mrs. Sorenson stood to help Josephine. "I think we all just want you to proceed with caution."

"To Mark's defense," Steven added, "it did seem like the date was lousy! I mean, poor guy! I have never blown a booger on a girl's leg, and I pray I never will!"

The room erupted in laughter. "That by far, is the funniest thing ever!" Nate agreed.

"Ok, ok!" Josephine sat back down. "I do admit, it was pretty funny! I would have died laughing if the look on his face wasn't so mortified!" Josephine laughed. "Can we please change the subject now? I promise I will proceed with caution, like Grandma said. Now, Steven, when do you think you will be back?"

"Probably in a month or so. The company wants to move

shortly after the new year. It's already the end of September, so that doesn't give them much time." Steven glanced at his parents. "I will let Mom and Dad know, and they can tell you all. I would love to have more get togethers like this! Especially if Josephine keeps having stories to tell of terrible dates!"

Again, everyone laughed. Josephine smiled and shook her head.

○ ○ ○ ○

The night ended well, with everyone saying good-bye to Steven. Brittany had walked away feeling a sense of dread.

"I really am having my doubts about this Mark guy," she confided in Luke that night. "I really wonder about him."

"I know, Brit," Luke put his arm around her, "but Jo is a big girl. She is going to have to figure out if this guy is good news or not. I know you want to tell her, but let her figure it out for herself. She'll talk with you more about it, and then you can tell her how you feel. But pray about it first, ok?"

Brittany kissed Luke before rolling over to sleep. "Ok. I will keep praying about it."

Something just didn't sit right with Brittany. She could feel it in the pit of her stomach. Mark was easily aggravated and Josephine was way too willing to give him another chance. Normally, people behave really well on first dates, even if things don't go well. Aren't people dating supposed to be on their best behavior, at least for the first month or so? Mark certainly wasn't on the best of behavior. Plus, Josephine was so lonely; she would go for any guy who took an interest in her. Brittany rolled over onto her side. Perhaps she was just being the overprotective sister.

God, please be in the midst of this entire situation.

With that, nevertheless, she fell into a restless sleep.

○ ○ ○ ○

Josephine dropped Steven off at his car and waved good-bye to him. He got in and sat for a few moments before starting it up and heading to his parents' house. It was a fun evening, cracking jokes about Josephine's terrible first date.

Poor guy, Steven thought, shaking his head.

Steven was really enjoying this family. He was finally able to connect with a group of people. Sure, he connected with the people at his church back east, but this was something different. He didn't have to try to meet them. They were already there, welcoming him into their family with open arms, just like they had done with his parents. His parents were the best people in the world. They had always been an example of Christ, even in the midst of difficult circumstances. They had a love for each other and a love for people that they passed on to Steven. They were the most encouraging people in Steven's life, and he was grateful for them, even when his mom made little comments at times about finding a "nice girl and settling down."

Truth was, Steven really wanted to get married.. Ever since he could remember, he wanted to have a wife and have a family. Steven even dated a few women back east, but no spark, nothing seemed to happen that would want Steven to pursue any of them any farther. He turned down the street to his parents' house. What would it be like to own a home one day, to have it filled with the love and laughter, the same as in his parents' house? What would it be like to finally share his heart with a woman who would willingly share her heart with him? Steven didn't know, but perhaps moving back to Colorado was a way to find out. Perhaps love was waiting for him here.

He didn't really have a clue. He knew he would pray because there was always hope for tomorrow.

Chapter 8

*I*t was a beautiful fall day. The sun was shining high in the sky, and there was not a cloud in sight. The temperature was supposed to be warmer than what it had been.

Welcome to an Indian summer! Sue thought, listening to the pastor speak. Sue loved going to this church. This is the church she grew up in. Looking around the sanctuary, she could almost see her parents sitting in the second row, like they used to do every Sunday. Sue loved Pastor Jack Reynolds. He had taken the place of the former senior pastor, Ron Donaldson. Ron had said it was time to retire, and so the torch had been passed to Pastor Jack. Jack was amazing! He was passionate every single time he spoke. He wore his heart on his sleeve and made known his heart to the congregation. He was so real and honest. Jack wasn't the most eloquent of speakers, and perhaps that is why she loved him so much. He never pretended to be someone he was not..

Sue sighed contentedly, glancing over at Nate. He sat next to her, attentive to what the pastor was saying. He nodded his agreement when Pastor Kevin said something about Jesus not coming to be served, but to serve and we ought to follow in His footsteps. Kevin rambled off a list of organizations the members of the church could get involved in, all the while not condemning the congregation, but encouraging them to do something outside of themselves. Sue squeezed Nate's hand, which brought a smile to his face. She felt so blessed to be married to this great man! Sue thought back to that wonderful night when she first met Nate.

Growing up in the church, Sue had some amazing youth

sponsors. These were college age adults who volunteered their time to work with the youth group. Sue had grown close to a few of them during her teenage years, and because of them, she wanted to volunteer her time and influence lives the way hers was influenced so long ago. It was Friday Fun Night, the night when the junior high kids were able to gather and just have fun. The youth pastor told Sue to come that night before attending the junior high Bible study. He felt it would allow her to get to know the kids in a fun setting first. Sue was excited as she stepped out of her car and shut the door. Just then, another car pulled up and parked next to Sue. A handsome gentleman with gentle eyes got out and smiled at Sue.

"Hi." He pulled out his guitar from the trunk of his car.

"Hi!" Sue smiled back at him.

"I'm sort of new here," the guy explained. "Could you tell me where the junior high group meets?"

"Actually, I am headed there myself. My name's Sue." Sue stuck out her hand.

His hand shake was firm, yet gentle. "I'm Nate. I'm a friend of Mike's, the youth pastor."

Sue nodded. "It's nice to meet you. Are you working with the youth group?"

"Mm, sort of. Mike asked if I could play a few songs tonight while the kids hung out." Nate fell into step beside her.

"I see. Have you known Mike a long time?"

"Yeah. We were in a band together in high school. We've kept in touch since then." Nate held the door open for Sue.

"Thank you." She walked through. "So, what kind of band were you in?"

"The typical heavy metal band almost every kid dreams about being in." Nate laughed, shaking his head. "It was a fun time, but I wouldn't want to go back to those days."

"How come?" Sue raised her eye brows.

Nate leaned closer, like he was telling her a secret. "Between you and me, Mike isn't the best singer. He plays better drums than he does sing, but sometimes, I needed a back up singer, and he was it!" Nate followed Sue down the hallway. "One day, you'll have to ask Mike to listen to the tape." Nate's smile made it all the way to his eyes.

Sue laughed. "Oh, now I am intrigued! I am definitely going to have to ask Mike for that tape!"

They entered the junior high room. Nate spotted Mike and nodded in his direction.

"It was nice meeting you, Sue. Thanks for leading me here. I wouldn't have found it without you." Nate turned to walk away.

"Not a problem, Nate. Have fun tonight." She waved and headed for the kids she had already met.

That night, Nate seemed content to play his guitar in the background while the kids played games, ate pizza, drank soda, and had a fun night. Sue would glance in his direction every so often and catch his eye. She would blush from embarrassment and Nate would just smile at her. After the kids had gone home and Sue was done cleaning up, Mike had asked if Sue and a few of the other youth sponsors wanted to join him, his wife Grace, and Nate for some coffee. Sue agreed to go.

"So, Mike." Sue sat down next to Nate at the table, "I hear you used to be in a band back in the day."

Mike shook his head and smiled. "Yep. Sure did. It was a pretty awesome band, too. I think we had the best drummer in town!"

Nate groaned. "And the most humble, too!"

Sue laughed. "Care to spare a CD so I can hear your talent?"

Mike rubbed his chin thoughtfully. "I'll have to think about that. It would depend. Would it be the one where I am singing back up? Because if so, no way! Only God and Grace should be subjected to my awful singing!"

The group laughed. Nate pretended to be shocked. "No! You weren't *that* bad, were you?"

"By the way, Nate," Mike leaned forward. "What did you ever do with the music you wrote?"

"Not much yet." Nate shook his head sadly. "It's just sitting in my notebook. Why?"

"I have a friend who has a recording studio. Care to put

some of your music on a cd for the rest of the world to hear?"

Nate's eyes were as big as saucers. "No way! Are you serious? Man, that'd be a dream come true!"

Mike's grin spread from ear to ear. "Perfect. Let's make it happen within the month."

"You don't have to tell me twice!" Nate slapped Mike on the back, his gratitude written all over his face.

The rest of the night went on with playful teasing. Sue felt a camaraderie she hadn't felt in a long time. As she was walking to her car, Nate fell in step beside her.

"I would love to hear your music when you are done recording." She looked down, shyness overtaking her.

"I will definitely give you a copy of the cd." Nate grinned.

"Thanks! I would love that!"

"So," he stammered. "Will you be at next Friday's Fun night?"

"Definitely!" Sue's eyes lit up with excitement. "Those kids have so much joy and life! I wouldn't miss it!"

"Great! Perhaps I will see you there." Nate stopped beside her car.

"You'll be coming back then?" Sue felt her spirit lift even higher.

"Yeah. Mike asked if I could make this a regular thing."

"Oh fun! I'm glad to hear that!" Sue hadn't expected to be as happy as she felt about the news. She opened her car door and was about to climb in. Nate stuck out his hand. Sue shook his hand and smiled.

"Again, Sue, it really was nice meeting you."

"Same here, Nate. I'll see you next Friday."

"You can count on it." Nate let go of her hand and walked away.

Sue started her car, grinning from ear to ear. She liked Nate, and hoped they would become good friends.

○ ○ ○ ○

Now, sitting next to Nate at church, she never would have guessed God had planned that night for this very reason. She was so blessed to be married to Nate! What started out as a friendship quickly grew into something so much more! Nate put his arm around her shoulders and smiled at her. She leaned close to Nate and smiled back. *Jesus,* she prayed, *thank You for my husband.*

When the service was over, she and Nate headed to the toddler room to pick up DJ.

"Hey," Sue was thoughtful for a moment, "let's do something fun today. It's a beautiful day. I hate to waste it inside."

"What do you have in mind?" Nate waited for the toddlers' room assistant to get DJ.

"Hold on a second," Sue turned her attention to the worker. "How was he today?"

"Little DJ?" the elderly woman asked, squeezing DJ in a big hug and handing him to Sue. "Perfect, as usual. He is such an angel! We love having him!"

Sue smiled. "Thanks. We think so, too."

"Daddy! I made you, see?" DJ shoved a piece of paper toward Nate. On it was a stick figure with purple hair standing straight up.

"That's me?" Nate pretended to be in awe. "Buddy, it looks exactly like me!"

Nate swung DJ around and waved good-bye to the child care attendants..

"Back to your suggestion." Nate set DJ down and took his hand.

"Yes. I think we should go to a park and just play. What do you think? We could swing by some place and pick up lunch and go to the park down the street."

"Sounds like a plan. What do you say, pal?" Nate put DJ in his car seat. "Do you want to go play at a park?"

DJ's eyes lit up. "Yeah! Play! Will you swing me, Daddy?"

Nate got in the car and turned in on. As he drove out of the parking lot, he glanced over his shoulder at DJ. "Of course! I would love to push you on the swings!"

A smile formed at the corner of Sue's mouth. "I love days like this!"

"What do you mean?"

"I love days when we can just go play and have fun as a family. Times like this will go by so fast! We'll look back in a few years and wonder how the time flew!" Sue looked wistfully out the window.

Nate nodded. "I agree. So, we'll make the most of our time now, how about that?"

Sue placed her hand on Nate's leg. "Sounds great to me!"

Nate drove through a fast food place and headed to the park. They sat at one of the tables there, prayed for their meal, and talked.

"How was church today, DJ?" Sue watched DJ bite his chicken nuggets.

"Fun! I like church!" DJ put his chicken in the container and sipped his milk.

Nate grinned. "I'm glad, buddy. Now, let's finish eating so we can go swing and play!"

DJ gulped down the rest of his food, and Nate and DJ headed off toward the swings. Sue followed after she was finished cleaning up.

Nate put DJ on the swings and pushed him gently at first.

"Faster, Daddy, faster!" DJ yelled with excitement.

Nate laughed a hearty laugh and pushed DJ higher. Sue smiled, watching the two of them. When DJ was finished on the swings, Nate walked him up the steps to the slide.

"Want to race?" Nate challenged him.

"Yep!" DJ answered.

Nate sat down, and so did DJ. "Ready, set, go!" Nate called, and pushed himself down. DJ did the same. DJ got to the bottom of the slide just before Nate did.

"Good job, DJ!" Sue ran over to the bottom of the slide. "You beat Daddy!"

"No fair! I think DJ pushed off before I did!" Nate teased, rubbing DJ's head. "I'm just kidding, DJ! Good job!"

DJ grinned. "Chase me!" and with that, he started to run.

Nate ran slowly after DJ, yelling all the while, "Oh, there's a storm comin', Buddy! When I catch you, I'm gonna tickle you!"

Sue could hear DJ's giggle from where she was standing. When Nate caught up with DJ, he gently tackled him on the grass and began tickling him. DJ laughed until he could barely breathe. Sue was caught up watching the interaction between father and son. She knew this time would go so quickly, she wanted to cherish every single moment they had together. She locked the entire day up in her heart, storing it for a time when DJ was grown and out of the house. She would want to revisit this day and many like it. Tears sprung to her eyes. She brushed them away with the back of her hand, not wanting to get lost in what the future held, but trying to savor every moment of today.

"Now you get Daddy!" Nate stood up and started to run.

DJ laughed some more. "I get you! Storm comin', Daddy!"

Nate laughed and fell to the grass. DJ pounced on Nate and started tickling him just like a two year old would do.

Sue came up and started helping DJ tickle Nate.

"Hey! DJ has an ally!" Nate grabbed Sue around her waist and tickled her back.

By the time they were done, they were all laughing, lying on the grass.

Nate put his hands behind his head. DJ looked over at him and did the same.

"This has been a fun day," Nate commented.

"Fun day," DJ agreed.

"Well, boys, I say it is almost nap time! After a fun time like that, Mommy needs a nap!" Sue stood up.

Nate and DJ followed. Sue grabbed DJ's hand, and Nate held on to Sue's hand.

"I love our family," he leaned close to her, kissing her on the cheek.

"Mm. Me, too."

Sue was the happiest she had been in a long time. As they walked to her car, she thought about how blessed she was. She loved being a wife and a mom. Sue remembered her parents, and the love they had for one another.

God, please allow Nate and me to have that kind of love. She looked out the car window. *Please allow us to be the kind of parents my parents were to me, Brittany, and Josephine.*

Her thoughts went to Josephine. Sue thanked God for her sacrifice.

Bless Josephine, Lord. Please give her wisdom as she goes on her second date today with Mark. Let her know what it is You desire for her.

Nate reached over and took her hand. "Whatcha thinking'?"

"Just thanking God for my many blessings," Sue replied with a smile, glancing at Nate and back at DJ.

○ ○ ○ ○

Josephine peered at herself in the full length mirror. Her black pants fit nicely today. With her white shirt accenting her waist, she felt she looked pretty good. She grabbed her black jacket, brushed her hand through her hair, and ran to answer the door.

Oh, Lord, please let today's date be a lot better than the last one!

"Hi, Mark." Josephine swung the door open.

"Josephine," Mark eyed her up and down, "you look beautiful. Are you ready?"

"Yes. Let me grab my purse, and I'm all set to go." Josephine ushered him into the living room as she got her purse.

"So, what are the plans for today?" She looked up at him. She caught her breath when his eyes met hers.

"Today, I wanted to take you to the Cheyenne Mountain Zoo." Mark paused for a moment. "I know it's over an hour away, but I thought that would give us time to talk and get to know more about each other. Does that sound all right?"

Her heart skipped a beat as their arms brushed against each other.

"That sounds wonderful, Mark. I'm glad you thought of it. I have taken my niece there a few times, and I really love that zoo." Josephine climbed in the car and buckled her seat belt.

"Perfect. I'm glad to hear it." Mark started the car and drove toward the freeway.

They sat in silence for a few minutes.

Mark cleared his throat and glanced at her from the corner of his eye.

"Listen," he began nervously, "I really am sorry about our first date. Thank you for giving me a second chance."

Josephine smiled at him. "No problem. After thinking about it a little bit more, I can understand why you were so upset. But this is a new day, and I look forward to having a good time with you."

"Same here. How was church today?" Mark looked over his shoulder before changing lanes.

"It was wonderful! I loved the worship today, and the message was awesome!" Josephine went into a description about the message. She was really convicted sitting at church today. The pastor was talking about how Jesus forgives and forgets our past mistakes. He doesn't want people holding onto past hurts. "I really felt God speaking to me today." She placed her hand over her heart, tears filling her eyes. "I know God doesn't hold my past against me. So, I figure, why hold someone else's against them?"

Mark patted her hand. "Sounds like an amazing sermon. I wish I was there to hear it. I agree with your pastor. The past is the past."

Josephine eased back into the seat and sighed inwardly. Hearing Mark say that calmed her fears. She had wondered throughout the day if Mark would hold her relationship with Jim against her. Now, she knew everything was going to be fine. Breathing a sigh of relief, she turned her attention back to Mark. "How was your church today?"

"It was pretty good." Mark shrugged his shoulders. "It wasn't anything I hadn't heard before, but it was a good sermon. The pastor was talking about being a true disciple of Jesus. He was talking a lot about how we need to sit at Jesus' feet and spend time in His Word."

"Oh," Josephine breathed, "I love that! Did he use Martha and Mary as an example?"

"Yes, he did." Mark nodded his appreciation of Josephine knowing her Bible. "I suppose you've heard a sermon like that?"

"I haven't for a long time, but before I made poor choices, my parents' pastor used to talk a lot about being a disciple, and he would use that illustration."

"Gotcha. I like hearing that. It's a good reminder to keep doing what I am already doing, you know?" Mark pulled into the parking lot of the zoo.

"Absolutely." Josephine nodded, walking beside Mark toward the entrance. "Not to change the subject or anything, but what made you decide to come here today?"

Mark paid for the tickets and entered the zoo with Josephine.

"Well," he placed his hand on the small of her back, allowing her to walk in front of him. "I really wanted to do something fun, but something that would give us a chance to talk at the same time. I thought about the movies, but I just wanted a chance to get to know you better, and for you to get to know me a little better, too."

Josephine took a map from the employee. "Thank you," she said politely to her. She opened her map. "Where to first?"

"What's your favorite attraction here?" Mark looked around them.

"That's a tough one." Josephine tapped the tip of her nose. "I just love that this is the only zoo in America that is in the mountains!" Her eyes lit up. "I know! How about we check out the lions? I think those cats are simply majestic."

"Sure. That sounds good to me." Mark took her hand and led her through the crowd.

"What's your favorite attraction?" Josephine was a little light-headed from the way that Mark's fingers felt wrapped around hers.

"I like the Mountaineer Sky ride. I definitely want to take you on that. Have you ever been on it?" Mark tipped his head to one side.

"No, actually, I haven't. It seems every time I come, it's either shut down or I just never make it that way. Have you?"

"Yes. It is truly amazing to fly up over the zoo on a ski lift and look down at God's creation of the mountains." He shook his head. "It is breath taking."

"Wow. It sounds wonderful! I would love to do that with you!" Josephine was excited the date was already going a lot better than the previous one. Her mind drifted back to their first date and how awful it was. She quickly cleared her head. This was a new day, a new date, and apparently, a new Mark.

Time to move on, she told herself sternly.

They stopped in front of the lion exhibit. "Look at those magnificent creatures." Josephine was in awe. "Aren't they amazing?"

Mark looked down at Josephine. "Not as amazing as you are, Josephine."

Josephine looked down shyly. "Thanks Mark."

"I mean it." His tone was serious. "You really are an amazing woman. I don't know what I would have done had I been in your shoes the other night. It shocks me that I am standing here with you."

"Mark," Josephine wrinkled her brow, "I already told you that all is forgotten. No reason to bring it up. We all make mistakes. I'm just really happy to be here with you."

"I'm happy to be here with you, too." Mark gave her a sideways hug. "Ok, I won't bring it up anymore." He started walking toward the bald eagle exhibit. "I love the eagles. I think they are pretty cool, too."

"Oh yeah? How come?" Josephine fell into step beside him.

"I think it is awesome that they mate for life. I like how God uses them in Isaiah 40:31 'but those who hope in the LORD will renew their strength. They will soar on wings like eagles; they will run and not grow weary, they will walk and not be faint.' I just find that I would love to soar like the eagles do. Wouldn't that be cool?" Mark stopped in front of the exhibit.

"They mate for life? Really? What happens if one dies?"

"That's the cool thing, too." Mark faced Josephine, excitement pouring from his voice. "Just like the Bible says if one person in a marriage dies, the other can remarry the same goes for an eagle. It won't hesitate to find a new mate. But when they do find their mate, even if the female is falling, the male will hold on to her and fall with her. He will never let her go. Crazy, huh? Even if it means death, he is totally committed to her."

Josephine's eyes grew wide. "I never knew that before! How do you know so much about eagles?"

"I did a study on them one time in high school. The lessons I had learned stuck with me." Mark lifted one shoulder. "Sorry to bore you with all of this."

"You're not boring me. I find it interesting!" Josephine took his hand in hers. "Besides, I like learning new things." "Good. I enjoy sharing the things I learn." Mark squeezed her hand.

Josephine felt her whole body relax being near Mark. She was enjoying spending this time with him. This date had definitely made up for the previous one! As they walked in silence, her mind began to drift toward the future. Josephine saw herself falling head over heals for Mark, telling him she loved him for the first time. She could picture him taking her in his arms, kissing her gently and passionately. She shook her head, pleading with herself to take things slowly. Letting her mind drift like this wouldn't help her at all! She needed to get to know him better before she made a lifelong commitment to him.

"Last time, we talked so much about me, I feel like you should tell me about you." Josephine slowed down to look at the grizzly bears.

"What would you like to know?" Mark leaned against the fence.

"Well, you said you grew up in a Christian home. Have you been at the same church all of your life? When was it that you knew you wanted to follow Jesus?"

"My parents are pretty active in their church. Shortly after high school, I realized I needed to find a church on my own, to kind of have my own identity. So, I found a church that loves Jesus and that had opportunities for me to serve. My parents were fine with me going to this church. They knew of the pastor and knew it was a God-fearing church." He paused. "I like having my parents' support on things. Family, like I told you before, is very important to me."

Josephine nodded. "I know what you mean. It meant the world to me, knowing my parents were not disappointed in me when I chose to be a hairstylist and not a teacher or missionary. Now that they are gone, my sisters have really taken on that role, as well as the Sorensons.."

"I imagine it must have been hard, your parents' death, I mean." Mark's gaze was fixed on hers, sympathy pouring from his eyes.

"Yes, but we aren't talking about that, remember?" She gave him a playful shove. "Answer my next question. When did you know you wanted to follow Jesus?"

Mark laughed and held up his hands in surrender. "Ok! Ok! I knew I wanted to follow Jesus at a young age, even before I was ten. My folks did such a great job on living Christ at home that I knew He was real and wanted me to live for Him."

"Did you ever feel at times it was too hard?"

"Sure. I think everybody feels that way at times." Mark shrugged his shoulders. "But then I would remember that God died for me, and that wasn't easy at all. I just keep going back to what the Bible says, about denying myself, taking up my cross, and following Him."

"Hm. I guess I never thought of that." Josephine studied Mark. Confidence poured from him. She secretly wished she had some of that confidence for herself.

"What made you decide to come back to Jesus?" Mark straightened and started walking again.

Josephine followed him. "Well, it was a long process, as I am sure my sisters can tell you." She smiled a sad smile. "I wish I'd never walked away in the first place, but God is good and took me back with open arms! Anyway, Mr. Sorenson was a regular customer of mine, and a very strong believer. He and his wife were really friendly to me when I started working at the shop. When my parents died, they were really there for me, letting me cry, never telling me how I should feel. They accepted my choices, even when I moved in with Jim."

"Did they ever tell you it was wrong?" Mark's eyes narrowed ever so slightly.

Josephine huffed. "Oh yeah they did! They let me know they did not condone my choice at all, but that they were not going to turn me away either. So, with the Sorensons loving me and my sisters loving me, one day, I was sitting at home, and I realized what a fool I had been. Things with Jim and I were fine, but I was still lonely. There was a place in my heart that Jim couldn't fill. I knew what it was. It was the place that God Himself can fill. Jim and I sat down that night and talked about it. He didn't understand, but he respected my decision. I knew at that moment that I wasn't in love with Jim, but he had become a really good friend, you know?"

"I've never been in love before, so I don't really know, but I can kind of understand." Mark sat down on a bench.

"Really? You've never been in love?" Josephine let the shock she felt show on her face.

"Really. I haven't really dated a lot of women." Mark raised his shoulders. "I wanted to be careful with whom I gave my heart to."

"Wow, Mark! That is amazing. I just can't imagine you not dating more. I mean, you're good looking and you love Jesus. Why weren't the girls knocking down your door?"

Mark smiled. "Thanks for the compliment. I just never had many girls really interested in me, and I wasn't interested in them, either. I know it seems strange, but I think it was a good thing."

"Totally a good thing."

Josephine was really enjoying herself and their talk. She was able to be honest and share her heart with him, and he was, too. Josephine felt a bond begin to grow between them.

They walked some more and talked some more, sometimes about important things, other times not. Josephine was a little nervous going on the Mountaineer Sky Ride, but once she was on the lift, next to Mark who had his arm around her shoulders, her fear subsided. She saw the beauty of the mountains and how small the animals looked from way up high. When they disembarked, they saw the rock wall.

"Do you want to try climbing it?" Mark suggested.

"On one condition." Josephine's eyes twinkled.

"What?" Mark crossed his arms in front of him.

"No competing!" Josephine laughed, playfully punching Mark's arm.

Mark laughed, too. "Deal." He took her in his arms and gave her a hug.

They climbed the rock wall and had a great time. When they were done, Mark bought them a drink to share. As they strolled out of the zoo, Josephine was content with how the date was turning out.

"How about a bite to eat?" Mark took her hand in his.

"Sure!" Josephine couldn't stop her heart from racing every time Mark touched her.

"Can we steer clear of Italian food tonight?" Mark gave her a wink.

"Absolutely!" Josephine nodded emphatically.

By the end of the evening, Josephine knew the date was a success.

Mark walked her to her front door. "I had a terrific time tonight, Josephine."

She shyly looked up at him. "Me, too. Thanks for a great day!"

"No, thank you. It's because you forgave me that we had such a great time. I hope we can do it again and soon." Mark's voice was thick and husky.

"I would like to make you dinner, if that's all right with you." Josephine lifted her eyebrows in hopeful expectation.

"That sounds good to me. When would you like to have me over?" Mark caressed her arm.

"Would Friday be too soon?" Chills ran up and down her body at his touch.

"Friday is perfect." Mark leaned closer to her. Then he kissed her ever so gently on her lips.

Her heart was beating rapidly when he pulled away. His lips

were so soft and sweet! But there was something in the back of her mind that told her this was a little too soon. She quickly pushed those thoughts out of her head.

"I'll see you Friday," Mark whispered, backing up.

Josephine didn't say a word. She only waved good bye and let herself in the door to her apartment. Closing the door, she leaned against it and sighed dreamily. Things were going so well already! What a great date! Josephine didn't think the date could have gone any better. Now, if only Friday would come quickly!

She knew she would have to keep herself pretty occupied.

Chapter 9

*B*rittany stretched and glanced at the clock. Nine o'clock in the morning. *Wow!* She thought. *I was able to sleep late today!* Climbing out of bed, she headed to the kitchen to make herself a cup of tea. She loved Saturday mornings. Luke took the kids to breakfast every Saturday to spend some time with them. He missed the kids while he was at work and enjoyed having this time alone with them. Luke had said that he also wanted to give Brittany a chance to sleep in and have time to herself. She loved her husband. He was always so thoughtful!

Looking out the window, she noticed clouds rolling in. Normally by Halloween, they would have gotten their first snow. This year, though, with Halloween only a few weeks away, snow hadn't come at all.

Perhaps we could get a little snow today, Lord?

Brittany enjoyed the snow and was looking forward to it. She loved the way the snow covered the mountains like a big white blanket. She was anxious to see the trees in her front yard draped with white. Snow made anything look beautiful. She was always telling Luke if they were ever to buy a new house, it couldn't be in winter because snow made even the ugliest house breath taking!

Just as she was about to sit down in her favorite chair with her tea, her phone rang.

"Hello?" She paused before taking a sip of her tea.

"Happy Saturday!" Sue's voice was cheerful on the other end.

"And to you, Sue! Did Nate take DJ out to breakfast?" Brittany held the phone with her shoulder and wrapped her hands around the cup.

Sue sighed happily. "Yes, he did. Thank Luke for me for giving Nate that idea. I adore my Saturday mornings! Don't get me wrong. I love my son, but sometimes, I just need some me time, you know what I mean?"

"Absolutely!" Brittany took a slow sip of her tea. "I just got up not too long ago. I don't get to sleep in Sunday through Friday, so I make the most of my Saturday mornings."

"I wish I could. I am just an early bird by nature I suppose."

"Yes you are! You always have been." Brittany leaned back in her chair, completely relaxed. "So, what's up?"

"Have you talked with Josephine today?" Sue's joyful tone turned to one of concern.

Brittany gulped and tried to settle the sinking feeling in her stomach. "No. Why?"

"She had her third date with Mark last night. I was wondering if she called you yet to tell you about it." Brittany could hear Sue fidgeting in the background.

"Nope. She probably knew I was going to sleep in." Brittany ran her hand through her hair.

"Yeah, that's true."

"Did she call you?" Brittany sighed, trying not to let her mind get the better of her.

"Yep."

"And?" Brittany prompted.

"I don't know, Brit," Sue hesitated. "There's just something with this whole thing that doesn't sit well."

"What do you mean?" Brittany leaned her head against the back of her chair.

"Jo told me all about their date," Sue began with a heavy sigh. "She told me how he came over to her place so she could make them dinner."

"Ok," Brittany tried to take a neutral position. "Doesn't sound too bad so far."

"No, but it was just her wording, I guess. Almost like, she is going to walk down the aisle with him next Saturday. Anyway, I'm getting ahead of myself. So, he came over and brought her flowers, which is sweet. I always find that a good thing. Jo told me she made them her famous Chicken Marsala, and he really enjoyed it. He complimented her all during dinner about what a great cook she is." Sue paused and suddenly laughed. "I'm sorry. I know I shouldn't laugh. I know Jo is a great cook *now*; she's certainly come a long way!"

"You mean from the spaghetti and syrup days? Yes, she has!" Brittany giggled.

"So, after dinner, she puts on a movie," Sue continued. "He puts his arm around her, she snuggles closer, which is normal. It just seems that they are moving a little fast. Plus, they are all alone in her apartment. Anything could happen. You know he kissed her on their second date, right?"

"I know. I told her to be careful and take things slow. This doesn't seem slow, does it?" Brittany thought for a second. "Nothing did happen, right?"

"Nothing happened, thank God. And no! This isn't taking things slow! And that's what worries me. Red flags are going up everywhere! Josephine told me Mark might be the one for her. Brit, this is only their third date! She's already thinking about marriage. I think she is jumping in way too soon."

"Hm," Brittany was quiet. "Why do you think that is?"

"I think it is stemming from her loneliness. She so desperately wants to be in a relationship. I think she wants what we have. I understand that, I really do. But, at the same time, she has to be careful. I wonder if she is clinging to the first guy who has shown interest in her. I asked her whether or not she had prayed about all of this. You know what she told me?" Shock registered in Sue's voice..

"What?"

"She said she prayed about her being lonely and all of a sudden, Mark came along. I know God answers prayers quickly, but at the same time, she needs to use discernment. What if this isn't God's answer to that prayer? What if this is a test? What if God has someone else in store for Jo and she is going to miss it because of Mark? Ugh!" Sue groaned. "There are so many what ifs!"

"We can't base our life on what ifs, Sue. You know that."

Brittany tucked her feet underneath her. "We just need to pray God will reveal His plan to Josephine and that she will know for certain what it is."

"I know. But what if He tries and she doesn't listen? I'm just worried. Remember what happened last time she was lonely?"

"Yes," Brittany gently lowered her voice to make her point. "You have an amazing son because of it."

Conviction poured from Sue. "I do. You're right. And I wouldn't change any of that for the world. But what if something good doesn't come out of it this time?"

"Sue," Brittany chastised, "what are you talking about? You know God's promises. He makes all things work together for good for those who love Him. Even in our sin and rebellion, good can come."

"I hate it when you are right; you know that, don't you?" Sue teased.

Brittany smiled. She could hear the scowl on Sue's face through her voice. "I know. I'm not trying to sound mean or anything. We need to let Jo live her life, even if that means with her doing things we don't agree with or jumping into relationships we think she isn't ready for. I agree she needs to take things slowly, but all we can do is advise her to do just that. It's up to her what she does with our advice."

"Ok, ok," Sue conceded. "I won't get on her case. I'll just encourage her to take things slowly."

"Does she even know how to do that?" Brittany wondered out loud.

Sue was quiet for a moment. "I don't know. I never thought of that before. Maybe that's the problem."

Brittany relaxed a little in her chair. "Maybe. But either way, commit this to prayer and see what God does. He may change her heart, He may change ours. Who knows? Let's just hold each other accountable to praying, alright? You know what Mom used to say? Just wait and see what tomorrow brings."

Sue's sigh sounded heavy. "Brit, sometimes, you remind me so much of Mom, ya know that?"

"Thanks, Sue." Brittany wiped her eyes. "But truthfully,

that's what we need to do."

"All right," Sue agreed. "So, what are your plans for the rest of the morning?"

"Well, I figure the kids and Luke will be home by eleven, and since I have spent most of my time talking with you, not much else," Brittany teased.

"I guess that's my cue!" Sue laughed, pretending to be hurt. "You are so lucky I love you, big sis!"

"I sure am, and I love you, too, little sis!" Brittany set her cup down on the table beside the chair.

She hung up the phone. She knew she had given Sue great advice, yet her heart felt strangely unsettled. Brittany hadn't met Mark as of yet. She didn't want to rush things by inviting Mark and Josephine over to the house for dinner. She wanted to make sure this was the guy Josephine was going to date. Brittany walked to the sliding glass door and opened the curtains. She had an incredible view of the mountains from her backyard. Just as she was about to open the door and step outside, she noticed snow flurries beginning to fall. How would her parents respond to Josephine? What would they say to her to help her slow down? Now that they were gone, Brittany and Sue have done their best to be there for Josephine, even if they disagreed with her choices. Brittany's eyes followed the snowflakes as they gently hit the ground. Gently. Maybe that's what the Lord wanted her and Sue to do, or be, rather. Gentle. Speak the truth in love, right? When the time came, perhaps Brittany can speak the truth in love with Josephine, telling her to be careful and take things slow. Sure, she had already done that, but it was mostly in passing. Yes, Brittany decided with a firm nod, that's what she would do. Speak lovingly to Josephine about not rushing into anything. Take a step back and continue to pray.

Brittany wrapped her arms around herself and stared out the window. Her mind drifted back to when she was in her late teens. She had just finished praying about Luke. Brittany knew their relationship was headed somewhere serious. She sat with her journal on her lap, her Bible open, and her eyes fixed on the gorgeous view of the mountains. Her mom had walked past the living room and saw her sitting there.

"Honey," her mom's eyes were filled with concern. "Are you all right?"

"Yeah. I was just praying about Luke." Brittany tried to sound nonchalant.

Her mother sat down across from her. "What about?"

"Mom, I know our relationship is getting more serious. We've talked about marriage already." Brittany loved the relationship she had with her mom. She was always willing to listen to Brittany share her heart and never judged her. Her mom had always given her room to make mistakes, but always gave her grace and compassion. Not only that, Brittany's mom was a godly woman, filled with wisdom. Now as she poured her heart out to her mom about Luke, her mom sat, waiting patiently to share her thoughts with her oldest daughter. Brittany and Luke had discussed marriage. That's what was bothering Brittany. They were so young! She and Sue were in the process of moving in together. And now, Luke was talking marriage with her. Yes, they had been dating ever since she was a freshman in high school. But should they get married this early? She just didn't know the answers.

"I imagine you would talk about marriage. You've been dating for a long time now." Her mom tilted her head to one side.

Brittany nodded. "We have, I know. I just want to make sure this is what God wants, you know?"

"And what do you think that is?"

"I'm not sure yet. I know I love Luke. I know he is an incredible man who loves Jesus. I just want to make sure I am in the center of God's will."

Her mom had smiled and had gotten up to sit next to her. She put her arm around her. "Oh, Brittany, I know exactly what you mean. I prayed that same thing in regards to your father."

"You did?" Brittany's eyes widened.

Her mother had nodded. "I did. I can't tell you how happy it makes me that you desire Jesus more than anything, including the love of a fine young man."

"Thanks, Mom." Brittany cocked her head to one side and grinned. "You really think he's a fine young man?"

"Uh-huh. Your father and I both do." Her mom had squeezed her shoulder and stood up, tears coming to her eyes. "And Brittany," her mom continued almost in a whisper, "if this is who God has for you, we support you one hundred percent."

Brittany jumped up and hugged her mom. "Thanks, Mom! I love you!"

"I love you, too, Brittany."

Oh, Lord, if only Josephine had Mom here to help her and guide her like she did for me! And let's be real, Lord, I miss Mom.. Jesus, I miss her so much. I wish she were here for me, too! Brittany wiped her tears with the back of her hand. She walked to her chair, picked up her tea and took it back to the kitchen to be reheated. As she was walking toward the living room, Brittany felt a peace come over her and felt God speak to her once again.

I'm here for you, Daughter, and for Josephine, too.

Brittany felt chills run up and down her body. She sank into her chair and closed her eyes.

Thank you, Daddy, she whispered.

Josephine peered out of her window blinds. Snow. The one day she had off and it was snowing. Josephine enjoyed the snow, but today, she wished it wasn't snowing. She wanted to be out of her apartment. She wanted to be somewhere that would occupy her mind. Since her date with Mark last night, she could hardly concentrate on anything. She felt his arm around her shoulders and how good it felt to rest her head on his chest during the movie. She looked at the dining room table and saw the flowers he had brought her. They were so beautiful! The vibrant purples and reds were accented with the white baby's breath. It was a lovely sight. She could picture him sitting at the head of the table. He looked so natural there, like he was meant to be there.

Josephine plopped down on the sofa and blew her bangs out of her eyes. She really felt she and Mark were connecting and wanted to know how he was feeling. She didn't want to rush into things, but the more time she spent with him, the more she liked him. They had spent every day talking on the phone prior to their last date. Josephine really enjoyed those talks. She laughed a lot at his silly jokes. She was impressed by how spiritual he was, and how he knew the Bible so well. Mark spent a lot of time opening up to her, being honest with his feelings about family, and how someday, he wanted one. Unfortunately, she hadn't heard from Mark at all today and was concerned that maybe she had done something during the date that would change his mind about the two of them.

Josephine thought about how different things were with Mark than they were with Jim. She tried tucking the memories away, but they came back to life as if they were yesterday. Jim was standing in the door way of the apartment they shared. He didn't want to talk about their relationship. They had been living together for a year and a half, and Josephine had felt something was missing. She couldn't put her finger on it, and she really needed to talk. Jim was unresponsive. He kept telling her they were fine, that they enjoyed each other's company and had a good time together.

"Something's missing, Jim." She searched his eyes and face.

"Babe, nothing's missing." He crossed the room and sat next to her. "You are just imagining things, that's all. I still love you." He turned on the television. And that was the end of their conversation.

At the time, she had loved Jim, or so she thought. Did she even know what love was? Was Jim just a friend? She didn't know. Maybe she was imagining things. Maybe this was how love really was. Sighing, she had sat back and watched whatever Jim had put on the TV. But Mark was a different story. He was communicative, giving her his undivided attention, listening to her when she spoke. He complimented her and prayed with her. Jim had never done those things!

Josephine jumped when the door bell rang. She walked to

the door with a slight frown on her face. She wasn't expecting anyone to come over today.

I wonder who that could be.

Opening the door, she saw Mark standing there, all bundled up in snow gear.

"Hi!" He smiled through his scarf. "Wanna come out and play?"

Josephine laughed. "What?"

"I said," Mark leaned forward, and spoke more slowly, "do you want to come out and play?"

"Play what?"

"Play in the snow! It's supposed to snow pretty good today, and by the looks of it, it already has! I'd say it's been snowing for at least three hours now." He stomped his feet on the door mat before coming in her front door. "Come on! Don't just stand there. Go get dressed!" Mark gave her a gentle push from behind.

Josephine walked to her bedroom. "Ok! But where are we going to go?" she called from behind her door.

"Actually, I know a great sledding hill not too far from here," Mark answered loud enough for her to hear. "I put two sleds in the trunk of my car, just in case you agreed to come out and play."

A few moments later, Josephine came out from her room with dark blue fitted snow bibs on, a warm snow jacket, a beanie, snow gloves, and a scarf.

"I've never known someone to look so beautiful dressed like a giant marshmallow. But you sure do!" Mark grinned.

Josephine giggled. "Thanks, I think," she added "All right. I'm ready to go."

They drove over to the park with the sledding hill. Mark was right. This was a great place to go sledding! Josephine and Mark had fun going down the giant hill and crashing at the bottom. After five times of doing that, they decided to have a snowball fight. The snow wasn't too soft, so it was perfect for making snowballs. Josephine hid behind a tree and launched a snowball in Mark's direction. It hit him square in the chest.

She jumped up and down with delight only to be pelted a few seconds later with a few of his own snowballs. Josephine fell over from laughing so hard. Mark came over and joined her. Sitting in the snow, looking at Mark, Josephine's heart skipped a beat. This is what she had been hoping for. She had desperately wanted someone to have fun with, to talk seriously with, and to share her heart and soul with. Mark seemed to fit all of those things and more.

Mark slowly rose to his feet. "We have to do one more thing before we leave." He pulled her up to her feet.

"What's that?" Josephine wiped the snow off of her pants.

"Why, build a snowman of course!" Mark told her, with mock surprise. "Everyone knows that you have to build one snowman on the first day of really good snow!"

"Oh, that's right!" Josephine pretended to remember.

Together, they built the most lopsided snowman Josephine had ever seen. But in her eyes, it was perfect!

As they were driving back to her apartment, she sighed happily. "Want to come in for some hot tea or hot chocolate?"

"Hm," he answered, rubbing his chin, "perhaps you have some coffee instead?"

"Yes, I do." She made a mental note of Mark preferring coffee over hot chocolate. "I could make us up some. Unless you have somewhere you need to be."

"The only place I need and want to be is with you," Mark took her hand and squeezed it before letting go. "I was so glad you had today off of work, especially when I saw it was snowing outside. All I could think about was wanting to be with you today."

"I'm glad." Her voice was soft. She got out of the car and walked with him back to her apartment. "I wanted to be with you, too."

She let them both in and headed to the kitchen to start the coffee. "Go ahead and put your stuff on the coat rack by the door."

Mark took off his snow gear and underneath he was wearing a pair of jeans with a light blue sweater

"Wow!" Josephine felt heat rising to her cheeks. "You look

amazing. That's a great color on you."

"Thanks. I knew you'd like it." Mark sat down on the couch. "You told me blue was one of your favorite colors, and I just happened to have this in my closet." He smiled, and it melted Josephine's heart. "Why don't you go change? I'll keep an eye on the coffee."

Josephine quickly changed and came back to see two cups of coffee on the coffee table. "Can I get you anything to eat?" She sat down.

"No thanks. I'm fine."

They sat side by side sipping their coffee. Neither one of them spoke for a few minutes. It was a comfortable silence. Every time Mark's arm gently brushed against hers, her heart soared to new heights.

Finally, Mark broke the silence. "I had a wonderful time last night."

"So did I. I had a fun time today, too." Josephine's eyes sparkled.

"I'm glad we had today to spend together. It seems I want to spend all of my free time with you," Mark admitted, putting his coffee down and turning to face Josephine.

"I feel the same way. You are all I could think about today."

"Josephine, I know we have only been on three dates, but I want to date only you." Mark paused, staring into her eyes with sudden intensity. "I guess what I am trying to say is, I want you to be my girlfriend."

Josephine's mouth dropped. She hadn't expected this to happen so quickly. She had hoped it would, but she hadn't expected it.

"Mark," A shyness suddenly came over her. "I would like that, too."

Mark leaned over and kissed her gently. "Fantastic." He grinned. "That was the answer I was hoping for."

Josephine tucked a piece of hair behind her ear. She lowered her eyes, hoping her would kiss her again. She lifted her eyes to Mark's. She didn't want her time with Mark to end, especially now. She cleared her throat. "So, what do you want to do now?"

"Let's go celebrate," Mark stood up.

"Celebrate how?" Josephine stood up.

"Let's go to dinner."

Mark walked to the coat rack and helped Josephine on with her coat. "I know this great little Mexican place. Would you mind if I took you there?"

"Not at all!" Josephine followed Mark to his car. He opened her door, but before she got in, he pulled her into a warm embrace. His arms around her felt natural. Josephine didn't want the moment to end. When he finally let go, he brushed his lips against her cheek and smiled. She got in the car and tried to still her ever racing heart.

After they were on their way, Mark confided in her. "I was really nervous about today."

"You were? I couldn't tell." Josephine turned to look at him.

Mark nodded his head. "I knew last night I wanted you to be my girlfriend. I just didn't know how to ask you. After a perfect day like today, I couldn't pass up the chance." He reached over and took her hand. He kissed her hand. "You have made me so happy, Josephine."

She gave his hand a squeeze. "And you have made me so happy, Mark."

They arrived at the restaurant and entered the building hand in hand. Much to their surprise, Brittany and Luke were waiting to be seated.

"Jo!" Brittany crossed the room to give her a hug. "What are you doing here?"

"Mark and I just had fun playing in the snow, and he suggested coming here for dinner. What are you doing here? Where are the kiddos?" Josephine looked around.

"Sue offered to take them so Luke and I could have a date." Brittany glanced from Mark to Josephine.

Catching on to her clue, Luke reached out his hand to Mark. "Hey, man, I'm Luke."

Mark shook Luke's hand. "I'm Mark. It's nice to meet you."

"Same here." Luke put his arm around Brittany's waist.

"I'm sorry, guys." Josephine shook her head. "This is Mark. Mark, this is Brittany and my brother-in-law, Luke." Josephine made the introductions.

"Hi, Mark," Brittany gave him a hug. "I've heard so much about you; it's nice to finally meet you."

The hostess called from the podium. "Luke, party of two," she called, "your table is now available. Luke, party of two."

Brittany glanced at Luke who nodded in her direction. "You two are more than welcome to join us."

"Really? We don't want to intrude." Josephine's eyes lit up.

"No, it's fine." Luke waved his hand. "We'll go ask the hostess if our table will fit four."

Luke and Brittany walked away.

Mark leaned over to Josephine and said tensely, "Is this really a good idea? I mean, I was really hoping it would be just the two of us."

"Oh, Mark!" Josephine bit her lip, taking a step back. "I'm so sorry! I was just so excited to share our news with them; I thought it would be fun to have dinner together."

Mark eased up a bit and stepped closer to Josephine. "I didn't think of that." He sighed, taking her in his arms. "Sure. I guess we can have dinner with them."

Josephine hugged him. "Thanks Mark. I know you won't regret this!"

Luke walked up and coughed slightly. "Hope I'm not interrupting, but its all set."

Mark and Josephine let go of each other and walked side by side behind Luke. Luke led them to the table the hostess had shown them. Brittany was seated already. Luke sat next to her, with Mark and Josephine sitting across from them.

"So, you two had a snow date, huh?" Brittany leaned her elbows on the table.

"Mark showed up today unexpectedly. He said when he saw it was snowing, he just wanted to spend the day with me." Josephine looked at Mark joy radiating from her eyes. Mark leaned back against the booth. "Yeah.. I just wanted to share the first snow of the season with Josephine. I took her to a park not far from her house where there is great sledding."

"Oh yeah. I know that park," Luke nodded his agreement. He nudged Brittany. "He's right. Awesome park! Especially for sledding!"

The waitress came and took their order. When she left, the conversation resumed.

"So, you two must have had a great time! It was the perfect day to play in the snow," Brittany took a drink of her diet Coke.

"It was." Josephine took Mark's hand in hers.

"It was such a perfect day today, playing in the snow, spending time together, that I asked Josephine to be my girlfriend." Mark leaned back and put his arm around Josephine.

Luke's eyes widened, and disappointment colored Brittany's eyes.

"That's, that's fast!" Brittany finally managed to say.

"Not really, when you think about it." Josephine's eyes narrowed a bit. "We have known each other for over a month, you know."

Luke cleared his throat. "Congratulations, you two," he said tentatively.

"Thanks." Josephine rested her head on Mark's shoulder. "It is pretty exciting. It was so unexpected, but I am glad it happened!"

Luke took a drink of his soda. "Wow. I guess I didn't expect it to happen so soon."

Mark straightened a little. "Yeah, well, when you know something is from the Lord, you just don't need to wait to make it happen."

"Hm. That's an interesting point of view," Brittany began tilting her head to one side, but stopped when she saw Luke's look from the corner of her eye. "Well, maybe we can all have dinner together to get to know each other a little better. We can invite Sue, Nate, and the Sorenson's. How does that sound?"

Josephine's eyes widened with excitement. "I would love that! What'd you think, Mark?"

Mark nodded slowly. "Sure. That sounds like a good idea. When would you like to do it?"

Brittany thought for a moment. "We could plan for either tomorrow after church or next Friday. Which would be better for you both?"

"I'm okay with tomorrow," Mark shrugged his shoulders. Suddenly, his phone rang. "Would you excuse me while I take this?"

The others nodded as he walked away.

"You sure you don't think this is a little fast, Sis?" Brittany's face was full of concern.

A crease of doubt crawled across her face. "I don't think so. Like I said earlier, we have known each other for over a month now."

Brittany smiled, but it didn't make it to her eyes. "I know, Jo, but I just want to make sure you aren't jumping into anything. I love you, that's all."

Josephine returned her sister's disappointed gaze. "I know you do. I just don't want to be alone anymore, and God seems to have placed Mark in my path right when I was at my loneliest. So, I think this is what He wants for me, ok?"

Brittany spotted Mark heading their way again and picked up the conversation from before. "Ok. I will ask Sue tonight when I go pick up the kids, and then I will call the Sorensons on the way home."

"Perfect." Josephine nodded her agreement.

The waitress came with their food and set it down before them.

"Mark, would you pray for the food, please?" Josephine asked him.

"Dear Lord, thank you for this food. We ask You to help it nourish our bodies. Thank you for the time I had with Josephine today and the steps we have taken in our relationship. Thank You for the opportunity to spend time with her family. In Jesus' Name, Amen."

They ate their food while continuing to talk. Brittany asked how Mark came to Jesus, about his family, and where he was headed in life.

Mark answered each question with ease and confidence.

Josephine was impressed how quickly he answered her sister's questions. At one point, however, she was a little annoyed with all the questions Brittany was asking him.

When Mark excused himself to use the restroom, Josephine turned on her sister, "Gosh, Brit, talk about putting him on the spot!"

"What do you mean?" Brittany's hand flew to her chest.

"I mean, what's with the twenty questions?" Josephine's voice had an edge to it.

"I'm sorry, Jo. I didn't mean for it to come across that way. I don't know very much about him, and I wanted to get to know him a little better." Brittany set down her fork.

Josephine's eyes softened, ashamed at getting frustrated so quickly. "No, I'm sorry. I just don't want Mark getting the wrong idea. I don't want him to think he is being interrogated. He was a little leery about having dinner tonight with you guys. He wanted it to be just the two of us, but I was so excited to share the news with you, that he went along with it." Josephine gave a lengthy sigh.

"He didn't want to have dinner with us?" Confusion was written all over Luke's face.

"He just wanted to celebrate with the two of us. I don't think it was anything personal. I mean, he doesn't even know you. I'm not sure. Maybe he doesn't do well with last minute changes once he has his mind set on something. Anyway, sorry."

Mark came back to the table. "What did I miss?"

Josephine was quick to answer, "Nothing. So, are we just about ready to go?"

Mark looked at the bill. "Sure."

Luke took the bill. "I'll pay for this one. You can do it next time."

Mark smiled and patted him on the back. "Thanks, man."

"So, we're on for tomorrow night, right? Say six?" Brittany stood and put on her jacket.

"Absolutely," Josephine confirmed. She hugged Brittany as they were heading out of the restaurant. "Again, sorry for getting defensive. I didn't mean to." She whispered. "I just really want you guys to like him and to make him feel as comfortable as possible."

"I understand. No worries. I love you and will see you tomorrow night." Brittany hugged her back.

Josephine and Mark said their good-byes and drove away.

"What did you think of my sister and Luke?" Josephine shifted to get a better view of Mark.

"They seem nice." Mark lifted a shoulder.

"Yeah. I love them both very much." Josephine didn't know how to bring up her frustration with Brittany. She felt she needed to apologize to Mark for her sister's many questions. "I'm sorry if she put you on the spot, though, by asking you so many questions, I mean."

Mark shook his head. "It's all right. I figured she was just trying to get to know me, that's all."

"I didn't want you to be uncomfortable, though. You didn't want to have dinner with them initially, so I was hoping for more casual talking and less questioning."

"I didn't want to have dinner with them because I wanted to cherish every second I had with you in celebrating our new relationship. Not because I didn't want to get to know them. I had my heart on just the two of us spending time together. Does that make sense?" Mark pulled into her apartment complex and turned off the car.

"Sure. I totally understand. Well," Josephine continued, "just be prepared for a lot of questions tomorrow night."

Mark walked her to her front door. "I'm not going to come in. I want to get a good night's sleep tonight and be well rested for tomorrow night. Can I pick you up early so we can be alone before we have to be at your sister's house?"

Josephine wrapped her arms around his waist. "That would be wonderful. Any time we can be alone sounds great to me."

He kissed her cheek and hugged her tightly. "Awesome. I'll see you tomorrow around 3."

"Bye, Mark. Drive safely," Josephine called as he strolled away.

With a happy sigh, Josephine closed and locked the door behind her. This could not have been a better day! Putting the coffee cups in the dishwasher, she smiled thinking of how good it felt to be in a relationship once again. It had been a few years since her last one. She was ecstatic that this one was with a Christian man. She paused for a brief moment to wonder if it was all happening a little fast. Was Brittany right? Should she have gotten to know him more before deciding to be his girlfriend? Should she have spent more time in prayer about Mark? What if he wasn't the one for her? With a shake of her head, she brushed those thoughts away. Mark was an amazing guy who loved the Lord. She had spent lots of time praying about him, hadn't she? Who else would God have for her? Mark was the only man who showed any interest in her at all. No, she decided matter of fact; things were not going too fast. This is exactly where God wanted her....wasn't it?

Just then, her cell phone rang. She answered it quickly, expecting Mark on the other end. She was surprised when she heard Steven's voice instead.

"Steven! How's it going?"

"Good, Josephine! I hope you don't mind me calling you."

Josephine smiled. "Not at all. Mark just left and I was just settling down for the night."

Josephine told Steven about their day and how Mark asked her to be his girlfriend. She rattled on about how great Mark was and how thankful she was to be in a relationship again.

Steven was quiet for some time. Josephine hadn't picked up on his quietness, and thirty minutes later, when she was off the phone, she realized she hadn't asked Steven why he had called.

Oh well. I'll call him tomorrow night after dinner and find out what was up.

She climbed into bed, suddenly realizing how tired she was. She quickly fell fast asleep.

Chapter 10

Sue walked into Brittany's house followed by Nate and DJ.

Tonight should be interesting, she thought, carrying drinks and a chocolate cake. When Brittany told her the news last night of Josephine's relationship with Mark, Sue found herself caught in a wave of emotions. She knew Josephine was happy. She felt she should be happy for her, but she just wasn't. For some reason, she was disappointed. Sue desired only the best for Josephine. Whether Mark was that or not had yet to be seen. Today, however, she was determined to have a positive attitude.

Sue had talked with Kayla about Mark before coming to Brittany's.

"Sue, I understand your frustration," her friend empathized. "But be careful. You don't want to drive Jo away. The more opposition you show, the further she'll go. Plus, your relationship with her will change."

"What do you mean?" Sue's brow furrowed.

"She won't want to be as close to you as she is now. You'll suddenly become the enemy. She will know you aren't excited about her relationship with Mark and will keep most of it a secret from you." Kayla's voice was filled with warning.

It was good advice, and Sue knew it. She really did want to get to know Mark. She had met him only briefly at the birthday party for DJ and Gideon. *It's important to go into the evening being positive,* she kept telling herself. Sue didn't even have a problem with Mark. It was Josephine she was concerned about. Josephine was impulsive at times, not thinking before she acted. Sue worried that was what was happening with Mark. Sue smiled to herself. Not only was she getting to know Mark, but the Sorenson's were going to be there. She was also looking forward to spending time with them. To Sue, the Sorensons had become an important part of her family. They would never take the place of her parents, but she was glad to call them her grandparents. She loved them dearly, and was very happy to hear they were able to make the get together. She was equally pleased Steven would be joining them, too.

"Hey Sister!" Sue called from the entry way. "We're here! Where would you like the drinks and dessert?"

"I'm in the kitchen. Come on back and we'll get things together." Brittany poked her head out.

Sue walked back to the kitchen. Brittany had set out a long plastic table for the kids to sit at and had the dining room table already set for dinner.

"Wow!" Sue commented. "Look at you! You already have the place half done! Why did you want me to come early again?"

"Oh, don't be silly! You are free labor, of course! And Nate, too!" Brittany teased, bumping her sister with her hip.

Sue set down the drinks and dessert. "Well, then, put me to work!"

Sue and Brittany worked in silence preparing the evening's meal. Before long, Brittany's doorbell rang.

"Are you expecting anyone else to come early?" Sue wiped her hands on a towel and walked to the front door.

Brittany shook her head. "Nope. Only you guys. I wonder who that could be."

Sue opened the door.

"Grandpa, Grandma, Steven!" Sue swung the door open wide enough for them to enter. "What are you all doing here so early?"

"Well, dear," Mrs. Sorenson gently pushed her way past Sue, "this is a special occasion, and we thought we would come over early to help."

"Thank you very much." Brittany hugged each of them. "We're almost done, but we would love to spend extra time with you all!"

Steven took the salad out of his mom's hands. "Where can I put this?"

"In the refrigerator for now, please," Brittany directed. "And Steven, I am so glad you could come tonight! I didn't expect you to be in town so soon!"

Steven closed the fridge. "I know. I'm excited to be back this quickly. My boss sent me out here. He said it's cheaper to send me instead of anyone else because I have family I can stay with and he won't have to pay for a hotel for me." Steven laughed. "I don't mind, though. I enjoy coming home. Actually, now I can start looking for a place of my own."

"We enjoy having him stay with us, too," Mr. Sorenson piped in. "He helps with the dishes and cooking." He patted his stomach. "Ah, good food! I've missed some of his famous dishes he used to make for us!"

Steven slapped his dad on the back. "It's good to be home, Dad!"

"I haven't had time to call Josephine to tell her you'll be here," Brittany suddenly remembered, moving around the kitchen. "I'm sure she'll be happy you're here, too!"

"I tried to tell her last night when we talked on the phone that I was in town. She was so excited about her and Mark, I barely got a word in edge wise! This is the perfect weekend to come home." Steven's eyes twinkled as he rubbed his chin. "I really wanted to meet the guy who had such a horrible first date and lived to tell about it!"

Everyone laughed. "But we certainly won't bring that up, will we dear?" Mrs. Sorenson gave Steven a firm look.

"No, Mom." Steven shook his head with mock obedience. "I won't say a word."

More laughter came from the group. "Ok. Let's continue setting up. How's dinner coming along?" Luke took a sip his coke.

"Fine. It's almost ready. I love buying ready-made lasagna!" Brittany grinned. "It's so easy to prepare, and doesn't take any extra work!"

"Luke," Mr. Sorenson gave him a firm nod, "you keep an eye on that coke of yours, got it?"

Luke placed his hand over his heart. "I promise! I will!"

The group finished getting things ready and headed to the living room to sit and talk a little more before the guests of honor arrived.

○ ○ ○ ○

It was almost five, and Mark and Josephine were seated on her couch.

"Ok. Tell me about your family." Mark rested his head against the back of the couch.

"Well," Josephine put her feet on Mark's lap. "Sue and Nate were married just a few years ago. They have a son, Daniel James." Josephine was quiet. Should she tell Mark DJ was her son? What if he didn't want to be with her after he heard that? Is it too early in their relationship to be so honest? She subtly glanced at Mark. He was nodding his head.

"Yes. I remember DJ. He's the reason I met you." Mark looked at her and smiled. "One of the best days of my life."

Josephine giggled, forgetting her previous concerns. "Me, too. Ok. So, Sue and Nate." She focused on the topic at hand. "They are a great couple. He is perfect for her in every way. Not only does their personalities match, but they look like they fit together, you know what I mean? Nate has a great sense of humor and keeps us all laughing. But he isn't a clown. He has his serious side, too. I love that guy."

"Sounds like you do." Mark nodded absently. "Are Sue and Nate planning on having more kids?"

"They may. They are still looking into that." Josephine was careful with her words. She wasn't ready to tell Mark DJ was adopted just yet.

"Brittany and Luke have been married for about six years now."

Mark interrupted her. "Six years! Wow! They got married young!"

"Yep. They were high school sweethearts, so a year or so after Brit graduated, they got engaged, and then married." Josephine waived her hand. "Anyway, they have a daughter,

Joslyn who is four and a son, Gideon who is two. He was born the day DJ was born. Joslyn is adorable! She loves to be in front of a crowd, and will sing or dance or do whatever it takes to draw some attention! And Gideon! Well, you remember him singing to us at his birthday party? He loves music. Those kids are truly amazing! Brittany and Luke are wonderful parents." Josephine couldn't say enough wonderful things about her family. It was important to her that Mark loved them as much as she did.

Mark began rubbing Josephine's feet. "Okay. And the Sorensons? Tell me about them."

Josephine's eyes glowed. "They are spectacular! I can't say enough about them! I already told you they helped me come back to Jesus, but they have done so much more than that! They loved me through my sin; they made me apart of their family. Not just me, but my sisters, too. They welcomed us with opened arms. Truly, Mark," her eyes shined with admiration, "without them, I don't think I would be walking with the Lord."

"I owe them huge thanks, then." Mark leaned toward her and kissed her cheek. "Do they have any children?"

Josephine nodded. "Yes. Steven is their only child."

"What's his story?"

"Well, he is in his late twenties. Twenty-six, I think. He works back east and is about to move here with his company. He will be coming back and forth, trying to look for a place to live."

"He seems young. Why did his parents wait so long to have him?"

"I think because they wanted to make sure they were financially stable before they had kids. Steven is a nice guy. I met him not too long ago. He seems to have a great relationship with is parents."

"You've known his parents for a long time and are just now meeting him? How come?" Mark slipped his fingers through hers.

"It wasn't until after my parents died that my relationship with the Sorensons got deeper. They really stepped in at a time when I needed love and guidance. So, I guess it didn't seem necessary to meet Steven before. Then the Sorensons embraced the rest of my family, and I suppose they wanted to share their family with us, too." Josephine shrugged her shoulders. "I doubt you'll be meeting Steven any time soon, though. He won't be in town for another month."

"Hm. Interesting. Sounds like a fun family. I look forward to meeting them all and getting to know them." Mark put his feet up on the coffee table. "Do you think they will like me?" Doubt clouded Mark's features.

"What's there not to like? You love Jesus, and that's the most important thing. You are kind and funny. We have a great time together. They know these things already. Don't worry." Josephine rubbed his arm, trying to ease his worries. "They are going to love you."

Mark stretched. "I guess you're right. Well, we ought to be heading over there, right?"

"So soon?" Josephine pretended to pout. "Brittany doesn't live that far. We can leave in ten minutes and still be there on time."

"I want to be a little early so I can make a good impression." Mark helped her up.

Josephine sighed. "Oh, alright. I'll grab my coat."

"Can you believe this weather? Yesterday it was cold and snowing. Today it's in the sixties. I love Colorado!" Mark held her sweater for her as she put it on.

Josephine turned and looked at him. "I know. It's pretty amazing. Colorado is a great place to live." She stood on her tip toes and kissed his cheek. "Now that I have you, it's even better."

Mark took her hand and looked deeply into her eyes. "I feel that way, too."

○ ○ ○ ○

"What time are they supposed to be here?" Luke squinted out the front window.

"Six." Brittany walked over to the window, too. "Why?"

"Because they're here." Luke set down his Coke and strolled over to the front door.

"That's odd," Sue piped in. "Jo's never early to anything!"

"Apparently," Brittany raised one eye brow, "this is a big deal!"

Luke opened the door for Mark and Josephine and looked over his shoulder to quiet the women down. "Mark, good to see you again."

Mark shook his hand. "Good to see you, too, Luke."

"Hi, Jo! Hi, Mark!" Brittany walked toward them. "You're here early!"

"Yeah." Mark took off his jacket. "I knew this was an important day, and even though Josephine didn't want to, I told her we needed to be here early."

Sue had her back turned to Mark and Josephine. When she heard that comment, she stifled a snicker. What a weird thing for someone to say! She wondered if Mark had a low self esteem. It seemed to Sue he needed to make himself feel good.

"Sue," Josephine touched her arm, "you remember Mark, right?"

Sue turned around and plastered a smile on her face. "Hi, Mark."

Mark hugged her. "Hi, Sue! How's Martha doing?"

"She's doing well. Thanks for asking," Sue slipped her arm through Nate's. "This is my husband, Nate."

Nate reached over and shook Mark's hand. "My mom told me how great you were with Becca! Maybe when DJ gets a little older, you can teach him a thing or two about swimming, as well."

Mark smiled. "I would love to." He reached down and tousled DJ's hair. "DJ is a natural in the water. I could tell from those few interactions I had with him."

"Thanks." Sue picked DJ up and hugged him tightly.

A throat was cleared behind Josephine. J o s e p h i n e turned to see Steven standing in the kitchen doorway.

"Steven!" Josephine gave him a giant hug. "What are you doing here?"

Steven hugged her back and laughed. "I see you're surprised!"

"Yes! I didn't expect to see you so soon!" Josephine laughed along with him. "When we talked last night, you didn't tell me you were in town!"

"You pretty much carried that conversation all on your own! My boss sent me. He wanted me to check on a few things. Perfect timing, I say," he added, nodding toward Mark.

"Hey, Mark. I've heard a lot about you. I'm Steven."

Mark's posture straightened. "Hey." He raised his hand slightly, eyes narrowing.

Josephine finished introducing Mark to the rest of the group. The Sorensons fell into conversation with Josephine about work and some of her friends there. Mr. Sorenson sat down and motioned for his wife to do the same. Josephine sat down on the couch next to Mark. Sue noticed how Mark's mood changed once he had been introduced to Steven. He suddenly didn't seem as relaxed as opposed to when they first arrived.

I wonder what that's all about, she thought, watching him closely.

Brittany came out of the kitchen. "Ok, folks." she announced. "Dinner is ready!"

Everyone stood up. As they were walking into the dining room, Sue overheard Josephine say to Mark,

"Everything all right?"

Sue leaned back a little to catch his response. "We'll talk about it later," she heard him say tensely.

Sue frowned slightly. *Oh, brother*, she thought annoyed. *What could possibly be the matter?*

Josephine sat next to Mark, her mind whirling. *What could I have done to cause such a cold reaction?* She replayed the events of the evening in her mind, trying to figure out what she could have done. *Please, Lord*, she begged, *don't let me mess this up! Mark is a neat guy! I don't want to ruin what has only just begun!*

Just then, she noticed all eyes were on her.

"I'm sorry," she stammered, cheeks turning pink. "What?"

Nate laughed. "I asked if you would please pass the salad."

"Oh!" Josephine reached over and handed the salad to Nate. "Here you go."

"It looked like you were in deep thought," Steven met her gaze. "What are you thinkin'?"

Josephine waved her hand in front of her. "Nothing. I was just thinking about the day, that's all."

She stole a sideways glance at Mark. He had his eyes down, like he was concentrating on eating. "So," Josephine tried to take the focus off of her, "Grandma, what's new with you? How are things at church?"

"Fine. Not much is going on except Steven being home for a bit," Mrs. Sorenson replied, patting his arm.

Steven smiled. "I love these impromptu trips. They are so much fun, especially when they surprise people." A teasing smile turned the corners of his lips.

Josephine laughed, almost forgetting her previous worries. "It was fun to be surprised. But Brit, why didn't you tell me?"

Brittany shook her head. "I only found out this afternoon! Sorry! Besides, some surprises are nice, don't you think?"

"I have to agree." Josephine smiled when Steven winked at her.

"When can you go look at apartments with me?" Steven took a bite of his lasagna.

Josephine thought for a moment. "I can go tomorrow. I have the day off of work."

"Perfect. Pick you up at about 10?"

"Sounds like a plan," Josephine nodded.

"So, Mark," Brittany interjected, "tell us a little bit about your family."

Mark looked up. "There's really not much to tell. I grew up in a Christian home. My parents raised my siblings and myself to put Jesus first in our lives. My mom was a stay at home mom until we went to school and then she became a teacher's aid."

"Does your mom still work?" Sue sipped her water.

"She does. She says being around the little kids keeps her young." Mark seemed less tense to Josephine as he began answering her sisters' questions. Maybe she was just imaging things. Perhaps things were fine between the two of them.

"What does your dad do?" Steven sat back in his chair.

Josephine looked at Mark just in time to see his eyes narrow a bit. She frowned slightly, wondering what that was for.

"He works for the university. He teaches for the liberal studies department." Mark's answer was sharp.

"That must have been cool to have your dad home during the summer while you were growing up." Steven glanced at his dad. "I would have loved that!"

Mr. Sorenson smiled at his son. "Me, too, son."

Josephine waited for Mark to reply. Instead, he took a bite of his bread as if he didn't hear Steven.

"I imagine it must have been fun to have your dad around during the summer," Steven tried again.

"Mm hm." Mark's cold response toward Steven started to make Josephine's blood boil.

Josephine shot Brittany a panicked look. Brittany caught on and spoke up.

"Mark," she said quickly, "do you live at home or on your own?"

"I live with my parents." Mark set his fork down. "They're pretty great. They let me live there rent free right now so I can finish at the university and not go into debt trying to pay for school."

Josephine stopped paying attention to the conversation. What was going on? Why was Mark being so cold to Steven? He seemed fine with everyone else. She didn't understand and the more she thought about it, the more frustrated she became. She found herself not enjoying the dinner or conversation because she just couldn't shake her irritation. Finally, after dinner was over, she leaned over to Brittany.

"I need to run to the store really quick. Would you mind if I took Mark and we came right back?"

Brittany nodded her head. "Sure. Would you mind picking up an extra gallon of ice cream while you're out?"

"No problem." Josephine patted Mark's arm. "Mark, come

with me to the store really quick please."

Mark stood up. "Ok." He slowly pushed his chair in. "I guess we'll be back."

"We'll try not to eat all the cake while you're gone," Steven joked.

Mark glared at him. "Thanks," he said sarcastically. "I appreciate that."

Josephine grabbed his hand, her eyes wide. When they closed the door behind them, she turned on him. "What's wrong with you? Why are you treating my friend so meanly?"

"What's wrong with me?" Mark's eyes were hard. "Oh, I don't know. My girlfriend of only a few days seems to be flirting with the first guy she sees!"

Josephine winced. "What?!"

Mark got in the car and slammed the door. "Oh come on! You threw your arms around him and completely ignored me. You have secret phone calls with him you don't bother telling me about, and then you go and make a date with him!"

Josephine angrily snapped her seat belt on. "You're kidding me, right? I gave Steven a hug, Mark, and that was it! I was shocked to see him, and I was glad he was here to meet you. He called me last night, probably to tell me he was going to be here, but I spent the entire time talking to him about you. And me going with him tomorrow isn't a date. Before we even started going out, I told him I would help him find a place to live."

"Oh," Mark looked sheepish. "I didn't know you talked about me the entire time. But can't he ask a different person to help him? Why not Sue or Brittany or even his mom or dad?"

"He asked me, Mark, not anyone else. I offered to help him a while ago, and he took me up on it. I am not going to take back my offer because you are feeling insecure." Josephine tried to keep her voice steady.

"I didn't know you offered to help him." Mark's anger was subsiding. "And I am feeling insecure. I meet some of your family for the first time tonight, and I just wanted to have a good time. I wanted them to like me. And then all of this happens. I wondered if maybe you should be dating him instead of me. On top of all that, I just didn't understand why you were so excited to see him and then why you would make plans with this guy. Its weird having you hang out with another man besides myself."

"It doesn't matter if it's weird to you or not. You were purposely rude to a friend of mine." She crossed her arms in front of her as she walked down the isle of the store. "I can't believe you could be that way."

"How can he be a friend of yours already? You just recently met him, didn't you?"

"I met him around the same time I met you, come to think of it, and you and I are dating. Do you think I can't make a friend in that same amount of time?" Josephine whirled around and faced him. When he didn't respond right away, she continued down the aisle.

Mark came up behind her and gently took her by the shoulders and made her look at him. "I'm sorry," he said. "I was wrong. I know I shouldn't feel insecure. Would you please forgive me?"

Josephine looked up into his eyes. She let her arms fall by her side, and breathed a heavy sigh. "I don't want to date anyone else but you. That's why I said yes to you, Mark. Don't feel insecure. Steven is just a friend of mine, that's it. Nothing more."

"I believe you." Mark took her into his arms. "You didn't answer me, though. Forgive me?"

Josephine nodded her head. "I forgive you." She wrapped her arms around his waist. "Let's get back before they start to miss us."

"Ok," Mark agreed, paying for the ice cream. "We're okay then?"

"We're okay." Josephine gave him a small smile.

○ ○ ○ ○

"What was that all about?" Nate asked Luke as they cleared off the table.

Steven took the salad bowl off the table. "I think he likes me!"

Nate snorted. "You think so, do you?"

"Oh, I totally do! Did you see how nice and friendly he was to me? Man," Steven paused and shook his head. "I think we have a lifelong friendship already developing!"

"I don't know." Luke eyes were wide. "If I were you, I think you just developed an enemy!"

Steven shrugged. "No matter. Don't worry about it, guys. I'm sure my presence here just threw him off."

"I'm just surprised he didn't hide it better." Brittany gave a long sigh. "The entire dinner was weird."

Sue nodded in agreement. "Steven, I'm sorry you had to go through that." She patted his arm.

"Sue, it's okay, really."

"Why don't you go sit while we finish up the dishes?" Sue suggested to the guys.

If the truth was told, Steven had sensed Mark's uneasiness from the moment he entered the living room. At first, he thought maybe it was just because Mark didn't know Steven was going to be there. But as the night wore on, Steven knew something else was wrong. He wondered if Mark was jealous- but of what? He and Josephine were friends. They met for the first time not too long ago. Sure, talking with her was easy. She was funny and smart. He liked how easy it was getting to know her, but nothing was going on between them. It was odd that Mark would jump to that conclusion so quickly. Steven hoped everything was all right between Mark and Josephine. They had been gone for quite some time. Steven rubbed his temples.

Lord, I hope Josephine knows what she is getting herself into by dating this man!

Steven knew that jealousy was a strong emotion. If Mark was jealous this early in their relationship, no telling how jealous he would get later on!

Chapter 11

*J*osephine turned off her alarm and lay still in her bed. Stretching, she glanced at the clock to make sure it had the right time. Nine o'clock, it read. Steven would be arriving in an hour to pick her up to go looking for apartments. She slowly climbed out of bed and headed toward the kitchen. The coffee was already made due to the automatic timer she had set the night before. She grabbed a cup from the cupboard, filled it up, and sat down on her couch. With a sigh, she picked up her Bible and began praying.

Lord, last night was not perfect, to say the least. I admit I am still annoyed with how Mark treated Steven. I know he asked for forgiveness, and I really do forgive him, but, ugh, she groaned, *I don't know. I just pray Steven didn't notice how rude Mark was, and if he did, help him to be understanding, if the subject comes up. As for the rest of the day, I pray Steven will find something he really likes. I pray we will have a great conversation, one that gives You glory and praise. Lord, I pray this will be a great day. I love You, Jesus, very much. Speak to me as I study Your word right now.*

Josephine opened the Bible to Philippians. It was one of her favorite books in the Bible. She loved the simple message it gave. She read the first chapter, soaking it all in.

Now, as she read chapter two, verse five jumped off the pages and landed straight on her heart,

"Let this attitude be in you which was also in Christ Jesus."

She paused, praying that she would have the same attitude and mind that Jesus had. She prayed she would have it at work, loving people the way Jesus did. She asked God to help her with her family, that she would love them as Jesus did, including the

Sorensons. She prayed she would love all with whom she came in contact. She didn't want to only love people, but she wanted to serve them, as well, just as Jesus had done. She sat with her Bible open on her lap, eyes closed, and in deep prayer. She finished her prayer and then continued reading the chapter.

Again, a verse jumped out at her.

"Do all things without grumbling and complaining," Josephine stopped reading, and humbly asked for forgiveness for complaining about Mark and how frustrated she was. She knew she needed to not complain about anything, and decided that today, she would do just that.

"No more complaining," she said out loud. She finished reading the chapter and was startled by the ringing of her door bell.

Josephine quickly jumped up and looked at the clock. Ten o'clock!

She threw open the door. "Steven! I am so sorry!"

Standing there in a long coat and a beanie, Steven smiled. "I see you are already to go!" He eyed her up and down, taking note of her gray sweatpants and oversized sweatshirt.

Josephine groaned. "Come in! I was reading my Bible and I lost track of time!" She opened the door wider for him to come in.

"No problem. I can't think of a better way to lose track of time than in the word of God." Steven walked in her apartment and looked around. "Nice place. I like it."

Josephine walked toward her room. "I'll be right out, I promise. It will only take me a minute to get ready."

Steven sat down. "Don't worry about it. I'm in no hurry. Take your time."

"So," she called through her closed door, "do you have any idea where you would like to look?"

"Well," he raised his voice a little, "I like the looks of this place. Any vacancies?"

"Not that I'm aware of!" Her voice became muffled. "But we can check with the manager."

A few moments later, Josephine walked out and grabbed

her jacket. "Wow, you look nice." An easy smile crossed Steven's lips.

Josephine blushed. "Thanks. But really, I just threw this on."

"Well, I'd love to see you when you actually have time to get ready!!" Steven's eyes danced.

Josephine playfully pushed him toward the front door. "Yeah, yeah. Okay. All set?"

"Yup. Let's go!" Steven held the door open for her and walked out behind her. "What were you reading in your Bible this morning?"

"Philippians. I love that book!" Josephine fell into step beside him.

"Me, too. It's so simple, yet so deep at the same time."

"Yes! I totally agree!" Josephine went into detail about her morning reading and how it really spoke to her heart.

"That's so awesome, Josephine!" Steven exclaimed. "I love it when the Bible isn't just a book, but active in our lives!"

"So do I." She paused a moment.

"You okay?" Steven glanced her way.

She nodded. "Yeah. I just realized you called me Josephine. I'm not used to that with friends. They normally call me Jo."

"Should I call you something else? Like Bigfoot or Whale?" Steven teased.

Josephine groaned. "You must have talked with my sisters!"

"Well, I don't know the entire story, but last night before I left, they suggested I call you one of those things to see what you would do." Steven smiled slyly. "So, what's the story?"

"Well, Bigfoot came from my sister wanting to see if I would answer to it. For some reason, when I was little, I would answer to almost anything. Sue would call my name, and I would respond. Then she shortened it to 'Jo' to see if I would answer. When I did, she thought it would be funny to see what else I would answer to, and Bigfoot just stuck."

Steven chuckled. "That's funny! What about Whale? Did you answer to that, too?"

Josephine shook her head, her blonde hair bouncing. "No! I don't even know why this happened, but one day, about a year ago now, Brittany was looking at pictures with Gideon on her lap. She flipped to a picture of me, and he pointed to it and said, 'Whale!' Don't even ask me why!" Josephine laughed shaking her blonde head. "I wasn't fat or anything, and by that time, I had lost the baby weight!" Josephine stopped abruptly and covered her mouth.

Steven had stopped at a red light. "Jo," he gently took her hand, realizing what she had just done, "I already know about DJ. It's totally all right."

Tears swelled up in her eyes. "You do?"

Steven squeezed her hand in a friendly gesture. "I do. When that all had happened, my parents were considering adopting your baby if you hadn't told them about Sue and Nate. They asked me what I thought and how I felt, being older and all."

Josephine's eyebrows rose. "Really?" she asked softly, looking into his compassion filled eyes.

Steven nodded. "Really."

"I didn't know that." Josephine turned her head, staring out the window.

"They were going to talk to you about it one day when you came over to the house. I guess you had told them before they could tell you their thoughts that Sue and Nate had agreed to adopt the baby," Steven explained. "They kept silent because they knew that was the best choice, and afterwards, they didn't feel it necessary to say anything."

"I love them!" Josephine whispered.

The Sorensons never stopped amazing Josephine! They were actually talking about adopting DJ! Her heart soaked in this newfound information. What a blessing these people were in her life! But, that also means they had talked with Steven in depth about the adoption. What would he think of her? Did he look down on her for giving up her only son? Did he think she was selfish? If he, being a friend, would think that, what would Mark think if and when she told him the truth?

Steven waited for her to say more, and when she didn't, he

prodded, "What's going on in your head?"

"You must think I'm terrible, giving up my baby." Shame filled her eyes.

Steven parked the car and turned toward her. "Why would I think that?"

"Because I could have taken care of him, I just didn't want to." She wiped her eyes with the sleeve of her jacket.

Steven dug for a tissue and handed it her way. "True. But you also did the right thing by giving DJ the chance to have a mother and a father."

"I know I did the right thing. Sometimes I just worry about what others think of me." Josephine looked out the window.

"Jo, don't worry about what others think. It's what God thinks that matters the most," Steven encouraged her. "Hey, look at me." When she did, he continued, "As for my measly opinion, I think you did the right thing. I think it takes courage and strength to give up your son to a family member, where you see him all of the time. I think it is amazing that you did that!"

"As a man, I need your opinion on this. What do you think my future husband will say?" Josephine looked deeply into his eyes, and for the first time, noticed how beautiful they were. She quickly brushed the thought out of her mind.

"That's a hard one. I can only speak from my perspective." Steven raised his brow. "I don't think it matters. DJ is happy with Sue and Nate. He would be happy with you, too, but would you be capable right now of that arrangement? I don't think so."

"Steven," Josephine climbed out of the car, "you are an amazing man! Some girl is going to be pretty blessed to have you in her life!"

Steven dug his hands in his pockets and pretended to be embarrassed. "Aw, shucks," he kicked the ground, "thanks. When she comes into my life, tell her that for me, okay?"

Josephine laughed and walked with him toward the manager's office.

"These apartments are pretty nice." She looked around, taking notice of the trees and the play area for little kids.

They walked into the building and spoke with the manager who gave them a tour of the facilities. She showed them the two different available units, a one bedroom and a two bedroom apartment. Steven thanked her for her time and headed to the car.

"What do you think?" He started the car and pulled out onto the street.

"I don't know," she answered, unsure. "It seemed alright. Just a little too expensive for not having a garage."

"I thought so, too." Steven nodded. "With the snow, I think I would want some covering for my car. My parents told me about some crazy hail they got last year! If my dad's car had been in the driveway, it would have shattered the windshield!"

"I know! I remember that! It was insane!" Josephine turned up the radio. "I love this song!" It was Toby Mac's, City on Our Knees. She hummed the words. "Remember when he was in DC Talk? I used to love them growing up!"

Steven laughed. "Even in their rap days? That's funny!"

They drove to a few more places, all of which, according to Josephine, didn't seem quite right.

"There has to be something that would fit you." She slumped her shoulders, discouraged.

"I'm sure there is." Steven seemed less worried. "We just need to find it, that's all."

During lunch, Josephine kept going back to the moment she looked in Steven's eyes. They were deep and intense. She hadn't noticed them before today, and wondered why that was. Steven was good looking, no doubt about that. She knew if she wasn't dating Mark, she would definitely be attracted to Steven. Once again, she pushed those thoughts away and focused on what Steven was saying. She needed to get through this day without wondering what would had happened if she hadn't found Mark first.

They were just pulling out of the restaurant parking lot when Josephine noticed a sign for a house for sale. "Steven, pull over."

"Why?" Looking over his shoulder so he wouldn't hit another

car, he pulled over.

"Okay. See that sign over there?" Josephine pointed across the way.

"Yeah."

"Follow it."

"You want me to buy a house?" Steven was skeptical.

"I haven't decided yet." She leaned forward, trying to figure out which way to go. "But maybe we are going about this all wrong. Perhaps you should be looking at houses for sale. I mean, why not? Why waste money on rent when you can buy? You know the area pretty well. You used to live here. You could put an offer in and have escrow close by the time your company moved here."

Steven turned the car around and began following the sign. "Hm. I never thought of that. Maybe you are right. Let's go check it out."

They drove up to a gray house with white trim. It had an enclosed, raised porch that chairs could set on so one could over look the street. The house sat at the end of a cul-de-sac. The lawn looked freshly mowed.

Steven took out his cell phone and began dialing.

"What are you doing?" Josephine running up beside him.

"I'm calling the realtor. Maybe we can look inside."

Josephine looked through the windows of the house. It was truly an adorable house.

Steven closed his phone. "Let's go," he announced.

"What do you mean?"

"He gave me the code to the lock box. He said he knew my dad and trusted that I wouldn't do anything illegal." Steven put the code in and stepped inside.

Upon entering the house, she realized looks were nicely deceiving. The house looked small from the outside, but on the inside, it was much bigger than what it appeared to be! The tan carpet was accented by beige walls. The kitchen looked updated with newer appliances. It even had an island in the middle! The dining room was big enough to fit a table for eight and then some. Walking into the living room, she noticed the beautiful brick fireplace. Josephine loved the way the rooms were designed. She was surprised there was even a family room, and right off the family room, with stairs leading down, a finished basement.

"Steven." She was breathless! "This house is gorgeous!"

Steven was wide-eyed and speechless himself. "I know. I wonder if I can afford something like this? And, also, do I even need a place this big?"

"Well, call the realtor back and ask him how much it's going for." Josephine turned around in circles, in awe of the beauty the house possessed.

Steven did just that. When he got off the phone, she looked at him expectantly. "Well?"

"Well," he hesitated, "well," he said again.

Josephine punched him in the arm. "Tell me already!"

"Ow! Okay! Okay!" Steven rubbed the spot on his arm where she hit him. "Well, I think I can afford it without going broke." He grinned. "I need to pray about it and ask my parents' opinion."

Josephine already had her phone out and dialed when he finished his sentence.

"Who are you calling?"

"Your parents! They need to come here right now!" Josephine's smile lit up her entire face.

Steven laughed. "Okay!"

Steven wandered around the house a little bit more. He opened up the blinds that lead to the backyard and saw a swing set left by the previous owners. His mind began to drift. He envisioned his own children one day playing on the swings. He could hear their laughter in his head as they tumbled down the slide together. He imagined him and his wife, sipping their coffee, watching them play. Suddenly, his heart ached. He longed for that day. It had been a desire of his for a few years now, to start a family. For some reason, the Lord hadn't allowed the right woman to come into his life just yet. Steven knew she was out there, he just didn't know where. He knew he would meet her, BUT he just didn't know when. He began to pray.

Lord, You know the desires of my heart. You know how lonely I can get. If You want me to buy this house, I pray it will all work out. I pray my future wife will love it. I pray You will be with her right now at this moment, blessing her, guiding her, showering her with Your love. Have us come together soon. Lord, thank You for this opportunity. I pray You will guide and lead me this very moment.

Steven felt Josephine slowly come up beside him.

"Oh my goodness!" Josephine's hand flew to her mouth. "What an adorable backyard! I love the swing set! If you get this house, Steven, we'll have to have our gatherings here where the kids can really enjoy that!"

Steven looked down at Josephine, a slight sadness filling his eyes. "Steven," Josephine's brow furrowed, "what is it? Are you having second thoughts?"

"No, I'm not having second thoughts," he replied, turning away from the window. "I was just praying about this, and for my future wife."

He sat down on the carpet. "It's hard sometimes, being alone, I mean."

Josephine sat across from him, waiting for him to continue.

"I'm twenty-six. I have wanted a family for as long as I can remember. Yet, the Lord hasn't allowed that. Looking outside made my heart ache for that family that has yet to come." He paused, making circles in the carpet with his finger. "I want what God wants. Right now, He wants me to be single. Okay, I can do that. But I can't wait for the day He allows me to get married! I just pray it won't be too long, you know what I mean?"

"What do you want her to be like, your future wife?" Josephine tilted her head to one side.

"Well, I want her to love Jesus with all of her heart. I don't care if she grew up in a Christian family or not. Her past isn't what matters to me. It's who she is now and what she desires to be in the future that matters the most. I want her to be passionate for the Lord. I love talking about Jesus, and I want her to, as well. It's important that she wants to grow and learn, not only about spiritual things but in life, too. Does any of this make sense?" He took off his beanie and ran his hand through his thick, dark hair.

Josephine stood up and walked to the fire place. "It does. I know what you mean, not wanting to be alone, and wanting to find someone you can spend your life with."

"Do you think you have found that in Mark?" Steven stood up and walked over to her. He ran his hand on the mantle.

"I don't know," Josephine answered truthfully. "I hope so, but I seriously don't know. I think it's too early to tell in our relationship. I just met him a few weeks ago, and I've only been on a few dates with him. Between you and me, I wonder sometimes if this is all a little too fast. But please don't tell my sisters or anyone else I said that!" She fixed her gaze on his.

"You can trust me." Steven put his hand on her head and messed up her hair.

Josephine giggled and ran her fingers through her hair. "You know what? I truly believe I can trust you. You're a good friend, Steven."

Steven hugged her briefly. "So are you, Jo. I look forward getting to know you more and spending time with you. Maybe one day, when Mark decides he likes me, we can all go out together."

Josephine gasped and stepped back. "What do you mean?"

Steven raised one eye brow. "C'mon. You and I both know he did not take an instant liking to me last night."

Josephine looked down, ashamed. "I'm sorry. Was it that obvious?"

"Only if you could see." Steven snorted. "But it's fine. I wasn't expected to be at dinner, so I can see how it would throw him off a bit."

"Don't make excuses for him, Steven. He knows he was wrong. I'm just sorry he was so rude to you."

"Don't worry about it. Hey," Steven switched gears suddenly. "What did my parents say?"

"Oh yeah! I almost forgot!" Josephine slapped her forehead. "They are on their way!"

Right as she finished her sentence, the Sorenson's knocked

on the door. Josephine ran to open it for them.

"Hi!" Steven laughed as Josephine's excitement radiated from her. "You two are going to love this place!"

Josephine gave them the grand tour, talking a mile a minute about how Steven could decorate each room and where to put what.

"Actually," she stopped in the kitchen, "I don't even know what your style is!"

Steven smiled. "It's similar to what you have been describing, to be honest! If you could see my apartment back east, you would laugh! I think I have a few of the things you just mentioned!"

"Oh, Steven!" Mrs. Sorenson clasped her hands in front of her. "This is just a great house! Would you really want to buy it? Could you afford it?"

"Well, Mom, I have been saving for quite some time now. I have enough money for a down payment, I think. I was praying about it before you guys got here. I don't know. What do you both think?" Steven leaned against the kitchen counter.

"Well, Son," Mr. Sorenson began, "we prayed about it on our way over here, and we, too, have been setting money aside for you. We thought it would be for your wedding, but if you would rather, we could give it to you for the house."

"Mom, Dad, you two are the best!" Steven hugged them both. "We can talk about all that later. Let's say we call the realtor and put an offer in. What do you all think?"

"Yes!"

"Definitely!"

"Yay!"

A few hours later, after signing the paper work, Steven was driving Josephine home.

"Thanks for today, Jo." He pulled into her apartment complex.

"Thank you! That was so much fun! I can hardly wait to hear if your offer gets accepted!" Josephine's eyes beamed.

"I'll call you as soon as I hear something," Steven promised.

"Good! Thanks for letting me be a part of this. I will keep you in prayer about our conversation about your future wife. I know God has someone special for you, Steve," Josephine encouraged, reaching over and patting his hand.

"Steve, huh?" Steven looked up as if in thought. "I don't know if anyone has ever called me Steve before. It's always been Steven."

"I'm sorry!" Josephine was quick to apologize. "I didn't mean to offend you!"

Steven laughed. "You didn't. I like the sound of it. All right, you can call me Steve!"

"You had me all worried! You turkey!" Josephine punched him in the arm again.

Steven laughed. "Alright! I deserved that! Now head home before Mark thinks I took you to Vegas to elope or something!"

"You are terrible!" Josephine giggled. "Call me when you hear from the realtor!"

"You got it! 'Bye, Jo!"

"'Bye, Steve!"

Josephine walked to her apartment, praying God would bless Steven beyond all he could ask, hope, think, or even imagine.

Just then, her cell phone rang.

"Hi, Mark!" She could feel her smile cover her face.

"Hi, Josephine! How are you?"

"I'm good. I was just heading into my apartment, and I was going to call you."

"You're done, huh? How did it all go?"

"It went so good! Well, at first, it didn't. We couldn't find the right place for Steven. But then, this is so cool, I saw a sign for a house for sale. I told him to follow that sign, and guess what?" She was talking a mile a minute, but she couldn't help it. It had been such a great day, she couldn't wait to share it with Mark.

"What?" Mark laughed at her enthusiasm.

"He put an offer in on the house!"

"Really? What made him decide to do that?" Mark's tone was light.

"Oh, Mark, if you were to see this place, you would have loved it! It is truly a lovely home! He called the realtor and asked if we could see it. Then, we called his parents, and they fell in love with it, too. It is awesome!" Josephine went into detail about the beauty of the house and the layout.

"Wow!" Mark commented when she was done. "It sounds cool. I'm glad you had a good time."

"I did, thanks." Josephine felt herself coming down from cloud nine.

"So," Mark hesitated, "did my name come up?"

"What do you mean?" Josephine tried not to react.

"Well, you were with another man all day. Did you talk about me at all?"

Josephine's defenses went up. "How am I supposed to answer that, Mark? If we did, would that be a good thing? And if we didn't, is that a good thing?"

"I guess it depends," Mark snapped back. "If you talked about me positively, it would be good. If it is negative, it wouldn't be. So, which is it?"

Josephine stood motionless in the middle of her apartment, dumbfounded. She couldn't believe her ears. Placing one hand on her hip, she answered,

"Actually, yes, your name did come up. Steven mentioned that you didn't like him. I was hoping he wouldn't have caught on to your rudeness last night, but he did."

She plopped down on the couch, angry.

"Oh." Remorse instantly filled his voice. "I was hoping he wouldn't have caught on. I really do feel badly about the way I acted toward him last night."

Josephine's anger subsided. "I know you do. And he said he understood. His presence there caught you off guard. He was pretty cool about the whole thing."

Mark sighed. "Good. I'm glad." He paused slightly. "What else did you talk about?"

Josephine stopped for a moment, wondering how to answer. She didn't want to tell Mark about DJ yet, and she wasn't sure how he would respond to Steven's feelings about being alone.

With Mark's insecurities, she wondered if he would look more into the conversation than what it really was.

"Josephine? You still there?"

"Yeah, sorry," Josephine apologized. "I was just thinking about mine and Steve's conversation, trying to remember what we talked about."

"Steve? You call him Steve?"

"Yeah," Josephine said cautiously.

"Does anyone else call him Steve?" Mark's questions were starting to get on her nerves. She breathed in, trying to be patient. "I don't know, to tell you the truth. He was introduced to me as Steven, and he said no one has really called him Steve before."

"So why are you calling him Steve?"

"Because it just slipped out today and he said he didn't mind." She took a deep breath. "Mark let's not turn this into a big deal. So what if I call him Steve? It's a friend having a nickname for another friend. That's it. Plain and simple."

"And there's nothing going on between you two?" Accusation filled his voice.

"No, there isn't. Like I said, he is a friend. Seriously Mark, I can't handle these insecurities." Josephine tried to keep her voice steady. "If this is going to work, you are going to have to trust me."

Josephine heard Mark sigh. "I know. I'm sorry. Can I make it up to you?"

Josephine didn't know if she was in the mood to see Mark, but she answered instead, "What did you have in mind?"

"Dinner. Can I take you out tonight?"

"That's fine," she relented. "What time?"

"I'll be there at five thirty, okay?"

"Ok, Mark. I'll see you then."

Josephine hung up the phone and kicked her shoes off. She rested her head back on the arm of the couch and put her fee up. Lying down, she wondered, how could a wonderful day turn out to be so frustrating? It was so much fun looking at apartments and really connecting with Steven. She knew he was going to turn out to be a great friend. And now, she just made a date with Mark. She was anything but excited to see him tonight. She really wanted to stay at home and have a relaxing night. She closed her eyes and tried to pray. When she couldn't find the words, she drifted off to sleep.

Mark arrived at precisely five thirty. When Josephine opened the door, he was standing there with a sheepish grin on his face and a dozen red roses.

"Hi." He shyly handed her the flowers.

"Mark, these are beautiful!" Josephine inhaled the aroma of the flowers.

"I wanted you to know how sorry I was about last night and today. I really enjoy having this relationship with you, Josephine, and I don't want to do anything to mess it up," he explained eagerly.

Josephine hugged him as her frustration ceased. "Thank you. Let me put these in some water before we go. Where are we going?" She walked into the kitchen and put the flowers in a vase.

"I thought I would take you back to the Mexican restaurant, where we celebrated us with your sister and Luke. Does that sound good?" Mark walked into the kitchen and took her hand.

"It does. Let's go." She led him into the living room and put on her coat.

The rest of the evening was a good one. Josephine and Mark spent a lot of time talking and laughing.

"So, you know what my most embarrassing moment is," Mark began, "tell me yours."

"What was yours again?" Josephine wrinkled her nose, trying to remember.

"Our first date." Mark took a bite of food.

"Oh, yep, now I remember." Josephine took a drink of her soda. "Okay. My most embarrassing moment. It was a long time ago, but it was pretty embarrassing."

"Go on, go on," Mark encouraged.

"Well, several years ago, I was at church on a Sunday night. Our church was pretty big at the time. We had three services on Sunday, two in the morning and one in the evening. I had decided to go to the night service. That night, our pastor gave an amazing sermon! I remember sitting in my chair thinking how appropriate it was for my life. He had just finished giving the salvation invitation, and a friend of mine came over to me and asked if I would go into the back room and pray with her. I grabbed my Bible and headed back there."

Josephine paused to take a sip again. "So, after we had prayed, communion had just been given out. It was pitch black in the sanctuary. I couldn't see a thing. Anyway, I was walking back to my seat. I didn't notice a square box in the middle of the aisle."

"Oh no," Mark groaned, seeing where this was going.

"Yup. Good thing for me, people didn't see me. But, much to my surprise, I flew over the box and landed with a loud thud!"

Mark started laughing, as did Josephine.

"My friend heard the thud and looked behind her only to see me sprawled out across the floor. My Bible went flying down the aisle. It just so happened to land in front of a guy I was very interested in at the time!"

"No! What happened after that?"

"Well, my friend began laughing. I couldn't control it, either, and I burst out laughing. There were at least five hundred people in the sanctuary, and unfortunately, it was really quiet when I hit the floor, except for the noise I made, of course. Our laughter was uncontrollable, so after I got up, I hurried to get out of the sanctuary so I wouldn't disturb the communion time. I had completely forgotten about my Bible!"

Mark's laughter grew a little louder. "I have a bad feeling about this!"

Josephine giggled. "It does get pretty bad! So," she inhaled between giggles, "my friend and I are practically holding each other up because we are laughing so hard. The next thing I know, Matt, the guy I liked at the time, walks over to me, and hands me my Bible." Josephine wiped her eyes. "Are you okay? He asks me. My face is beet red; I casually take my Bible from him, and continue laughing! I just couldn't stop!"

"He must have thought you were nuts!" Mark leaned back in his chair, holding his stomach.

"He actually started laughing, too. By this time, the service had ended. I was still talking or laughing, rather, with Matt and my friend, when another friend came up. He walks over and whispers, 'Man, did you guys hear that thud during communion? I wonder what happened!' Seriously, it threw us into another fit of giggles! It was a pretty embarrassing moment, but it was so much fun at the same time!" Josephine sighed and shook her head. "Good times, good times!"

Mark's laughter quieted down. "Okay. That does sound embarrassing, but it sounds like a lot of fun, too! I wish I could have been there to see it all happen!"

"Oh, believe me; I am so glad you weren't there! Having Matt there was bad enough!"

Mark leaned over and held her hand. "Thanks for sharing that with me. It was pretty funny! I needed a good laugh today."

"Me, too! It's fun remembering things like that. I'm sure during our relationship, we will both have many, many stories to tell each other!" Josephine squeezed his hand.

She enjoyed this side of Mark, the light-hearted and easy-to-talk-to guy she was first interested in. As the night drew to a close, he took her in his arms and kissed her gently. All of her irritations from the last few days melted away. She was glad to have this time together and felt a little guilty for not being excited about it when he first suggested them going out. Now as she kissed him back, she was thrilled to be his girlfriend and prayed that their relationship would grow stronger and stronger with each passing day.

Steven bid his parents good night and headed toward his room. He flipped on the light and tossed his wallet on the dresser. Sitting down on the edge of his bed, his mind began to replay the events of the day. He actually put an offer down on a house! Steven slapped his forehead! How did that even happen? He woke up this morning, thinking he would put a security deposit on an apartment. Instead, Steven felt he had signed his life away on a house.

A house!

The house was much too big for him right now, and he knew it. However, Steven was the type of guy who didn't just look at the here and now. He looked toward the future. He didn't see any sense on buying a small house for a bachelor. Besides, as Josephine had pointed out, they could have plenty of family gatherings at his house. The kids would love the big backyard. He could buy toys and games for them to play with whenever they came over. He lay down on the pillow and sighed. Josephine. She was a handful, to say the least! A bundle of energy! Her heart for the Lord was inspiring. Steven hadn't clicked with someone that fast in a long time. If she wasn't already dating someone, Steven would have asked her out by now. But, he knew better than to mess with another man's girl.

Oh well, he thought a twinge of sadness piercing his heart. *I guess I'll have to keep waiting.*

With those words playing over in his mind, he fell asleep.

Chapter 12

*J*osephine woke with a start.

What am I doing today? She rubbed her eyes, trying not to be so groggy. *I know I am doing something, but what is it?* She tapped her forehead, trying to remember. Suddenly, it came to her! It's the Un-Packing Party! Escrow had closed on Steven's house in late November, and his company had moved all of his belongings out already. Josephine's sisters and Steven's parents had decided to meet at his house today to help him get unpacked and settled. Josephine had asked Mark to join them. She really wanted Mark and Steven to get along. Steven was turning out to be one of her closest friends. She enjoyed her phone calls with Steven, often talking about Jesus or just laughing with each other. Josephine wanted Mark to like Steven as much as she did. Mark had agreed to help. He said he would pick her up at nine. Glancing at the clock, Josephine realized she didn't have a lot of time. She sprung out of bed and jumped in the shower. She knew she would have to make it a quick one. After the shower, she dashed around her apartment, getting ready, and praying silently for the day to go well. She looked around the apartment, making sure she had everything she needed. As an early Christmas present for Steven, she had gotten him an area rug to go underneath his dining room table. She just knew it would be the perfect accent to the room. Now, she picked it up and walked to her front door. Looking over her shoulder, she walked out just in time to hit Mark in the stomach with the rug.

"Ugh!" Mark gasped, doubling over.

"Mark! I'm so sorry!" Josephine dropped the rug and ran to his side.

Mark laughed. "I'm fine. Really. You caught me by surprise!"

Josephine picked up the rug and started walking toward his car. "I was coming out here to meet you, and glanced over my shoulder to make sure I didn't forget anything. I'm really sorry!"

Mark took the rug from Josephine. "No problem, really. It was actually funny!"

Mark put the rug in the back of the car. "What's the rug for?"

"I bought Steven an early Christmas gift. It will look perfect in his dining room under his table. Oh, Mark!" Josephine smiled up at him. "You are going to love this house! It is so adorable!"

Mark returned her smile. "You really like it, huh?"

"I do! It looks small on the outside, but on the inside, it is really quite big! The floor plan is amazing! The backyard is a good size, and it has a great swing set the previous owners left behind."

"Wow! So far, it sounds pretty cool." Mark followed the directions Josephine was silently giving.

"It is. I really think you'll love it!"

They drove a few more minutes in silence. As they rounded the corner, Josephine saw her sisters had already arrived.

"Oh good! My sisters are already here! Maybe we can get Luke or Nate to get the rug!"

Mark's brow furrowed. "Why? Don't you think I can carry it on my own?"

"That's not what I was saying, Mark!" Josephine defended herself. "I was actually trying to protect you from getting hurt again!"

"Oh," Mark nodded his understanding. "I didn't get your joke. Sorry."

Josephine relaxed a little bit. "It's all right.. Did you want to get the rug?"

"Yeah. I'll get it. I don't want your brothers-in-law to think I am not capable of carrying it in by myself." Mark said, pulled it out of the trunk.

Josephine waved her hand. "They wouldn't think that.. Let's go. I can't wait to show you around the place!"

They walked up to the house and came in without knocking. "Hello!" Josephine called. "We come bearing gifts!"

Steven came out of the kitchen. "Hey!" He gave her a hug, and patted Mark on the back. "What's this?" Steven pointed to the rug.

"It's an early Christmas gift." Josephine's eyes shone with joy. "I have the perfect place for it, too!"

Steven laughed, taking the rug from Mark and opening it up. "Wow, Jo! This is awesome! You really shouldn't have!"

Josephine squealed with delight. "I knew you would love it! Can you guess where I had envisioned it to go?"

"Hm," Steven pretended to be thinking. "My guess is the dining room, under that table. Am I right?"

Josephine smiled. "Yes you are! What do you think?"

"I think it will look great there. Mark, buddy, would you mind helping me move the table? I would ask Luke, but he hasn't finished his morning Coke yet, and I don't want him to do much before he does! And Nate, well, he loves the decorating thing, so I don't want to pull him away from that!"

Mark chuckled. "Sure. Just lead the way."

Josephine smiled, watching the two of them walk toward the dining room.

Good, she thought. *If they could continue to get along, this day was going to be perfect!*

"Josephine!" Grandma called from the kitchen. "Come on in! We could use some help in here!"

"Hi Grandma!" Josephine gave her a hug. "How are things coming along?"

"Slowly. For a bachelor, he sure does have a lot of stuff!" Mrs. Sorenson wrinkled her nose.

"That's because I like to cook," Steven retorted, coming back into the kitchen.

The women laughed. "That is what every girl desires!" Sue put her arm around Steven's shoulders. "A man who likes to cook!"

Brittany nodded her head. "It's true," she agreed. "One of my favorite things is when Luke is cooking. And he enjoys it, too!"

"Mm, hm. Nate, too," Sue glanced over her shoulder at Mrs. Sorenson. "He really wants Grandpa's noodle recipe. Do you think we could get that, Grandma?"

"Of course, dear!" Mrs. Sorenson smiled at Sue. "Invite us over when he makes it, alright?" Sue nodded and grinned.

"Well," Josephine cut in, "where do you want me and Mark to go?"

Steven paused. "I suppose we can have two of us in the living room, taking out the books and putting them on the bookshelves next to the fire place. I don't think our presence is needed in here. Is that alright with you ladies?"

Brittany nodded. "That's fine. Go get to work."

"She's a slave driver." Steven pointed at Brittany. "You'd think it was her house or something!" he added teasingly.

Brittany snapped a towel in his direction.

"Back to work!" she ordered, teasing Steven back.

Steven and Mark walked out together, both chuckling.

"So, what would you like me to do?" Josephine surveyed the scene.

"I was thinking we should start putting the dishes away," Mrs. Sorenson suggested.

"I can do that." Josephine opened a box and got right to work.

"Should we ask Steven where he wants these things?" Sue pulled out some pans.

"Nah. Steve and I seem to be on the same page with stuff like this," Josephine answered with a waive of her hand. "I can pretty much guess where he'll want them."

"And if we are wrong," Mrs. Sorenson added, "he can move things around later."

"Did you just call Steven 'Steve'?" Sue said, with a quizzical look on her face.

"Yes." Josephine bent down and put the pans away.

"Has anyone ever called him that?" Sue handed her another pan.

"When Grandpa and I named him, we vowed never to call him Steve. We just felt he looked more like a Steven. So, whenever we introduced him to people, we would call him Steven, and no one ever really questioned it. Even growing up with friends, they never bothered to call him Steve," Mrs. Sorenson explained.

"What made you decide to call him Steve, Jo?" Brittany angled her head.

"I don't know. We were talking the day he put the offer in on this house, and it just came out. It seemed like a natural thing, so I did it. Why is this a big deal?"
Josephine looked from one sister to another.

Sue shrugged her shoulders. "It isn't, really. It's just that in the time of knowing him, I haven't heard anyone call or mention the name Steve before." She patted Josephine on the shoulder. "Really. It's no big deal."

"Mark was a little annoyed with it at first, too. I still don't get why," Josephine confided. "It's just a nickname, like how you guys call me Jo or Bigfoot. Although, I do appreciate you guys not calling me Bigfoot as much!"

"Yeah, Jo seems to fit you better now than Bigfoot does." Sue stacked some plates on top of each other.

"That's true," Brittany piped in. "I always thought it was funny that you answered to Bigfoot!"

Josephine laughed and rolled her eyes. "One time I answer to anything, and unfortunately, it sticks for life!"

Brittany took out a white coffee maker from a box. "Hm. Where should this go?"

All four women stopped and looked around the kitchen. The doors to the cherry wood cabinets were all wide open, waiting to be filled. The black appliances set off the hard wood kitchen floors. The women looked back at the coffee maker and then at each other.

"Um," Mrs. Sorenson tentatively took it out of Brittany's hands, "I think it is going to have to go in the yard sale pile."

Sue and Josephine nodded their agreement. "It just doesn't go with the look of the kitchen. The microwave, stove, fridge, and oven are all black," Josephine said. "The whiteness of the coffee maker will just make it stand out like a sore thumb."

"It looks like I am going to have to get Steven a new coffee pot." Mrs. Sorenson set the coffee pot back in the box and marked 'Yard Sale' on the lid.

"Yes indeed!" The sisters agreed.

The women worked in the kitchen for a few more hours, unpacking and getting things set up until lunch time.

"There is so much talking and laughing coming from in here," Luke commented, , "I didn't think any work was actually getting done!"

Brittany pretended to be hurt. "What? You don't think we can multitask? That's just silly!"

Luke glanced around. "It does look pretty good in here. Are you almost finished?"

"Yes. Actually, this is the last dish that needed to be put away," Mrs. Sorenson answered, closing the kitchen cupboard.

"Did I hear someone say the kitchen is finished?" Mr. Sorenson walked into the kitchen.

"You sure did, dear." Mrs. Sorenson hugged her husband. "What do you say you treat us to a late lunch? I'm sure everyone is starving by now! How about pizza?"

"I think I can manage that." Mr. Sorenson pulled out his wallet and thumbed through the bills.

"Did someone say pizza?" Nate poked his head into the kitchen.

"Hi, hon!" Sue walked over to Nate and kissing him on the cheek. "Where have you been hiding today?"

"Hiding? Ha! Steven has been working like a mule!" Nate placed a hand on his lower back.

"Working like a mule!" Steven retorted. "Every time Nate would take out a book, he would ask me about it! I don't think we got nearly as much done as you ladies! It's a good thing I had Mark helping me out there, too!"

Nate sheepishly looked at Steven. "What can I say? I love to read! Anyone who has this many books ought to be prepared to give an answer as to why he has them!"

Josephine grabbed Marks' hand. "While they are talking and hopefully ordering pizza, I want to give you the grand tour."

Mark followed Josephine out of the kitchen. "Looks like I am being pulled away!"

They left the kitchen followed by more talking and laughter. "Ok, you already saw the kitchen and dining room, and the living room, right?"

"Right. I haven't seen the bedrooms, bathrooms, basement, or back yard." Mark counted each room on his fingers.

"I'll show you the basement first." Josephine pulled him toward the stairs.

She turned on the light and walked down the short flight of stairs. "This is the basement, or the rec room, as Steven calls it. Over there is a bathroom with a full shower and toilet." She pointed to a closed door. "That over there is a pantry of sorts. I'm figuring if there is an emergency, it would be stocked with plenty of food or something."

Mark nodded. "Hm. Interesting."

"It's a pretty big space, don't you think? It would be fun to put a pool table or air hockey table down here. I like how big it is."

"Show me more of upstairs." Mark didn't appear impressed. He took her hand and went to the stairs.

"Upstairs is pretty neat, too. The master bedroom is really big. I'll show you that next."

The walked up the two flights of stairs to get to the second story, and then down the hallway to the last door. Josephine opened the door. Once inside, the room was a nice size.. It had a recessed sitting area with two small, but comfortable looking easy chairs. . A fireplace took one side of the wall and Steven's bed was placed against the other wall.. A bench placed underneath the window gave a place to view the mountains.

Josephine guided Mark to the five piece bathroom. The double sink was accented with a few candles already. The shower was set apart from the Jacuzzi style bathtub.

"I just can't get enough of this bathroom!" Josephine turned in circles, gazing at the largeness of the room.

"What does a single guy need with all of this stuff?" Mark picked up a candle and smelled it.

"I think he was thinking about the future, when he gets married." Josephine took the candle and put it down.

"Does he have someone in mind?" Mark raised an eyebrow.

"No," Josephine said slowly. "I think he just has hope that one day, he will get married and his wife will enjoy having her own sink."

"Weird. I guess I wouldn't have thought that far ahead."

Josephine lifted her shoulders. "It's not a bad thing to think ahead. We just need to pray his wife will enjoy the house and all it has to offer."

"Show me more." Mark walked out of the bathroom.

Josephine showed Mark the two extra bedrooms and then took him back downstairs to where the dining room sliding glass door lead to the back yard.

Walking out onto the patio, she gestured grandly with her arms, "And this," she breathed in the air, "this is the back yard. Isn't it lovely?"

Mark looked around, still unimpressed. "It just looks like a back yard to me."

Josephine looked up at him in surprise. "Really? I love this back yard. It's big enough for the kids to play in, big enough to have a swing set in, big enough to entertain during the summer months. It has a wonderful view of the mountains. See over there?"

Mark looked to where she was pointing, a skeptical look crossing his face.

"Josephine, everyone in Colorado has the view of the mountains, either from their back yard or from one of their windows in the house," he reminded her.

Josephine cocked her head to one side. "I know. And that's the beauty of living in Colorado! No matter where you live, the mountains are always right there. So," she linked her arm with his, "what do you think of the house?"

"It's fine.. I just don't see why he would need something so big." Mark looked down at her.

"It's just fine? Really?" Josephine couldn't hide her shock.

Mark shrugged. "I guess I just don't feel the same way about it as you do. It's big, that's for sure. The rooms are all right. I don't really care for the layout of the house. I think having a formal dining room and a kitchen breakfast nook is a little much. Why would a person need two places to eat? Just have a dining room. Then, he has a living room and another whole room in the basement. Why? What's the purpose to that? And why would he even bother living in a place this big? I still don't understand that. One person living here all alone? Seems like it would be too much to take care of."

Josephine was stunned. "I'm not even sure I know how to answer all of those questions."

"I'm not really looking for answers." Mark was unaware of Josephine's expression. "I was more thinking out loud."

"Oh," Josephine tried to hide the disappointment written allover her face. "I guess I was just hoping you would love it as much as I do."

"Why? It's not like we're going to be coming here all that often, you know what I mean?" Mark turned toward the house to go back in. "Hey, I think I just saw Nate walk by with the pizza! Let's go inside and have some!"

Josephine stopped for a moment. "You go ahead. I'll be right in."

"You sure?" Mark turned slightly toward her.

"I'm sure." She turned her back to him.

"Ok. I'll save you a slice."

Josephine nodded briefly. She looked at the gorgeous view of the mountains, and couldn't help feeling a little sad. She had fallen in love with the house the moment she and Steven stepped through the front door. Everything about the house was inviting to her. Her heart was a little heavy as she stood staring at the mountains. She didn't know why it was so important that Mark liked the house. For some reason, it just was. That was why she didn't mention anything to Mark. She felt she needed to discover on her own why she felt so let down and disappointed. She was so deep in thought, she didn't hear the sliding glass door open and close behind her.

"Hey, Sis," Brittany handed her a piece of pizza. "You all right?"

Josephine took the pizza half heartedly. "I'm fine."

Brittany looked at her, puzzled. "You don't seem fine."

Josephine sighed. "I just got done showing Mark the house."

"Uh-huh." Brittany took a bite of her pizza.

"He doesn't really like it all that much," Josephine confided in her.

"Okay-. This is a problem because...?" Brittany gently asked.

"I'm not sure. I just felt really let down. I was standing out here, trying to figure out why I was feeling this way."

"Interesting. Do you think it has anything to do with the fact that you found this house for Steven?" Brittany suggested.

"Maybe. I don't know. I guess I just need to pray about it some more. I don't want to say anything to Mark about being disappointed without knowing completely why I feel this way."

"That's a good idea," Brittany agreed. She put her arm around Josephine's shoulder. "Why don't we head back inside, then? Just so that Mark won't think anything is wrong."

Josephine nodded. "Sounds good." She sighed one more time before entering the dining room with Brittany.

"So, Mark," Nate set down his paper plate, "how is school going?"

"Pretty good," Mark answered, taking another bite of pizza. "I'm enjoying it."

"How many more years do you foresee being in school?" Brittany sat down by Luke.

"Only a few more. I sort of got a late start." Mark leaned back. "I didn't know what I wanted to do with my life, and so it took me a little while to figure it out. But once I got on the right track, I should be done pretty quickly. Maybe a few more semesters, and that's it."

"What are you going to school for?" Steven wiped his hands on his napkin.

"I'm going to be a teacher. I love working with kids, and right now, I have been volunteering my time at our church, helping the children's pastor."

"That's cool," Steven said. "I think it takes a special kind of person to be a teacher for children."

"What do you do?" Mark nodded in toward Steven.

"I work with an aerospace company. It was getting a little too expensive back east, so the company decided to move out here. Colorado's also more centrally located to our customers," Steven informed him.

"Wow. Aerospace! That's pretty high tech." Mark seemed slightly impressed.

"Eh, it could be, I guess. I try not to think too much about it when I am off of work. I'm not one of those guys who likes to bring their work home with them," Steven admitted.

"My dad felt that way, too." Sue voice was soft. "He didn't want a stressful day to affect his attitude when he came home."

"That's true," Brittany's eyes were moist. "I remember him telling us when he had a rough day, but he did his best to leave work at work."

"I wish we could have met your parents," Regret filled Mrs. Sorenson's eyes.

"Me, too," Josephine squeezed Mrs. Sorenson's hand. "They would have loved you guys!"

Steven stood up. "I'm going to get something more to drink. Anyone want anything? Luke, do you know where your Coke is?"

Luke groaned while the group tried to hide their giggles.

"No, thanks," came the reply from the rest of the gang.

"Jo?" Steven turned toward her when she hadn't answered.

"I'm still debating about that." Josephine jumped up. "I'll just go with you."

Josephine followed Steven into the kitchen.

"You all right?" Steven turned toward her once they were out of ear shot.

"I'm fine." She opened his fridge. "Why do you ask?"

"You just seem quieter than when you first got here. I just wanted to make sure everything was fine."

"I'm okay. I was just thinking about how much I love this

house." Josephine looked around the kitchen wistfully.

"I love it, too!" Steven agreed. "Thanks for finding it for me. I'm glad you were with me that day."

Josephine smiled. "It was a good day. All right, where do you want us to focus on next?"

"Well," Steven thought for a moment. "We have some of the decorations up already, thanks to Nate. The couches are already in place, as well as the dining room table. I have my bedroom set up already. I don't have a lot to put in the basement yet. The books are all done, and so is the kitchen. I don't know if we have a whole lot to do."

Josephine glanced around the house. "That's true. Most of the boxes are done. Do you need to go shopping for anything?"

"I'm sure I will," Steven held her gaze. "But I think I want to make a list first, so I don't buy things I already have."

"Good point." Josephine glanced away quickly, hoping Steven wouldn't notice her cheeks turning pink. Why was she suddenly embarrassed? She shook her head.

"I think this is all we really need to do today," Steven concluded as if he hadn't seen her act any differently.

"Well," she cleared her throat, "if and when you need to go shopping, call me. I love spending other people's money!"

"Sounds like a plan," Steven laughed, walking toward the living room.

"Well, everyone," he addressed the group, "I think we can call it a day."

"What?" Luke appeared shocked.

"I was just talking with Josephine, and really, we've finished most of the unpacking. I do need to go shopping, but Jo has offered to go with me when I am ready, and that is not today." He winked at her.

Brittany stood up. "Ok, Steven, if you say we're done, then I guess we're done."

Sue and Nate followed suit. "I guess so. Do let us know if you need anything, alright?" Sue gave Steven a warm hug.

"I will. And thanks, you guys, for all of your help. I really appreciate it. This place is starting to look like home."

And Steven walked the whole group to the door.

○ ○ ○ ○

Steven closed the door and looked around. Home. His home. Who would have thought buying a house could have been this easy? He chuckled to himself thinking about his realtor. He had told Steven it is hardly ever this easy, putting an offer in, having it get accepted right away with no counter offer. Escrow had closed so quickly. Steven was thrilled to have a house all of his own. Sue and Brittany were in awe of the home, almost as much as Josephine was. Steven walked to the basement. It would be a lot of fun decorating the basement, having it as a recreation room. He could put a couch by the wall, perhaps a television on the opposite wall. There was enough room for a pool table or air hockey table. He'd have to wait on those purchases, though. He still wanted to make the house more of a home first, which meant taking care of upstairs and buying games the little ones would enjoy.

He breathed a lengthy sigh. Little ones. When would his day come to be a husband and a father? Steven hated dwelling on his loneliness and what he wanted but didn't have. He knew he needed to be content in all things. It was difficult for him tonight, however. Sue and Nate had each other. They had DJ, although Nate's mom had watched him today, along with Gideon and Joslyn. Brittany and Luke had each other and two wonderful children. Josephine also had someone special.

When, Lord? When will it be my turn? Be content, he felt the Lord whisper to his soul.

Yes, that's what he needed to do. Be content with what he has. With new resolve, Steven walked upstairs to the living room and pulled out his Bible.

Time in God's word always gave him perspective. Tonight would be no different.

○ ○ ○ ○

Josephine and Mark walked to the car. After getting in,

Josephine sighed and sat back. "Well, that was fun." She glanced his way and gave him a tired smile.

Mark nodded slowly. "It wasn't too bad. I thought it was going to be more work."

"Steven doesn't have that much stuff yet. I'm glad it wasn't too much."

"Hey, can I ask you a question?" Mark turned to her suddenly.

"Sure," Josephine answered.

"When did he start calling you Jo?" Hurt filled his voice.

"A little while ago, I guess. Why?" Josephine wondered where this was going.

"I just noticed a few times today, he called you Jo. I was wondering if you told him to call you that or if he just felt comfortable enough with your friendship to start calling you that."

"I told him the day we went looking for the house he could call me Jo." Josephine lifted a shoulder and let it drop casually.

"Oh." Mark said and then was silent.

"Mark, is there something wrong/"

"I guess my feelings are a little hurt, that's all." Mark pulled into the driveway at her apartment.

"Why don't you come in and we can talk about that?" Josephine got out of the car.

Mark hesitated. "Are you sure? I don't want to be a bother."

"Mark, you're my boyfriend. If I hurt you somehow, I would like to know so I can correct that."

Mark slowly got out of the car. They walked to the apartment silently. When Josephine let them in, she closed the door behind her and sat down on the couch. Mark sat down across from her.

"Ok. Tell me again why I hurt your feelings." She put her hand on his knee.

Mark looked down at his hands. "Well, we've been dating for about three months now. I have always called you Josephine, wondering if you would ever tell me to call you Jo. And you and Steven met around the same time you and I did, and he is already calling you by your nickname."

Josephine nodded, understanding. "And you were waiting for me to tell you that you could call me Jo, right?"

Mark nodded. "Yes. I was hoping you would offer that to me."

"Oh Mark. I'm sorry," Josephine apologized. "You are completely right. I should have been the one to offer that to you. Please forgive me for that. I didn't mean to hurt your feelings or make you feel like you weren't included."

"Thanks." Mark leaned toward her and kissing her cheek. "I appreciate that."

"You can call me Jo, you know that, right?"

"I know. I think for now I will stick with Josephine." Mark leaned back.

"How come?"

"Well, everyone seems to call you Jo. Thinking about it now, I'm not just anyone. I am your boyfriend. I don't want to be like everyone else who is close to you. Does that make sense?"

Josephine thought his explanation a little odd, but accepted it all the same. "I suppose so."

"So, what would you like to do now?" Mark ran his hand through his hair.

"I was thinking maybe we could go in the Jacuzzi. Does that sound fun?"

"It's a little cold outside. Are you up for walking in the cold all wet?"

"I'm fine with that. I think a nice warm spa sounds good." Josephine stood up. "Did you take your trunks home from last time?" She looked under her bathroom sink.

"No. They should still be there."

"Oh, here they are," Josephine tossed them his way. "I'll change in my room and leave the bathroom for you."

"Thanks. See you in a minute."

A few minutes later, they were sitting in the hot spa, relaxing and talking about nothing in particular.

"I love spas." Josephine felt her entire body relax. "It just feels so good to sit in something warm and feel all your tight muscles relax."

"I think spas are all right." Mark shifted uncomfortably. "But truthfully, it's like taking a bath to me."

"Really? Even with the jets and stuff?"

"I know it sounds weird. Most people like spas,, but it's not my favorite thing to do."

"Hm. That's interesting. What would you do instead? To relax I mean?"

"Normally, when I'm stressed, I like to sit by myself and read my Bible. I don't rely on outward things to help me de-stress." Mark's whole body seemed to radiate confidence.

"That's cool. For me, I like having outward things help my body. Then, after I de-stress, I make myself a cup of coffee, unwind, and then I can enjoy my Bible times. I find for me, then I can focus on what God is trying to say to me."

"I never thought of it that way before." Mark was thoughtful. "I guess people have different ways of doing things."

"That's what makes the human race so interesting. God created us all so differently. If we were all the same, life would be pretty boring."

"Well," Mark scooted over to Josephine, "life with you is not boring, and for that, I am thankful."

Josephine kissed him on the lips. "I feel that way about you, too."

They sat for a while more in the spa, and then headed back to Josephine's to change. Mark left shortly after that. Josephine was left alone, thinking about the day and her feelings. What she had said in the spa was true: God did make them different for a reason. Life would be boring if people were all the same.

I guess it doesn't matter if Mark didn't like Steven's house. It's not my house, after all. Besides, our differences are good. I don't want to date someone who is exactly like me. That would be way too boring!

She went to bed that night, sleeping more peacefully than she had in a long time

Chapter 13

*B*efore Sue knew it, the week of Christmas had arrived. Sue loved Christmas! It was a time to focus on Jesus. It was a time of giving and sharing, a time of loving and caring. *Christmas*, Sue thought fondly. Christmas had always been her father's favorite time of year. It wasn't about the presents, but about the reason for the season. Jesus came, willingly, to live as a normal man would. He came to walk in the shoes of the people He Himself created. He gave Himself up for mankind, which is why her father gave gifts. The gifts her dad had given weren't thoughtless gifts. They were always special. The gifts had a reason behind them. Sue walked over to the trunk her dad had made for her the Christmas before he had died. It was one of her most cherished gifts of all time.

It took so long for Dad to make this! A sad smile crossed her lips. She ran her hand over the top of the trunk.It was a dark wood, with hand carving of the bible verse 'Philippians 4:1' on it. Sue hadn't memorized that verse until after her parents went home to be with Jesus.

It said, "So, brothers and sisters, I love you and miss you. You are my joy and my crown. Therefore, dear friends, keep your relationship with the Lord firm!"

Tears sprung to her eyes as she thought about those words.

"Suzy," her dad had said to her that Christmas, "I miss you being my little girl. You were so willing to jump onto my lap and ask me a million questions about everything! But now, look at you! You are no longer Daddy's little girl. You are more than that now. You are my friend. And I love you very much!"

She had cried when he finished talking. She had wrapped her arms around him, and held him for a very long time.

"Dad, no matter how big or old I get, I will always be your little girl," she had whispered to him.

When she pulled away, she noticed he had been crying, too. It was a tender moment she will never forget.

Christmas was a time to remember her parents and the traditions they left behind. It was a time to bring those traditions into her family. And it was a time to create new ones with Nate and DJ.

Sue picked up the gifts she had made for the men in her life. She had been busy during the month of November, making special blankets for DJ and Nate. Kayla was kind enough to help her make them. She was brilliant at sewing. Sue knew without Kayla's help and expertise, she would never have gotten them finished. Sue knew Nate and DJ would love them.

DJ loved superheroes. He had never seen a cartoon or movie of one, just the characters. So Sue had looked high and low for Superman material. She finally found it! She excitedly started sewing DJ's blanket, and finished just before Thanksgiving. It was more difficult keeping Nate's hidden from him. Kayla offered to keep them at her house so he wouldn't find the blanket. Sue knew he would love his material. It had musical notes and guitars all over it. Nate loved music. Sue was always saying he was the most talented man when it came to music. Not only did he play a number of instruments, but he had an amazing voice that made Sue smile every time she heard him singing! She remembered the cd he had made when they were just getting to know each other. It was all of his original music.

One song in particular was her favorite. It was called "Rest and know." The chorus rang through her mind whenever she felt hopeless.

"There is hope through the darkness. Something to hold on to. Your anchor waits to hold you, hold you through the storm, rest and know... rest and know....He is God." She loved that song! Sue sighed contently, looking forward to Nate's response when he saw the blanket.

Sue loved to give. Christmas was a favorite holiday for her for that simple reason. She spent time creating scrapbooks for Nate's mom and step-dad as well as his dad and step-mom. Sue also included the Sorensons, knowing they would adore the scrapbook, too. She wanted to capture each moment with DJ and share it with his grandparents. She knew they would love and cherish the books, just as she cherished her own. For her own family members, she spent time searching the stores for what they would like. Sue loved to buy the gifts she knew people would love. It was fun searching for things for Brittany and Luke and their kids. As a joke, Sue bought a red t-shirt for Luke, printed in the coca-cola font, that said, "Where's my Coke?"! She laughed to herself, thinking of his response.

Sue had the most fun shopping for Steven. She and Josephine had gone shopping together. Sue loved Steven's house and wanted to get something that would fit his personality as well as his house. She found a picture of Jesus laughing. Once Josephine had seen the picture, she informed Sue of how perfect it would fit in the house. Sue quickly purchased it.

Mark's gift was the hardest for Sue to find. She wasn't sure what he was interested in, and it was tough for her to get an answer from Josephine on what he would like. Sue shopped and shopped. Sue tried paying extra close attention to Mark might like. When the family gathered together for Thanksgiving, she purposely asked him questions about his wants and needs. She listened when he talked with others to see if his interests would come up. The more she listened to him, the more she realized a self-help book on his insecurities might be what he needed. Upon discussing it with Nate, she realized that would probably offend him and decided against it. Sue finally decided on a Christmas cd by Chris Tomlin. She had heard Mark say he enjoyed Chris Tomlin.

Thanksgiving was a relaxing day, filled with family visiting from house to house, enjoying the day together. Grandma and Grandpa were there, talking joyfully about Steven moving back to Colorado. Steven himself was still back east, wrapping things up for the company's move.

Joslyn made everyone laugh as she sang and danced. Gideon brought his guitar, so while he played his guitar, Joslyn sang and DJ played his bongos. Everyone had a wonderful time watching their performance. Even Mark seemed to be enjoying himself. Her attitude toward Mark had gotten better. She no longer rolled her eyes every time he came in the room or said anything.

Since Steven's house was all decorated and ready for the holidays, everyone decided to meet there on Christmas Day to celebrate together. Brittany and Sue offered to come early to help prepare the food and set the table. Mrs. Sorenson was to drop off Mr. Sorenson at Sue's. He was going to ride over to Steven's with Nate and DJ followed by Luke and the kids.

Josephine said she would love to come early, but she had made plans to be with Mark's family earlier that day.

○ ○ ○ ○

"Merry Christmas!" Josephine sang out when Mark opened the door to his parents' house.

"Merry Christmas!" He gave her a hug and invited her in.

Josephine walked in to a whole different world than the one outside! It was cold and grey outside, with clouds threatening to burst at any given moment. Inside, the fire was burning cherrily in the fireplace and a Christmas tree was the focal point of the room. It was elegantly decorated, as was the rest of the house. The room looked as if it was from a Better Homes and Garden Magazine! Stockings hung from the fireplace, but Josephine wondered if they were ever filled. A porcelain manager scene was carefully displayed on the hearth of the fireplace. The room was altogether beautiful and warm. More than that, it was perfect.

A pang of sadness filled her heart, however. As lovely as the room was, it wasn't like how her parents' house used to be. Home-made tree ornaments always decorated the tree. Josephine and her sisters would string popcorn and drape it through the branches of the tree. Her mom loved snowmen, and all throughout the house there was evidence of that. Her dad would proudly display the girls' decorations they had either painted or handmade. As beautiful as Mark's parents' house was, it wasn't anything like the home she grew up in. Forcing a smile, she turned her attention back to Mark and his family. His sister, Ally, and her husband, Ben was already there. His older brother's family had yet to arrive.

"Josephine," Mrs. Littleton extended her hands. "How are you?"

"Fine, Mrs. Littleton." Josephine squeezed her hands. "Merry Christmas!"

"And to you," Mr. Littleton's rough voice sang out. "It's nice to see you again!"

Josephine smiled warmly. "Thank you. It's nice to see you, as well. Thank you so much for inviting me over today!"

Mrs. Littleton's eyes glowed. "Not a problem, dear. We are just so happy Mark has someone special in his life."

"Mom!" Mark groaned and rolled his eyes. "Please ignore them."

Josephine laughed. "I will do no such thing!"

Mark's parents laughed and led them into the living room. The conversation was light and easy. Josephine really liked Ally, Mark's twin sister. She was so down-to-earth. Ally and Ben went to the Littleton's church and loved it. They were in the process of talking about moving out of state, though. Ben had gotten a job offer in Pennsylvania. Ally's parents weren't too happy to have their only daughter move so far away, but they would support their decision no matter what happened. Josephine thought about her parents and what they would have done if they were still alive. How would they respond if she would move away? She quickly dismissed those thoughts. They weren't there. There was no use in dwelling on the what-ifs of life.

The morning and afternoon flew by quickly. Before too long, it was time that she and Mark should head over to Steven's to celebrate Christmas with her family. Josephine gathered up her presents, thanked the Littleton's, and headed to her car. Mark said he would follow her to her house, and then they could drive over to Steven's together. Josephine looked forward to being with her family.

Christmas just wasn't the same unless they could all be together!

○ ○ ○ ○

Christmas couldn't come quickly enough for Sue! She had been up for at least two hours, anxiously awaiting the moment she could wake up the men in her life. Sue excitedly woke up Nate and DJ. Neither of her men were morning people, but Sue just couldn't bear it any longer! She desperately wanted to give them their gifts, and start the day.

Sue and Nate had filled DJ's stocking the night before. Nate had put special things in her own stocking, just as she had done for him. Together, all three opened their stockings. Then it was time for the gifts to be passed out. Sue handed DJ the wrapped blanket. He opened it and gently touched the material to his cheek.

"Mommy, I wuv it!" His adorable blue eyes were shining with joy.

He ran over and gave her a big hug and kiss.

"Merry Christmas, baby." She squeezed him tightly.

Nate opened his next. The look of shock and excitement poured from his face.

"Honey!" Nate ran his thumb across the material. "When did you have the time to do this?"

"It wasn't easy! But with Kayla's help, I was able to pull it off. Do you like it?" Sue wrung her hands nervously together.

"I love it! Thanks, love!" He leaned over and kissed her.

Sue opened her present. It was a special 'mommy' box. The box was decorated with pictures of DJ and special things he had painted.

"Oh, Nate! Thank you! I will cherish this always!" Her eyes blurred with unshed tears.

"I will put all of DJ's special drawings in here."

"That's what it's intended for." Nate smiled. "I'm glad you like it."

The rest of the morning was spent enjoying each other. Nate

took out the Bible and read the birth story of Jesus. Sue sat in awe of the simplicity of how her savior entered the world. Even DJ sat, transfixed by the story. When the reading was over, DJ said to Nate and Sue, "I wuv Jesus." It brought tears of joy to their eyes!

Sue and Nate got dressed and helped DJ get dressed. The Sorensons were due any minute, and they wanted to be ready. When the door bell rang, Sue dashed around the house, trying to remember last minute items she was to bring to Steven's.

"Merry Christmas!" Mrs. Sorenson sang out. She was dressed in a cheerful red and green Christmas sweater.

"Merry Christmas!" Nate wrapped her in a big bear hug. "You look festive today."

"Thank you, Nate." Mrs. Sorenson grinned from ear to ear.

Mr. Sorenson gave Sue a hug. "Are you all set to drive over to Steven's with my wife?"

"I am! Are you all set to play with my boys before you head over there?" She tilted her head playfully.

Mr. Sorenson chuckled. "I am. I think I lucked out, though. I get to play, you get to work."

Sue laughed. "True, true. It will be a joy all the same."

Kissing Nate on the cheek, she left with Mrs. Sorenson.

The rest of the afternoon was a blur. Sue, Brittany, Mrs. Sorenson and Steven flew around the house, preparing it for the day's festivities. When everyone else arrived, dinner was almost all on the table. Christmas music was playing in the background, and there was a special section in the living room for the kids to play with the toys Steven had bought them for when they come over his house. The house suddenly became more alive with the bustle of activity. Once everyone was seated around the table, and the prayer was given, did conversation really begin to flow. Everyone was talking to each other, asking about the day they had had, wondering what each person had gotten for Christmas. Even New Year's Day had come up, wondering what each one was doing, whether or not they should have a fun family gathering. Some time during dinner, DJ ran over to Josephine.

"Auntie Jo," he bounced up and down, "Mommy made supa-man bwanket!"

Josephine scooped him up onto her lap and rubbed noses with him. "Really, buddy? Do you love it?"

DJ's eyes grew big and he nodded emphatically. "Yeah! It's soft!"

"You'll have to show it to me next time I come over, okay? I would love to see it!" Josephine snuggled close to him.

"Wow, Josephine!" Mark angled his head to one side. "I know family members look alike, but DJ looks like he could pass for your son!"

Nate dropped his fork on his plate, and Sue's mouth hung open. The room became strangely quiet.

Finally, after what seemed like an eternity to Sue, Steven said smoothly, "It's true, isn't it? They are definitely related!"

Luke joined in, "A buddy of mine has a niece who looks just like him! Poor thing! She'll be really ugly when she gets older if her looks don't gradually change!"

Mr. Sorenson started off the laughter until the rest of the group joined in. It appeared to be uncomfortable laughter at first, but then, after glancing at Mark, and realizing he didn't catch on, Sue's laughter was more from relief than anything.

Was it really that obvious that DJ was Josephine's son? Why hadn't Sue thought about that before? Of course Josephine would date someone and possibly get married. What would her significant other think and feel? Sue wondered if maybe it was time to tell Mark the truth. Should he know this early on in his and Josephine's relationship? What would he say? What would he do? Would Josephine lose him because of it? Sue didn't know what to think.

All she could do was pray, and pray she did!

○ ○ ○ ○

The moment the words were out of Mark's mouth, Josephine felt sick to her stomach. She should have known something like this was bound to happen. What was she thinking? How could she ever be in a normal relationship with someone who didn't know the truth?

"DJ, thanks for telling me about your blanket. I will come by another day, and you can show it to me, okay?" She patted DJ's head half-heartedly.

"Otay!" DJ enthusiastically replied.

Josephine picked up her fork and began eating. Every bite was a forced one. She felt sick. Her head began to pound.

Mark put his arm around her. "Hey. You don't look so good."

Josephine gave a weak smile. "I'm fine. My head just started hurting, that's all."

Mark massaged the back of her neck. "Can I do anything for you?"

"No. I'm fine. I'm just going to see if Steven has any medicine." She got up from the table. "Steven, do you have anything for a headache?"

Steven quickly got up. "Sure. Follow me."

Steven led her to the nearest bathroom and took out two pills from the medicine cabinet.

"What am I doing?" Josephine fought back the tears that threatened to spill onto her cheeks.

"What do you mean?" Steven handed her the medicine.

She gulped them down. "Can I really be in a relationship and keep DJ a secret?"

Steven looked down. "I don't know the answer to that, Jo."

"Ugh! I know you don't." Frustration filled her eyes. She shook her head sadly. "One mistake and I seriously think I'll be paying for it the rest of my life."

"DJ wasn't a mistake, Josephine." Steven's voice was kinder than before. "He is a remarkable little boy. Sue and Nate are blessed because of him. And he is blessed because of them."

Josephine nodded. "I know. What am I going to do, Steven?"

Steven hugged her as she started to cry. "Pray. See if God wants you to tell Mark about DJ. But wait to be sure it is the Lord answering you." He rubbed her back. "When we act on our own initiative, things never go the way they should."

Josephine pulled away. Wiping her eyes, she sniffed. "Thanks. I will. I better get back out there. Thanks for listening. I needed it."

Steven shrugged his shoulders. "As the songs all say, " That's what friends are for." He gently brushed away the tears that continued to come.

Josephine took his hand in hers and squeezed it. She walked back to the dining room, praying.

Lord, is it time to tell Mark the truth? What if he doesn't want to be with me anymore? What if he looks at me differently? Oh, Jesus, show me what the right thing to do is!

Josephine's heart was still in turmoil, but she hoped her facial expression didn't show it.

"How's your head?" Genuine concern poured from Mark.

"It still hurts, but I'm sure it will be better soon. Thanks for asking." Josephine squeezed his hand.

Looking around at the couples seated at the table, Josephine realized her chances of having a relationship like any of theirs was close to impossible. She had two choices: keep the secret, and hope Mark would never find out. That would be ideal, but she knew she would be living a lie. Or she could tell Mark, and soon, and risk losing him.

Josephine looked at the natural was Brittany responded to Luke. She knew Brittany had no secrets from Luke. They were always open and honest with each other, even if the truth hurt. "Speak the truth in love," she could hear Brittany say. Brittany laughed at something Luke said, tossing her hair over her shoulder. What it would be like to be that carefree! Brittany never had to wonder if Luke was going to leave her. *Unlike me*, Josephine thought dejectedly. She glanced at Sue and Nate, wondering how they were dealing with Mark's observation. It seemed as if they had moved on. DJ sat on Nate's lap, trying to finish Nate's food. Nate kept pushing his plate further and further away from DJ's grabby hands. Sue laughed at the game father and son were playing.

It couldn't possibly affect them if I were to tell Mark. Josephine massaged her temples. *Why should they be acting and feeling any differently?*

With her headache starting to go away, she pushed her plate back, resolved as to what she needed to do.

○ ○ ○ ○

Brittany watched Josephine's reaction to Mark's comment, with a sinking feeling in her stomach. She had seen that look on her sister's face before, and it was never a good sign. Josephine could be very impulsive at times. She seldom gave forethought to her actions. Josephine was one to act without thinking, to do as she felt she ought to instead of thinking things through. Brittany sighed silently. The look on Josephine's face was one of determination.

This can't be good. Brittany placed a hand on her stomach.

"Hey, Jo?" Brittany caught her sister's gaze from across the table. "Why don't you and I go get dessert ready?"

"So soon?" Luke gave Brittany an odd look.

Brittany patted his hand and smiled. "Oh, honey, you know Grandpa. He has a wedged-shaped cavity that needs to get filled."

Mr. Sorenson pounded his fist on the table. "That's right! Where's the pie?"

The group all laughed as Josephine and Brittany walked out of the kitchen.

"Should we take orders, or just bring it all to the table?" Josephine took the pies out of the refrigerator.

"Let's see what we have first, and then decide." Brittany cleared her throat. "So, how are you, with Mark's comment, I mean?"

Josephine's back straightened a little. "Fine. I was upset at first, but I think I'm okay now."

"Good." Brittany tried not to overstep her boundaries. "Why were you upset?"

"I think I didn't expect him to notice the resemblance. It caught me off guard, you know?"

Brittany nodded. "Sure. I can see that." She waited for Josephine to continue. When she didn't, she added, "And what are you thinking?"

"What do you mean?" Josephine narrowed her eyes.

"I mean, I know you, Jo. I know that look on your face. What are you thinking?" Brittany set down another pie.

"I'm not too sure yet. I have an idea, but I don't know entirely what I am going to do. Truthfully, Brit, I don't mean to be rude, but I don't want to talk about this right now. Can we just take the dessert out and have a nice Christmas?" Josephine put her hand on her hip and sighed.

Brittany was taken aback. She hadn't expected Josephine to be unwilling to talk about her feelings and her heart. "Sure, Jo. I didn't mean to pressure you. I just wanted you to know that I am here if you need anything."

"I know you are. I appreciate that." Josephine's answer was short and firm. With that, she turned around and walked out of the room holding the dessert in her hands.

Brittany's heart sank. When Josephine acted distant and aloof, nothing good came out of her actions.

Josephine was not being very open, and that caused deep concern for Brittany.

○ ○ ○ ○

"So, Mark," Josephine began hesitantly as they were driving to her apartment. "How did you enjoy Christmas with my family?"

"It was fun!" Mark smiled joyfully.

"I'm glad you thought so. Did you enjoy the gifts they gave you?"

Mark nodded. "I did. I know I am hard to shop for, especially since they still don't know me very well. It was nice of them to think of me. I have to say, I like my gifts far more than I liked what Sue had gotten Steven!"

Josephine's mouth hung open in shock. She loved the picture of Jesus laughing that Sue had bought for Steven. It was one of her favorite pictures of all time!

"Seriously?" Josephine was still uncertain she heard him correctly.

"I'm totally serious. I didn't care for it at all!"

"I love that picture! I thought it really captured Jesus' character!"

Mark raised one shoulder and patted her leg. "Okay. We can have our different opinions. It's really all right."

Josephine was quiet for a moment. "I suppose it is." She rubbed her forehead. "Hey, when we get to my house, can you come in for a few moments? I want to talk to you about something."

Mark looked at her from the corner of his eye. "Is everything okay?"

"I'm not sure yet. I'd like to talk to you about it and get your opinion." Josephine knew she was being vague, but she had no choice. She didn't want to give too much away. She was afraid if she did talk to him now, he would toss her out of the car before she could explain everything to him.

"Sure, I'll come in," Mark said, curiosity filling his voice.

They reached her apartment and walked in silence. Josephine wondered how she was going to start the conversation.

God, please help me!, she cried silently, but she didn't feel any better than before her little prayer.

Sitting on her couch, she faced Mark. Taking a deep breath, she began, "Mark, we've been dating a few months now." Mark leaned over and kissed her gently on the lips. "Best few months of my life."

She smiled half heartedly. "Thanks. But before you say that, you might want to hear what I have to say." Mark's brow wrinkled as he slowly sat back. "Okay."

"Mark, tonight, you said DJ could pass for my son." Josephine paused, tears filling her eyes. "Well, that's because he is. I gave him up for adoption a few years ago to Sue and Nate."

Mark sat back on the couch. "What....what do you mean? DJ's *your* son?"

Josephine launched into the story of her and Jim's one night stand. She explained how she wasn't ready to be a mom and felt, after a lot of prayer, that Sue and Nate could take better care of DJ and give him all she could not. By the end of the story, tears were pouring down her cheeks, and she was sobbing uncontrollably.

Mark stood up and slowly began pacing the floor.

"So why are you telling me all of this now? Why not before?"

Josephine looked up, her eyes pleading for him to understand.

"Mark, I didn't know where this was going. I didn't want to spring this on you if we decided it wasn't going to work out between us. But then, you made the comment at dinner tonight, and I panicked! I never thought anyone would see the resemblance between DJ and me! All through dinner, I kept wondering what you would say, what you would do! I couldn't keep this a secret any longer."

Mark finally sat back down. "Wow, Josephine, this is a lot to take in. I don't know if I completely understand why you gave DJ up to Sue and Nate. Is it legal? Or are they just taking care of him until you can? And if so, what does that mean? Until you get married?"

Josephine wiped her eyes. "Everything's legal. And no, I have no intention of reclaiming my son. I promised them this would be a final decision." She sniffed. "As for why I gave him to Sue and Nate, well, it's a long story. Nate can't have kids. He had testicular cancer when he was younger. Sue had always wanted to have kids of her own, and when she and Nate became serious, she gave up that dream. Well, not really. She said she wanted to adopt. And this was her opportunity."

Mark closed his eyes. Josephine couldn't tell what he was thinking or how he was feeling. Did he think she was completely awful? Did he want to end their relationship right then and there? What was going on in his head? Why wasn't he speaking?

"Please say something!" Josephine begged.

"I'm still trying to process all of this. And Jim gave up all parental rights, you said?"

"Yes, he did. He never wanted to have kids, even while we were together. When I told him I was pregnant, he wanted me to have an abortion." Josephine's eyes suddenly became hard. "No matter what mistakes he and I made, terminating a life is absolutely out of the question! DJ was not going to suffer for our mistakes!"

"I'm glad you felt that way, even in the midst of the crisis." Mark rubbed the back of his neck.

"What are you thinking, Mark? I need to know. Do you want to end our relationship?"

"Do I want to do what? Why would I want to do that?" Mark snapped his head up.

"Well, I thought," Josephine stammered, "I thought once you found out, you would think I was a terrible person for giving up my son."

Mark gently took Josephine in his arms. "Oh, sweetie, I couldn't think that about you. What I actually think is that Sue and Nate took advantage of your situation and used it to benefit themselves."

Josephine pulled back, alarmed. "No! Mark, that's not how it was at all! They didn't ask me if they could adopt DJ, I asked them!"

"I understand all of that. But let's be honest, you were hormonal, scared, and not really of sound mind. Did they try to talk you out of it at all?" Mark scratched his head.

"They asked me a lot of questions. They made sure this is what I really wanted. And, believe me, it was!"

"And now? Now, seeing DJ all the time, is that what you wanted?" Mark pointed to a picture of DJ and Gideon on her wall. "Can you honestly say you don't want him to be *your* son?"

"Yes, I can. He's happy, Mark, really happy. He doesn't even know I am his birth mom. He loves Sue and Nate, very much, and they love him equally as much. Before I even asked them, I prayed. I prayed and prayed! I knew, once I had talked with Sue about it, that that is what God wanted me to do."

"Josephine, I don't mean to doubt what you felt God was telling you, but maybe it wasn't God. Maybe it was you just trying to find a way out and not listening to what God really wanted. Why would God want you to give up your baby? Why wouldn't He want you and DJ to be together?"

"I'm not sure I like where this is going, Mark. I know what I felt. I know that at the time, it was the right thing to do." Josephine got up and stood above him.

"Okay. Let me give you another scenario. What if God wanted Sue and Nate to take care of DJ until you were able? What about that?"

"That wouldn't be right." Josephine was quick to answer.

"Why not? Why wouldn't that be right?" Mark took her hands in his and gently pulled her down to the couch again.

"When would that be? And why would He want me to tear apart a family? Besides, I gave my word to them. I promised them that I wouldn't try to take him back." Josephine pounded her chest.

"I don't think it's fair of them to hold you to that. After all, you were emotional and in shock. And, you wouldn't be tearing apart a family. You would be reuniting yourself to your son, your son, not their son, but yours."

"You didn't answer my first question," Josephine pointed out. "When would I be able to take care of DJ?"

"Why not now? I mean, you are financially better off than before, you said so yourself. You are spiritually a strong person. I can testify to that. And now, you have me. We can raise him together." Mark leaned back and rested his arm on the back of her couch.

"You....you would want to raise DJ with me?"

Mark nodded. "I would. I wouldn't let you do it alone, Josephine. I'm not in this relationship short term. I'm in it for the long haul. I know we've only been together for a few months, but I truly believe you have the qualities I want in a wife. So, yes, I would help you raise DJ."

The room began to spin. This was just too much to handle in one night. Josephine didn't think she could handle anymore of this conversation.

"Mark, I don't think I can do this tonight. I am emotionally drained, and now, with all you said spinning in my mind, I need some time to think." Josephine stood up and walked toward the door.

Mark stood up, too. "I understand. Listen," he took her in his arms, "I want you to pray about what I have said. The more I think about all of this, the more I feel I am right. I think you should be the one raising DJ, and I will be here to help you. But enough said. I will let you spend time with the Lord. Pray, and I will, as well." He kissed her forehead and walked to the door. "And I know I haven't told you this yet, but I love you, Josephine."

With that, he closed the door and left her standing in the middle of her living room, shocked at his declaration of love.

Mark shut the door gently behind him. He had wondered why he had gone through so much pain and agony in his life. Now he knew. He went through all of that to help Josephine. A smile tugged at Mark's lips. It would all be worth it if he could get her to do the right thing. Mark finally had a purpose, a calling. He was excited to help lead and guide her down this road. Now, he prayed she would only let him!

Chapter 14

*J*osephine barely slept that night. She spent most of the night tossing and turning. By the time she woke up, she had bags under her eyes and her feelings were in turmoil. Claim DJ as her own son? Could she really do that to Sue and Nate? How would they respond? She promised them she would never try to take DJ back. She had all the paper work drawn up and signed. Would she be able to say she wasn't mentally sound when she signed the papers? Would that even hold up in a court of law? What would this do to her family? Would they understand? If they didn't, would they recover? Josephine slowly climbed out of bed and walked to the kitchen. Pouring herself a cup of coffee, she sighed. She sat down on the couch. Josephine tilted her head from side to side trying to ease the tension that was building in her neck. Tension filled every ounce of her being. She had never considered raising DJ as her own. The thought never occurred to her, until now.

On top of that, Mark loved her. He said so last night as he was leaving. Did she love him? If she didn't, would she want him to take that role in DJ's life? Wasn't that one of the reasons why she gave DJ up in the first place? He wouldn't have a dad. Now, with Mark in her life, he could potentially. He would have a mother *and* a father. Plus, Mark's right. She was in a better position financially, spiritually, and emotionally. She was able to give DJ all she couldn't before. Josephine groaned. With all these thoughts playing ping pong in her mind, she wasn't able to think clearly.

"Lord!" She cried and looked up. "What am I supposed to do? What do you want me to do? Do I break my promise to Sue and Nate? Do I fight them so I can raise DJ? What? Did I really hear You right? You did want me to give him up for adoption, didn't You? Jesus! I need answers! Please help me!"

When her door bell rang, she jumped. Setting down her coffee, she slowly walked to the door.

"Steven." She gave him a smile that didn't quite make it to her eyes. "What's up?"

"Hey." His soft blue eyes showed concern. "You don't look good."

Josephine gave a short laugh. "Thanks. Do you say that to all the girls?"

Steven smile and shuffled his feet. "Nah. Just the pretty ones," he responded with a wink.

"Come on in. Can I get you a cup of coffee?" She wearily walked into the living room.

"Sure. But really, what' going on?" Steven took off his coat and sat down.

"Oh, Steve, it's a long story. Do you have anywhere to be anytime soon?" She handed him his coffee and plopped down in the chair opposite him.

Steven took a sip. "Nope, no plans to be anywhere but here."

She bit her bottom lip. "Well, I ended up telling Mark about DJ last night."

Steven let out a low whistle. "How'd that go?"

"Interestingly, actually. Where do I even begin?" Josephine sat back and closed her eyes.

"Hey," Steven leaned forward. "It's not that bad, right?"

"I'm not too sure, yet. Mark doesn't hate me, so that's good."

Steven nodded and leaned back against the couch. "So, you two are still together?"

"Yeah, we are. I asked him if he thought any less of me, and he said no." Josephine felt exhausted.

"Jo, that's what you were hoping for, right?" Steven wrinkled his brow.

Josephine nodded. "But then he started bringing up things

I hadn't thought of before. He said I'm ready now to raise DJ as my own son, that spiritually, financially, and emotionally, I'm stable. And Steven, he even said he would help me raise DJ!"

"Whoa, wait a second." Steven held up his hand. "Jo, are you really considering doing that? What about Sue and Nate?"

"Well," Josephine pursed her lips together. "That's the thing. I never had thought about all of this before. I don't want to hurt Sue and Nate. I know they have spent the last few years raising him, but he is my son, right? Don't I have the right to fight for him now that I am able?"

"Jo, seriously. You really think Sue is just going to hand you over DJ? You made it legal by signing the paperwork." Steven leaned over and gently took her hand. "She's going to fight for him. Biologically, yes, you are his mom, but that's it."

"Mark feels Nate and Sue took advantage of the situation." Josephine's voice was barely above a whisper.

"I'm not following."

"I was scared. I found out I was pregnant and worried about what I was going to do. The only thing I could think of was giving the baby up for adoption. I was emotional, and as Mark said, not really in my right mind. Sue and Nate took advantage of that to get a child." Even to Josephine, this didn't sound right. "Saying it out loud doesn't sound good."

"Oh, okay. So all of this is coming from Mark. That makes more sense to me now." Comprehension crossed over Steven's face.

"What's that supposed to mean?" Josephine yanked her hand away.

"Jo, this is Sue and Nate we're talking about," Steven reminded her, sternly. "These people weren't trying to steal your son. They are your family. Why, why would they take advantage of you?"

"That's just it, friend. I know they wouldn't. That's why I am having a hard time with this. Mark says they did. He says God wouldn't want me to give up my son. But I know what I felt that day! I knew what the right thing to do was!" Tears spilled down her cheeks.

"So, what's the problem then? Why are you listening to

Mark in all of this if you know what you did was right?" Steven handed her a tissue.

She wiped her nose. "Because I am afraid if I don't fight for DJ, then I will lose Mark all together."

"Is he really worth the heart ache that is going to come if you do decide to fight for DJ?" Steven's voice was gentle.

"Steven, you told me not too long ago you were lonely." Josephine's eyes became hard. "I felt that way before Mark came along. He has been the only one who has shown any interest in me. Now you are telling me to break up with him just because he feels he is looking out for me? So I can go back to being lonely?"

"He's not the only one who has feelings for you, Jo, or who looks out for you."

Josephine narrowed her eyes. "What do you mean?" Was Steven about to declare he had feelings for her? What if he did? Could she handle any more than what she was going through already? What if Steven did have feelings for her? Would that change anything? Did she have feelings for him? Her heart beat rapidly in her chest as she waited for his answer.

Steven looked down. When he looked up at her again, his eyes said what his words didn't. "Your family cares for you. They love you more than you know. If you did go through with this, you would destroy your family."

Disappointment clouded her face. "What do you know about my family? Being around for a few months doesn't make you an expert, Steven!"

Steven's face turned red. "And the same can be said for Mark! Who does he think he is, coming into this family, thinking he knew Nate and Sue's intentions? When did he become the expert on them, Jo? Can you tell me that?" Steven eyes flashed.

"Mark is an outsider, telling me what he sees, that's all. Sometimes I need an outsider's opinion, not someone who is emotionally involved in the matter." Josephine was positively exhausted and didn't know if she wanted to discuss this any further.

"And that's what I am, Jo." Steven's voice became gentle.

"I'm here to tell you that Sue and Nate would not have taken advantage of the situation. Why would they do that?"

"Honestly, Steven, I don't think they would have intentionally taken advantage of that. Don't you think we do things without realizing the real reasons behind them?" She lifted her eyebrows, hoping to have Steven understand her point of view.

"And you honestly believe that? C'mon, Jo! Think!"

"I am thinking! At least that's what I am trying to do! Who says what I am saying isn't the truth?"

Steven sprung to his feet. "Josephine! Are you even listening to yourself? This is ludicrous! I can't believe these things are coming from your mouth!"

"Look, you came over here. I didn't ask you to come; I didn't even ask you for your opinion. You asked me what was wrong, I told you. Now you are getting upset with me? What kind of friend are you?" Blood rushed to her face.

Bewilderment was written all over his face. Steven slowly sat back down. "I guess I thought I knew you better. I thought you cared about your family."

"I do care about my family! I'm confused, and I don't know what to do! I have Mark's voice in my head. I have your voice in my head. I don't know what truth is anymore. Was it God I heard or was it me?" A groan came from deep within her. "Steven, I don't need you to sit there and judge me."

Steven sighed. "I'm not trying to judge you, Jo, honestly, I am not. I just want you to think before you decide to act. This is a big decision. You don't want to listen to Mark on everything. He doesn't know your family, and he doesn't know what really took place that day."

"And you do? How could you know what went on that day? Because your mom and dad told you? Well, I love your parents, but they don't know everything! What if I was wrong? What if God wants me to have DJ back?"

Josephine fought back the tears that threatened to spill once again. She covered her face. She knew she shouldn't be talking to Steven like this. She should be watching the words that were coming out of her mouth. But she was angry! She felt he was attacking her and Mark.

"Steven, I need you to go. I don't want to say anything else I will later regret. Please, please, just leave." She started sobbing quietly.

Steven got up, grabbed his jacket, and headed for the door. "I'm sorry, Josephine. I'm sorry I made you angry, but I think if you were to go after your son, let me rephrase that--- *Sue's* son--- you would be ripping apart a family. I don't just mean DJ, Sue, and Nate. I'm talking about your *entire* family. Before you do or say anything, please spend some time in prayer."

With that, he was gone, slamming the door behind him.

Josephine's head jerked up. *How dare he! How dare he come into my home and treat like I am some monster for thinking about wanting to be with my son! He's supposed to be my friend, Jesus! He's supposed to encourage me, not tear me down!*

Her phone rang. "Hello?" she snapped.

"Josephine? You okay?"

"Oh, hi, Sue," Josephine answered, sniffing.

"Hey, Sis, what's the matter?"

"Steven and I just had an argument." Josephine took a few deep breaths.

"You and Steven? That's odd. What happened?"

"He just thinks he knows everything. I mean, even before he left, he told me I should pray. Can you believe that? Like I am the one at fault here!"

"What was your fight even about, Jo?" Confusion drifted over the telephone line.

"I don't want to get into it right now, Anyway," she added, changing the subject, "what's up?"

"Oh, DJ wanted to know if you could come over today so he can show you his blanket. He's really excited about it! And he loved how excited you were about it, too!"

Josephine smiled. DJ wanted her to come over? That made her heart a little lighter.

"DJ wants me to come over? You tell that sweet boy that yes, I will be there!"

She arrived at Sue's in just a few minutes. Walking into

her house, Josephine heard laughter coming from DJ's room. She tiptoed toward his room, to see what the laughter was all about. Josephine peered around the door frame, careful not to be seen.

DJ was hiding under his new blanket. Sue was pretending not to know where DJ was. She would look around the room, and say aloud, "Hm. I wonder where DJ went. Did he go to work with Daddy?" DJ would giggle under the blanket. Sue walked over to the blanket. "Wow! This blanket looks so comfortable. Maybe I should lay on it and take a little nap!" Sue slowly knelt down beside the blanket. Then she put her head right on the lump that was DJ. DJ's giggle was muffled under the blanket.

"Mommy! It's me! I under the bwanket!" DJ called out.

Sue sat up, looking around confused. "I heard DJ's voice. Where did it come from?

DJ peered out from under the blanket. "Here I am!"

He threw his arms around Sue's neck and they fell backwards, laughing.

Josephine watched this interaction, her feelings all jumbled up inside of her. What was she thinking? Could she really take DJ away from Sue, after all she had done for her? Could she really separate this family? How would DJ handle that? How would Sue and Nate handle that? Josephine leaned against the wall, wondering if perhaps Mark was wrong on this. She just couldn't see herself causing so much pain and devastation to her entire family. She shook her head. In time, if she fought to take DJ back, wouldn't he forget that Sue and Nate were ever his parents? Josephine imagined herself playing with DJ like Sue had been. Her stomach was in knots. She didn't know what to do just yet, but for now, he was her nephew, and no more than that.

When she had control of her feelings, she walked into the room. "What's all the noise about?"

DJ jumped up. "Auntie Jo!" He ran to her and threw his arms around her waist. "You came!"

Josephine scooped him up and swung him around. "Of course I came! One of my favorite nephews asks me to come over to see his new blanket. I am definitely going to come over and see it!"

DJ ran over and grabbed his blanket. "See? Supa-man! I wuv it!"

"I can see that!" Josephine touched the fabric, realizing all the time and energy Sue had spent in making it. Her heart was suddenly pierced with guilt.

Sue got up off the floor. "Hey, Sis. You look better than you sounded earlier."

"Yeah. I feel better. I need to call Steven and apologize to him. When it comes down to it, the argument wasn't really his fault. It was mine. I think I got defensive too early on in our conversation." Josephine took DJ's hand. "Hey, don't you have those special cookies downstairs?"

"The cookies?" DJ's eyes lit up. "Mommy, can we have some?"

Sue gave Josephine a reprimanding look. "We do have the cookies downstairs. But did you eat all of your lunch?"

DJ looked at the floor. "No."

Josephine spoke up. "But, Mommy, his auntie is over. Couldn't you just let this slide this one time?"

Sue rolled her eyes. Giving DJ a stern look, she added, "You are lucky, pal, that Auntie Jo is here today. You may have one cookie, and only one!"

Josephine shot Sue a grin over her shoulder. "Sweet. Let's go, buddy!"

Josephine and DJ walked hand in hand down the stairs and to the kitchen. She took out the cookies and two cups for milk.

"Mm," she said between bites. "These are yummy cookies. Which ones are you favorites?"

DJ cocked his head to one side. "The mint ones!"

Josephine smiled. "Those are mine, too. I love these cookies!"

"So, Jo," Sue began, "you really think the argument was your fault?"

Josephine nodded slowly as Sue sat down at the kitchen table. "I do. I hear what he's saying now, but at the time, oh, he made me so mad!"

"Are you sure you don't want to tell me what the fight was about? You really struck my curiosity!" Sue leaned forward in anticipation.

Josephine shook her head. "No. I don't really want to get into it. Let's just say I really do need to spend some time in prayer."

"Auntie Jo, wanna play outside?" DJ finished his milk and wiped his mouth with the back of his hand.

"You bet!" Josephine jumped up and grabbed a ball to play catch with DJ.

Josephine spent the rest of the afternoon at Sue's. When DJ went down for a nap, Josephine sat down on Sue's couch, a glass of water in her hand.

"So, what's been going on, Sis?" Josephine took a sip of her water.

Sue smiled excitedly and took a deep breath. "Well," she began, "Nate and I have begun the international process of adopting!"

Josephine's eyes grew wide. "Really? What made you guys decide that?"

"Well, when DJ was one, we knew it was time to begin the process, since it can take time. We really wanted DJ to have siblings, even if they are from different countries. We've been working with an agency for over a year. Now, we have to go through the house inspection again, making sure everything is safe still. We have been assigned to a social worker already, and our agency is looking over our paper work, as well as the orphanage in Ethiopia."

"Why haven't you said anything before now?" Josephine rested her head on her hand.

Sue smiled sadly. "I have known so many people who have wanted to adopt internationally, and it took years, years to even get the process started. I didn't want to say anything, and then have nothing to report. We did tell the Sorenson's because they watched DJ for us while we were going to the classes and stuff. Brittany asked during the boys' birthday party, so she knows, too. I asked her not to say anything, though. But since things are moving smoothly, I thought I ought to tell you and get you ready for another little one!"

"Wow, Sue! This is huge! The Sorensons are great secret keepers! They never said a word to anyone, not even Steven! He would have told me for sure! And Brittany! Wow! She's good! So, what age group are you thinking about?"

"Nate and I really want DJ to be the oldest. We're thinking maybe a one year old or a baby." Sue sat back, her eyes shining. "It's an amazing thing, knowing we can give another child hope!"

Sue's phone rang. "Excuse me, Jo. I should grab that."

"Sure, Sue, no problem."

Josephine leaned forward, placing her chin in her hand. Would taking DJ back be a good thing? Would it cause harm to her relationship with her sisters? Would it be worth all the pain she would put everyone through? With the new information about Sue and Nate adopting, what impact would fighting for DJ make? Josephine shook her head and sighed. Is she really in a place to raise a child? She knew Mark said he would help, but what if things didn't work out with Mark? What if he decided somewhere down the road he didn't want her or DJ? Then where would she be? And what if she decided Mark wasn't the one for her? Would having him in DJ's life for only a short time be a good thing or would it cause more harm to DJ? Josephine was more confused now than ever!

Just then, Sue sat down across from her, in a sort of daze.

Setting aside her own thoughts, Josephine's face showed concern for her sister. "Sue? What is it?"-

"That was the agency. They've found a child for us to adopt."

Josephine jumped up and hugged her sister. "That's great! Sue! How wonderful!"

"It is wonderful. But there's more."

Josephine wrinkled her brow. "More? What do you mean?"

Sue spoke slowly. "Well, the little boy has a sister- baby-to be exact!"

"Wait a second!" Josephine held up her hand. "You're telling me the agency found you siblings to adopt? What are the ages?"

"The little boy is almost two, and the little girl is not even one yet!" Sue's head fell back. "I can't believe this! I don't know. I know I need to talk with Nate about it all, but three kids under three? And a little girl on top of that? I always thought we would adopt boys!"

"Sue, if there is anyone who could handle three kids under three it would be you!" Josephine encouraged her sister. "You should call Nate and talk with him about it! I will leave you to pray and talk with Nate. Let me know what you decide, but I think, no, I know you can do it!"

Josephine kissed Sue on the cheek, grabbed her purse, and walked out the door.

Lord, please give Sue and Nate wisdom on what to do! She silently and quickly prayed.

As she drove away, she knew she needed to talk with Steven. Glancing at her watch, she knew exactly what she needed to do.

She also knew she needed to spend time in prayer. Whether or not she would fight to take DJ back was a big decision that she didn't want to make without first talking things over with God and counting the cost of what it would do to her family.

Sue didn't move. Three? Three kids under three? Could she do it? Is this what the Lord really wanted? She wanted to laugh and cry at the same time. Sue covered her face with her hands as the tears slid down her cheeks. This was amazing news! Never would she have thought that she would be a mom of three in less than four years! When Sue and Nate began dating, he was upfront with her about him not being able to have kids. It pierced her heart, not being able to go through pregnancy and having the bond that occurs between a child and its mother during that time. However, the Lord had shown her she could still have that bond. She had once heard that adoption means growing inside of your mother's heart instead of her body. Sue loved that definition! She could bond with a child knowing that she and Nate picked them specifically to be their child. God had worked so much on her heart. When she had told Nate a few weeks later it didn't matter if they could have kids of their own,

Nate practically wept with delight! He talked about adoption, and from the very beginning they had been on the same page, both wanting to adopt internationally. Josephine had thrown a wrench in their plans, but they were okay with that. When they decided to begin the adoption process again, they figured it would take a long time to find a child they could adopt. Now, here they were, a little over a year later, and not only could they possibly adopt one child, but two! Sue laughed joyously! What a wonderful opportunity for them! Standing up, Sue headed to the kitchen to call Nate. The sooner they could talk and pray about this the better. Sue picked up the phone and dialed his work number.

"Honey, you better be sitting down!" Sue giggled. "Have I got some news for you!"

Chapter 15

Steven paced back and forth in the living room. His mind was reeling from his conversation with Josephine. Pausing in front of the sliding glass door, he ran his fingers through his hair in frustration. He had the perfect opportunity to tell her how he felt. She talked about being lonely, and if she broke up with Mark, she would have no one. He had sat on her couch, wrestling with his feelings. He desperately wanted to take her in his arms and tell her that he cared for her. He would be there for her. Steven went to Josephine's to see how she was doing after the previous night. He hadn't expected her to pour her heart out to him about her feelings of loneliness. He suddenly found himself faced with telling her the truth. Somewhere in the course of their friendship, his feelings for her had begun to change. He didn't know exactly how or when. Perhaps it was the many phone conversations they had shared. Or maybe it was all the time they spent together. She had gone shopping with him on several occasions, helping him buy things for the house and getting the basement set up as a recreation room. He thought back to their talks about Jesus and the life He called them to live. He and Josephine had connected in so many ways. But how was he supposed to tell her how much he admired her and wanted them to be more than friends when she was dating Mark? He just couldn't. He knew it was the right thing to do, to keep his feelings to himself. Then there was Mark. Mark. His name sounded bitter on Steven's tongue! He was never too fond of Mark but even less now! How could he even suggest to Josephine that she take DJ back? What right did he have? Steven turned away from the sliding glass door and slumped down on the couch. Mark was quick to blame Sue and Nate. He judged their actions and motives without knowing anything about them. Steven shook his head, sadness filling his soul. Why would Josephine even listen to Mark? Steven already knew the answer to that. She was letting her loneliness control her actions yet again, just like she had done with her one-night stand with Jim. If there was only some way Steven could get through to Josephine. Make her realize the reason she was considering taking DJ back was because of her loneliness. But fighting for DJ wouldn't solve her ache, would it?

Then there was Nate and Sue to think about. Nate, Sue, and DJ would be devastated. Looking up to heaven, he sighed. His heart was in agony, and it wasn't even his family who could be torn apart. He had half a mind to go over to Mark's place and punch him in the nose. Steven knew, though, that would not be the right thing to do. James 1:19 came into his head. "Let every man be quick to hear, slow to speak, and slow to get angry. For the anger of man does not produce God's righteousness." Steven stood up, not sure what to do. Now, he was fuming and frustrated and down right disappointed. *Ugh!* He groaned. What was he supposed to do now?

Needing to do something, Steven walked into the kitchen. He loved cooking and baking, and since he needed to keep himself busy, he decided to do a little of both. He took out ingredients to one of his favorite desserts. If nothing else, he was going to show Sue and Nate how much he loved them by baking them a mouth watering cake! Rummaging through his kitchen as he prepared the cake was a good distraction. He finally placed the cake in the oven, and was about to take out makings for his dinner when the door bell rang. He contemplated not answering since he wasn't in the mood for guests, but changed his mind. Whoever it was would know he was home by his car out front. He had forgotten to put it into the garage when he first came home.

Wiping his hands on a dish towel, Steven walked to the door.

"Jo!" Steven didn't know what else to say. He wasn't in the mood for another heated discussion. He sighed inwardly. He noticed she had a pizza box in her hand. "What are you doing here?"

Josephine smiled sheepishly. "Hey. I brought this as a peace offering." She handed him the pizza.

Steven tentatively took the pizza box from her hand. "You didn't have to do this." He stepped aside as she swept past him, her perfume lingering behind her.

"Open it."

Steven slowly opened the lid and saw written in pepperoni slices, "I am sorry."

He chuckled softly. "How did you manage to pull that off?"

"I just asked the employee helping me very nicely, that's all." Josephine stepped closer to him. "It's true, though. What it says. I really am sorry."

Steven looked down at her, studying her features. He brushed her hair away from her face. He suddenly felt himself getting lost in her beautiful eyes. Steven needed to get some distance between them. "Are you hungry? Should we eat this before it gets too cold?"

Josephine followed him into the kitchen and took out two plates. "Sure. So, will you forgive me?"

Steven nodded his back to her. "Of course I do." He knew they needed to talk some more about their conversation. Maybe he would be able to tell her his thoughts on her loneliness. He silently prayed for wisdom.

"Mm. Something smells good. Whatcha baking?" Josephine peered into the oven.

"I'm making chocolate cake for Sue and Nate. I thought they might like something yummy."

"I see." Josephine filled two glasses with soda. Steven watched her as she walked into the dining room, noting how well she fit in at his house. *Stop it, Steven!* he chastised himself.

"I was over there today." Josephine sat down at the table.

"Really?" Steven tried to hide his shock. "Why?"

"Well, I got a call from Sue today," Josephine began.

"Wait," Steven said holding up his hand. "Let's pray before we continue our conversation." Steven bowed his head and prayed. When he was finished, he continued. "So, what did you go there for?"

"DJ wanted to show me his new blanket. I thought it would be fun to play with him for a bit." Josephine took a bite of the pizza.

"Hm. How did that go?"

"It went well. After DJ went down for a nap, Sue told me she and Nate have begun the adoption process internationally."

"Good for them! I wondered how long it would take for them to adopt again!" Steven could see she was struggling with what to say next.

Finally, Josephine put her thoughts into words. "I always thought DJ would be enough."

"It isn't that DJ isn't enough. Trust me. Coming from an only child, DJ would much rather have a sibling!" Steven shook his head. "It gets pretty lonely being an only child."

"Hm. I guess I had never thought of that. The interesting thing is, while I was there, Sue got a call from the agency. They had sent Sue and Nate a few pictures of the kids they are going to adopt. Siblings! I can hardly believe it. Anyway, it appears the adoption could take place sooner than they thought."

"How old are they?" Steven set down the pizza.

"The little boy is almost two, and the little girl isn't quite one yet."

"Three under three? Sounds tough, but she can do it!"

Josephine laughed. "That's what I said!"

Steven was amazed at how much they thought alike. He and Josephine seemed to be on the same page about most things. They had their differences for sure, but he enjoyed the fact that they seemed to have the same ideas and interests. He needed to say something before she questioned his silence. "Do they have everything in order? Visas, etc.?"

"I don't know. They've been going through this for a while, so I assume so."

"Good." Steven knew it was time to bring up their conversation. "And what about you? Have you been praying more about your idea since this morning?"

She shrugged her shoulders. "Off and on. I don't know, Steven. I need more time to think about it before I make any real decisions."

Steven placed his elbows on the table. Leaning forward, he said softly, "Count the cost, Jo. Think about all the pain that could come from your decision. And remember, not much has changed from when you gave DJ up in the first place." Josephine shook her head emphatically.

"Not true. I'm stronger now. I am more firm in my faith. I am better off financially. Plus, I have Mark. He said he would help me as much as he could."

"Ok. I see I'm wrong in regards to you spiritually, financially, and emotionally. Just because Mark is there now doesn't mean he will be in the future. You admitted to me not too long ago you didn't know if he was the one for you or not. Do you really want a string of men walking in and out of DJ's life? Don't you want more stability than that, especially for DJ?"

Josephine's eyes drifted to her plate. She was quiet for a moment. "I do want more than that for DJ. That's why I gave him up in the first place. But what if Mark is the one for me?"

"That's a big what if, Josephine." Steven tilted his chair back on its hind legs and put his hands behind his head. .

Josephine looked down and began playing with her crust. "I know. My thoughts are still all jumbled. I haven't made any decisions yet, Steve. Just know that I hear you and will take what you are saying into consideration, ok?"

Steven let the chair drop and placed his elbows on the table. "Jo, you mentioned today you didn't want to be alone. Don't let that be the deciding factor in your decision. You don't want to settle on dating Mark just because you are afraid to be alone. You know what I mean?"

Josephine tilted her head sideways. "I hate loneliness, Steven. I hate coming home to an empty house. I know I haven't dated much before Mark in the last two years, but it feels right having someone by my side. What if this is the way I am supposed to finally have my own family?"

Steven shook his head gently. "Not this way, friend. God

wouldn't want you to settle on someone just so you won't be lonely. He wants the best for you. Tearing apart your family by trying to take DJ away from his parents isn't what is best for you. I think deep down inside, you know that."

"Maybe I do." Josephine sighed heavily. "But what about dating? Is there someone out there for me, really?"

Steven placed his hand over hers. "There is, I can promise you that."

"Who? Who, if not Mark?" Josephine's eyes pleaded for an answer.

Steven rubbed the back of his neck and sighed. "Josephine, why are you so focused on who to date?"

"I'm tired of being alone, Steven. I want what your parents have and what my sisters have. I want that companionship. I want to feel like I am adored by someone. I want to be loved and valued and cherished. Mark makes me feel special. He even said he loves me." Tears filled her eyes.

Steven's eyes widened. "Really? I didn't know that."

Josephine raked her hand through her hair. "He just told me last night."

Steven rubbed his chin thoughtfully. "How do you feel?"

Josephine huffed. "I'm not in love with him, I know that."

Relief flooded through Steven. "I don't know if you are to marry Mark or not. I don't know what the future holds for you, my friend. I can tell you I value you and your friendship. I cherish you and desire the best for you. Can I give you some friendly advice?"

When Josephine nodded, Steven continued, "Instead of looking to a man for what you desire, look to Jesus. He can fill that void. I know He isn't here physically, but He is here. He adores you more than Mark and more than I do. You are the apple of His eye. I know that you are lonely. But no man is going to fill that void which only the Lord Himself can fill. I think once you have that figured out and allow Him to be your everything, the rest will fall into place. Now, as for DJ, please, I beg you, don't do anything rash. Pray about it."

Josephine stood to clear the table. "I will. I won't do anything just yet. I promise you that much."

Steven nodded firmly. "Good. Now, how about a mean game of Wii?" Steven suggested playfully.

"Ohhhh! You are on! You are so going down!"

An hour later, Josephine drove home and Steven drove over to Nate and Sue's, cake setting next to him. He was glad Josephine had come by and apologized. His heart was still uneasy about her fighting for DJ, but he knew it was best to leave his troubles in the loving hands of his Heavenly Father. He knew he had the perfect chance to tell her his feelings. Steven really wanted to let her know she had another admirer, someone who wanted to date her. But he didn't feel the timing was right.

And timing, particularly in this situation, was everything.

Sue opened her door, a beautiful smiling lighting up her face.

"Steven!" she exclaimed giving him a hug. "It is so nice to see you! Come on in!"

Steven smiled in return. "Thanks. I hope I'm not interrupting anything."

"Not at all. What brings you by?" Sue ushered him into the living room.

"I was thinking about you guys today, and I thought I would make you a little something to enjoy." Steven handed her the cake.

"Oh, this looks fantastic!" Sue licked her lips.

Nate walked in from the kitchen. "Steven!" he said happily. "How's it goin'?"

"Good, thanks. You guys seem like you are in a great mood!" Steven sat down.

"I'm going to go cut this up and pass it out. I'll let Nate fill you in," Sue winked at Nate.

Steven looked around. "Where is little DJ?"

Sue called over her shoulder, "We put him to bed early today."

Nate grinned. "It's been an exciting day around here," he began. "We have been going through the process of adopting internationally, and it looks as if the brother and sister we are going to adopt are almost ready for us to pick up."

"Yeah. I heard somethin' about that today."

"You did?" Nate appeared confused. "How? We just found out today."

"Jo came by today and told me all about it. I guess she was here when Sue got the call." Steven crossed his leg.

"Did I hear you say Jo came by your house today?" Sue walked into the room with a tray in her hands.

"Yes you did." Steven answered, taking a plate from her.

"So you worked everything out then? The two of you are fine?" She sat down and took a bite of her cake. "This is excellent, Steven!"

Steven shifted uncomfortably. "Thanks. You, you knew we had an argument?"

"Uh-huh. I am just glad you two worked it out. It's never a good thing to let an argument last a long time. It does more harm than good," Sue advised.

"I knew Josephine had come over today, but I had no idea she told you about our disagreement." Steven was shocked Josephine had mentioned anything to Sue. It made him uncomfortable. She should have prayed more about her dilemma before talking with Sue about it. He sighed. "I must admit, I am a little surprised."

"You're surprised she told Sue she had a fight with you? Why?" Nate took a gulp of his milk.

"Well, I didn't know she was ready to go public with it yet. She told me she would spend time in prayer." Steven shook his head. "How do you feel about it?"

Sue knit her eyebrows together. "I'm not sure, to tell you the truth. I was a little surprised, but I am glad she is thinking things through and coming to her own conclusions."

Steven's eyes grew wide. "Ok. Hold on a second. You're glad she's thinking things through?"

Sue laughed. "Of course! With Jo, she is so impulsive, as I am sure you gathered from your argument. So, it made me happy when she told me what she needed to do."

"Sue! I'm shocked!" Steven couldn't stop the

disappointment from coming through his words. "You would be fine with her decision?"

"I don't understand." Confusion danced its way across her face.

"Mark is trying to talk Jo into taking DJ back and you're okay with that?"

"What??" Nate and Sue said in unison.

"What do you mean, what? You said she told you about her decision."

"Yes. Her decision to apologize to you and to tell you she was wrong. She never told me what the argument was about. Steven, what's going on?" Sue said slowly.

Steven groaned. "Oh, Lord, what I have done?" He put his head in his hands.

Nate stood up and walked over to Steven. Placing a hand on Steven's shoulder, he said gently, but firmly,

"Steven, what's happening here? I'm in the dark, and you seem to be the one who can shed a little light on this situation for me. What did you say Mark was trying to get Jo to do?"

"Oh my gosh, you guys. I am so sorry! I thought she had told you all of this, and I was shocked. I should have asked more questions before saying anything. It's just that, nothing made sense, Sue." Steven quickly added, "I thought she told you everything, and you were ok with it all. I couldn't believe you would be so willing to give up your son!"

Sue's hand flew to her heart. "I'm not okay with giving up my son!"

"I can see that now," Steven whispered. "What was I thinking?"

"Steven, I'm still not understanding." Nate walked back over to Sue and sat down.

Steven told them about how he had dropped by Josephine's and she informed him of her discussion with Mark. He explained how he and Josephine argued, and how she came and apologized for the things she said.

"Did she say if she was going to go through with it, though?" Fear and anger colored Nate's eyes.

Steven glanced from Sue to Nate and shook his head sadly. "No. She didn't."

Throughout listening to Steven, Sue's face went from ash white to beet red. "How dare she!" She slammed her fist on the arm of the couch. "She came over here today, doesn't say a single word about any of this, listens to me about adopting again, and is still considering taking DJ away from us? How could she?" Sue cried, tears streaming down her face.

"You said, Steven, Mark was the one who put the thought in her head?" Nate's eyes were hard and full of anger.

Steven nodded. "Yep. But listen, guys, Josephine wouldn't do that, would she? I mean, just because Mark put the idea in her head, she wouldn't listen to him, right?"

"I don't know. Josephine is quite impulsive. If she's afraid of losing Mark, she might do anything to keep him, including something like this." Sue wiped her eyes with the back of her hand.

Nate stood up and began pacing the floor. "Oh, if I knew where he lived, I would go over to Mark's and give him a piece of my mind!"

Steven chuckled bitterly. "You are a better man than I, Nate. I wanted to punch him in the nose!"

Sue laughed despite the tears still streaming down her cheeks. "Thanks, Steven."

"So, what are you guys going to do?"

"We need to spend time in prayer, that's for sure," Nate said, finally sitting down.

Steven leaned forward, his elbows resting on his knees. "Listen, if you need to tell her I told you about this, please do. I shouldn't have told you in the first place. If she gets angry with me, I will deal with that."

"Thanks, Steven, we appreciate that." Nate glanced at Sue. "But, as angry and upset as I am right now, I think we need to pray. Let's take it before the Lord and leave it there. We will see what He tells us to do."

Sue nodded slowly. "I agree. I don't want to, but I agree."

"Then let's take it to Jesus now." Steven gathered around his friends, placing a hand on each of their shoulders.

Sue and Nate bowed their heads, and for the next twenty minutes, all three were in agreement before the Lord.

When Steven left that night, he felt a surge of different emotions. He felt heartbroken for telling Nate and Sue about Josephine, and he felt strangely at peace, knowing God was going to work through this situation, no matter what the results.

The next morning, Josephine woke up to the sound of her phone ringing.

"Hello?" She rubbed her sleepy eyes.

"Good morning, beautiful. Did I wake you?"

"Yeah, Mark, but it's all right.

"Well, since you are awake, can I come by and take you to breakfast?"

Josephine blinked her eyes, adjusting to the sunlight shining through her window. "Sure. How long do I have to get ready?"

"Actually, I am outside your front door. Just let me in, and I'll wait while you get ready."

Josephine laughed. "Ok. I'll be right there."

Josephine got out of bed, and slowly walked to the front door. "Hey there! I didn't hear from you at all yesterday."

Kissing her on the cheek, he smiled. "I wanted to give you time to think about what we talked about. But let's not get into that now. Let's talk more at breakfast. Go get ready." He gently pushed her toward her room.

"Okay, okay! I'm going! I'll be out in a few minutes."

A few minutes later, they were on their way to the restaurant. Once they were seated, Mark began asking her questions.

"So, what do you think? Have you given it any thought?"

"I have. I don't know, Mark. Yesterday, DJ called and asked if I could come over and see his new blanket. I walked in and headed upstairs. I saw Sue playing so sweetly with him! It was a very tender moment between the two of them. I just don't think I can take him away from her and Nate." Josephine's eyes were troubled. She sipped her coffee and continued, "I really think he is better off with Nate and Sue."

Mark gently took hold of Josephine's hand. "I know you are very sensitive in regards to this whole thing, Josephine. Sue's your sister, after all. What do you feel in your heart?"

Josephine shook her head. "That's just it. My heart tells me he is better off with Nate and Sue. I don't have that much to offer him."

Mark cocked his head to one side. "But you do. I think you aren't giving yourself enough credit, Jo. You are an amazing woman! You are strong in the Lord, doing great financially, and you have me to help you along the way."

"Mark, what if you aren't around anymore? What if we don't work out?"

"Oh Josephine," Mark's eyes grew soft. "I'm not planning on going anywhere. I'll be here for the long haul."

"Thanks, Mark. I don't know, though. When I was there yesterday, seeing Sue and DJ, and then hearing about Sue's new adoption, I just kept thinking that what I decided a few years ago was the right choice."

Mark's eyes narrowed.

"What do you mean new adoption?"

"Nate and Sue have started the adoption process internationally. While I was there, she got a call saying the agency saying they need to be ready to pick up the kids soon."

"What? DJ's not enough for them?" Sarcasm tinted his voice.

"I thought that at first, too. Then, I realized that of course they would want to adopt again. It's always been a dream of theirs to adopt internationally." Josephine set her coffee cup down.

"Okay. So you said they are adopting siblings?"

"Yep. A boy and a girl." Josephine took a bite of her food.

"Josephine! This is great! Don't you see?"

Josephine wiped her mouth with her napkin. "Don't I see what?"

"This could be an answer to prayer! If they adopt siblings, they don't really need to have DJ, right? They would still have two kids!" Mark was enthusiastic. "I knew God wanted you to fight for your son! This just proves it!"

"I'm sorry, Mark. I am having a hard time following what you mean." Josephine wasn't sure she wanted to find out. She suddenly felt uneasy.

"One reason you wouldn't want to take DJ from them is because you wouldn't want to leave them childless, right?" When Josephine nodded, he continued, "All right. So yesterday, you found out that they are adopting again. Now, you probably wouldn't want to leave the adopted child without a sibling. Now you won't have to! The two kids will have each other, and Sue and Nate won't need to have DJ around! Don't you get it?"

Josephine set down her fork. Understanding crossed her face. "I think I am beginning to. But I am not sure if I want to take DJ back just because they adopt two more kids."

Josephine shook her head slowly. "But Mark, this doesn't feel right. I don't want to fight for DJ because I know he belongs with Sue and Nate. That's why I gave him up in the first place."

Mark placed his hand over Josephine's. "Sweetie, just keep an open mind. By them adopting the siblings, maybe this is God's way to show you He wants you to have DJ back."

"I know what God wanted, Mark." Josephine's defenses rose. "I know He wanted me to give him up."

Mark squeezed her hand. "I think you were too emotional to know what God was saying to you, sweetie."

Josephine felt her cheeks grow warm. She kept her voice low, but it was tense.

"Mark, you don't know what I was feeling then!"

"I'm not doubting your relationship with God, Josephine. I'm just saying that you had recently come back to know the Lord. Sometimes, it's hard to tell what He wants when we are so new in walking with Him. Listen, let's drop the discussion for now. But continue to pray about it, all right?"

Josephine took a deep breath. "Okay. We'll drop it for now."

Josephine ate her breakfast in silence. What Mark was saying, was it true? Was she too new in her walk with Jesus that she didn't hear Him correctly? Could that really be the truth? She was more confused than ever. Her head swam with unanswered questions. She didn't know who to turn to. She couldn't go to Sue or Nate because then she would have to tell them everything. Same for Brittany and Luke. The Sorensons were always a possibility. They never judged her in recent choices. Maybe she would talk with them or Steven. She needed to sort things out and soon.

Her life was getting more complicated as each day passed.

Chapter 16

Sue opened her Bible, but her mind wouldn't focus. Flipping the pages of her journal, she tried to start writing, but all she could think about was Josephine. Sue was still reeling from the news Steven had given them a few days beforehand. She went through several different emotions: anger, betrayal, hurt, sadness, fear. Sue was an emotional wreck. She didn't want to call Brittany. She knew that if she were to tell Brittany, Brittany would step in and confront Josephine. Sue had gone before the Lord over the last few days, but she still didn't feel at peace. Closing her Bible in frustration, Sue grabbed the phone and dialed.

"Kayla?" she asked as soon as she heard her friend's voice.

"Sue, my friend! How are you?"

"Ugh. I've been better. What are you doing in about an hour?" Sue was desperate to talk to someone.

"Nothing. Why? What's up?" Concern traced her voice.

"I'll explain when we see each other. Would you and Taylor mind coming over here? I'll put on some coffee and throw some cookies in the oven."

"No problem, Sue. We'll be there in a bit. See you soon."

Sue got up. Kayla was such a great friend. She knew her friend would give her wisdom. A smile tugged at Sue's lips, thinking how precious her friend and her family were to Sue. And now that Kayla was four months pregnant, DJ and the new little ones would have a new friend to play with. Sue went to find DJ. He was playing quietly in his room.

"Honey, would you like to see Taylor today?"

"Taylor? Yay! Taylor!" DJ jumped up and down.

"Let's go downstairs and make some cookies for you two.".Sue picked up DJ and gave him a big hug. "When they get here, Mommy and Kay are going to spend time talking. Will you play nicely with Taylor?"

DJ nodded his eyes wide and serious. "I make sure Taylor and I play nice, Mommy."

Sue laughed. "Thank you, honey. Now, let's go make some cookies!"

DJ giggled with delight. "Yeah!"

Sue enjoyed every moment baking with DJ. He was so fun to watch. He sat on the counter while she put the ingredients together. She let him add the chocolate chips, and then let him lick the spoon. Every moment she spent with him she treasured in her heart, not knowing what her future held.

A little while later, her doorbell rang. DJ went running to the door first, followed by Sue.

"Hi Taylor!" DJ gave his friend a hug.

"Daniel James!" Taylor squeezed him tightly. She was the only one who would not call him DJ. DJ loved it!

"Friend!" Sue welcomed her friend inside.

"Sue! You look like you haven't slept in a few days!" Kayla hugged Sue.

"Kids, why don't you go on upstairs? Play nicely, ok?" Sue ruffled DJ's hair.

After getting her friend a cup of coffee with a few cookies, Sue sank down onto the sofa next to Kayla.

"What's going on? Why the long face? Are you and Nate ok?" Kayla took a bite of the cookie.

"We're fine. It's just-- just--" Sue couldn't continue without tears spilling down her cheeks.

Kayla reached over and grabbed her friend's hand, not saying anything. When Sue had composed herself enough to talk, she replayed the events from the other night. Kayla's expression showed shock, then anger. Sue grabbed a tissue and wiped her eyes.

"I just don't know what to do," she confessed. "A part of me wants to run over there and shake Josephine. I want to remind her of her promise that once she agreed to this, there was no going back. I want to cry with her, asking her why she would even entertain Mark's crazy thoughts. Then I want to smack Mark upside his knuckle brained head! We welcomed him into our family, and this is what he does? Ugh!"

Kayla drew a deep breath. "I understand your feelings of frustration. What does Brit say about all this?"

Sue shook her head. "I haven't told her yet. I don't want her intervening. I know she would. I also don't want Josephine to feel like we are ganging up on her. That would drive her further away, and who knows what she would do then?"

"And you said you told her about the adoption coming up? With the kids, I mean?"

"I did! She just sat there, not saying a word! That's aggravating, too! She could have told me what she was thinking, after all." Sue groaned and sipped her coffee.

"Well, I see why she didn't say anything. I mean, would you want to tell me you were thinking about taking Taylor away if you were her biological mother? Maybe she's still praying about it and will come to the conclusion that it isn't a good idea," Kayla added hopefully.

Sue nodded. "That is a possibility. I guess I am just thinking the worst. What if she decides to fight for DJ? What if I lose him? He's my son, Kay! I know I didn't give birth to him, but he is a part of me. My mind just automatically goes to the worst case scenario. I shouldn't do that, I know. It's just so hard! I don't want to lose my baby, Kayla."

Kayla's eyes were sympathetic as she reached for her friend's hand. "You shouldn't let your mind go there, I agree. Don't let your mind go to the worst case scenario. Just remember Philippians 4:8

"Finally, brothers, whatever is true, whatever is honorable, whatever is right, whatever is pure, whatever is lovely, whatever is of good report, if there is any excellence and if anything worthy of praise, dwell on these things."

Sue's eyes swelled up with tears again. "Thanks, Kay. I appreciate you more than you know!"

Kayla's eyes were moist. "I am so glad we met at the adoption support group! That was a blessing to me, you have no idea!"

"I feel the same way!" Sue nodded. "So, how does Taylor feel about having a little sibling on the way?" Sue needed to change the subject.

Kayla patted her stomach. "She is absolutely thrilled! She can hardly believe it! By the time this little one is born, they will be almost three years apart. I think any more than that wouldn't be good."

"I understand. If the adoption goes through with the siblings, then we will have three under three! Can you believe that?" Sue laughed. "I may go out of my mind!"

"I guess it could be worse. The kids could be twins!" Kayla giggled.

"Can I get you some more coffee?" Sue offered. "It's decaf, you know."

"I know. I would love some, thank you!"

The two friends chatted for a few more minutes before they heard feet running down the stairs.

"Is it cookie time, Mommy?" DJ peered down the stairs carefully.

Sue nodded her head. "Yes, sweetie, it is!"

She poured two glasses of milk and put some cookies on a plate. The kids sat at the table, talking and laughing and eating. Sue smiled, listening to their conversation.

"My mommy's giving me a little sister," Taylor sang happily.

"My mommy's giving me a sister and a brother," DJ retorted.

Taylor gave him a doubtful smile. "Her tummy's not big."

"That's cuz our babies are in Africa." DJ took a sip of his milk, a mustache outlining his upper lip.

"Really, Mommy? Is that true?" Taylor looked doubtfully at her mom.

Kayla nodded. "Yes, Tay, it is. They are going to have little ones in their home, too! Isn't that exciting?"

Taylor clapped her hands. "Yay for us! We get to be big brothers and sisters!"

DJ clapped, too. "Yay for us!" he mimicked.

Sue and Kayla laughed. They spent the rest of the day together. By the time good-byes were said, Sue was feeling a hundred percent better. She knew she didn't need to worry about what the future held. No matter what, God would see her through. Her mind would dwell on Philippians 4:8.

Nate walked in just as the phone rang. Sue gave him a quick kiss and answered the phone.

"Sandy!" Sue said, smiling at Nate. "How are you?"

Sue was quiet. She glanced over at Nate, her eyes as wide as saucers.

"What is it?" Nate mouthed.

Sue held up her hand. "That soon? Really? No, I don't think it'll be a problem. I need to talk with Nate. Can I call you right back? At this number? Great. Thanks, Sandy."

"What?" Nate asked, sitting down at the kitchen table.

"It appears we need to be getting some plane tickets!" Sue couldn't contain the excitement in her voice.

"Why?" Nate was confused.

"The kids' paper work has gone through. Everything is all set. We need to be in Ethiopia by next Sunday!"

Nate jumped up and swung Sue around. "Really? I mean, really?"

Sue giggled. "Yes! Can you get the time off?"

Nate set Sue down. "I had already talked with my boss and let him know that any day now we could be getting the call. He said it was fine, just let him know! This is great, Sue! Do we take DJ with us?"

Sue nodded. "Yes. Sandy thinks we should take him since we will be there for two weeks."

Nate sat down again. "I'm glad she said that! I didn't want to experience this without him. He's going to be affected by this as much as we are! Oh, honey, this is wonderful!"

"I know! Let me call Sandy, and I will get all the information from her. Then we need to jump online and get some tickets booked! We have a lot of shopping to do this week!" Sue smiled. A few hours ago, her heart was in turmoil. Now, she was beyond thrilled!

Nate smiled back. "Ask Sandy what the sizes of the kids are! I want to go shopping for some clothes, too. I want to make this feel like it is their home. I can hardly wait!"

Sue was already writing down the information Sandy was giving her. She and Nate booked the flight, and then Sue called Brittany and Kayla. Both women were excited for Sue and Nate. They both talked about having a "Welcome Home" party after the kids were all settled. Sue grinned. She felt so blessed to have these women in her life! They were her very best friends!

She was so grateful for their wisdom and encouragement!

Chapter 17

*A*lly sat in her living room watching her brother's animated face explain what was taking place in his life. It had been a long time since she had seen him this excited! Her head turned and followed his rapid pace across the carpeted floor. Running a hand through his hair, he turned abruptly toward her.

"Don't you see, Sis? This could be the reason I went through so much heartache in my life! I have been wondering why for so long! Now, this is the answer."

He sounded so sure of himself, so confident. That was one thing Mark didn't lack, confidence. Neither did she for that matter, but hers was a different confidence. She was confident in who God created her to be no matter what life brought her way. Her brother was much more arrogant. A twinge of guilt ripped through her. She knew it wasn't nice thinking such things about her own twin. Sometimes, though, she wondered if maybe they were switched at birth! They viewed things so differently, and this was no exception.

"Mark, listen to me. You really think this is it? Have you really thought this through, all the trouble that can and probably will come from this?"

"I have thought this through! I thought you would understand. Of all people, Ally, I thought you would see where I was coming from." He sat down across from her on her brown sofa. He frowned at her as he leaned back.

The sad thing was, she didn't understand. She couldn't fathom why Mark would encourage Josephine to fight for the son she had given up a few short years beforehand.

She shook her head sadly. "But I don't, Bro, that's what I am saying."

"Think of all we have gone through! Don't you think life would have been better had things been different?"

Better? Would her life be any better had things been different? No, she never even contemplated the idea. Such thoughts never crossed her mind. She wouldn't allow them, first of all. And second, she felt as if she were betraying those she loved most in the world. No, her life wouldn't have been better had she not gone through what she and Mark had. As a matter of fact, she practically guaranteed life would have been harder, more of a struggle. And who knows if she would have found the Lord or her wonderful husband?

"Listen, I don't think our life would have been any better. Especially after the information you found out a few years back. Why would you even think that?"

Mark rubbed his forehead and sighed. "Because I have a feeling. If things were different, who knows?"

Ally groaned inwardly. She knew if she said too much, she would push her brother away. He had been so distant the last few years. Family had always mattered to him. He still came to the family functions. But ever since he found out the truth, he put a barrier between him and the rest of the family, even Ally herself! Twins were supposed to have a special bond, and she had felt she and Mark did until a few years ago. Ally didn't want to say too much to drive him away again, but she couldn't just stand by and let Mark's personal feelings try to push Josephine into doing something that could literally tear her family apart. Ally didn't know Josephine's sister at all, but she could practically guarantee Josephine's family wouldn't recover if Mark had his way.

Ally crossed the room and sat down next to her brother. Gently putting a hand on his leg, she held his gaze, hoping to convey the love she was feeling for him. "Mark, I know you are still hurting. I can see that. But I don't think you should project how you feel onto Josephine."

Mark glared at her. "That's what you think this is about?"

She nodded. "I do. I really do. And I can understand why you would do that," she quickly added, sensing Mark pulling back from her.

"I'm not doing that!" Mark got up defensively. "I think this is the reason why we went through what we did. Because I am supposed to help Josephine in her decision to move forward. That's all this is about, Al. You should know me better than that!"

The problem was she did know him better than that which is why she knew she struck a nerve with him. She knew Mark's real reasoning behind his actions, and it saddened her deeply. She slowly stood up and walked to Mark leaning against the mantle on the fireplace. She wrapped her arms around his waist, hugging him from behind.

"I love you, Mark. Growing up, you were the best friend I ever had! We were always there for each other, just like I am here for you now. I just don't want you to do anything rash. I want you to keep praying about this, but not from your eyes. From Josephine's eyes and from her family's eyes. Because once she moves forward, there is no turning back and undoing the pain that can be caused."

Mark turned to face her as she continued. "And pray about your motives. What are they really? Sometimes, we do things without realizing why, and then when the truth hits us like a ton of bricks, the damage we have caused can't be fixed." She looked up into his eyes and saw a hardness that hadn't been there when he first arrived.

She was losing him, and she knew it. There was nothing she could do at this point but pray and hold her ground. Ally knew what she was saying was good advice. She also knew her twin. She exhaled softly and let go of Mark.

"Well," he said absently, "it's not like she can do anything now. Her sister and Nate are out of the country, so she's going to have to wait until they return."

Ally looked up into his eyes. Although they were twins, they looked nothing alike. He was tall, she was petite. She was a blonde while he was darker. She had green eyes which changed colors with whatever she wore; his were definitely blue.. Right now, those blue eyes were laced with disappointment that she hadn't supported him or reacted the way he had hoped she would. Ally felt his sadness. But in the Bible, James, chapter 4:17 said that if someone knows to do good and doesn't do it, it's a sin.

Ally wasn't confrontational by nature. It had taken her many months of meditating on this verse for her to put it into action. Now that she had, she knew her brother's heart was troubled.

Ally squeezed her brother's hand before turning away. "Well, I'll keep you all in prayer. If you want to talk, let me know. I'm here if you need me."

Mark nodded shortly, put on his jacket and left. Ally sat back down on the couch and blew her hair out of her face. Well, she had done the right thing, she knew she had. At the moment, it didn't feel too good.

But she also knew God was bigger than her feelings and would do what needed to be done, even if that meant using her in the process.

Chapter 18

"*I* can hardly believe the last two weeks have flown by so quickly!" Brittany exclaimed, her tea steaming from her cup.

"I know!" Josephine agreed, drinking her coffee. "Nate and Sue will be back in a day or two. I wonder what the kids look like. I wonder if the kids have changed much from their photos! This is so great!"

Brittany grinned. "I can't wait to meet them!"

"Me, too! Are we meeting them at the airport or at their house?"

"Neither. Sue thought it would be best to let them get settled before we meet them. She said about a week or so."

Josephine groaned. "Seriously? This is going to kill me!"

"Tell me about it! I understand her thought process, though. The kids need to adjust a little bit before we overwhelm them. You know what I mean?" Brittany explained.

"Yeah," Josephine said, disappointment showing in her eyes. "I understand. I wonder how DJ is handling all of this."

Brittany leaned back in the chair and glanced around the coffee shop. "I imagine he's pretty thrilled. He gets to have a brother and a sister in one day!"

"What if the kids don't get along?" Josephine raised her eyes slightly above the rim of her cup to see Brittany.

"I think it might take them time, but I think they'll be fine." Brittany nibbled at her muffin.

"Ok. But let's just say what if. What if the kids don't get along? Sue just can't ship the kids back to Ethiopia, can she? Would she?"

"No. Sue wouldn't do that. I think she would just make it work," Brittany reassured Josephine.

"I'm excited to meet the kids, but I worry for DJ's sake. Is he going to be alright through all of this? What if he suffers serious trauma?"

"I highly doubt he will suffer trauma, Jo. He's only two years old.. He may not even remember any of this!" Brittany laughed.

"You don't think he'll remember anything at all? When do kids start remembering things?" Josephine tilted her head to one side.

"Oh, some kids remember a lot at this age. Then other kids don't remember a thing. I just think that DJ will be fine." Brittany waved her hand. "I truly believe God will work it all out for everyone involved."

"But Brit," Josephine persisted, "what if this is really a bad thing for DJ? What if he does come out of it harmed? What if he grows up resenting Nate and Sue? That would defeat the purpose of me giving him up in the first place." Josephine knew she didn't sound convincing, not even to herself.

Brittany leaned forward, her brow furrowed. "Sis, where is this all coming from? You haven't brought up DJ being your son in a long, long time. What's really going on here?"

Josephine sank back into her chair and sighed. "I don't know. Maybe I'm just concerned?"

"Hm. Why am I having trouble believing that's all it is?" Brittany crossed her arms in front of her.

Josephine took a deep breath. Well, she thought, she might as well tell Brittany her thoughts. Doing it in a public place would be better. That way, if Brittany disagreed with her, she couldn't kill her in public.

"I've been thinking what it would be like to have DJ as my son," Josephine began.

"DJ? Or just to have a child of your own?" Brittany clarified.

"DJ," Josephine said quickly and lowered her eyes.

Brittany's mouth dropped open. "Like trying to take him back?"

Josephine nodded her head, a look of guilt crossing her face. "I haven't done anything about it. I've just been thinking about it, that's all."

"Jo," Brittany put her hand on Josephine's leg. "You're not really serious, are you?"

"So what if I am? Don't you think I have a right to mother my own son?" Josephine's defenses rose.

"He's not your son! You gave him up!" Brittany retorted, pulling her hand away.

"I only gave him up because I was emotional and confused. It was brought to my attention that maybe Nate and Sue took advantage of that just to have a child of their own."

Brittany's eyes grew wide. "You honestly don't think that happened. I know you better than that. Who brought this to your attention?"

Josephine was silent for a moment. "I told Mark what happened between me and Jim, and that DJ was a result of that night," Josephine confessed. "He and I were talking, and have been for a little while now. He said he would be willing to help me raise DJ, that now I am in a better place than I was before."

Josephine watched Brittany collect herself and look out the window at the snowflakes falling peacefully from the sky.

"Josephine, please tell me you have not said anything to Sue about this," Brittany pleaded.

"I haven't. I didn't think it would be good timing to do it now. I thought that maybe after they get things settled I could talk this through with them."

"Do you really think this is a good idea? How do you foresee this all turning out?" Brittany's eyes held an intensity Josephine hadn't seen since her parents' died.

"I don't really know how this would turn out. I've just been thinking about it, that's all."

"And how do you think Sue and Nate will feel?" Brittany probed.

"I think they will be fine since they would have just adopted two other kids. They don't need DJ now." Josephine couldn't believe she was actually saying these things. Guilt pierced through her.

"What?" Brittany asked appalled.

Josephine knew she had to finish what she had started. "They just adopted two kids. They don't need to have three. They won't miss DJ now that they will have their hands full with the new little ones. Besides, don't you think DJ could get overlooked?"

Brittany snorted. "I won't even comment on that just yet. Jo, DJ could never be replaced. If Gideon were to die, Luke and I wouldn't have another one to replace him. You just don't do that."

"People do that all the time!" Josephine made sure her tone was sharp so Brittany wouldn't see the doubt that was plaguing her.

"Really? Like who? Who do you know who does that?"

"I can't think of names right now. Brittany, stop attacking me!"

"I'm not attacking you, Jo. I'm really trying to make sense out of this bombshell you just dropped. You want to take DJ back because Mark thinks it's a good idea. You think Nate and Sue took advantage of your situation just to get a child. Never mind the fact they were just married slightly before you had DJ. Never mind the fact that adoption in the United States was something they never wanted to do. Never mind the fact that you promised, *you promised*, Jo, that you would never take him back. Never mind these things. What do you think this will do to yours and Sue's relationship? Have you thought that far ahead? What will this do to the family?"

"I didn't say I was actually going to do this. I just said I was thinking about it, Brit!" Josephine brightened suddenly. "What if I presented it to her like I was doing her a favor? Taking DJ off of her hands!"

Brittany laughed sarcastically. "Josephine Johnson! A favor would be willing to take DJ for a few nights, not for the rest of his life! Don't you see how absurd that sounds?"

Josephine sat silently for a moment. How would Sue feel about all of this? Would she fight her? Of course Sue would fight her! DJ was Sue's son, after all! How would it affect their relationship? Would they ever be able to have family gatherings? Would they be civil with each other? Would Sue even show up at the family gatherings if Josephine won the court battle?

"Josephine, look at me," Brittany said sternly. "We haven't even talked about Mark. What if he bails on you? What if he isn't the one you are supposed to marry? What if you go through with all of this only to find out that you two are not compatible? Where would you be? Think, Josephine. Think." Brittany tapped her head.

Josephine sighed. "I don't know, Brit. I don't know how Sue would respond. I don't know the future."

"That's a cop out, Josephine, and you know it." Brittany pointed her finger at Josephine. "None of us know the future, but we need to count the cost of our actions. Think before you plow ahead with this."

"I have been thinking. I really think I could raise DJ," Josephine's voice was suddenly mousy. She ran her hand through her hair.

"I have no doubt you can raise DJ. I know you'll be a great mom one day. I really believe that! But that's not what I am referring to. What about everything else? What about Sue and Nate? What if you and Mark don't work out? What about you working? Who's going to take care of DJ then?"

"Mark's family can help," Josephine whispered.

"Mark's family. Sure. And if Mark is out of the picture? Who would help you then?"

"You mean you wouldn't help me?" Josephine asked, stunned.

Brittany shrugged her shoulders. "No I would not, Jo. I could not and would not support you in any way, shape, or form!"

"What kind of sister would you be, not helping me?" Josephine accused Brittany, anger filling her features.

"I would be a sister forced to choose sides, Jo. It wouldn't be my doing, but yours. You would put me in this position. Don't do that to me or anyone else who cares for our family. Now, answer my question. What about Sue?"

"I think Sue is a very forgiving person. I think she would help me." Josephine nodded her head, suddenly sure of herself.

Brittany shook her head, sadness filling her beautiful

features. "Then you don't know Sue very well. She is a forgiving person, yes. But she would have nothing to do with you."

"Then she wouldn't really have forgiven me, would she? And she would be in sin because God tells us to forgive," Josephine retorted harshly.

"No, Jo. You are very wrong about that. She can forgive you and have nothing to do with you. Forgiveness doesn't mean forgetting. It means not holding onto the hurt and pain, but that doesn't mean putting yourself in harm's way again. And she would be if she had a relationship with you. Because every time she saw you, she would battle anger and hurt. She would look at you like you betrayed her, and with good reason. If you won custody of DJ, and I say if because there is no guarantee you would, she wouldn't be able to be near you."

"So if I don't win custody, you think we could have a relationship?" Hope filled Josephine's eyes.

"I don't think so. If she was able to keep DJ, perhaps she would cut you out of her life altogether because of fear you may try to do this again. Who knows?" Brittany raised her shoulders.

"You are just speaking from how you would feel. We don't know for sure how Sue would take any of this." Josephine tried to cling to hope that this wouldn't tear her relationship apart with Sue.

"Maybe. Maybe not. I don't know. What I do know is this; this idea is not a good one. I can't see one good thing coming from it, and that includes you raising DJ. You could end up alone, and I know that is not what you want for DJ," Brittany concluded.

Josephine set down her cup. "I know I have a lot to think about. I need to go. I'm meeting Mark at his house in a few minutes. Thanks for talking with me. I love you, Sis." Josephine bent down and kissed Brittany's cheek.

"I love you, too, Jo. I'll be praying for you."

"Thanks."

Josephine left feeling more confused than ever. She didn't know what to do.

Lord, I am so confused. I don't know what to do anymore! Do I fight for DJ? Do I let this all go? What do you want, Lord? I just don't know! Please, please show me! Is there any truth to what Brittany was saying? Give me wisdom, Jesus!

Brittany sat at the coffee shop, her heart breaking into a million little pieces. The news Josephine dropped on her hit her like a ton of bricks. Brittany didn't foresee any good thing coming from this. She knew Sue would be devastated.

How could Jo be thinking these things? Why would Mark even suggest these things? Was Jo that gullible? Lord, this could forever change our family. With Mom and Dad gone, my sisters are all I have left. I don't want to see them destroyed. This has potential to destroy us. God, please, speak to Josephine. Touch her heart. Help her to see this can't be a good decision. Jesus, I just don't know what else to say. Help!

Brittany gathered her belongings and headed out the door. She was about to get into her car, when she heard a car honk behind her. Glancing over her shoulder, she saw Steven waving. Steven rolled down his window.

"Hey there," Brittany said, trying to brush away her troubled thoughts.

"Hey Brittany," Steven smiled at her.

"Whatcha up to?" Brittany prayed Steven couldn't see her shattered heart through her eyes.

"Just grabbing a cup of coffee before heading over to my parents' house. They are so excited about Nate and Sue! They want to go shopping today, so I offered to tag a long. How about you?" Steven rolled his window up and got out of his car.

"I was just having coffee with Josephine. Luke has the kids this morning. I love Saturdays!"

"How is Jo doing today?" Steven leaned against his car door.

Brittany rolled her eyes. "I don't know. Fine, I suppose."

"Did she tell you about our argument a while ago?" Steven sounded hesitant.

"No. But she did share some disturbing news."

"Ah. She told you about DJ." A look of understanding crossed his face.

"You know?" Brittany couldn't hide her surprise.

Steven stood up. "Do you have a few minutes to go inside? It's cold out here. I don't think the snow is going to let up anytime soon."

Brittany looked at her watch. "I have about ten minutes."

"Great. I'll fill you in."

Walking back inside, Brittany sat down while Steven ordered his coffee. She closed her eyes, praying things would turn out ok.

"When did you find out?" Brittany asked as he sat down.

"A few weeks ago. I dropped by Jo's and she told me. Then we fought. I went home, angry. Then I decided to make a cake for Sue and Nate, and Jo dropped by, apologizing. After Jo left, I went to Sue's to give them the cake."

"I can't imagine what this is going to do to Sue and Nate if they find out."

Brittany knew Sue well enough to know her heart. Sue would be devastated and angry. Brittany felt her eyes fill with tears.

Steven looked sheepish. "They already know," he answered quietly.

"What was that?" Brittany leaned forward as if she was suddenly punched in the stomach.

"I accidentally told them."

Tears spilled from her eyes. "How did that happen?" she whispered.

"Sue asked me if Jo and I were better. I thought Jo had told Sue what she was thinking. When Sue was so nonchalant about it, I was appalled. I blurted it out! I seriously thought she knew!"

Brittany covered her mouth with her hand. "Oh, Steven! How did they take it?"

"Heartbroken. Angry. Scared."

Brittany wiped her tears with a napkin. "I can only imagine. Why hasn't she told me if she's known so long?"

Steven sipped his coffee. "Probably because she was so caught up in the adoption process, maybe it slipped her mind?"

"Or maybe she knew I would jump right in and start fighting this battle," Brittany smiled through her tears. "Kind of like what I did today."

"Mm. Perhaps that is the reason. I take it things didn't go so well?" Steven crossed his leg.

"I don't know, friend, I really don't know. Jo's on her way to Mark's, and I have a feeling he is behind all of this. I'm so mad at him, I could kick him!"

"We really should have come from the same family!" Steven chuckled. "I wanted to punch him in the nose!"

Brittany laughed. "We do have a bit of a temper, don't we? Well, I guess we can only pray. Oh, Steven, I really hope Josephine doesn't go through with it!"

Steven stood up. "Me, too. But something tells me she will. And Mark will be the driving force behind it all."

Chapter 19

Steven's heart pounded against his rib cage as he hung up his phone. He knew it was time to talk with Josephine which is why he had called Sue. It had been a few weeks since Nate and Sue had brought home the kids from Ethiopia. Steven had met the kids a week after they got home. They were adorable, to say the least! Steven watched Nate and Sue interact with the three kids. Although Sue felt overwhelmed, Steven knew she and Nate were going to be great with all three of them! But whenever Steven looked into Sue's eyes, he saw fear hidden in them. Josephine still hadn't mentioned anything to them about what Mark was suggesting she do. Sue had confided in Steven that she was up at night, worried one day Josephine was going to drop the bombshell and destroy their lives forever. Steven had known for some time he needed to talk with Josephine about what he had done. He had called Sue to make sure it was all right with her before he went ahead with his plans. She had told him she and Nate were fine with him telling Josephine, but she cautioned him.

"She is going to be angry, my friend! I want to warn you, this could destroy what you two have. Are you prepared for that?"

Steven slumped further into his couch. "Yeah, unfortunately, I am. The last several weeks have been weighing on my heart, Sue. I need to be the one to tell her what I have done. If she hears it from you, she'll be even more upset with me. Just pray for me, ok? I am going to call her soon."

Sue's voice filled with compassion. "Nate and I will be. Keep us posted on what happens, okay? We love you, Steven!"

"I love you guys, too. Thanks, Sue."

Now, sitting on his couch, his heart beating rapidly, he found Josephine's number on his cell phone and clicked send. A moment later, her perky voice answered.

"Hey Steve! What's up?"

"Hey yourself, Jo! Not much. How about you?"

"I was just relaxing after a long day at work."

Steven could picture her sitting in her recliner, her feet tucked under her body. She probably had a cup of steaming coffee sitting beside her on the end table.

"How's the coffee?" he asked, a smile tugging at the corner of his lips.

Josephine laughed. "Am I that predictable?"

"Sometimes. Other times, you throw me off completely."

Let this be one of those times! he anxiously prayed.

"So, what's going on? I am positive you didn't call me to talk about my coffee!"

"You got me there. Actually, I was wondering if we could hang out a bit tonight. Are you busy?"

"No, I'm not. Are you wanting a rematch on the wii? Because you know I can take you down!"

"Well, that hadn't crossed my mind, but maybe. You want to come over in a few minutes? Would that be alright?"

"Sure. See you soon."

Steven clicked his phone off and set it down on the arm of his couch. His heart finally seemed to stop beating so fast. He caught his breath, feeling tension run up and down his body. He was about to tell one of his best friends he made a huge mistake. His mind ran with the possibilities of how this conversation could go. He could lose Josephine's friendship for good or she might see that she was wrong in even considering taking DJ back. She might even break up with Mark! Steven shook his head. Nah, that wasn't even a possibility. He wished it were, but he knew deep down it wasn't. The only thing he knew to do was pray.

Lord, I'm worried about what is about to happen. You know the future already. You know the outcome. I just ask that You give me peace, guidance, and courage to do what I need to do. Please prepare Josephine. Be with her. Give her ears to hear what I am about to say. Be in the very center of our talk, please, Lord. Thank You in advance. I know You are always with me.

Josephine knew Mark wouldn't be happy with her going to Steven's house tonight. But she needed time to laugh. She hadn't had that with Mark as of late. Lately, he seemed more concerned with her trying to get DJ back than anything. Instead of talking about little things, Mark was bent on talking about DJ every time they had gotten together. It was starting to get on Josephine's nerves. She still hadn't decided on anything. As a matter of fact, the more she thought about it, the more she felt DJ belonged with Nate and Sue. Josephine knew what God had spoken to her, and she knew she had done the right thing. For some reason, though, Mark doubted that when they were together. When she was in Mark's presence, she doubted it herself. When Mark would leave, the cloud would lift from her heart, and she would chastise herself for being controlled by Mark's over powering ideas. She pulled into Steven's driveway and bounced toward the front door. She needed to have fun tonight. Josephine was still very much interested in Mark, but Steven had a light-heartedness about him that drew her. She needed that in her life, especially now.

When Steven answered the door, concern filled her being. He didn't look right. Come to think of it, he didn't sound right on the phone, either, like he was carrying the weight of the world on his shoulders.

"Steven, is everything alright?"

Steven's eyes flickered with something she couldn't quite put her finger on. Sadness? Pain? Guilt? What could it be?

Steven let her in and guided her to the living room. "Can I get you something to drink?"

"No, thanks. What's the matter?" Concern filled her eyes.

Steven looked away as she sat down. "I need to talk to you about DJ."

Josephine groaned. "Ugh. Not you, too! That's the only thing Mark is interested in lately! DJ! I love the boy, I really do, but my life isn't all about DJ!"

Steven nodded. "I understand. It must be frustrating talking about it all the time. Have you come up with anything yet?"

Josephine kicked her shoes off and put her feet on the couch. She grabbed an extra couch pillow and hugged it to her body. "No. Mark keeps pushing me to 'do the right thing'." She deepened her voice as if she were Mark. "But I thought I did do the right thing. I keep telling Mark that, but he keeps questioning me. I don't know." She sighed and looked down at the pattern on the pillow.

Steven was quiet as if he were weighing what she had said. Finally, he spoke, "What's Mark's motivation?"

Motivation? Josephine didn't think he had any motivation. Sure, he was pushy at times, but she thought it was only because he cared for her and wanted her to be happy.

"I don't think he has any. Why?"

"Well," Steven put his feet on the foot stool, "I can't help but wonder, why is he so interested in you fighting for DJ? What is driving him to push you to do this? What's in it for him? He hasn't proposed, right?"

Josephine chuckled. "No, he hasn't proposed. But why would he need a motivation? Wouldn't he just want what's best for me?"

"Of course. But who's to say what's best for you is fighting for DJ? Everything was going smoothly until Mark brought this up, right? Nate and Sue were happy. You were happy. DJ is certainly happy. Why is you having DJ back best for you? Isn't that selfish?"

Josephine paused, letting what Steven had to say sink in. Why hadn't she thought of that before? Why *was* Mark pushing her so hard? Having DJ back wouldn't be easy for her, that's for sure. It would be tough being a single parent. So, is that what is best for her and DJ? To be raised without a dad? He had one already, Nate. DJ was already in a happy family, now the oldest to two siblings. What was the *real* reason Mark wanted her to move forward?

"That's a good point, my friend." Josephine pointed a finger at him. "I'm going to need to talk to him about that. I don't know why I never thought about that." She got up from the couch and walked toward his television set. "Now, how about that wii tournament? Are you ready for the fight of your life?" She knelt down, pushing buttons to set it up.

Steven came up beside her and touched her hand. "Not yet. I need to tell you something, Josephine."

She turned around, startled by the serious tone in his voice. "I knew there was something wrong, Steven! Tell me! What is it? Are your parents sick? Did something happen at work? Do you have to move back east again?"

Steven shook his head firmly. "No, no. Nothing like that."

Relief swept over her. "Whew! What are you doing, scaring me like that?" She wiped her forehead. "Whatever it is can't be all that bad."

A sad chuckle sounded from deep within Steven's chest. "We'll see about that."

He led her back to the couch and sat down next to her. "Jo, I need to tell you this before you accidentally hear it from someone else." He cleared his throat. "I told Nate and Sue about what Mark is trying to get you to do."

The room began to spin. "You, you did what?" she whispered.

As Steven launched into the story of what had happened, Josephine felt her blood begin to boil. When he was finished, she exploded. "I can't believe you would do that! How could you even think for a second I would go over there and tell her what Mark wanted me to do?" She felt her cheeks getting redder and redder from the anger that was burning inside her.

Steven wrung his hands together. "I know."

"Steven," Josephine shot up from the couch, "I came over here to apologize to you that day. I never told you we even talked about Mark. Why? Why would you think that?"

"Jo, I don't have an answer. I was shocked when Sue told me she had talked with you. I couldn't understand why she was so flippant about you thinking about taking DJ." He sighed and ran a hand through his hair, clearly distressed.

Josephine didn't care how weary Steven looked. She didn't

care if he was in pain. She didn't care that he had become her best friend In the past months. All she knew was she felt betrayed. She had told him what had happened between her and Mark, and the first chance he got, he ran to Sue and Nate with the information!

"So how long did it take you until you told them? Did Sue answer the door and then you blurted it out? Bet you couldn't wait to get over there to tell them how horrible of a sister I am! Am I right?" She spat out the words through clenched teeth.

"No," Steven shook his head vehemently. "I didn't go over with that intention! Sue took the cake in the kitchen and was cutting it up. Nate told me about the adoption, and I told him I had heard about that from you. That's when Sue came out. I told you this, Jo. I didn't mean to tell them!"

"Sure you didn't, Steven! You probably had it all planned out the moment you left my house that morning after our fight! You probably figured you ought to tell them so you could get in even better with my family! Well, how do you feel now? Are you glad you told them?" Angry tears blurred her vision. Josephine put her shoes on as if, ready to leave at any given moment.

"No, I'm not glad I told them. Every time I see Sue, I see the hurt in her eyes. Every time I talk to Nate, there is an underlined fear in his voice that one day, DJ may not be with them. No, friend, I am not glad I told them. As I said before, it was a mistake, and I am deeply sorry about that."

Josephine could tell Steven was sincere, but she didn't care. Her sister knew and she wasn't the one who told her. Steven had betrayed her trust.

"You betrayed my trust, Steven. Friends don't do that. They keep each other's secrets. They listen and don't go tattle-telling to each other's family. What you did makes me question our friendship." Josephine placed a hand over her heart, tears sliding down her face.

"I didn't mean to!" Steven got up and paced the living room floor. "Jo," he knelt down in front of her, "please, believe me when I tell you this! I had no intention of telling Nate and Sue about this! I should have thought everything through! I know that! As soon as I said the words, I knew that! But I didn't mean to betray your trust! You don't know how much you mean to me, Josephine! I would never do anything to hurt you intentionally!"

Josephine jerked her body away from him and stood up. "Tell me, Steven, is that why you brought up Mark tonight? To try to get me not to take DJ away so we can be fine? Are you trying to get me to doubt Mark's intentions so I can leave him and not fight for DJ? Is that *your* motive, Steven?"

Steven sat heavily down on the couch again and turned away from Josephine. Tears glistened in the corner of his eyes, but Josephine didn't have any sympathy for him. She couldn't believe he would do this! Her best friend in the entire world just broke her heart! And now he was the one crying? Well, too bad for him! He was not about to get any sympathy from her, no way! He deserved to feel bad! He broke her confidence, and now he can suffer the consequences!

"I don't have a motive, Josephine, believe me in that. I asked you to come over tonight, not to get you to doubt Mark, but to get you to know the truth. I told you the truth, and I didn't have to." Steven's voice held emotion deeper than anything Josephine had ever heard.

She refused to be affected by it, though. "You said you wanted me to hear it from you and no one else. That is the only reason you told me, so that no one else would." Josephine pointed an accusing finger in his direction. "It had nothing to do with you being honest and truthful."

"Not so, Jo, not so," Steven shook his head. Anger flickered in his eyes but only for a moment. "I asked you to come over so I could be the one to tell you. I should have done it a long time ago, but I didn't. I didn't care if you found out, but I cared how you found out. The last thing I wanted was for you to confront Sue and Nate only to find out they already knew. That would have thrown you off. I wanted you to know the facts before you moved ahead. Can Mark say that? Has he been honest with you?"

Josephine winced at his words. "How dare you bring Mark into any of this! He told me how he felt, Steven! That is important!

So what I don't know what his motives are? He probably doesn't even have them! That's how selfless and devoted he is! Can you say the same? Are you selfless and devoted? No! You are not! Had you been, none of this would have happened! You aren't devoted to me or our friendship!" Josephine grabbed her keys and headed for the door.

"Josephine! Wait!" she heard Steven call as she slammed the door behind her.

She ran to the car and quickly peeled away without even buckling her seat belt. She couldn't sit there another minute, listening to the pack of lies Steven was throwing at her. And then on top of all he had done, he tried to make her think less of Mark! How dare he! She considered him her friend, her best friend! Not after tonight!

Not ever!

Sue hung up the phone and turned her worried eyes to Nate.

"It didn't go well, huh?" Nate put his arms around her and pulled her close.

Sue shook her head sadly. "No. I better put on some tea. I think we are going to have a visitor tonight."

"You think Jo will come over here? Now?" Nate's handsome features twisted in concern.

Sue nodded. "Yep. Go put the kids to bed. I don't want them to hear what she has to say. And if I know my sister, she will have a lot to say."

Nate gathered the three kids and walked slowly up the stairs. Within ten minutes, the door bell rang. Sue answered the door, praying for the peace of God to rule the conversation she was about to have. Josephine stormed in and turned angry eyes on her sister.

"So, you know." It wasn't a question, more of a statement.

"Can I get you some tea to help you calm down?" Sue did her best not to get defensive, but needed to have a gentle voice. She had been meditating on verses in the bible that had said things about a harsh word stirs up anger, but a soft answer turns away wrath. Now, with everything in her, she forced herself to be calm.

"Tea? Are you kidding me?" Josephine's look was flabbergasted. "I came over here to talk to you. I can only assume you talked with Steven since he has a habit of running to you whenever there is a problem with me. And you want me to have tea?"

Sue gently took Josephine by the hand and drew her into the living room. "Isn't that what Mom would have done? Wouldn't she have said, "Let's start this conversation out with a bit of tea?"

"Well, you are not Mom, and she isn't here, so why bother?" Josephine tossed her keys down on the coffee table and turned on Sue.

"Jo, I know I'm not Mom. I never claimed to be. I happen to agree with her, though. Tea has a calming effect on a conversation. First of all, it takes a bit of time for the water to boil, so we don't have to hurry. We can sit and think before we say anything. Second, the tea is hot and takes time to drink. That is good because instead of saying things quickly, we can sip the tea and relax. Third, I enjoy the taste of tea." Sue noticed Josephine had calmed down a little. Taking that as a good sign, she motioned for Josephine to come with her in the kitchen.

Sue took out three cups and placed a tea bag in each one. She took out the sugar and cream, just in case anyone wanted to add anything. By the time the water was done boiling, Nate had entered the adjoining dining room and sat down at the table. Josephine followed his lead as Sue poured the water in the mugs.

"Would you like to stay in here or head into the living room?" She glanced from Nate to Josephine.

Nate raised his eyebrows at Josephine who sighed deeply. "Living room. Let's get comfortable," Josephine answered, taking the mug from Sue's hands.

When everyone was settled, Sue spoke up. "And yes, Steven did call me to tell me he spoke with you. That's how I knew you would be coming over here tonight." She sipped her tea, peace filling her soul. Sue knew it wasn't the tea that calmed her heart, but the Lord.

Josephine's eyes were red from crying. She sniffed and took a tissue from the box Nate offered. "So, you know," she said more gently this time.

Nate nodded. "We know."

"I don't know what I'm going to do yet." Josephine looked at Sue and Nate, despair filling her eyes. "Mark wants me to take DJ back. Steven doesn't. I can only imagine you both don't, and I know Brittany doesn't. I should have known she would have taken your side. You two have been best friends since the day you were born."

Sue set down her mug. "It's not about taking sides, Josephine. I think it's about what is right. You gave DJ up without us asking you to. We didn't offer to adopt him from you. You came up with that on your own. Now, Mark comes in to your life, and he thinks he knows what's best for you?" Sue tried to keep the edge out of her voice, but failed. "Who does he think he is?"

Nate put his hand over Sue's. "What I think Sue is saying is, why would he care so much? And why would you entertain such thoughts?"

Josephine ran her hand across her forehead. "I don't know why he cares so much. I doubt there is any deep reason for it. I think he just feels families should be together."

"But we are his family," Sue retorted. "We have raised Daniel James from day one. He was ours from the beginning. You know that. Why would you let him talk you into such a thing?"

"He hasn't talked me into anything, Sue." Josephine's eyes flashed with anger. "If he had, I would have filed weeks ago!"

"Filed? For what? Permanent custody?" Sue leaned forward. "What judge would give that to you? You gave up your rights years ago! What makes you think you have any rights now?"

"I don't know what my rights are, to tell you the truth. I haven't looked into it legally. I do know that I have been praying about it and thinking long and hard about it. As of today, I don't know what to do. I lean toward telling Mark no, I'm not going forward, and then I lean toward wanting to have DJ back. Life has gotten more confusing! I don't know what to do anymore!"

Josephine sobbed quietly into her tissue.

Nate got up and walked over to where she was sitting. He put a comforting arm around her shoulders. "Josephine, you have been like a little sister to me for quite some time now. We love you very much. We haven't always liked your choices, and I think we are safe to say we have made that pretty clear." Nate grinned at her. Josephine met his gaze and gave a slight smile in return. "But I think that if you do go through with this, nothing will be the same for anyone. Have you thought that far ahead?"

Josephine nodded. "A little. Brittany told me that, too, as well as Steven. So, what you are saying is, if I did go through with it and you guys lost custody, you wouldn't be a part of my life, right?"

"How could we?" Sue whispered. "How could you be a part of someone's life who took your son away?"

Josephine's shoulders sank. "But you guys took my son away, didn't you? And I'm a part of your life."

"No, Jo, don't go mixing up words. There is a big difference between taking away and giving up. We didn't take DJ away, you gave him up. Do you see the difference?" Nate's voice was gentle, yet firm.

"I have to be honest here, Sis," Sue's elbows rested on her knees. "When I heard what Mark wanted you to do, I was mad, mad as I think I could ever be.! I could hardly believe you would listen to him! He just came into your life a few months ago. I have known you from day one! I was angry that you didn't talk to me about what he was saying. Instead, you kept it all to yourself. Truthfully, I'm still a little angry."

"That's because I wanted time to think things through. I need to figure out if what he is saying is true or not. I have to come to this conclusion on my own. I don't want other people telling me what to do!" Josephine's voice rose slightly in defense.

"I get that, but by not talking to us, aren't you letting Mark tell you what to do? Would you have ever thought of doing this before Mark brought it up? You never said anything about this for two years, Jo! Two years! And now, Mark waltzes in your life, tells you to get DJ back, and you are thinking things over?

What's there to think? You should tell him no!" Sue's cheeks were red with sudden anger. Mark had become a bad name to her. Here he was trying to destroy the only family she had left! Nate saw the pain in his wife's eyes and moved to her side.

"If I tell Mark no, I could lose him forever." Josephine's voice was barely above a whisper.

Sue suddenly felt nauseous. What? If Josephine told Mark no, she could lose him forever? Is that what she heard? No, it couldn't be! Josephine wouldn't be that desperate! She wouldn't date the first guy who finds her interesting and cling to him like this! She wouldn't compromise what she knows to be truth just so she wouldn't be lonely! She wouldn't put her family at risk just to fill a void, would she? But that is what Sue had heard!

Sue placed her hand over her stomach. "Let me get this straight. You are thinking about this only because you don't want to lose Mark?"

"You make it sound like a bad thing, Sue," Josephine said harshly.

"But wouldn't you have done anything to keep Nate in your life?"

"No!" Sue answered quickly. "I would not have! I love Nate, but if he were telling me to do something I knew was wrong, we would be over in a heart beat!"

"You expect me to believe that?" Josephine's eyes were doubtful. "I know how much you had fallen for him! I saw the look in your eyes every time he came in the room! There is no way you would have given him up!"

"Josephine, Nate never would have asked me to do anything like this! There's no point in even discussing it! He never would have mentioned it!"

"Mark isn't a bad guy; he's just looking out for my interests."

Looking out for her interests? How could that be? Raising a child on your own would be difficult! It would be time consuming, and it requires a lot of energy! Sue knew a lot of people did it, but that isn't the life Josephine had wanted nor had she chosen. How could Mark suggest it be looking out for her? What ulterior motives did that man have, anyway?

Sue inhaled deeply. Pausing for a moment, she exhaled, trying to get her thoughts to calm down. "Look, Sis, what's the reason Mark is telling you these things? Have you thought about that?"

Josephine's eyes flashed. "Oh, so you are in on it, too!"

Sue was confused. "What do you mean?"

"Steven said the same thing tonight! Oh, I should have known you three would be working together on this! You are trying to get me to doubt Mark so I will break up with him! What was I thinking, coming over here, and trying to talk to you?" Josephine stood up abruptly.

"Jo," Sue stammered, "I have no idea what you are talking about. I don't know what Steven said to you tonight, but I am not in cahoots with him on anything! All I wanted to know was why Mark wanted you to do this! That's it!"

Josephine rushed to the front door. "Sure! You expect me to believe that? Well, I don't! You said yourself you talked with Steven tonight! I'm such an idiot! And to think I almost let you two talk me out of going through with this! Well, you haven't, and neither has Steven! I don't know what I'm going to do, but I do know this; I won't be talking with you about this anymore! Not until I reach my decision! Good night!" With that, she stormed out of the house and slammed the door.

Sue turned, stunned and confused. "I don't know what just happened."

Nate shook his head, concern filling his eyes. "Me neither, but I can pretty much guarantee, it wasn't good."

Chapter 20

*H*ow could it be March already? Sue thought wistfully, folding the laundry. It seemed like it was only yesterday when she and Nate had brought the little ones home. They were doing surprisingly well. Miles, the little boy, was a trooper, and took to the family right away. He and DJ now shared a room, although it wasn't always that way. Nate had suggested putting Miles and Ella in the same room so they had some form of routine in their lives. After a month or so, though, Miles loved playing with DJ, and when DJ asked if Miles could sleep in his room, Miles was so excited. Miles and DJ had become fast friends. Of course, there were some disagreements, but nothing out of the ordinary.

Ella was a different story. She required a lot of attention. It was difficult getting anything done! Ella wanted to be near Sue all of the time, and anytime she was put down, she would cry and throw a fit. Nate had taken the first month off from work so he could become a part of the routine and make things easier. But with Nate at work, the last month had been trying, to say the least. Sue knew Ella would adjust, that it would take a little more time. She continued being patient, doing her best to give Miles and DJ the attention they so desperately needed and she desperately desired to give. Brittany and Kayla called often, asking when they could throw the "Welcome Home" party for the kids. Sue just didn't have things all together yet, and wanted a little more time. The kids did get a chance to meet Kayla and her family as well as Sue's sisters, the Sorensons and Steven. The kids were withdrawn and shy around everyone, but over the course of the month, they came out of their shells and interacted well with the other kids. Sue was excited and thrilled and looked forward to scheduling the party. She knew the kids would be great.

Sue picked up DJ's little shirt and folded it. Her eyes drifted around the room. Her gazed lingered on a picture of Josephine, Brittany, and herself. She sighed heavily. Sue still hadn't heard anything from Josephine about fighting for DJ. Deep down, she had hoped that Josephine had decided against it. After all, it had been a few months now and nothing had been done. Sue hoped against all hope that is how it would stay. She had barely spoken to Josephine since the day she had stormed out of her and Nate's home. Her conversations were brief and somewhat strained. There were many times Sue had wanted to talk with Josephine about what she was thinking she was going to do. When she tried to approach the subject, Josephine had eyed her coolly.

"I don't know yet, Sue. Don't push me," Josephine would warn.

So, she held her tongue. If Josephine doubted her decision, Sue didn't want to be the cause of her going ahead with it. Sue's mind drifted to her conversation with Brittany just a week after their return from Ethiopia.

"Why didn't you tell me about Josephine?" Brittany demanded gently.

Sue held the phone up with her shoulder while picking up Ella. "Because I knew how you would react. Who told you?"

Brittany sighed. "Jo."

Sue grunted. "Well, at least you heard it from the horse's mouth. What all did she say?"

Brittany replayed her time with Josephine and running into Steven.

Sue had sunk to the couch in shock. "Wow. I'm amazed she even told you about it!"

"I know. But I tell you, Sue, she hasn't really thought things through. She honestly feels you two would have a relationship if she went through with it."

"It wouldn't come easy nor right away, if at all," Sue admitted. "Not very Christian of me, is it?"

"Oh Sue," Brittany said soothingly, "That's not it at all. I know you love Jesus, and so does anyone who comes in contact with you. If Josephine goes through with this thing, I wouldn't expect you to have a relationship with her."

"It's hard even now," Sue confided. "I mean, she's thinking about taking my son away. I have to wait and see what she decides. Why does she even get the right to decide? And then there is Mark in all of this! Oh, he makes me so mad!"

Brittany was silent for a moment and then spoke, "I understand. I will continue to pray for you and Jo about this. Keep praying. And if there is anything I can do to help you with Miles and Ella, let me know. And Sue, you guys might need to contact a lawyer about all of this."

Sue sat down, feeling the weight of the world was on her shoulders. "Yeah, Kayla said the same thing. I'll talk with Nate about it. And thanks, Brit. Love you."

Sue shook her head, bringing her back to the present. With Easter right around the corner, Sue was glad for the distraction. Easter would be celebrated at Brittany's house. Sue was thankful! Nate's family would be there. His dad and step-mom were planning on coming in from Texas. Nate's dad was looking forward to meeting his newest grandchildren! Luke's family had said they were going to join in on the festivities, as well. Luke's mom and dad were visiting from California. Sue knew it would be a crowded house, but was glad for it all the same. Josephine was the only family member who wasn't going to be there. She had made plans with Mark's family. Just as well, since almost everyone knew what she was thinking about doing. Sue didn't know if she could handle pretending everything was fine if Josephine and Mark had shown up.

Sighing, she folded one of Ella's shirts. Easter was a little of a week away. *Just a few more days,* Sue thought. *I really need to get the Easter basket stuff.*

Sue yawned, and looked around the living room. One could tell she had three little ones. Her living room hadn't looked the same since Miles and Ella came home. There were toys strewn all over the floor, and a basket full of diapers and wipes. Laundry was separated on the couch, waiting to be put away. With a sigh, Sue stood up and picked up the laundry basket. *No time like the present!* She thought with a silent laugh. With the kids all napping, she started in her room. By the time she was done putting away clothes, Ella had started to cry.

Sue walked quietly passed the boys' room, not wanting to wake them. She opened the door and looked into the crib.

"Hi Ella," she cooed softly.

Ella reached up and smiled. Sue noticed for the first time just how breathtaking Ella really was. She had beautiful dark skin, big brown olive shaped eyes, and dark curly hair. Dressed in her blue sweats outfit, she looked absolutely adorable. Sue picked her up and kissed her cheek.

"How's Mommy's little girl?" She asked gently.

Ella wrapped her arms around Sue's neck and nestled her head on her shoulder. Sue went downstairs and glanced at the clock. Nate should be home from work any minute. He had called earlier and asked if Sue needed anything.

"Yes!" Sue answered emphatically. "A large, double stuffed pizza with olives and pepperoni, please!"

Nate's hearty laugh sounded like music to Sue's ears. "Anything for you, my love."

"Mommy!" DJ called from the top of the stairs. "Wake up time please?"

"Sure, sweetie. Is Miles awake?"

"Yep!"

"Perfect. Come on down. Daddy will be home any minute. You guys hungry for some pizza?" Sue felt the hint of a smile form across her lips as the boys came down. They looked sleepy at first, but at the mention of pizza, both of their eyes lit up.

Pizza was one of DJ's favorite meals. "Yay!" he yelled excitedly.

"Yay!" Miles mimicked.

The boys ran downstairs, and immediately started playing with the toys on the floor.

"Hey, boys. Why don't we pick up some toys before Daddy gets home? Who's going to win? Will Daddy be here first or will you pick up the toys first?" Sue challenged.

"We will win, Mommy." DJ's face looked serious.

Miles nodded his head. "Yes. We win."

Sue smiled and set Ella down. Ella began playing with a toy while the boys picked up the other toys. Sue made her way to the kitchen and began making a salad to go with the pizza.

"Honey! I'm home!" Nate called from the front door.

"Daddy!" DJ declared, running to hug Nate's knees.

Miles ran up behind DJ and did the same.

Wiping her hands on a towel, Sue came out from the kitchen and kissed Nate on the cheek. Taking the pizza from her hand, she headed back to the kitchen.

"Hey, kiddos!" Nate bent down and wrapped all three kids in a giant bear hug.

Sue listened with a smile on her face. She loved this time of day. Nate had really embraced the kids, all three of them, as his own. From the first day he held Ella in his arms, tears streaming down his face, he became their Daddy. It didn't take long for Miles and Ella to call them Mommy and Daddy. The social worker said that was normal. Kids normally do what they see and hear other kids do, and since DJ called her and Nate Mommy and Daddy, it was natural for the other two to do so, as well. Ella barely spoke, but when she said "Dadda" for the first time, Sue's heart swelled, especially from the look on Nate's face. Miles was already a little talker. He seemed more than willing to accept her and Nate as his parents.

Sue poked her head around the kitchen wall and watched Nate playing with the kids on the floor. She loved watching them all interact with one another. They were the oddest of families, but they were her family.

Sue quickly set the table and called everyone into the dining room for dinner. Putting the kids in the high chair and booster seats, she and Nate took their places. Nate bowed his head for prayer.

"Jesus," he began, "we thank you for this food and for always providing our every need. We thank you for the wonderful gift of our children. Bless them and keep them in your loving hands. Thank you, Father, for my beautiful wife. Keep her sane during this crazy time. Amen."

Sue looked up and smiled at Nate. "Thank you."

Nate winked at her. Taking a bite of his pizza, Nate listened intently as the boys began telling him all about their day. Nate gave them his undivided attention and asked several questions throughout dinner. Once dinner was finished and the dishes were done, Nate gave the three kids a bath and read them a bed time story. After praying with the kids, Nate and Sue sank onto the couch, wrapped in each other's arms.

"What a great day," Sue murmured contentedly.

Nate kissed Sue and nodded his head. "I agree. Those three kids are simply perfect! We have a wonderful little family here, Sue. I am truly blessed."

Sue agreed. "Me, too. I am so thankful for the little ones! DJ has done a great job taking Miles under his wing. And Ella is doing better with not needing to be held all of the time."

"I'm glad to hear that. You are doing a marvelous job with all three kids," Nate complimented her.

Sue blushed. "I wish I were doing better. It's all I can do to keep them clothed and fed! This poor house! I hate seeing it so messy!"

"I don't care about the house, Honey. I care about your sanity, and from what I can see, you are doing great. Hey, have you heard from Jo at all?"

Sue's shoulders fell. "No. I was hoping we would by now. Have you thought more about us contacting a lawyer?"

Nate nodded. "Yes, I have. I think we should. It's good to know what we may be up against."

"Okay. I'll do that tomorrow." Sue suddenly felt very tired.

They sat in comfortable silence. Then Nate kissed her again, this time a little longer. Sue sank further into his arms, kissing him back, enjoying their time alone together.

Just then, DJ called from his room, "Mommy! I have to go potty!"

Sue pulled back and laughed. "It was fun while it lasted," she said, a hint of disappointment in her voice.

"No way. We're picking up where we left off when you come back," Nate teased her.

Walking up the stairs, Sue added a little swing to her hips for Nate's sake. Nate sighed and wiped his forehead. Sue looked over her shoulder and laughed and quickly climbed the rest of the stairs.

○ ○ ○ ○

Josephine sat in her living room, feeling depressed. She hadn't talked much with her sisters since they found out the truth. She missed them and the relationship they all shared. Will they ever be the same again? Since her and Steven's argument, she hadn't spoken to him, either. Now, as she sat next to Mark watching a movie, she wondered if she was making a mistake. Maybe she had let her anger get the better of her. She shouldn't have stormed out of Sue's that day. She should have called her the next day and smoothed things over. That was over a month ago now. Josephine felt as if it were too late. She couldn't just call her and act as if nothing had happened. She wanted to, but she knew she couldn't do that. And then there was Steven. She was hurt that he had told Nate and Sue, but at the same time, she understood. Josephine desperately wanted to call him, talk things out, and see if they could still be friends. But when she had told Mark what Steven had done, he acted like it was unforgivable. He went on and on about how friends keep each other's secrets, how he never really liked Steven, and he was glad Josephine was done with him.

The problem was Josephine didn't want to be done with Steven. She missed him. She missed their talks and the many times they laughed together. She felt like she was all alone in the world yet again, but this time was worse than anything she had ever felt before.

Josephine stole a quick glance at Mark. He seemed so content with the way things were playing out. He was fine with her not having a close relationship with her sisters. He said they had too much control over her and felt it was time she lived life out from under their shadows. He was especially glad Steven was out of the picture. Suddenly, Steven's questions came back to her. She pushed them out of her head after their argument, but now, she couldn't shake them no matter how hard she tried. She grabbed the remote and pushed pause. She needed answers and needed them now.

She turned to face Mark. "I have to ask you something." Josephine continued when she had his attention. "Why do you want me to get DJ back so much?"

Something flickered in Mark's eyes, and then quickly disappeared. "Why do you ask?"

"Well, I had wondered that a while ago, but I never asked you about it. I forgot, I guess. Why is this such a big deal to you?"

Mark took her in his arms and caressed her arm. "Sweetie, I care about you, you know that."

His answer didn't sit well with her. "I know you do. I'm not questioning your feelings toward me. I'm questioning why you want me to do this."

"Why are you questioning me at all?" Josephine could feel Mark's body tense up. She pulled away from him so she could look into his eyes. "Do you think I have a motive or something?"

"I don't know. That's why I am asking. Steven and Sue said something about why you want me to do this."

Mark stood up, anger flashing in his eyes. "Oh, I see. So that's what this is about. They want you to doubt me so you can break up with me and not go through with it. And you are letting them get into your head!"

"Mark! I'm not!" Josephine rose and put her hands on his shoulders. "I'm not saying you have an ulterior motive! I just want to know if there is any other reason, that's all. I'm not letting them get into my head."

Mark's face relaxed. "Sorry I got so defensive. I just hate that your family and friends are trying to tear us apart."

Josephine put her arms around his waist and hugged him.

"They aren't. I won't let them."

Mark sighed. "There is no other reason. I love you. I told you that. I really think God wants families together, not torn apart." He looked deeply into her eyes. "Do you believe me?"

Josephine tried to push the doubt she felt out of her heart and prayed Mark wouldn't see it in her eyes. "I know how you feel about me, Mark. Like I said before, I do not doubt that."

Mark breathed a sigh of relief. "Good. Now let's finish our movie. Have you decided what you are going to do yet?"

Josephine sat back down on the couch. She shook her head. "Not yet."

"Don't take too long. I think if you act quickly, you could win custody of DJ." Mark picked up the remote.

"Is that what your lawyer friend told you?"

Mark shook his head. "No. But I can't imagine why a judge would keep the two of you apart."

"Hm." Josephine didn't feel as confident as Mark did.

She had signed papers giving up her son. What judge would waive those just because she wanted him back? And did she want him back? Did Josephine really want to separate a family? Could she really raise DJ on her own? Would she even want to? The questions still loomed over her like a heavy rain cloud. Josephine didn't have the answers. She hated feeling torn between her family and Mark. She knew she had to keep praying and let God guide her.

"Mark," Josephine paused the movie again. "I'm so confused. I have been battling my decision for a few months now. I still don't have answers!"

Mark took her hand in his. "Josephine, confusion is from the devil. That's not from God. You need to spend time alone; praying about what God wants you to do."

"I have been, though. That's just it. I still don't have any answers." Josephine looked down at the couch, her eyes filling with tears.

"Have you thought about fasting? I mean, Easter is a week or so away, right? So, why don't you fast from people from now until then. Don't answer your phone or go to work. Pray about what God wants you to do, and then move forward."

Josephine felt herself relax. That was a great idea! Fast from people! Why hadn't she thought of that before? She wouldn't talk to anyone, including her sisters or Mark for a week. She will spend time in prayer and seek God in all of it. "Brilliant idea, Mark! That's what I will do! As soon as you leave tonight, I will begin fasting. I better make some calls to see if anyone wants my shifts at work."

Mark nodded as she picked up the phone and made some calls. After she got her shifts covered, she sat back, content. Fasting is exactly what she needed. She looked forward to the peace that would come from spending time with the Lord and the Lord only. Now if she could only experience that peace now. Perhaps she would feel better.

Chapter 21

*M*ark left Josephine's house, a smug expression on his face. Things were going so well! Who would have thought he would finally be able to see good come from his past? He had experienced so much hurt and pain. It finally dawned on him why the Lord had let him go through so much. It was because of Josephine. He didn't know if she was the one he was supposed to marry. But Mark knew he was supposed to help her fight for her son. He was supposed to reunite them and help them be a family, like they should have been from the beginning. Like he should have been with his parents. Only that didn't happen. Mark brushed the thoughts away as soon as they had come. Now wasn't the time to dwell on what should have happened. Now is the time to dwell on what will be. Mark pulled out of Josephine's complex. He had the rest of the day all to himself. He didn't have classes today. He thought about going to see his sister, but wasn't ready for a confrontation on what he should or shouldn't be doing. She just didn't understand. How could the two of them be siblings, let alone twins? How could they have been through the same thing as children, yet see things so differently? He didn't know, and he didn't care. At this point, he was pushing forward, with or without her blessing. Mark hadn't told his parents about what he was pushing Josephine to do. He could see the disappointment in their eyes if he did tell them. He knew it would only cause them more pain. But hadn't they caused him pain years ago? Hadn't they brought all this on themselves? No! Mark didn't want to go back there and forced himself to focus. What should he do with the rest of his day? Suddenly, an idea hit him. He quickly turned the car around.

Sue smiled softly to herself as she listened to Nate's voice sing from the cd player. She loved listening to the cd he had made years ago. When the doorbell rang, she turned the music down ever so slightly. Sue opened the door, surprised to see Mark standing there. "Mark," she said stiffly. "What can I do for you?"

Mark looked past her. "Can I come in? I need to talk to you."

Sue opened the door slowly. "Sure. But please keep your voice down. The kids just fell asleep."

Mark nodded respectfully. "Sure."

What was *he* doing here? What could he possibly have to say? Sue knew she should be hospitable, but there was no sense in pretending she didn't know what he was doing to her family. He was the enemy, after all. Sue sat down and offered Mark a seat. "Can I get you anything to drink?"

Mark shook his head. "No. This isn't a social call."

"What's this about then?" Sue's body was tense.

"Josephine doesn't know I'm here, for starters," Mark began, leaning forward, his elbows resting on his knees.

"All right..." Sue didn't like the way things were going already. If Josephine didn't know he was here, then he was being secretive. Sue didn't like secrets. And she didn't like Mark.

"Listen, Sue, I wanted to give you a heads up that Josephine's going to fight for DJ," Mark's look spoke the confidence she didn't feel. "I think it would be in your best interest if you gave him up without a fight."

Sue's eyes grew wide. "What? How do you know she's going through with it?"

"She's fasting from people over the next week so she can clear her head. I think when she is done, she will come to the conclusion that she will want DJ back."

"Why is she fasting from people? How would that help her?" Sue had to remind herself the kids were napping. She kept her voice low and tried to keep her voice even. She knew it was a losing battle. Anger poured forth from her like a busted pipe.

"You and your family, and other people she knows are confusing her. She doesn't need that. She needs love and encouragement and support. I suggested she fast from everyone so she can spend some time with the Lord and find out what He wants." Mark paused, a sly grin pulling at the edges of his mouth. "I think you and I both know what that will be."

Sue's mouth twisted. What? What was he talking about? How does Mark know what the Lord wants from Josephine? How could he come into their family and pretend to know anything about them? She felt sick to her stomach. She closed her eyes and inhaled. Slowly, she exhaled and tried to push out all the frustration she felt boiling inside of her.

"What makes you think God wants her to fight for DJ? DJ already has a family, Mark. Why would God want us to be separated?"

"Sue," Mark's words were on the border of patronizing, "why would God want Josephine to give up DJ in the first place? This isn't a matter of family now, but then. He never should have been separated from her to begin with. You and Nate were in sin by thinking otherwise."

"Oh, you are insane! Where do you even come up with this garbage?" Sue's eyes flashed with anger.

"I know from experience, lets just say that." Mark sighed. "I just think it is in your best interest to not fight us on this."

"Why's that, Mark?" Sue could tell she was losing the battle of self control.

"Because I think you will lose," Mark answered calmly. "Most family court judges would rather see the child back with its biological parent that with an adoptive parent."

"And you know this how?" Sue's eyes narrowed.

"My family has friends who are lawyers. I think they will agree with me."

Sue stood up angrily. "And you think I am just going to give up my son? Without a fight?"

"Sue," Mark said condescendingly, "he's not your son. He's Josephine's son. The sooner you realize and accept that, the better off you'll be."

"She only gave birth to him, Mark, nothing else," Sue said through clenched teeth. "I am his mother." She pounded her chest.

Mark shook his head. "That may not be how the court looks at it."

"You might want to check your facts, Mark. From what our lawyer says, once a parent's rights are terminated, they cannot be restored, no matter what." Sue sat back on the couch, satisfaction creeping into her as she saw Mark flinch.

"Hm. Well, I don't know about that. Anyway, I just wanted to come by and forewarn you. It may be easier for you if you just didn't fight us on this. I'm not here to gloat. I just wanted to prepare you, that's all."

Mark stood to leave. "Before you go, Mark, I just have one question for you." Sue fought back angry tears.

Mark turned toward her. "What?"

"Why would you even suggest to Josephine to take back DJ?" Sue's heart was showing on her sleeve.

Mark paused. "Sue, I firmly believe God wants families together. I don't think He would want Josephine and DJ to be living separate lives. I think you and Nate are hindering God's will for their lives."

"Mark, you weren't there when this all started. How can you say you know what God's will is?" Sue pointed an accusing finger at him.

"Sometimes, Sue, it takes an outsider to see people not obeying the voice of the Lord. That's all I am, an outsider, helping you all to see the error of your ways and trying to help fix them." Mark lifted one shoulder and let it fall.

"The error of my ways? How did you come to that conclusion?" Sue asked incredulously.

"You manipulated Josephine for your own personal gain. That's the error I am referring to. And Josephine's error was believing she couldn't take care of DJ on her own."

"You are an arrogant, pompous man! I can't believe you would even judge another that way. You know nothing about our family or the events that took place during that time." Sue shook from anger.

"Sue, I didn't come over here to be called names. I was just coming over to warn you and give you some friendly advice. Take it or leave it. Enjoy your day," Mark spouted over his shoulder and closed the door behind him.

Sue stormed around the living room, fuming. She couldn't stand that man! Everything within her being wanted to call Josephine and scream and yell at her. She knew that would do no good. Instead, she walked over to the book shelf and grabbed the precious book filled with memories. She sank sullenly into the couch and opened to the first page. Staring back at her was DJ's sweet face, the day he was born. Nate was holding him, proud as ever. Sue turned to the next page. Her heart broke as she saw herself, DJ, and Nate standing in the hospital. The caption read: One Happy Family. Tears slid down her cheeks. Could this really be happening? Could the next family portrait they take really be without her son?

Sue sat on her couch, tears streaming down her face. Her whole world was crashing, and she had no way of knowing how to stop it. She didn't know why she was torturing herself this way, looking at a book with precious memories she had painstakingly put together, not knowing the future would look this bleak. In any given moment, everything could change. Sobbing quietly, she flipped another page, one that took her breath away. The page showed her family, all together, happy and joyful. *Will we ever be that way again?* She wondered. Her family was about to be torn apart, never to be the same again, all because of one choice. *Why, Lord? Why is this happening?* She questioned. No answer came. Sue was devastated. Her heart felt as if it were being smashed into tiny pieces. How could things have turned out this way? How could one person change the course of their lives without even realizing the consequences of their actions? Sue sighed heavily and closing her eyes, she leaned heavily against the couch

Nate's voice rang through the house. Sue had forgotten she

had put on his cd he had made years ago.

"There is hope in the darkness. Something to hold on to. Your anchor waits to hold you, hold you through the storm, rest and know, He is God." Sue was definitely going through a storm. Her emotions were all over the place. She couldn't see through the darkness that lay ahead of her. Rest and know, Nate's voice resonated through her soul. He is God.

The ringing of the phone brought Sue back to the present.

"Hello?" she choked out.

"Sue, honey, what is it? Are you okay?" Nate's voice was etched with concern.

"Mark was just here," Sue answered weakly.

Nate groaned. "That doesn't sound good. What happened?"

Sue described the scene that took place between her and Mark and the awful news he brought over with him.

"Now can I go punch him? I could grab Steven and the two of us could take him out together. You know, the bible does say two are better than one!"

Sue laughed in spite of herself. "I love you, Nate. But no, you cannot. And I think you took that verse out of context."

Nate sighed. "I know. I thought I should at least try. Seriously, though, Sweetie, don't worry. Or try not to, at least. We will continue to leave this in God's hands and fight them every step of the way."

"Thanks. The kids will be up soon. I better go compose myself before they get up."

"Ok. I love you, Sue," Nate said softly.

"I love you, too, Baby," Sue replied gently.

When she hung up the phone, Sue sat back down on the couch. She wiped her face with a tissue, and took a few deep breaths. Her heart rate had settled down and she was finally calm when the kids woke up. Sue didn't know what the future held. She trusted God, though. Her world may be in utter darkness, but she was bound and determined to cling to her Anchor.

She knew no other way to live her life but to trust the One who held her life in the palm of His hands.

Chapter 22

*E*ddie sat across from Sue, holding Ella in his arms. He was a tall man, with graying hair. His ocean blue eyes sparkled as Ella grabbed a fist full of his goatee. He opened and closed his mouth, making it seem like she was doing it by pulling on him. Miles sat to his left and giggled at the show Eddie was putting on. DJ nestled next to Sue, hiding his grin behind his hand. Sue was so glad Eddie and his wife, Carol, had come to visit! It had been almost a year since she had seen her in-laws. She had a fun relationship with her father-in-law. They often joked with one another. Her step-mother-in-law called it a battle of the wits. More often than not, Sue felt she had won. Sue stifled a giggled and focused on the people sitting across from her.

"Can I get you two some coffee or tea?"

Both of them shook their heads. Carol got up. "No thank you. I'm going to take these kiddos into their room to play with them." She scooped up Ella and motioned for the boys to follow her.

Eddie sat back and smiled. "You have a great family, Sue. I'm proud to be their papa."

Sue's heart melted with gratitude. "Thanks, Dad. I'm glad you and Mom can be here to finally meet them."

Eddie's brow knit together as he leaned forward. "How are things going? What's the word with your sister?"

Sue ran her hand through her thick hair. "Not much. She's fasting this week from people, so her boyfriend informs me. I don't know, Dad." Tears filled her eyes. "I just don't know what's going to happen. I'm scared and angry all at the same time. I know from talking with the lawyer that there is a good possibility we won't lose DJ, but you never know. We could get a judge that favors on reuniting families. And, I'm so mad at her, I could scream! She lied to me! She is threatening to take away my son! That is something she promised she would never do, Dad! Every time I think about it, I get more and more angry!"

Eddie nodded sympathetically. "I can understand that. I see the hurt she has caused you. You must be wondering how you can ever trust her again, right?"

When Sue nodded, he continued, "Trust is difficult to earn back once it has been lost. But it can be earned again. Remember that. Give things time. You don't know what will happen in the future. Shoot, we don't even know what the next hour holds, right?"

Sue sighed, the weight of the world resting on her shoulders. "I can't picture my life without DJ. My life just wouldn't be the same."

Eddie played with his chin thoughtfully. "I understand. We never know what the future holds. Keep praying about it." He patted her hand. "It is difficult losing a child."

Sue cocked her head to one side. "You've lost a child?"

Eddie nodded slowly. "When Nate was two, his mom and I had a little girl, Hope. She was beautiful." Eddie's voice broke. He paused before going on. "She wasn't even two months old when we found her one morning, gone home to be with Jesus."

Sue watched Eddie compose himself. She hadn't known this story before. Sue was surprised Nate never talked about it. "Does Nate remember any of this?"

Eddie shook his head. "Not really."

"Oh, Dad, I am so sorry. I didn't know you and Martha went through that. What a horrible time for you!"

Eddie dabbed at his eyes. "It was hard, that's for sure. No parent should have to bury their child."

Sue felt her heart break for the man sitting across from her. It would be hard to give up DJ if Josephine fought for him and won. But to have him die? She didn't know if she could handle the pain.

"In this life, Sue, we are never guaranteed a tomorrow. We

only have today. Treasure each day you have with your kids and Nate. You never know when your last one will be." Eddie began. "I know you must be thinking it was hard for us to go through that, and it was. Years after I gave my life to the Lord, I heard a pastor say our goal in raising children is to teach them about Jesus so that one day we can all be together again. I have hope that one day, I will see my little Hope in heaven."

Sue nodded, tears spilling down her cheeks. She brushed them away with the back of her hand. "So, what you are saying is, no matter what happens with DJ, as long as he loves Jesus, even if I don't get to spend time with him here on earth, I will in heaven."

Eddie gently smiled at her. "I knew you would catch on. I always tell Nate you are a bright girl!"

Sue laughed. "Thanks, Dad!"

Eddie looked at the clock. "What time is that son of mine due home from work?"

"Anytime now," Sue glanced toward the front door.

"Good! I want to take us to dinner!" Eddie stood up. "Until then, I have some grandkids I need to play with! Here comes Papa!"

Eddie bellowed as he headed up the stairs. Sue heard Carol tell the kids they better hide! Squeals of delight flowed down the stairs. Sue stood up and stretched, smiling at the noise from upstairs. She enjoyed her talk with Eddie.

She said a silent prayer thanking God for her in-laws.

Good Friday, Josephine thought as she sat down on her couch. She had spent the last week fasting from people. She had spent a lot of time reading God's word, and even more time praying. She searched for answers and tried to listen intently. It was hard for her. She didn't have the radio on or the television. She literally spent the week in solitude, praying God would reveal what He wanted her to do. She still didn't have answers, but she was filled with God's peace. She didn't know what that meant, only that He hadn't left her alone.

Alone. The word hurt her heart more than anything. She hated being alone. Ever since she could remember, she struggled with loneliness. That's what had gotten her pregnant, hadn't it? She was lonely. Instead of calling her sisters, she had called Jim. Of course, she never regretted DJ coming into the world as a result. She just wished she would have not given in to sin. Oh well. No sense in wishing. She couldn't change the past. Only the future. What did the future hold for her? She still didn't know. Josephine needed to figure things out and soon.

She glanced around her empty apartment. What would it be like to have a child here with her? She would have to share her bedroom, of course. What would she do with all of his toys? Where would she put them? Would she have to move? Could she afford to move? How much would her bills go up? How much would her life change? Did she really want the responsibility of raising a child on her own? Sure, Mark said he would help, but could she rely on that? Her mom would say not to count her chickens before they were hatched. Relying on Mark to be around the next eighteen years would be just that. She didn't know if she would end up marrying Mark. For some reason, she couldn't see him standing at the end of aisle as she walked down. She didn't picture anyone as of yet.

One thing she knew, however. She missed Steven. Throughout this time of fasting from people, she had the opportunity to reflect on her current relationships. Josephine hadn't spoken to the Sorenson's or her sisters in a long time. And she hadn't talked with Steven since her argument. That was over a month ago! She shook her head. Maybe she was just missing people.. She knew she needed to mend things with Steven so maybe that was a part of it, as well. Only one more day, and then she would call him, she thought with decisiveness. This feud had gone on long enough. It was time to make things right again.

As for DJ, what would she do about DJ?

o o o o

Ally leaned her elbows on her knees, tapping her fingers against her lips. She looked at the phone sitting across from her. It was one of the few things that weren't packed. She and her husband were moving soon. Her house had already sold. Escrow would close in less than two weeks. Ally had spent most of her time packing up their belongings, getting ready to move to Pennsylvania. She couldn't believe she was leaving her family and friends to move to a state where she knew no one! Ally knew it was for the best. Her husband had gotten an amazing job offer they couldn't pass up. It was everything he wanted to do and more! And the pay wasn't too bad, either.

Ally slowly stood up, begging her feet to move toward the phone. She needed to do this one last thing before she left. She knew she did. She groaned inwardly. The repercussions of her actions were going to be great. She had counted the cost of what she was about to do. She and Ben had talked extensively about it. Ally knew it was the right thing to do, and she knew it was time. Urging her feet forward and forcing her hand out, she picked up the phone. Sighing, she dialed the number.

"Josephine? It's Ally."

Chapter 23

*J*osephine absently stirred her coffee, waiting for Ally to arrive. She knew it was a few hours early before her fast was supposed to be over, but Ally sounded so distraught, she couldn't help but meet with her. Josephine wasn't going to answer her phone at all when it rang, but she hardly received calls from Ally. Since Ally was going to be moving, Josephine doubted she wanted to become close friends. So something must have been wrong. She had answered the phone, panic gripping her heart. The only reason Josephine could think of Ally calling her was because something had happened to Mark. But that wasn't the case, Ally assured her. She did sound bothered, however, and part of it was due to Mark.

Josephine's gaze traveled to the giant window, waiting for Ally to pull up. The sky was getting darker. The forecast called for a spring snow storm. Josephine couldn't remember the last time they had gotten snow for Easter, but that's what the weather men were predicting. Not a lot of snow, but an inch or two mixed with rain. Josephine loved the cold weather, but a part of her was ready for the warmth. She loved to feel the sun on her face. Today, she felt the wind whip her hair as she had walked to her car to meet with Ally, and then when she got to the coffee shop, the cold surrounded her like a cocoon. Summer can't come fast enough, she thought as she spotted Ally pulling up.

Ally waved slightly as she headed to the counter to order her drink. When her order was up, she quickly grabbed it and a beeline way to where Josephine sat.

Josephine stood and hugged her. "Hey Ally! How's the packing going?"

"Almost done, thanks for asking. We'll be leaving soon. It seems surreal, I tell you!" All sat down and slowly sipped her coffee.

"I believe it!" Josephine sat in silence, waiting for Ally to gather her thoughts. She had no idea what this was about, so she waited.

Ally cleared her throat nervously. "If Mark knew what I was doing, he would be so angry with me. But Josephine," her eyes shown with intensity Josephine hadn't seen before. "You need to know the truth before you move forward in fighting for DJ."

Josephine's cheek flushed from embarrassment. "You know about that?"

Ally nodded. "I do."

"I didn't know Mark told you about it. Truthfully, I'm still confused about what to do. When I think about it, I don't believe fighting for DJ is what I should do, but Mark is so persistent. When he talks with me, he is so passionate about it." Josephine shook her head, confusion written on her face.

Ally crossed her arms in front of her. "Did he ever tell you why he was so persistent?"

"Honestly, I asked him the other day. He said it was just because he loves me. That's the only reason he gave me." Josephine sipped her coffee, watching Ally struggle through her emotions.

Why was she so upset? Josephine had no idea why Ally wanted to meet with her, let alone why Mark's sister looked so bothered.

Ally sighed deeply. "That's it? That's the only reason? Don't you think it odd? What's his real motive? Did you ask him that?"

Josephine was caught off guard by the edge in Ally's voice. "I did, but he got defensive. He said I was letting everyone tear us apart. After that, I didn't bring it up again."

Ally rolled her eyes. "I swear, sometimes it amazes me we come from the same family! It amazes me we are even twins!"

Josephine gave an uncomfortable laugh. She still had no idea what this was all about. "Ally, you wanted to talk to me about something important, so what's going on?"

Ally shrugged off her jacket. "Ok. I'm about to tell you something, but you can't interrupt me until I am through, all right?"

Josephine rested her elbows on the table separating herself from Ally and placed her face in her hands.

"Okay,." she agreed.

"Mark and I are adopted," Ally stated quickly. When Josephine was about to speak, she held up her hand. "Hold on. Let me explain, and then you can ask me your questions if you still have them."

Adopted? Mark and Ally were adopted? How could that be? Josephine shifted in her chair, listening as Ally began explaining.

"Mark and I were only babies when we were taken away from our birth mom. My parents were foster parents, waiting for infants to be placed in their home. You see, once my brother, my oldest brother that is, was born, my parents realized they couldn't have any more children. So they decided to adopt through the foster care system. The social worker had called my parents and asked if they would be willing to take twins. They were beyond thrilled but never realized we would be able to be adopted. My birth mother had her rights terminated after many failed attempts at getting clean from her drug abuse. Never in all of my life did I ever think we were adopted. Not until we were fourteen. My parents sat us down and told us the truth. I was stunned at first. We were adopted? Oh, but Josephine, then the truth hit me. My parents wanted us! We weren't some accidents born and raised into a family. We were wanted! God adopting me took on a whole new meaning! I wept with my parents. I remember the day like it was yesterday. When the truth sank in, I ran to them, and threw my arms around them. I cried with them and thanked them for choosing me, for wanting me, for giving me a life I never would have known."

Josephine's eyes were filling with tears and threatening to spill onto her cheeks. She could see the joy in Ally's eyes. Ally's own eyes were moist as she spoke.

Ally took a deep breath. "But that's not how Mark took it." Her eyes suddenly turned dark. "He asked a lot of questions about our birth mom. He wanted to know if she had ever tried to contact us. My parents were open and honest. They informed us that she had indeed tried to contact us, but they wouldn't allow her to see us. Not too long after that, she died of a drug overdose. Mark was suddenly angry. He couldn't understand how my parents had kept this a secret so long. He didn't understand why my parents hadn't allowed us to see her. He felt that maybe if we were able to meet her and reestablish a relationship with her, perhaps we could have been her reason for getting clean. He even said that he could have won her over to Jesus, and they took that opportunity away from him. He started saying cruel things to them, hurtful things. Even though they had given him a good life, a life full of love and laughter and life. I knew in my heart they were trying to protect us. They didn't want us to have to deal with someone who was addicted to drugs. Seriously, Josephine, after fourteen years, she still wasn't clean! I tried to remind Mark of these things, how our adoptive parents brought us to Jesus and gave us a great life. He brushed me away. He said I was too emotional, that I see everything through rose colored glasses, not as they really were. My parents were heartbroken. They knew we might be upset, but my brother was way out of line. He stormed off that day, staying the night at a friend's house, not wanting to talk to us or be with us for a few days. Finally when he came home, he said he understood why they waited so long to tell us, but he still didn't understand why they wouldn't let us meet with our birth mom."

Ally shook her head. "I don't know, Josephine. It's like he felt it was their responsibility to reunite us with our birth parents. But my adopted parents didn't do anything wrong! They took us in. They protected us from what could have been a terrible relationship with our birth mom. But he didn't see it that way, I don't know why. I still don't understand his thought process. I can only imagine what kind of relationship we would have had with her. And believe me, it wouldn't have been pleasant."

Josephine held up her hand. "Wait a minute. You didn't want to know her?"

Ally shook her head vehemently. "Not at all! I didn't hold any animosity toward her, please understand that. But she was only my biological mom, nothing more. She didn't raise me, the Littletons did. They were the ones who sat up with me when I had nightmares. They were the ones who laughed with me, loved me. They were the ones who gave me a good home, a good life, and showed me how to live my life for Jesus. I didn't have a desire to know my birth parents. I had wonderful, godly parents already. That's all I needed."

"But Mark didn't see it that way?" Josephine sat back in her chair. She wanted to hear the rest of the story. She needed to hear the rest of the story. She was appalled Mark hadn't told her the truth. Why wouldn't he be honest with her? Why would he withhold this information from her?

Ally picked up a napkin and toyed with it. "Nope. He felt my parents robbed him of knowing his real parents, as he called them."

"So, how did he reconcile with your parents?"

Ally blew air from the side of her mouth that lifted her bangs slightly. "It took a long time, let me tell you. He was hurtful and angry most of his adolescent years. My parents finally talked him into going to counseling with them. That seemed to help, but that only happened a few years ago. It was a long and painful road we went down with him."

"Ok. So, Mark was grateful that he had the Littletons after that, right?"

Ally laughed, but it was void of humor. "You would think that, wouldn't you? But no, not my twin! In his twisted mind, my parents were the ones to blame. He said he forgave them, but he still held them at arm's length. We have never really been the same family since then."

"That's absurd!" Josephine exclaimed.

"I know. But he blamed my parents for everything, including her death."

"But Mark said family is very important to him. That's one

of the things he said when we first met! Why would he blame your parents for that?" Josephine was confused and shocked.

"Oh, family is important to him. It took him a long time to realize just how important family is. For a long time, Mark withdrew from us. He didn't want to have anything to do with us. He looked down on me for being so grateful; he looked down on my parents; and even on my big brother! Not until recently did his attitude start to change."

"Whew. This is a lot to take in, Ally. I'm not sure what to make of all of this." Josephine rubbed her forehead and closed her eyes.

"I know. I understand. But I thought you might need to know the real reason Mark is pushing you. He feels if you have DJ back, DJ won't go through the pain and agony he did when DJ finds out he is adopted. He feels families should have the opportunity to be with each other." Ally looked down. When she met Josephine's gaze, her eyes were brimming with unshed tears. "Josephine, I don't know if this is going to help you or not. All I know is this: I was grateful my parents adopted us. They gave me what my birthmother obviously could not. If you take nothing else from this conversation, take this: Let DJ have his family, the one with a mom and a dad, loving him and raising him as God intended. I'm not saying you wouldn't be a great mother, but don't take DJ away from the only mother he has ever known." Ally placed her hand on Josephine's and gave it a gentle squeeze.

"You're saying let DJ stay with my sister, right?" When Ally nodded solemnly, Josephine continued, "What is this going to do to your relationship with Mark? I mean, you know I am going to confront him on this, right?"

Ally withdrew her hand and leaned back. "I know. I have thought about that already. It will destroy our relationship, I know that. I'm prepared to fight to keep my relationship with him, but I know my brother. He will take my telling you as a betrayal. I'm ready to accept the consequences of my actions."

"You barely know me and my family. Why would you risk your relationship with Mark for us?" Josephine was astounded.

"Because I believe it is the right thing to do. You needed to know the truth, and I knew Mark wasn't going to tell you. DJ needs to stay with your sister. I believe that with all of my heart. And I think deep down, so do you, Josephine." Ally stood and put on her jacket. She gazed down at Josephine, a joy filling her eyes. "I know you'll do the right thing."

Josephine met her gaze, the truth sinking in. Suddenly, she pushed her chair back and wrapped Ally in a tight hug. "Ally, you have no idea what an answer to prayer this is! I spent all last week in prayer about this. I felt God's peace, but I didn't know what I was going to do. And now this! Thank you! Thank you for being honest with me! Thank you for telling me the truth, even though it is going to cost you your brother!"

Ally was crying softly by now, clinging to Josephine. "I don't know what's going to happen between you and my brother." She sniffed. "I am just thankful I had the opportunity to get to know you, Josephine. Take care of yourself. And take care of your family. Do whatever it takes to bring healing to you and your sister."

Josephine nodded and pulled away. "I will. Thanks, Ally. God bless you and your husband as you start a new life together in Pennsylvania!"

Ally smiled slightly **and waved good**-bye.

Josephine lay in bed, tossing and turning. She had gone to bed early, praying for the sweet embrace of sleep. But that is not what she had gotten. Instead, her mind replayed the information Ally had given her that afternoon. She hadn't spoken to anyone since that conversation. She knew Mark wouldn't be calling her or coming over until tomorrow. He had no idea Josephine had seen his sister.

Mark and Ally were adopted. That put a whole new spin on her decision whether or not to fight for DJ. What bothered her the most was that Mark flat out lied to her. She point blank asked him what was his motivation, and he said it was his love for her. Josephine snorted. Yeah, right. It was because of what he had gone through that prompted him to push her into fighting for DJ. Why wouldn't he just tell her the truth? Why wouldn't he be honest with her? Was he afraid that if he was honest perhaps she wouldn't go through with it?

Her mind raced looking for answers. Yet, she could find none.

His response to being adopted worried Josephine. She hoped and prayed DJ would never view adoption as Mark had. It shocked her, even, that he had such a negative view point. Why wouldn't Mark be happy knowing a couple wanted to raise him and love him and give him hope many kids nowadays longed for? Why would he resent them? It was obvious his biological mom wanted nothing to do with him or she wouldn't have given him up in the first place. And if she did want to have him and Ally in her life, she would have done her best to keep in contact with him. So, why was Mark so bent out of shape toward his adoptive parents? All of the information Ally had given her still wrestled in her heart and mind. What was she supposed to do now? What direction was she supposed to go in?

Josephine turned on her side, sleep still evading her. What was she supposed to do with her relationship with Mark? Could she trust him? Should she stay with him? Should she break up with him? If she did, would she be alone again? Who would love her? Who would she spend her time with? Obviously, she had alienated her sisters and Steven and even the Sorenson's. Josephine sighed. Why did she let her relationship with the Sorenson's go? She had guessed they knew all about what she was thinking in regards to DJ. Maybe she just didn't want to have another discussion about how she shouldn't fight for him. But in avoiding that discussion, she had avoided a relationship she treasured and valued through the years.

Josephine glanced at the clock. Nine o'clock, it read. She had been laying there for an hour. She needed to do something. Laying there wasn't going to solve anything, and it certainly wasn't going to bring sleep. She bounced out of bed, an idea suddenly hitting her. She quickly got dressed, ran a brush through her hair, and grabbed her keys.

As she left her apartment, she prayed God would go before her in what she knew she needed to do and prepare her heart for what needed to be said.

Steven sat on his couch, watching the basketball game that was on the television. He enjoyed basketball. His dad had taught him all about it, and every so often, they would have a one-on-one game. His father was a good basketball player. It always amazed Steven he never went into the NBA. When Steven asked his dad about it, his father would smile wistfully and put his arm around his mom and say there were more important things than the NBA. But that didn't stop them from playing hoops together or watching a few games throughout the week. Steven was a full-blown Laker fan. His dad had grown up in Southern California and passed along his love for the Lakers. Steven knew that was dangerous living in a city that loved its professional teams, but it was worth it. He enjoyed the playful banter he received from co-workers.

Steven chuckled, remembering the last game he and Nate watched together. Nate loved the Lakers, as well. It was fun hearing Nate argue with the referees even though he wasn't actually at the game. Steven understood. He'd done that a few times, too. It was fun, eating pizza with Nate and his family and watching the game. Even little DJ had gotten into it, saying adamantly,

"Pau Gasol is the best, huh, Dad?"

Nate had looked at DJ, pride showing in his eyes. "Yes, son, Pau is pretty awesome!"

Steven tousled DJ's hair and agreed with him.

Now as Steven sat alone, watching the game, he wondered yet again, if he was going to find that special someone. He continued to pray about it and wait on the Lord. It just seemed he would be alone for a little while longer. Proverbs 3:3-5 came into his head, "Trust in the Lord with all of your heart and lean not on your own understanding. In all your ways, acknowledge Him, and He shall direct your path."

Steven paused, letting the words sink in to his very soul. He decided that was the best thing for him to do.

Steven turned off the game when a knock sounded at his door. Slowly getting up, he checked his watch. Just after nine thirty. Who would be visiting him at this hour? Only one way to find out. He quickly went toward the door and opened it.

To his surprise, Josephine stood there, looking nervous and sheepish. Her beautiful eyes blinked back tears.

"Can I come in?" she asked tentatively.

Steven opened the door a little wider, allowing her to walk past him. He had no idea why she was there. They hadn't spoken since he told her the truth about Nate and Sue knowing. His heart quickened. Something must have happened to one of her family members. That's why she was there, to let him know in person.

"What happened? Is everyone all right?" He knew his voice sounded anxious, but after months of not speaking, he couldn't think of any other reason why she was there and obviously upset.

Josephine nodded her head, pressing her fingers to her lips before speaking.

"Everyone is fine. I'm sorry to scare you."

Steven motioned for her to sit down. He sat down across from her and wiped his forehead. "You scared me for a minute."

An uncomfortable silence fell between them. Steven didn't know what to say or how to start a conversation. She should be the one to say something first since she came to him. He knew that didn't seem like a godly thing to think, but at the same time, she hadn't answered any of his calls after she stormed out of his house. Josephine needed to be the one to begin the conversation. He didn't see any other way around it. So he sat, waiting for her to speak.

"Steven, I don't know where to begin." Her voice cracked. She looked down at her hands. When she looked back at him, tears filled her eyes. "I've been horrible to you. I know I have. The last few months, I have wanted to call you and apologize for that evening." She shook her head, sadness filling her beautiful features. "I just didn't know how. I realize it's been a long time coming, but I couldn't go another minute without telling you how sorry I am for the way I acted."

She's sorry? That was the last thing Steven had expected to hear her say. He sat, stunned. He needed to say something, but didn't know what.

"Can I get you something to drink?" He asked lamely.

The corner of Josephine's mouth turned up in a slight grin. "I tell you I'm sorry and all you can say is do you want something to drink?"

A quiet chuckle rumbled through Steven's throat. He gave a slight shrug. "Sorry. I'm not always eloquent with my words."

Josephine gently shook her blonde head. "I understand. Steven, I want you to know how sorry I am. I know I acted poorly. I wish I could go back and change what had happened between us."

Steven got up and sat next to her. "Jo, I know I said it a lot that night, but I am truly sorry for telling Nate and Sue. I need you to understand I never meant to hurt you." His eyes pleaded for her to understand.

"I know. That's just it. When I had time to process everything, I knew you hadn't done anything out of maliciousness. You didn't even intend to tell them. But by the time I realized that, it was too late to talk to you about it."

Steven leaned against the back of the couch. "It was never too late. If it were, would you be here now?"

"No, I guess not."

They sat in silence for a few more minutes. Steven knew their friendship needed mending, and he was willing to do his best to help the process. He missed Josephine, more than she knew. But before he could be friends with this blonde beauty sitting next to him, he needed to know a few things.

He cleared his throat. "Josephine, I have missed our friendship, but one thing seems to stand in the way of us being friends again."

"Mark," Josephine said matter-of-fact.

"No," Steven shook his head. "DJ."

Josephine's brow furrowed. "What do you mean?"

"Well, since I haven't heard from you, I figured you still haven't decided what to do about DJ. But I need you to know this right here and now, if you decide to claim DJ or try to anyway, I can't be friends with you." The words hurt, even as Steven said them. He didn't want to give up his friendship with Josephine, but he didn't agree with what she was thinking of doing. He knew he would be forced to pick sides, and he already knew he would choose Nate and Sue's.

Sadness filled her eyes. "I understand."

"Now I know you must be thinking-what did you say?" Again, Steven was surprised.

"I said I understand. I have given this a lot of thought, Steven, and I know what I would be doing. So, I am not surprised. But I don't think you have to worry."

Steven looked at her from the corner of his eye. "What do you mean?"

Josephine inhaled sharply and told Steven of her and Ally's conversation. While Josephine was talking, Steven found himself struggling with his feelings toward Mark. He was angry and annoyed. He felt saddened for Mark's parents and siblings. He knew they must be hurt by his reaction. And he felt angry. Mark had an agenda alright, and it didn't concern DJ or Josephine or their best interest. He was acting out on what he felt should have happened with him, no matter how delusional that thinking may be. Steven had to take deep breaths throughout Josephine talking, warning himself not to get too angry. Anger doesn't help anything. It can bring hurt and destruction. He needed to think about what he was going to say and how he was going to say it. Finally, Josephine finished.

"Have you told anyone else this?"

Josephine took off her shoes and tucked her feet underneath her. "No. I just found out today. I'm supposed to be on my people fast."

Steven ran his hand through his hair. "So Mark doesn't even know you know?"

"Nope. But he will." Josephine's eyes flickered with anger. "He lied to me, Steve! I asked him flat out why he wants me to do this. He said it was because he loved me. Would you lie to someone you loved? He deceived me! And he manipulated me!"

Steven silently applauded Josephine finally realizing who Mark really was. But he wasn't about to say that!

"So, where do you go from here?"

"Well, first I need to know that you forgive me." Josephine held her breath, waiting for his answer.

"Of course I forgive you, Silly." Steven threw a pillow at her.

Josephine smiled a grateful smile. "Thanks. You don't know how much I have missed you!"

"Oh, I think I can imagine. I am pretty miss-able, you know!" Steven laughed as Josephine threw the pillow back at him. "Seriously, though. I think every friendship has to go through something in order to be stronger, you know? I'm just glad it didn't ruin our friendship." Pausing briefly, he added, "But what's next for you?"

"Tomorrow I am going to talk with Mark. I seriously doubt I'll be spending Easter with his family." Josephine shook her head. "Why did I listen to him?"

"We all make mistakes, Jo. But, I think there are a lot of people you hurt in the process."

She sighed. "I know. Well, I'll have all weekend to think about how I am going to fix that."

Steven didn't know if it was a good one, but he had an idea. He prayed it would all turn out for the better. Leaning forward, he patted Josephine's knee. "I think I have an idea."

Chapter 24

*M*ark was humming as he sauntered up to Josephine's apartment. This was going to be a great day! He just knew Josephine was going to fight for DJ. When he left her apartment a little over a week ago, he felt a twinge of guilt. He knew suggesting she fast from people for a week was a little deceitful. He really wanted her to feel lonely so she would want to fight for DJ even more. If Josephine felt lonely enough, she would start to envision what it would be like to have her son with her all of the time, never having to be lonely again. His guilty feeling didn't last long, especially after he had left Sue's. She had called him arrogant and pompous. Did she even realize she was the same way? Well, after DJ was with his rightful mother, maybe she would see the error of her ways and beg Josephine for forgiveness for even being willing to adopt DJ. In and of itself, adoption wasn't all bad. There were kids in third world countries that needed to be adopted. But here is the United States of America, people should try to help the families heal and stay together. Not tear them apart, like what his parents had helped do. He forgave his parents, of course. They raised him. But he wished he had the opportunity to get to know his birth mom before she died. He was certain she would have gotten the help she needed if she had a family in her care.. Well, that was in the past. Now, he had a chance to reunite a mother and a son. And that's exactly what he was going to do.

Mark knocked on Josephine's door, whistling. This was going to be a great day, he just knew it!

Josephine braced herself and tried to steady her rapidly beating heart. This was it. She knew it was Mark at her door. Now was the moment of truth.

"Hi, honey!" Mark brushed his lips against her cheek. "How was your week?"

"Hey Mark." Josephine tried to keep her voice even. She didn't want to give anything away just yet. "My week was good. And yours?"

Mark waved his hand in the air. "We can talk about me later. I want to hear what the Lord told you. Come, sit next to me and tell me all about it!" He patted the spot next to him.

Josephine plastered a smile on her face. "Okay. But would you like something to drink first?"

"No, no. Just sit! Let's talk!" Mark was overly enthusiastic, Josephine noticed. He had no idea what was about to take place.

"Well, all right." Josephine sat next to him, but not too close. She wanted to be able to look him in the eyes. "I did come to a conclusion."

Mark's eyes were practically bursting with excitement! "Go on!"

"I've decided to leave well enough alone. I'm not going to fight for DJ."

Josephine studied Mark's reaction. His face went from excitement to astonishment to frustration.

"What?" Mark leapt up from the couch. "What do you mean? Why not?"

Josephine watched him move across the floor, trying to reel in his emotions. "I spent a lot of time in prayer, Mark. I don't think it is in DJ's best interest to rip him away from the only family he had ever known."

Josephine could hardly believe she had even considered it. Especially after her talk with Steven last night. She almost gave up everyone who mattered the most to her because she let this man put doubts about her family in her head. She obviously was not as strong as she had thought she was. She was thankful

Ally was willing to step out and speak the truth, even if that meant more trouble for her.

"I don't understand how you could come to that conclusion. Being here all alone, didn't it make you realize how lonely you were? Didn't it make you see how DJ could fill a void in your life?" Mark knelt down in front of her.

"No, it didn't. I was lonely, yes, but not for DJ. I was lonely for a husband."

"But, honey, I can help with that. I already told you I would be here for you, remember?"

"Mark, I also realized something else. You see, I was still confused on Friday, but God had given me peace. I didn't know what that meant until I got a call." Josephine waited for Mark to sit down again.

"You answered your phone? But you were still fasting." Mark gave her a disapproving look.

"I know. But when I saw who it was, I had to answer."

"Who was it?"

"Ally." Josephine watched Mark. He shifted uncomfortably.

"Oh? And why did you have to answer it?"

"Because I thought something was wrong with you. I was worried that something happened. So, I answered."

Mark looked nervous. "But obviously nothing was wrong with me. So what happened?"

Josephine caught his gaze and held on to it. "She told me the truth, Mark."

Mark's face became hard. "And what truth is that, Josephine?"

"The truth about why you want me to get DJ back." Josephine let her words sink in. "What I don't understand is, why didn't you tell me?"

"What was I supposed to say? I couldn't tell you the truth. You wouldn't have come this far if I did. But push that all aside. Think about what you're doing. You could have your son back and give him the opportunity to get to know you! Don't you see that?"

"Mark, DJ does know me. He knows me as his auntie. That's

all I want to be to him. Our situations are completely different. I still have contact with DJ. But he is happy. He has a mom and a dad and now siblings. It isn't the same as what you went through." She stood up to face him. "But the fact is you lied to me."

Mark put his hands on her shoulders. "I needed you to trust me. I still think you are making a huge mistake. I think he needs you more than just his auntie."

Josephine shrugged his hands off of her. Why won't he just let well enough alone? Mark wasn't listening to her! He wasn't understanding that he lied to her! All he can think of is fighting for DJ!

"Don't you understand, Mark? You *lied* to me! You made me think you were thinking of me and DJ! You weren't! You never told me the truth! Instead, Ally told me! How can I trust you?"

"Ally never should have told you. I don't see why she did. What place was it of hers?" Mark turned away and walked to her sliding glass door.

"What place? You're right. She shouldn't have told me; you should have! But you didn't'! You lied when I asked you for the truth! How can I trust you again?" Hot tears stung her eyes.

"My sister says she loves me and then she stabs me in the back! That's what I get for confiding in her!" Mark mumbled more to himself.

Josephine stared at him, appalled. "Oh my gosh! Are you serious? Do you even hear yourself?"

Mark turned slowly toward her. "Josephine, sweetheart, this has nothing to do with us. We can still be okay, can't we? You can trust me! I know I lied to you, but that won't happen again!"

She shook her head, brushing the tears off her face. "No. I can't trust you. You tell me you love me, that you want what's best for me, but you don't. You are selfish!" She pointed a shaky finger at him. "You thought of yourself when your parents told you the truth; you thought of yourself when Ally tells me the truth; and you thought only of yourself when you were pushing me to get DJ back. You never thought of what any of this would do to that sweet little boy!"

Mark grasped Josephine's hands and held them tightly. "Please! Understand that I was thinking of DJ! I only wanted him to be with the person who birthed him!"

"He belongs with his real mother! The one who is up with him when he has fevers and nightmares. The one who holds him when he is sick. The one who laughs and reads with him! That is who should have him!"

Mark's eyes looked deep into hers. "But what does this mean for us?"

"What do you think it means, Mark?" She spat the words out angrily. "We are done! I can't date you anymore!"

"Josephine! No! Don't you see I only want what's best for you? Can't you see that?"

"I see a selfish liar in front of me, that's who I see!" Josephine pulled her hands away from his. "Mark, we are through. I don't love you. You don't really love me. You don't know what love is. I should have listened to everyone! I could have saved us all from heartache!"

"By everyone, you mean Steven. Is that what this is all about? Are you going to him now?" Mark narrowed his eyes.

Josephine pursed her lips. "This has nothing to do with Steven! You are the one who lied to me, Mark. Steven has nothing to do with any of this!" Her cheeks flushed dark red with anger.

"Josephine, please give me another chance! I do love you! I promise I will gain your trust back."

"No. No, Mark. What's done is done. I can't trust you, and I don't want to try to trust you all over again. We are through."

"I can't accept that, Josephine! I won't." Mark tried to take her in his arms. "I thought you said you wouldn't let anyone break us up."

Josephine stepped back, glaring at him. "I didn't let anyone break us up. You did."

Mark pleaded with her one more time. "Please, sweetheart! One more chance."

Josephine shook her head vehemently. "No. Mark, I think

you ought to leave. This isn't getting us anywhere. You need to move on, and so do I."

She walked to the door, and held it open for him. Mark sighed heavily. "I wish you would reconsider. I think we are good together. And aside from that, I wish you would reconsider with DJ. He deserves to be with his real mother."

"We aren't really good together, Mark, you and I. And DJ is with his real mother, Sue. Oh, and please tell your parents I won't be there tomorrow."

Mark nodded absently. "If this is what you want, then I'll abide by your wishes."

"Good."

Mark leaned down and tried to kiss Josephine's lips but she turned her head so he kissed her cheek instead. "Have a good life, Josephine. I'm sorry it came to this." With that, he strode off, looking less confident than when he first arrived.

Josephine closed the door and crumbled to the floor, heartbroken that she had invested emotionally so much in that man.

When she did it again, she promised herself it would be with the right man.

Steven walked up the steps to Brittany's house with Josephine close by his side. He had given Brittany and Sue a heads up about what took place yesterday between Josephine and Mark. Steven glanced at Josephine, noticing the fear in her eyes. He had warned her that Sue was very angry. At first, Josephine didn't understand why. She had argued that she wasn't going to fight for DJ and that she and Mark were no longer together. Shouldn't that make up for what she had done? But Steven didn't think so and neither did Sue. Although Sue had admitted she was grateful Josephine wasn't pursuing the fight, she also admitted she didn't feel she could trust Josephine. Steven knew it would take time for Sue to heal and forgive. He just prayed Sue would allow that to happen.

"Just remember that bitterness and not forgiving hurts only one person, Sue- you," he had gently reminded her.

Sue said she appreciated Steven and all he meant to her family and that she would remember his words. She wasn't thrilled about Josephine coming to their Easter gathering, but she was thankful other family members would be present.

Steven knocked on the door and waited for someone to answer.

"Steven! Josephine! Glad you could make it, dear!" Mrs. Sorenson welcomed them in and gave Josephine a tight hug. "We love you, Jo; I hope you know that!"

Josephine returned the hug, tears brimming in the corner of her eyes.

"Thanks, Grandma. I love you, too."

Steven took off his scarf and jacket and put them away. The house was crowded because the snowy weather had brought everyone inside all at one time However, this didn't seem to bother this crowd!

Steven saw Sue's in-laws, all four of them, in one corner of the room. It amazed him that they all got along! What a blessing that was to Sue and Nate! In the dining room, Luke and his mom were talking, each holding a soda in their hands. Better keep a close eye on those two! They were bound to lose their sodas before the hour was done! Steven chuckled to himself as he remembered Luke confiding in him.

"Man! I finally know where I get losing my Coke from!"

Steven had smiled and asked, "Oh yeah? From who?"

"My mom! She asked me if I had seen where her Diet coke was!"

Steven slapped Luke on the back and shook his head.

In the living room, sitting on the couch, Sue sat holding Ella. Ella was a beautiful baby. Steven knew she had Nate wrapped around her finger already! Nate was sitting on the floor near Sue's feet, playing cars with DJ, Miles, and Gideon. Brittany was in the kitchen with Joslyn, getting her something to drink.

Just then, his dad grabbed Gideon from behind and pulled him over to the chair sitting near the fireplace.

"I got you in the critter trap!" his father bellowed.

Gideon's squeal of delight carried through the room.

Steven's dad had Gideon between his legs, squeezing gently, but hard enough not to let him be able to squirm free.

Gideon giggled and called for reinforcements. "Cousins, Sister, help me!"

DJ, Miles, and Joslyn ran to Gideon's aid. "Here we come, Gideon!" DJ yelled.

Steven laughed, placing his hand on the small of Josephine's back. "Looks like this is going to be a good day."

Josephine moved forward, being gently guided by Steven. "I hope so. I don't know if I should have come."

"Of course you should have. You have to make amends sometime. Why not now?" Steven whispered to her.

Josephine nodded slightly and made her way to the kitchen. Steven turned and sat beside Sue and Ella.

"Hey, Steven. Thanks for the heads up." Sue's eyes motioned toward Josephine.

"No problem, Friend. How are you?" His eyes showed his concern.

"I'm battling. It's a struggle to even be here with her right now." She shrugged her shoulders and set Ella down. Martha came promptly and scooped her up.

"Finally!" Martha exclaimed with mock frustration. "Now I get to hold my granddaughter!"

Sue smiled weakly and watched them walk away.

Steven gave Sue a sideways hug. "I understand your frustrations, Sue, yours and Nate's. Give it time."

Sue nodded. "I know." Sighing she continued, "I talked with Nate about this last night, too. I just don't know how much I can trust her not to go back on her word again. She was so easily convinced to think about it! What happens when the next guy comes along and tries to get her to do the same thing? What if she actually pursues it then?"

Steven saw the raw fear in her eyes. Nate got up and sat beside Sue, putting his arm around her. "We knew Jo had a tendency to be easily persuaded, Steven, we just didn't know it would affect us so much."

"I understand. Just remember this: Not every man is like

Mark. He had an agenda and tried to use Jo to accomplish that. Thank God for his sister coming to Jo before anything happened."

Nate squeezed Sue's shoulder. "I agree. It may take time, though."

"Wouldn't expect anything less, my friends. I'm praying for you guys."

Sue's smile didn't light up her face. "Thanks. I guess I ought to go talk to her, huh?" Sue stood up.

Nate looked up at her. "I better go with you."

Sue looked adoringly at her husband. "Yes, that you should. Be back soon, Steven."

Steven squeezed her hand and watched her walk into the kitchen.

Sue needed to forgive Josephine and even Mark in all of this, he knew that much. He prayed she would be able to do so and soon. Not forgiving someone leads to a life of bitterness and anger and pain, and not for the person in need of forgiveness. But for the person in need of forgiving.

Pushing his thoughts aside, Steven ran over to where the kids were still struggling to break free of his father's critter trap. Not only was Gideon trapped, but all the kids!

"Here I come, kiddos! I'll save you!"

Steven playfully began pulling his father's legs apart to get the kids free. He fell back to the ground and laughed. "Dog pile!" His father shouted as all the children threw themselves on top of Steven.

Steven loved this family with all of his heart. He was grateful they had accepted him and allowed him to be a part of their family. Now if only healing would come. Aside from Jesus resurrecting from the dead, that would be the biggest Easter miracle of all. Sitting back on his knees, Steven paused for a brief moment to watch the exchange between the sisters. Forgiveness was vital to keep this family close knit. Would Sue be able to forgive Josephine for all of the pain and heartache she had caused her? And could he possibly make clear the feelings he had for Jo to her? Steven ran his fingers through his hair.

He would just have to wait because he knew there was always hope for tomorrow.

A Note from the Author

Dear Readers,

Thank you for taking the time to read this book! It was a long time in the making! I appreciate you purchasing it and taking the time to share in the lives of the sisters and their friends!

I'm not sure if you caught the overall theme of the book or not. But it was my heart's desire to convey to you that our sin affects those around us. Josephine's sin of a one-night stand affected Sue and Nate. For Sue and Nate, it was a positive thing. But once Josephine decided to fight for DJ, her choices began affecting those around her even more. She and Steven almost lost their friendship; Josephine was forcing her family and friends to choose sides; and Josephine almost pushed everyone away from her because she chose to listen to Mark instead of wisdom.

Our choices, whether good or bad, affect those around us. They really do. We make choices everyday without thinking about them. They may not be as big as giving up our kids for adoption. But they can be as small as choosing the right thing to say in a time of crisis. We can choose to be encouraging to others or selfish in our thinking. We can choose to partake in lives around us or choose to live secluded, away from the world. God wants us to make choices based on what His word has to say. He calls us to live for Him, making Him the center of our lives. In so doing, our choices ought to have a positive effect on those we come in contact with. May I just give you this one encouragement? Make wise choices. Whether or not we mean to, what we do will affect every life we come in contact with.

God bless you as you seek to do His will!
In His Grip,

Joi

PS- Want to know what happens with Josephine and Sue? Does Sue reach a point in her life where she can forgive her sister? What about the relationship between Steven and Josephine? Does anything come of that? Find out in Hope for Today coming out soon!

LaVergne, TN USA
02 February 2011
214944LV00003B/8/P